DATING
GAMES

A NOVEL

RM JOHNSON

SIMON & SCHUSTER PAPERBACKS

NEW YORK   LONDON   TORONTO   SYDNEY

SIMON & SCHUSTER PAPERBACKS

Rockefeller Center

1230 Avenue of the Americas

New York, NY 10020

SIMON & SCHUSTER PAPERBACKS and colophon are registered trademarks
of Simon & Schuster, Inc.

First Simon & Schuster paperback edition 2004

For information regarding special discounts for bulk purchases,
please contact Simon & Schuster Special Sales:
1-800-456-6798 or business@simonandschuster.com

Designed by Lauren Simonetti

Manufactured in the United States of America

10 9 8 7

The Library of Congress has cataloged the hardcover edition as follows:
Johnson, R. M. (Rodney Marcus)

   Dating Games : a novel / RM Johnson

     p. cm.

       1. Dating (Social customs)—Fiction. 2. African American
women—Fiction. 3. Sisters—Fiction. 4. Twins—Fiction. I. Title

PS3560.O3834D37 2003
813'.54—dc21   2003050506
ISBN 0-7432-4455-9

    0-7434-6480-X (Pbk)

To my dear friend Shelia Sumners—
may you forever rest peacefully.

DATING
GAMES

ONE

LYING ON her back, still feeling the sensation of her boyfriend between her legs even after he had risen from her, Livvy knew she would become pregnant. She felt the warm fluid swim through her, making her certain of this. Her mother would kill her for wanting to have this child at sixteen years old. She'd do it anyway, that also she was sure of.

She waited four months to tell her boyfriend, Avery, for fear that he would run away. But the wait didn't matter, because he had disappeared only days after the news was given to him.

She finally called his house, then went over there, camping in front of his doorstep, wearing her big T-shirt, her belly big and round in front of her. His mother gave her no information, acting as if she had never met, or given birth, for that matter, to her son, Avery.

"Don't know where he is, and don't know when he's coming back," she said, slamming the door in Livvy's face.

Livvy walked home slowly, her head hung low, only to get harassed by her mother the moment she walked through the door of their apartment.

Livvy remembered their last argument in the kitchen. The place was a mess, as it had always been, and her mother had just walked in from her second job. Exhausted, she fell into one of the kitchen chairs, her hair wild about her head, her cheap clothes smelling like smoke from the lounge she worked at in the evenings. She had the strength to toe off only one of her high-heeled shoes, leaving the other one on. She blew out an exasperated sigh.

Livvy had walked out of her bedroom in a T-shirt and panties. She had not heard her mother come in, and when she caught sight of her, Livvy quickly turned around, hoping to disappear back into her room.

"Hold it."

Livvy froze.

"Why ain't this kitchen clean?"

"I was sick, Mama."

"What's wrong with you?"

"My stomach," Livvy said, a sour look on her face. She placed a hand on top of the curve of her belly.

"Livvy—"

"Mama, I ain't getting rid of it." Livvy knew what her mother was going to say, because she said it every night.

"Child, you see this place?"

Livvy looked at her uncertainly, not knowing where the question came from and what kind of answer was expected of her.

"You hear me?"

"Yes."

"It's a dump. Everything is falling apart. Ain't got living room furniture. Got to sit on folding chairs, because we can't afford nothin' else. Don't matter how many times we call the exterminator, don't matter how many bottles of Raid we spray, the roaches don't go away, and the damn rats think they got as much right to this place as we do." She paused, a look of disgust on her face, and glanced over the room.

"You like living like this, Livvy?"

Livvy tried holding her mother's stare but had to look away.

"Mama, I'm used to it."

"That's not what I asked you, child."

"It's our home, Mama." Livvy looked up at her mother, wanting to cry, feeling sorry and embarrassed for her.

"'It's our home' don't make it reason enough for us to have to live in this shit. This just how you gonna be living when you get my age. Is that what you want?"

Livvy didn't answer, knowing her mother's tactics for trying to get her to kill her unborn child.

"And you want your child living like this? You gonna have enough to worry about with diaper rash, and teething, and nonsense like that. You want to have to worry about looking down into your baby's crib and finding a rat sniffing around her? Constantly have to watch her while she's crawling on the floor, so she don't put lead paint chips or dead roaches in her mouth? Do you want that?"

"No," Livvy said, anger and frustration creeping into her voice.

"Then let me take you to the clinic. I'll be there with you, holding your hand all the way, baby. I'll be in the room with you."

Livvy let her mind wander down the street, into that room. She saw her legs hoisted up into those stirrups, heard the buzz of that blade, the suck of that vacuum, could almost feel her insides being yanked out of her.

"No!" she screamed, and turned, stumbling back on weary legs toward her room. But her mother was quickly up and out of that chair, had chased her down, one high-heeled shoe and all, and had spun Livvy around.

"Then what you gonna do, Livvy? You're sixteen years old, ain't finish high school. Ain't got no job, ain't got no skills to get a decent job, and you want to have a baby. How you gonna care for it?"

"We'll handle it."

"We? We!" Livvy's mother shouted. "Ain't nobody around here but you. Ain't nobody carrying that baby but you. Who the hell is we?"

"Me and Avery," Livvy whispered under her breath.

Livvy's mother sadly shook her head. "That boy is gone, and he ain't never coming back, child. You got to know that."

"He left, but once—"

"—once you have the baby, he gonna come back?" Livvy's mother finished for her. "No. He ain't. I thought the same thing when I had you, but don't no sixteen-year-old boy want to raise no child. He a child himself. But the difference between boys and you girls is that they smart enough to know they still children and got no business trying to raise one themself. Livvy . . ."

"I ain't killing my baby," Livvy protested, a tear slipping over the rim of her eyelid.

"Livvy, Baby—,"

"I ain't killing my child!"

"You gonna regret this your whole life."

"Like you regret having me?"

"No, no, Livvy," her mother said, stepping near to her, placing her arms around her, consoling her daughter. "You the best thing that ever happened to me. But why you gotta go and do it just because I did?"

Livvy stared into her mother's eyes, took a moment, then spoke. "Because I want somebody who really loves me."

"Livvy, I love you. You know that." Her mother tightened her arms around her child, but Livvy squirmed out of the embrace.

"You never here. You always at work, leaving me here by myself."

"Because I gotta take care of you. Pay rent, put food on the table."

"And what about Daddy? He didn't even stay around to raise me. Don't nobody love me. But my baby will when I have it. Even if Avery don't realize what a beautiful baby we made together, it won't matter, because my baby'll still love me." Livvy kept her eyes on her mother for a moment longer, then turned, and started back to her room.

"Livvy . . ."

"I'm having it, Mama."

"Livvy!" her mother called again.

"Ain't nothing more you can say. I said, I'm having it."

"Then you ain't having it here." Her mother's voice was low, but Livvy heard the words. She stopped dead, but did not turn and look around.

"That's right," Livvy's mother said. She sounded unsure, as if she questioned each word she said, but had to stay strong because of what she believed best for her child. "You heard me. You think you grown enough to bring a life into this world, then you grown enough to care for it yourself. I did what I was supposed to do. I had you when I was sixteen and would've cared for you until you was old enough to do it for yourself, but obviously that time is now. I ain't spending no more of my life raising somebody else child, even if it is yours. So I guess you got one more decision to make."

Livvy waited for a moment, making sure her mother was done saying what she had to say, then took the last few steps into her bedroom and closed the door behind her. There was no decision to make, Livvy thought, because it was made the night she got pregnant. She was having her baby.

SEVENTEEN YEARS later, Livvy Rodgers was thirty-three, working in a hospital as a nurse's assistant. She was proud of what she did, of what she accomplished, in light of the decisions she had made over the course her life. Yes, she could've done more, should've gotten further, but she took what she did very seriously.

The hospital uniform she wore was always spotless, brilliantly white, and sharply creased in all the appropriate places. Her curly, almost shoulder-length black hair was always pinned up in a bun, making her look very neat and professional. She kept herself in fairly good shape, although she could not seem to drop the fifteen pounds she had put on during her pregnancy. It had all gone to her hips and behind, making it necessary for everything she wore, including her uniforms, to be taken in at the waist in order for them to fit properly.

That evening, Livvy had been taking care of a new patient, a beautiful, fair-complexioned girl, with curly light brown hair, pulled back in a ponytail, and held with a single rubber band. She was the reason Livvy was having thoughts about her own childhood, about when she was pregnant.

Livvy assumed the girl couldn't have been any older than she was when she had given birth. If anything, she was probably a year or two younger.

The girl's belly was large and round under the blankets, for she was past due. She placed her hands over her stomach, shamefully trying to hide her unborn child from the nurses' assistant who was staring sympathetically down at her.

"You gonna have a baby," Livvy said, trying to smile in spite of the situation, sensing the girl's discomfort.

The girl smiled, slowly moving her hands. "Yeah. A baby girl."

"How old are you?"

"Fourteen."

The smile disappeared from Livvy's face.

LIVVY was in labor and screaming, clawing at the dashboard, feeling that something was clawing as ferociously at her insides to get out.

"Are we fucking there yet!" Livvy yelled out to her friend. Sharika drove the '73 Datsun B-210 as fast as the little engine would allow.

"We a block away, girl, just hold on. Don't be spillin' your insides all over my seats. Hold on!"

Not ten minutes later, Livvy was on her back in the delivery room of the Cook County Hospital, the free hospital. She was screaming and crying now, hot tears streaming down the sides of her face, and all the while she was trying to keep her eyes closed, trying to block out that damn bright-ass fluorescent light that burned her retinas like the sun. She had never felt pain like this before. Not even the first time she had sex.

Livvy screamed again, wanting to push, get this over with.

"Don't push. Don't push!" Livvy heard a voice coming from somewhere behind the sheet that hid her lower half.

"Fuck you!" Livvy spat and instead of pushing, squeezed the hell out of Sharika's hand. Her childhood friend was there by her side, dressed in blue hospital scrubs, mask and hat, like she was the other parent—the two of them a cute little lesbian couple.

"You feel any pain, you just squeeze my hand, all right, girl," Sharika had told her before the pain really started. Livvy squeezed all right, and she hoped she broke some bones so Sharika could feel pain close to what Livvy was feeling.

"All right, push. Push!" the doctor told her, and Livvy gave everything she had. The agony intensified, enveloping her entire body, but she continued, hoping it would stop, needing it to, because she felt she would surely die trying to give birth to her child if it didn't. Then just before she thought she would black out, the child passed out of her.

"Awww. Look what we have here," Livvy heard voices behind the sheet saying. She felt Sharika try to let go of her hand to see what was going on, but Livvy wouldn't let her go.

"What? What?" Livvy said, trying to raise her head, see over the sheet. She heard a smack, heard the baby start crying, and then almost simultaneously felt another pain.

"Hold it," the doctor commanded. "Hold it!" and Livvy knew something was wrong. Her baby was going to die. That's why it was crying. She just knew it.

She felt more pain, something else trying to push out of her, but she couldn't pay it any mind, because she was so worried about whether her baby would live or die.

"Surprise, surprise!" Livvy heard the doctor say through all her panicking and pain.

"What?" Livvy said, tears rolling over her cheeks. "Is my baby all right? Tell me!"

"I think we have a two-for-one."

Livvy turned to Sharika, still squeezing her hand. "What's wrong? What is he talking about?"

"Livvy, I want you to push again," the doctor told her.

"Why! What for?!" She felt another jolt of pain shoot through her belly.

Sharika pulled her mask down under her chin. "Because you're having twins," she smiled. "Now push!"

Five days later, Livvy lay in bed with her two little girls. Sharika's mother said she could stay at her house in the basement for a couple of weeks, till she found a job and a place of her own. Livvy thought of calling her mother, but the thought quickly passed. Her mother didn't want anything to do with her or her babies, so Livvy wouldn't force them on her. She thought of calling Avery, but had no clue of where to start. She called his mother to let her know the good news. His mother said nothing more than, "That's nice. But I still don't know where he is."

As Livvy lay there, her daughters in her arms, she realized that none of that made any difference. It didn't matter that no one cared about her anymore, because she would receive all the love she needed from her baby girls, Hennesey, and Alizé.

TWO

AT 8:45 P.M., Livvy finished her shift but was late getting off. One of the nurses had told her to clean up the patient in 316. The nurse knew Livvy was supposed to get off at eight, could see that she was walking in the direction of her locker, but she'd stopped her anyway.

Livvy could smell the stench from way down the hallway, and she almost bent over and puked heading toward the patient's room.

It was old Mr. Eisenbaum, one hundred if he was a day. All he did was lie in his bed with his eyes and mouth open, looking as stiff as if he was already dead, developing bed sores on his ass, and messing his sheets. This was the third time Livvy had to change him, and after the last time, she'd told herself she'd make it out of this place before she had to do it again.

"Hey Mr. Eisenbaum," Livvy said, loud enough for the patient in the next room to hear, because either old Eisenbaum was deaf or just didn't give a damn about what she had to say to him. "We're going to clean you up, okay?" There was no reply from him, just the cold, dead stare that had been on his face for the past few days.

"Okay," Livvy answered for him.

She cleaned him up, talking to him as she did, because she actually liked Mr. Eisenbaum. He had spoken only two words to her, and that was on the day he arrived. He was wheeled into the room on a gurney and lifted into his bed. He looked up at Livvy, who was standing off to the side, and greeted her, "Hi, nurse."

That comment had made her day—her entire week even.

Livvy wasn't a nurse, and although she had a disliking for all the nurses she worked with, or, as they would put it, worked *for*, Livvy desperately wanted to be one herself. That way, she would be able to care for the patients instead of just clean up the crap they spilled out onto their beds. But that would never happen, Livvy always told herself, stopping herself from getting her hopes up. She was thirty-three, too old to learn. All her learning years had been spent teaching Hennesey and Alizé, trying to raise them from babies, to girls, to respectful, decent young ladies.

Livvy had accomplished that, at least with Hennesey. She was smart as she could be, and that made Livvy smile as she drove away from the hospital toward home. Even though Livvy smelled like shit from the liquidy, pale brown mess that had splashed onto her forearm, and even though washing it off cleared it only off her arm and not out of her mind, she still had to smile when she thought of Hennesey. She was seventeen and had a full scholarship to the University of Illinois to study pre-med. She was going to be a doctor, and that made Livvy smile even more.

Her mom couldn't become a nurse, but her baby was going to be a doctor. "Take that!" Livvy said, steering her car, thinking about her daughter someday giving orders to the very nurses her mom once worked for. But almost immediately, Livvy became despondent when she thought about her other daughter, Alizé. Her daughters were twins, and they were both beautiful. But Livvy always asked herself, how could they have turned out so completely different?

Where Hennesey was confident about her intelligence, Alizé was confident about her looks. The child had grown breasts, it seemed, before she grew teeth, and she was very proud of that. She'd started wearing a bra when she was ten, makeup when she was eleven, and clothing that made men think she was twice her age when she was fourteen. Whereas the most important thing to Hennesey was her education, Alizé didn't care. The only thing important to her was how men felt about her, how much attention—and whatever else—she could get from them.

Livvy had noticed a difference in their behavior way back when they were toddlers. Alizé would finish all her food and start reaching over the table and taking her sister's. Seventeen years later, that behavior hadn't changed much. Only instead of Alizé's taking Hennesey's grapes, now she was taking her boyfriends.

Livvy tried so many times to convince Alizé to let her sister tutor her in school, help her try to find a career she would be interested in, or just to get away from her worthless friends and spend more time with her sister. Alizé wasn't hearing it. "What? You just want me to be like her! Well, let me tell you something, Mama. I ain't! We might look the same, but we ain't the same. All right."

Fine, Livvy would always think. She would smile a little bit, thinking about what her mother had told her before she had died. The girls were only five years old then, but her mother said to Livvy, "That Alizé is going to be a handful. That's payback for all the hell you gave me, child," she'd said, smiling. After the girls were a year old, Livvy's mother finally made her way over to her daughter's apartment. She said she couldn't have stayed away any longer. Livvy's mother had five good years with the girls before she passed, and even though Livvy and her mother weren't always the best of friends, she was glad her daughters had time to get to know their grandmother.

Livvy could remember the day she put her mother to rest, could remember standing there, looking down into her casket, both her daughters holding either of her hands.

"She sleepin', Mommy?" Hennesey asked, always the inquisitive one.

"Yeah, baby. She's sleeping, but it'll be forever," Livvy told her, still staring at her mother's waxen face. She thought about the hell they had been through with each other, the things that shouldn't have been said, shouldn't have been done, and then Livvy thought about the few good times they had together. Livvy promised herself that day that she would do everything in her power to give her daughters a better life, to give them more good times to remember than bad. On the day of her mother's death, she made that promise to her daughters.

Livvy turned into the parking lot of her apartment building, a smile reappearing on her face, as she thought about what was going to happen later tonight. She got out of the '91 Hyundai Excel, looked around, then slammed the door. She always had to look around to make sure there wasn't anyone trying to run up on her. She wasn't worried about the people who lived in the buildings. She knew all of them, even the roughneck little boys and the teens, most of them probably destined for jail. For the most part, she felt perfectly safe. She'd lived in this worn-down project building since the girls were babies, but this was still the 'hood, and many bad things could happen here.

Livvy walked up the stairs, greeting a group of boys.

"Hey, Ms. Rodgers," a couple of them said. Another boy in braids nodded his head.

"Boys, you stayin' out of trouble?" Livvy asked, as she walked past.

"Yeah."

"Don't want to see none of ya'll at my hospital, rollin' through the emergency room, okay?"

She stepped into the building, eyeing the fresh graffiti that had been applied to the fresh white paint that had just been applied yesterday over the old graffiti. She hoped the elevator was working, because after the long day at work, she didn't feel like climbing eleven flights of stairs, padded hospital shoes or not.

She pressed the button, listened for a moment, and smiled when she heard the noise of the machine starting to operate. The doors opened, and she was grateful that today, nobody had decided to empty their bladder in there or use it as a trash receptacle. The doors closed in front of her, and the elevator moved slowly, allowing her time to think about later tonight once again. She let her eyes fall closed, and the smile lengthened across her lips as she thought about Carlos. Make the best of things, her mother had told her. Well, that's what Livvy was going to do tonight.

Carlos Tillman was a beautiful, medium-dark-skinned man, with fine, wavy hair. His mother was Cuban, his father black, and Livvy would never have guessed that that combination could create a specimen as fine as Carlos. Carlos and Livvy had been seeing each other for eight years now. They met when they were twenty-five, and she couldn't wait to get into his pants and let him into hers. But she wanted to be respected, and didn't want him to think that just because she'd had two children when she was sixteen, she was giving booty away to every brotha who blinked his eye at her.

So Livvy waited. A whole two weeks. But when they finally got together, she wished she had given it up after two minutes. For the first month, they made love every day, twice sometimes. He made love to her like he really meant it, like his heart was into it, not like some of those other boys who would hump long enough to get off, then a second later go reaching over the side of the bed for the jeans they had just taken off.

Carlos would tempt her, tease her, and when they got to the love-making, it was slow, meaningful, and pleasureful. And when it was over, she wasn't looking at his ass as he slid his drawers up; she was looking into his eyes as he looked into hers. They would cuddle, and Carlos would tell her how he wasn't always going to be poor. He would speak of his dreams to change things around the projects, to start a real estate company, to give people of color in the community the opportunity to buy and own their own property.

"Because you know this is prime real estate, don't you," Livvy remembered him saying once after they made love. "This is Chicago lakefront property. And although the white folks are allowing us to live here now, one day they gonna realize that driving way into town from the burbs ain't cool no more. They gonna realize the water is nice to look at, and they gonna move us up out of here. You know that, don't you?"

Livvy didn't know none of that, but she smiled and kissed him on the lips, because she liked the way he spoke so passionately about the business. "I'm gonna make it, and you and the girls gonna be with me. Okay?"

"Okay," Livvy said, knowing that one day Carlos would actually make it, as he said he would.

Carlos did. Five years ago, he started a small real estate company, after buying an old apartment building that the city had sold for little. He bought the building with money he borrowed from family, friends, and anyone else who would loan him a dime. He rehabbed the place, rented the spaces out, and was on his way.

Now Carlos's company was thriving. He was buying and selling properties, giving loans, and even building. He had made good on his promise, but only part of it: he had not taken Livvy and her girls anywhere. But a year ago, he did move to a beautiful big house in a nearby historic district and since then had been seeing less and less of Livvy. It was business that was keeping him away, Carlos always said. Over the last two months, Livvy was lucky to see him once every two weeks.

A couple of her girlfriends told her that they had seen him with other women, but Livvy knew they were just saying that because they were jealous of her.

"That's why they sayin' that, right?" Livvy always asked Sharika, who lived upstairs from her.

"Yeah, I guess that's why they sayin' that," Sharika answered, saying what Livvy wanted her to say, and Livvy knew that's what she was doing. But until Livvy saw Carlos cheating with her own two eyes, these were all lies.

Carlos had called yesterday and apologized for faking the last two times he was supposed to have taken her out. He said that he would drive her around in his new Cadillac and show her the town.

"You look extra pretty for me, all right?" he said before hanging up.

Livvy was blushing as red as the dress she had rushed to the closet to pull out. She stepped in front of the mirror, held it up in front of her, and knew that it would cling perfectly in all the right places.

She had turned to the side, imagining how the dress would stick to that curve back there, and she knew that Carlos would be drooling. If he had been with other women, she told herself, he'll forget all about them after tomorrow night.

Livvy stepped out of the elevator, keys in one hand, purse and lunch bag in the other. She walked down the hall, toward apartment 1105. When she opened the door, Hennesey was stretched out across the floor, lying on a big pillow. The TV was on, but the volume was low, and her attention was focused on the pages of a big reference book.

"Hey, baby," Livvy said, smiling to herself, thinking, *My daughter never stops learning*. Livvy set her keys and bags down and received the hug that Hennesey gave to her.

"How was your day, Mama?"

"The typical, baby. All I can say is that I got dumped on in more ways than one. I really got to take a shower. Did you eat? Want me to fix you something?" Livvy asked, walking toward the bathroom.

"No, Mama, that's all right. I fixed something earlier," Hennesey called back.

After turning on the shower, Livvy stepped into her bedroom, stripped off her clothes, and with a turned-up nose dropped the soiled articles in the hamper. She really should've taken them down to the basement to burn them in the furnace, but washing them would have to do.

She walked back into the living room, wearing a bathrobe, asking herself why she was bothering to ask the question she was about to ask, when she knew the answer. She asked anyway.

"Hennesey, is your sister at home?"

Hennesey pulled her head out of the book, looked up at her mother as if she should've known better than to ask such a question. "Yeah, right, Mama."

"You know where she's at?"

"I don't know. She said she was going over to JJ's place."

Livvy shook her head, thinking about JJ, and the rest of Alizé's little no-good friends.

"Why, what's up?"

13

"Nothing. I just wanted to talk to her before I went out."

"Ooh, we going out, are we?" Hennesey smiled slyly. "I haven't heard anything about this."

"That's right, baby," Livvy said, sticking a hand on her hip, waving the other at her daughter. "Carlos is coming by here to pick me up soon, and he's going to show me the town. Gonna wear my little red dress that's just going to knock his socks off."

"Well, you do it, Mama," Hennesey waved back at her mother.

"It's already been done, he just don't know it yet." They both laughed, then Livvy hurried to the bathroom to get ready by nine-thirty, when Carlos said he'd pick her up.

LIVVY sat in the living room, her jacket on over the red dress she was so excited about. Her purse lay on the other end of the sofa. The television had been turned off, the same for the lights, save for the light over the kitchen sink. Hennesey had long ago taken her book into her bedroom.

"I don't want to wreck your flow when Carlos come to pick you up," Hennesey said, kissing her mother on the cheek, about two hours ago. "Have a good time, and I want you back in here by eleven-thirty," she said, joking.

This would've been impossible considering it was eleven-thirty now, and Livvy hadn't even left the house. All this time, Livvy had been sitting there, flicking the TV on and off, watching for ten minutes, then turning it off again, afraid that she'd be distracted and wouldn't hear Carlos knocking at the door, or calling her to let her know he was right outside. That was ridiculous, of course, but she didn't want to take any chances.

She rang his home phone a zillion times, his business phone more than that, and his cell even more, but all she got were recordings. She didn't bother to leave any messages because she knew he knew where he was supposed to be. He just hadn't made it yet. He must've gotten caught up in something . . . like some other woman's panties.

Livvy scolded herself for thinking like that. He would have a good reason for being late. She knew he would. And he would tell her when he came, because she knew he was still coming.

But would he *really* come? This would be the third time in a row that he had stood her up, so why should she think that he would come this time? Sad thing was, getting stood up was something that Livvy was getting used to, and not just by Carlos, but by other men she cared about as well.

She could remember when Avery finally reappeared after abandoning them. She was twenty-four, the kids were eight, and he had dropped back into her life like he had just fallen from the sky.

After opening her front door, finding Avery there, as thin as ever, his facial hair growing out of control, she couldn't believe the moment was actually happening. She wanted to claw his eyes out, but she also wanted to throw herself into him, wrap her arms tightly around him, tell him how much she still loved him. She did neither.

"I missed you," he had the nerve to say, and opened his arms for a hug. Livvy did not move.

After getting no response, Avery just walked into the house, as if he figured she always knew he would be coming.

"I want to meet my girls."

"How did you—"

"Mama told me."

Livvy narrowed her eyes at him. "Your mama could tell you everything that was going on here, but she couldn't tell me where you were?"

"It's a long story, Livvy."

"I got time." Livvy crossed her arms, anger on her face.

"I don't want to get into it right now. Besides . . . ," Avery said, nodding toward the hallway where Hennesey and Alizé were peeking their little heads around the corner.

"Come over here, girls," Livvy called. The girls came, Hennesey somewhat reluctant, Alizé almost running, a big smile on her face.

"There's someone I want to introduce you to." Livvy tried to break the news gently, but before she could, Avery said, "Girls, I'm your father."

A short gasp of surprise came from Hennesey, as a wide smile grew across Alizé's lips.

Livvy looked sharply at Avery, wanting to drag him toward the door, throw him out of her apartment for giving the news so abruptly, but he paid her no attention. His focus was on the girls. He had stooped down and opened his arms, bidding the two of them forward. Alizé ran quickly toward the man she had never seen before and jumped into his arms. Hennesey stood back, her arms crossed over her chest, scrutinizing the man with a cautious stare.

"It's okay," Avery said, holding tightly to a smiling Alizé. "I won't bite." He extended his hand out to Hennesey.

Hennesey looked up to her mother. Livvy nodded her head, giving her the okay to step closer.

Hennesey moved into Avery's other arm.

"Now," he said. "What are my daughter's names?"

"Hennesey," Hennesey said, softly. "And I'm Alizé!" Alizé said, almost yelling her own name.

Avery looked to Livvy as if to ask, *Why did you go and name my daughters after liquor?*

Livvy shot him a look back saying, *It's what we got fucked up on when you got me pregnant. Yo' ass wasn't around to stop me, so there!*

That same night, Avery announced that he was moving back in to help raise his daughters so they could be a family, even though all he ever brought was a half-empty gym bag full of clothes. He immediately started sleeping in Livvy's bed, butt naked, because that's how he said he always slept now. She hadn't had sex, decent sex, in over a year, and although she tried to fight it, she succumbed to his very first attempt at having her. And honestly, she didn't even know if it was a real pass or not. He brushed her nipple with his hand while raising it to scratch his cheek, and she was all over him after that.

Avery was there a week, spending huge amounts of time with the girls, because he was "in between jobs." Hennesey was indifferent. She had always been independent. Her head was always in a book before her father reappeared, and it was still in a book while he was there, so this new "dad thing" wasn't even interfering with her reading schedule. Alizé was loving every minute of the attention she was getting. She seemed like a different girl, laughing and smiling all the time, when normally she was frowning and finding a problem with every little thing.

Avery told Alizé he loved her after the second day he showed up, and Alizé told him she loved him back. All she talked about was how much she loved her daddy—until the day he disappeared again.

He disappeared as magically as he had reappeared, like the sky had sucked him back up through the clouds he had initially dropped down from. Nothing changed for Hennesey. She just went back to her books. But Alizé was in despair. Livvy would've been in just as bad shape if she didn't have to focus her attention on bringing her younger daughter (by one minute and thirty-six seconds) out of her funk.

Livvy tried locating Avery again, if for no other reason than to tell him how much both his daughters (that was a lie, just one of them, really) missed him, and to tell him he needed to start paying child support. But after a couple of halfhearted failed attempts, Livvy didn't bother anymore. A few months later, she met Carlos.

Livvy fidgeted with the buttons on her jacket, thinking that she would take it off, when she heard the doors of the elevator open. The sound was faint, but the elevator was just outside her door, so when there was no noise in the apartment, she could hear the doors slowly grinding open.

Livvy sprang to her feet, wanting to feel mad, wanting to appear angry, but she couldn't wipe the silly-ass grin that seemed to have a mind of its own off her face.

She fluffed her hair with her fingers, ran a tongue over her teeth to make sure there was no lipstick on them, then hurried to the door, and placed her ear to it. She heard footsteps approaching. She took a step back and stood up straight. She would wait 'til he knocked at least three times before answering, so as not to seem as if she'd been doing exactly what she had been doing, waiting for him.

Livvy took a deep breath in, the smile still glued to her face, anticipating his knock. But it never came. Instead the door just opened up, and Livvy was standing face to face with Alizé.

For all the makeup Alizé was wearing, the hip-hugging jeans, the high heels, and the clingy cotton top with the low bustline, she and Livvy looked more like sisters standing there than mother and daughter.

Alizé looked her mother up and down, disapproval on her face. She slammed the door without moving a step, then said, "All dressed up to get stood up again, hunh?"

Livvy wanted to slap her face after that remark, but she walked away. Alizé always had a way of cutting right to the chase. Livvy didn't like it, but she was right.

Alizé clip-clopped across the floor into the kitchen, sunk her head into the fridge, and pulled out a diet soda.

"Where have you been?" Livvy said, turning around to face her daughter.

"So who is it? Carlos again?" Alizé responded, ignoring her mother's question and sitting down on one of the dining room seats. The living room and kitchen made up one big open area. The space shared by the two rooms served as a dining room, where the table sat.

"You didn't answer my question. I asked—"

"Out with my girls."

"Doing what?"

"What we do. Mama, why you do this to yourself?" Alizé asked, a look of sympathy on her face now.

"I don't know what you're talking about," Livvy said, knowing full well what her daughter was asking her.

"Puttin' up with this nigga's bullshit," Alizé said, popping the top on her pop can.

"Don't talk that way in my house. I told you about that."

"All right, but it don't change the question. Why?"

Livvy smiled uncomfortably, squirming, looking for an answer. "He said he'd take me out. I can't remember the last time I been out for a good time. I can't accept an invitation to be taken out and treated like a lady, have some money spent on me?"

"I ain't sayin' that, Mama, but you know he ain't gonna show, and when he do, all he want to do is get in your panties." Alizé stood up, waving a frustrated hand about the air. "I can't stand niggas like that. Think because they got a little loot, that you should be all over they dick. Sorry," Alizé apologized. "Penis," she corrected, cutting a quick look at her mother. She walked over to Livvy, placed her hands on her shoulders.

"Mama, I know you got history with him, and I know there's probably some love stuff mixed up in there too, but you look good, and there's too many fine men out there to sit around and get played by this fool."

"I'm not getting played by nobody. And he's not a fool." Livvy stepped back, causing Alizé's hands to drop from off her shoulders. "But you know what?"

"What?"

"Next time I speak to him, I'm gonna tell him that I'm tired of his games," Livvy said, all of a sudden finding some heart.

Just then, a knock came at the door.

"Well, here's your chance," Alizé said, a smirk on her lips.

Livvy reluctantly turned toward the door. She reached out and was about to grab the knob, but turned around to see Alizé still standing behind her.

"What are you doing?" Livvy asked.

"I'm' makin' sure you tell him off, do what you said you was gonna do so you can be done with him."

"Ally, get your behind in your room."

"Fine, but Mama, handle your business, all right?" Alizé turned to go to her room.

Livvy waited 'til her daughter disappeared, fluffed her hair again, licked her teeth again, then opened the door. Carlos was standing outside of it, fine as ever, and all Livvy could do was smile.

THREE

ALIZÉ walked into the room she shared with Hennesey. Hennesey was lying on her stomach across her bed, reading some book. Alizé shook her head, walked over, and sat on her twin bed, across from her sister's.

"Damn, girl. It's almost midnight, and you still got your head in a book. You already got the damn scholarship. Relax, already."

"Maybe you ought to try it. Might learn something," Hennesey said, not taking her eyes off the page.

"All I need to know is right up here," Alizé said, tapping the side of her head, while she walked to the full-length closet mirror and started to undress. "And all I need to show is right back here," she said, as she slid the tight jeans off her round behind to expose a pink thong.

"Whatever," she heard her sister say. Henny wasn't up on what was happening in the real world, what was going on in the streets, Alizé told herself. All she knew about was that false paper-and-print world that went on in them books she was always reading. She didn't learn from firsthand experience like Ally did. Henny learned by reading stuff that other people wrote, from other people's experiences. She was second-hand learning and didn't even know it.

If Henny was as smart as she thought she was, as smart as their mama thought she was, she would've come to Ally to school her on what really mattered, like how a woman is supposed to look. Ally pulled her top over her head, reached back, and undid her bra. It was a nightly ritual for her: standing in front of the mirror butt-ass naked and looking at herself with a critical eye, checking for flaws, and then after finding none, praising herself for how damn fine she was.

Two perfect breasts bounced out of the garment and stood perky for her. The nipples were slightly erect, a result of the tiny bit of excitement Ally received from just looking at her own body. They weren't huge breasts—actually, a little smaller than normal—but that was okay, she thought, turning slightly around. Her ass more than made up for it. And that wasn't all she had. Some sistahs had ass and skinny little legs. Ally had ass, tight thighs that she worked, running or climbing stairs, and even had nice calves, which a lot of sistahs ain't got.

Her belly was flat, and beneath the thin layer of flesh was only slight evidence of a six-pack. That's how she wanted it. She wanted to be soft, because she knew that's how black men liked their women. She didn't want her stomach to look like cracked pavement, hard as stone, like Janet Jackson's. That's what white men wanted. Brothas wanted cushion for the pushin'.

On beautifully pedicured feet, she walked closer to the mirror, admiring her flawless berry-brown skin. She looked at her face, smooth as the surface of a puddle of still water. Her eyes were almond shape, lashes long, her nose a button (a diamond stud in her right nostril). Her lips were full, fat, juicy, and when she glossed them up, she knew brothas could damn near bust one just looking at them hard enough. She knew that every man who saw her had the fantasy of her lips around him, and she played that up to get whatever she wanted, knowing that it would never happen, had never happened, because some shit a sistah just couldn't do 'til she found the right man.

"Yes, I'm all of that," Alizé said to the mirror and blew a kiss at herself before closing the closet door and slipping a huge T-shirt over her head. The sad thing was, her plain-ass sister Henny over there could look exactly like her, but men would've never known, because she never wore makeup. She always wore jeans that just fit, not hugged, and a huge sweatshirt with a college name on it. She was a nerd, for sure.

"You done making love to yourself over there?" Hennesey said, closing her book.

"Yeah, and it was the best I ever had," Alizé said, pulling her blankets back and sitting on her bed.

Hennesey put her book down on the floor next to her bed, then rolled over on her back, sliding under her covers. "You should've seen Mama tonight. She really looked good, and she was really happy."

"Well, she ain't got no reason to be happy."

"Why you say that?" Henny wanted to know.

"Some fool who plays games with her head, make her think he loves her when he don't. She needs to get out and start playin' some of *them* fools, see how they like it."

"Everybody ain't like you. Running through men like paper towels. There's feelings involved. Mama loves Carlos."

"He don't love her." Alizé was sure of that.

"You don't know that."

"If he did, he wouldn't have stood her up for the third time in a row."

"What are you talking about? Mama was getting ready to leave when—"

"Dude was just getting here after I walked in," Alizé said, nodding her head toward the living room.

"So he came."

"But comin' ain't enough, Henny. Coming at the time he said he was going to is what Mama got to demand. She's too damn soft. I'm tired of seeing her get dogged. She let this Carlos dude walk all over her, just like she let Daddy get away without paying nothing for child support. I'm just glad I ain't like her." Alizé lay back in bed, crossing her arms under her head, and looking at the ceiling. She felt her sister's eyes on her, then turned to see Henny looking in her direction.

"What?"

"You shouldn't say stuff like that. Mama's a good woman."

"Ain't say she was a bad woman. I just said I'm glad I'm not her—meaning weak."

"She'll take care of that situation with Carlos when she's had enough," Henny said.

"Well, when he knocked on the door, she said she was going to take care of it tonight."

"Then that's what she's going to do."

"Wanna' bet?" asked Alizé.

"Yeah. You don't give Mama enough credit."

"You give her too much."

"I guess we'll find out in the morning."

"Guess so." Alizé reached over to turn off her bedside lamp, but before she clicked it off, both girls heard noise. It was the sound of voices, a man's and a woman's—their mother's and Carlos's—and they were both moaning in ecstasy. There was a single knock against the wall. The headboard, Alizé guessed. Then there was another, two more, then a constant rhythmic bump, bump, bump, bump.

A look of sadness and disappointment covered Alizé's face as she turned to Hennesey. "Don't have to wait 'til morning. I win." Alizé clicked off the lamp. Darkness.

FOUR

SLEEPING IN the bus station was worse than almost any night Raphiel Collins had spent in prison, he thought to himself. He was barely able to stand up straight after being roused awake by a police officer.

"What's your name, boy?" the bloated pink-faced officer said to him with a southern drawl .

"Rafe Collins," he said, then corrected himself. "I mean Raphiel."

"Which is it, boy?"

"It's Raphiel," Rafe said, telling himself that if this cop referred to him as boy one more time, he would be all over him, showing him just who the boy was. "But people call me Rafe."

"Go to a shelter if you want to sleep, Rafe." The cop said his name with sarcasm. He then eyed Rafe up and down as if looking for concealed weapons bulging from under his baggy T-shirt and jeans. "There's one down the street."

"I ain't homeless."

"Yeah, sure you aren't. Just move it along."

Rafe pulled his sore, tired body from the bench and started across the bus station floor. The cop believed that Rafe was homeless, and he was half right. Rafe had gotten out of prison three nights ago, after spending his twenty-fourth, twenty-fifth, and twenty-sixth birthdays inside. He had stood just outside that long, high, barb-wired prison gate with only a few dollars in his pockets, the clothes that he had been dragged into confinement wearing three years ago, and the realization that he could never go back home again after what he had done.

His first night out of prison, he slept in the shelter among all those other men, dirty and smelling from days and weeks on the streets, their long hair clumping together with the same dirt that darkened and dusted their clothes. When he walked in, he had wanted to turn back around, fearing that being around those men would make him start to look more like them, be like them. It was bad enough his clothes were old, hanging off his lean, muscular frame like rags. He needed to do something with the thick afro atop his head, the stubble growing wild on his face. He would have to find a place soon, but for now, he thought, this would have to do.

But Rafe couldn't sleep, for the stench from the man lying on the cot next to his was overpowering. Rafe pulled the neck of his T-shirt up over his face to try and filter out some of the funk, but when he saw one of the man's hands drop beneath his blanket, saw the blanket rising and lowering as the man started to groan and call out a woman's name, Rafe knew he couldn't stay there. He left and slept in the doorway of a boarded-up convenience store.

The following night, determined as he was not to, he ended up at his parents' house. He had no intention of climbing those steps, of ringing that doorbell, because he knew the frigid reception he would get. He just stood out there, sometime after midnight, wondering what they were doing inside, wondering if they had even thought of him over the past three years. He slept in his old backyard, pushed up near the house, curled in a ball, his knees pulled into his chest for warmth.

Now it was morning again. After the third night he had been out of prison, and after sleeping on that bus station bench, and running out of the little money he had spent on food, he knew he had to find a real home.

Rafe thought about people's houses he could crash at, thought about old friends, but there were very few of them, and he didn't want them to know that he was out. He didn't want to fall back into the circles he had been spinning around in, the ones that had ultimately landed him in prison.

It all seemed hopeless, Rafe thought, as he stood out on Canal Street, watching cars speed past him, thankful that it was spring and not snowing. He reached deep into his mind, trying to think of anyone who would give him shelter, even if for only a few days. After a moment, someone came to mind, and he wondered why he hadn't thought of her sooner.

Rafe begged for bus fare. It was beneath him, and he couldn't even turn his face up to look in the eyes of the two people who gave him the money. He had asked only black people, because he couldn't bear the idea of begging a white man, allowing him the opportunity to turn his nose up at Rafe and tell him to "get a job," as he walked away, a disgusted scowl on his face.

The ride took forty-five minutes, the majority of that time spent waiting for the transfer bus after getting off the El train. Some things never changed, Rafe thought, standing on the curb just under the bus stop beside a woman with a toddler in a stroller. It reminded him of when he was a child, when his whole life was in front of him, when he had the opportunity to be anything he wanted. But look where he was now.

The bus eventually came, and he was let off about two blocks from his destination. He walked through the nice neighborhood, a place he could remember visiting when he was younger. He had always looked up with wide eyes at the large houses and the nice cars parked in front of them.

It was Beverly Hills, a small, historic community in the city. In the seventies, no one but white people lived there, but in the late eighties and early nineties, blacks started moving in in droves. And as always, when blacks started moving in, whites started moving out.

Now the community was mostly black folks, but the houses were still nice, and despite the myth that some white folks believed, the grass on the front lawns hadn't started dying yet.

Rafe knocked on the door, then straightened his T-shirt and jeans, smoothed down his long, wild afro with his palms, and waited, hoping that she'd be home.

The door opened, and a large woman in her early fifties, wearing a brown wig, looked out. When she saw him, she almost stumbled backward with astonishment.

"Raphiel?" she said, gasping, placing a hand on her chest. "Is that you?"

"It's me, Aunt Dorothy," Rafe smiled.

She reached out, and wrapped her heavy arms around his body, giving him a huge hug, rocking him back and forth.

"It's so good to see you, baby."

"SO I KNOW your mother must have been happy to see you. Tell me what she said." Aunt Dorothy set some butter cookies and milk on the kitchen table for Rafe. She remembered that they were his favorite. As a child, he would stick cookies on each one of his five fingers, and nibble away at them until they were all gone.

"She ain't say nothin', Auntie, 'cause I ain't seen her or Pops. You know how they feel about me."

"I have to tell you that we don't speak about it that often, hurts her too much. But you know she had to have gotten over that by now. You're her son," Aunt Dorothy said, sitting down in the chair next to her nephew.

"I know, but so was Eric, and you know Mama. You're her sister, and you know she ain't lettin' go of nothing once she get it set in her head."

Aunt Dorothy nodded her head, looking as though she knew what Rafe had said was true.

"And that's one of the reasons I'm here, Auntie." Rafe looked down at his hands, as if ashamed by what he was about to say. "I ain't got nowhere to stay, and I know you be renting rooms here. I was wondering—"

"You know I only rent to men over fifty years old here. Less drama that way. And you know that I never have an open room. If anything, men waiting in line to be able to live in Beverly for $125 a week."

"Yeah, I know." Rafe felt as though now he really had nowhere to turn to.

"But it just turns out that somebody moved out yesterday, and I ain't had time to tell anybody about the room," Aunt Dorothy smiled at Rafe.

"But I ain't fifty years old."

"I know that. But that'll just be our little secret. I think you're mature enough not to cause any trouble. And if you do, you're still not too big for me to put you over my knee and spank your behind like I used to do when you were little."

AUNT DOROTHY opened the door to a small room with a full-size bed pushed up against one of the walls, a dresser against another, with a 19-inch television on top of it. "This'll be your room." Rafe looked over the small area, and thought that with a couple of air fresheners, he could call it home.

"I don't got any money on me now, Auntie," Rafe said, pulling at both his jeans pockets with his thumbs.

"You mean, you don't *have* any," she corrected him.

"Yeah. I don't have any, but I'm supposed to be going to see my parole officer tomorrow, and I'm sure he got a job set up for me."

"It's okay, sweetheart. There's no rush. You take your time. Do what you have to do, and pay me when you get ready. Okay?"

"All right." Rafe gave his aunt a hug. "Thank you so much for this," he called over her shoulder.

"It's what families are for. And what about your parents? You want me to call them? Talk to them for you? I'm sure they'd want to see you."

"No. No," Rafe said, leaning back so he could look into her face. "I'll get over there when I think it's right, okay?"

"Okay. Enjoy the room." Aunt Dorothy stepped into the hallway. "And you know if you get hungry, just come on downstairs, and I'll make you something to eat."

"Thanks, Auntie."

"And one more thing. The man across the hall from you, he's in his sixties. He never comes out of his room, but he can be a grouch. Don't pay him no mind. You'll probably never bump into him anyway. But the guy down the hall, Wade, is a sweetheart. You'll like him." She smiled, "You'll do just fine up here." She closed the door.

Yeah, Rafe thought, laying across his bed. He should be just fine here, and for the first time in three years, he was able to rest fully.

FIVE

THIS NEGRO had to be saving his money for something, Alizé thought, staring down at the bacon barbecue cheeseburger sitting unwrapped in her lap. She was on the passenger side of Steven's Toyota Corolla. Steve, a high school boy—not on the football team, or basketball, or any other team for that matter, but cute, 6'1" and every girl wanted him—was Alizé's boyfriend. At least he was for the moment. It was the following night, Saturday, and they had plans to go to a movie.

"I'm hungry," Ally said, just after he had picked her up.

Steve looked down at his watch. "We ain't got time. The movie's going to start in less than half an hour."

"And . . ." Alizé said, crossing her arms, twisting her lips. "What is that supposed to mean to me? I'm hungry, and I need something to eat, and you need to be taking me to get it."

Steve cut his eyes at her for a moment, then started the car and drove off. They ended up in the Burger King drive-through. He ordered what he wanted and asked Alizé what she'd like. She thought about saying "a decent place to eat," somewhere she could sit down on something other than plastic seats, or sit in the car and eat her meal off her thighs. She didn't say a thing. Just another strike against Steve, who would, if he messed up again, get dumped faster than he could say "Whopper Junior."

"So what you want, girl?" Steve asked, as if his time cost a million dollars a minute.

"Whatever," Alizé grunted. She ended up with a bacon barbecue cheeseburger combo meal. They sat in the parking lot, Alizé staring down at the top of her burger. It looked cold and stale, and the bun had a big dent in it, where one of the burger people had stuck his thumb into it.

"What's wrong?" Steve asked, through a mouthful of chicken sand-wich. "Why ain't you eating? Movie starts in ten minutes." He pushed the last of his sandwich into his mouth, sinking his finger in behind it, and sucking off whatever juice was on it, before he pulled it out.

"I ain't hungry no more." She started to wrap the burger back into its paper. "Let's go to the movie. I'll just throw it away."

"No, no." Steve quickly reached over and grabbed the burger out of her hand. He repackaged it carefully, slid it back into the Burger King bag, and placed it in the glove box. "I can eat that tomorrow for lunch."

"Sure you can," Alizé said, sarcastically. "How stupid of me."

By the time they got out of the car, Alizé had much attitude. Halfway there, she had noticed that they weren't headed to the nice movie theater on Michigan Avenue but toward the 'hood.

"Movie theater ain't this way," she noted.

"Dollar theater is." Steve kept his eyes on the road.

After Alizé and Steve parked the car, they walked toward the the-ater, turned the corner, and were met by the back of a line, thirty peo-ple long.

"Un-uh," Alizé said, looking at all the guys wearing their baggy jeans, hooded sweatshirts, and denim studded jackets. The women by their sides had gold teeth in their mouths, hair weaves and piece-ons flowing down their backs, makeup painting their faces like clowns, and outfits so bad that she wondered if they'd gotten dressed with their eyes closed.

"I'm not going in there with those fools!"

"But *Thug Life* is playing," Steve said, digging in his pockets, ready-ing his two dollars for whenever they made it to the ticket booth.

"*Thug Life*," Alizé said, loud enough for the people standing around her to hear. "We don't got to pay to see that. It's showin' right out here in this line."

Steve cut an evil look at Alizé, motioning for her to close her mouth.

"I'm not going up in that theater with these niggas to get shot by a stray bullet just because some fool is talking too loud."

"Well, take yo' ass home then," a woman's voice called out from somewhere in the middle of the line. There was a small swell of laugh-ter, which quickly died down.

Alizé craned her head, looking for the person who spoke. When she couldn't find her, she simply said, "Fuck whatever crack ho said that to me." Alizé turned to Steve. "Let's go." But Steve grabbed her by the arm, preventing her from leaving.

"We ain't going," he said, his voice low. "You wanted to go out and see a movie, so that's what we're doing."

Alizé's face showed mild shock. She looked at Steve as though he had lost his mind or maybe forgotten who the hell she was. She then let out a pathetic chuckle, still allowing herself to be held.

"Going out! You call going to Burger King, eating in you tore-up car, out?" Alizé said, speaking loud enough for everyone, from the front of the line to the back, to hear. Heads were turning, people tapping others on the shoulders, and drawing their attention to Alizé's tirade.

"And then you bring me to this nasty-ass movie theater," she continued, "that's showing year-old movies to motherfuckers who can't afford to see nothing better."

Another woman's voice, higher pitched this time, came from farther up in the line. "I'm gonna be one more motherfucker for that bitch, then it's on."

Alizé heard this and quickly turned in the direction of the remark. She stepped out of line and spread her arms wide, as if inviting confrontation.

"Somebody don't like it? Whassup? Step out. Let's do this," Alizé said, scanning all the women's eyes.

Steve stepped out to hook one of her arms, drag her back in, but she pulled away. "Naw, I told you, I ain't goin' in. I'm worth more than this." Alizé paced back toward him, her jeans hugging her curves just right, the eyes of so many of the men on her.

"I'm tired of this," she said.

"Well, roll wit' me, baby," a man called out.

"Yeah, she fine as hell," another agreed.

"Oh, ya'll like what you see," Alizé smiled, stepping back out in the front of the line.

"Hell, yeah!" a bunch of the guys answered enthusiastically.

"Ya'll really like it?" Alizé cooed, pulling off her jacket, showing off the tight-fitting T-shirt and the breasts pushing against the thin material. She spun around to give the guys a good look at her.

"I said, do ya'll really like what you see?"

A couple of guys started clapping, as if they were at a strip club and Alizé was about to start taking it off. Others shouted their approval.

Steve stood still at the end of the line, looking ashamed and embarrassed.

"So I should get wit' one of ya'll instead of my cheap-ass boyfriend?" Alizé called to the line filled with men.

"Oh, and you know it," some shouted.

"Mos def!" others agreed.

"Hmmm." Alizé rubbed her chin, as if giving it serious thought. Then a second later said, "But what good would that be doing me, 'cause ya'll cheap brothas brought ya'lls' dates to the dollar show too."

The women in the line laughed as Alizé walked off. "C'mon Steve," she motioned. He obediently followed, having no other choice.

OUTSIDE ALIZÉ'S apartment, she sat slumped down in the passenger seat of the car. They hadn't exchanged a word the entire way home.

"That show wasn't called for back there," Steve protested.

Alizé didn't speak, didn't even turn to face him.

"Callin' me out like that. Making me look like some punk. Calling me cheap."

"You are cheap!" Alizé told him, turning to look at him.

"I ain't cheap! I'm just in high school. How you expect me to be rollin'?"

"Much better than you are if you expect to be rollin' with me," Alizé pointed out, rolling her eyes.

"And what's that supposed to mean?"

"I meant what I said out there. I deserve better than this change you throwin' at me. Burgers and the dollar show ain't my idea of going out. Maybe you need to get a job."

"I'm not thinking about no job. I'm thinking about graduating from high school and then going to college, which is what you should be thinking about," Steve said, pointing a finger at Alizé, "instead of trying to be taken out for lobster dinners and expensive shows."

"So it's going to keep on being like this?" Alizé asked.

"What am I supposed to say, girl? I'm in high school."

Alizé shook her head sadly, placed her hand on the door handle, and popped it open. "Then you can't afford me," she said and got out.

As Alizé walked toward her apartment building, she heard Steve calling out to her for her to stop, for her to please stop and let him talk to her, but she kept walking, not even looking back once. This was how it would all start if she let it, Alizé thought. It was probably how it started for her mother. She let her father stick around when she shouldn't have with his cheap ass. Then he got her pregnant, and by that time it was too late. She had been mistreated by the man she loved most, and after that, she just got accustomed to it. So now every man she dealt with had an open invitation to walk all over her. They didn't have to treat her right, didn't have to take her out, buy her nice things, prove how much they wanted to be with her, because her mother was soft and didn't require them to.

But that wouldn't be Alizé. Hell, no, she thought as she stepped in the door, closing it behind her, finally blotting out Steve's pleading for her to come back, to reconsider. Alizé was worth much more than that.

When Alizé walked into the apartment, her mother had the phone to her ear. She was talking, lowering her voice as Alizé walked by, but she still heard what her mother was saying.

"I just wanted you to know that I had a really good time the other night, and I want to know when I can see you again," her mother said into the phone, her hand cupped over her mouth to keep Alizé from hearing her.

Alizé shook her head as she walked into her room. Isn't that nice? Her mother had a really good time, Alizé scoffed. She got all gussied up, put on her red dress, just to have it hiked up around her hips, and get done in the room next to her two daughters, when they were supposed to be painting the town. And now she calling that man, asking when they could do it all again. How sorry was that?

Alizé was right. Her mother had gotten used to being mistreated, and now it even sounded like she was beginning to enjoy it.

SIX

JANET JOHNSON'S apartment was on Thirty-Seventh Street, about ten minutes from where Alizé lived. The apartment was a huge two bedroom. Old as hell, but it was gigantic for the little that JJ paid in rent each month. The place was so big that when Sasha, one of Alizé's and JJ's mutual friends, was having problems with her boyfriend beating her, JJ said that that she could stay there until she got things together.

Sasha was nineteen and beautiful. Could've had any man she wanted with that pretty brown wavy hair she had on her head, that perfect smile, and that petite body. She looked like a model and dressed like one too, spending every dime she had on clothes. But she said she was done dating for a while, and Alizé could understand, remembering the time Sasha showed up at JJ's place, both eyes swollen so shut she could hardly see. She had stolen her man's credit card and had an all-day Gold Coast shopping spree, but she still didn't deserve to get worked over like that.

JJ was the opposite of everything Sasha was. Where Sasha was soft, JJ was hard. Where Sasha was quiet, polite, and submissive, JJ was loud, rude, and forceful. But she was like that for a reason. When she was younger, her mother's boyfriend used to rape her. JJ said that when she finally told her mother about it, her mother got all upset with her, said she was lying, and kicked her out, telling JJ that she wasn't going to let her mess up the good thing she had with that man. That had to be why JJ hated men so much.

Finally, there was Lisa, Ally's girl. She was average looking and didn't care how many times Alizé said she'd do her hair, face, and nails for her. The answer was no. She was plain as hell but had a cute smile. She was twenty years old and had had a baby when she was sixteen.

Now she was going to school and working full time, trying to provide for it but failing.

All four girls lay around the apartment sipping on beers and coolers. Alizé sat cross-legged in one of the big chairs, while Lisa's body was draped across the other one. JJ and Sasha sat on the sofa, Sasha turning the pages on a motorcycle magazine, while JJ puffed from a joint and sipped from a beer.

The 27-inch color tube played on in front of them, the volume down, lit candles placed here and there about the room flickering, as the girls continued to drink from their bottles and pass the joint around.

"Ya'll are getting me down," Lisa said, setting down her barely touched passion fruit wine cooler. "Ain't there something more to do than just lie around here and get drunk?"

"Like what?" JJ wondered, holding the joint to Sasha's lips, allowing her to take a puff.

"I don't know. Go and see a movie. Go out to dinner. Something."

"Movie playin' on the tube right there . . . ooh, ooh, go back to that page, girl," JJ said to Sasha, seeing a Harley she liked. "And don't got no money for dinner," she reminded them. "But there's a fresh box of Cap'n Crunch in the cabinet, and the milk should still be good."

"Do you even care about your future, JJ?" Lisa asked, sitting up in her chair. "Or is it all about bikes and beer?"

"Future? I'm twenty-two years old. My future is now."

"But you still need to be plannin' for—"

"I ain't got to plan for nothin'. Just because you messed up and let some nigga get you pregnant when you was a shorty don't mean that everybody got to be going to school and working they behinds off, tryin' to be a good mother, when kids is the furthest thing from they mind. Next time you need to make sure that fool put a condom on."

"I love my baby," Lisa said. "I'm glad I have my son. At least I have some priorities. At least I got direction," and she got up and headed toward the kitchen.

"Whatever, man," JJ said, blowing her off. "Why don't you direct your ass into getting me another Heineken." JJ looked over at Alizé, then tapped Sasha, bringing her attention to their brooding girlfriend.

"Damn, girl," JJ said. "Where your head at?"

Alizé didn't respond, just kept peeling the label from her wine cooler bottle.

"Alizé," Sasha called.

"Hunh."

"The sex must've been good last night, 'cause you still there."

"Naw, I was just thinking about what Lisa said. She was making sense, you know that, right."

"C'mon, Ally," JJ said, flopping backward into the sofa. "Not you too. Can't some girls just hang out and chill? Ya'll ain't even in your twenties yet. What's the damn rush?"

"Look at us. All we do is sit around, like Lisa said, and get drunk and high, and where's that gettin' us?"

"I ain't listening no more. You wreckin' my high, girl," JJ said. "Talking about the future and all that nonsense."

"I look at my mom," Alizé said, "and she just be letting dudes run all over her because she ain't got no leverage. She ain't got no power. You need money to have power, so you won't be in no situation where a man can just treat you any way he wants. Buy your ass a damn barbecue bacon cheeseburger, and expect you to be happy. Know what I'm sayin'?"

"I don't think it's all about just money," Lisa said, walking back in the room, handing JJ a fresh beer. "But I hear where you coming from."

"Ally just uptight, because she must be having problems with Steve again," JJ said.

"Ain't having no problems with Steve, because Steve is done."

"Yeah, we heard that the last time," Lisa remembered.

"Naw, I mean it now. Brotha ain't got no money, and I'm tired of being taken to cheap places to eat like I was in high school."

"But you *are* in high school," JJ said, drinking from the fresh beer Lisa brought her.

"But I don't look like it, and they're brothas out there that would lay out fat cash to get with a girl that look like me, know what I'm sayin'?"

"Naw, what you sayin'? That you gonna start dating men just because they got money to give you?"

"What's wrong with that? Men make money to spend it on women like me," Alizé said, stepping in front of the TV and demanding everyone's full attention. "Lisa, you sayin' you couldn't deal with having no man pay for the day care you need for Ricky in exchange for a little ass?"

Lisa looked to the ceiling, giving the question some thought, then shook her head. "I need some money, or I'm gonna have to stop going to school at night and get a second job, but I can't be selling my goods, Ally."

"And I thought you said you don't want to raise him in the 'hood. Thought you said if you had enough money, you'd go somewhere safer."

"I did say that. But there's better ways out there than spreading my legs."

"Sasha," Ally said, turning her attention over there. "You wouldn't do it if some fool was willing to buy you all the designer clothes you wanted?"

Sasha looked as though she was about to decline, then reconsidered. "Anything I wanted?"

"Anything."

"Aw, she don't count," Lisa said. "She a clothes ho."

"So you just gonna go out there, get you a baller, and start collecting, hunh?" JJ asked.

"If I'm gonna be spending time with a man, might as well be one with loot," Alizé said confidently.

"It ain't as easy as you think, baby. Some of those men ain't nothing nice. They take you to Red Lobster for steak and all the shrimp you can eat, and then think they own you. You saw what that fool was doin' to my girl," JJ said, sympathy on her face. She threw her arm around Sasha's shoulder, pulled her close, and kissed her on the cheek.

"Just glad she's out of that. But if you think you can do better, knock yaself out."

Alizé looked at her girls, took in what was said, but it didn't make any difference, because they weren't her.

"I'll make believers out of ya'll," Alizé said, digging into her purse and pulling out her cell phone. "There's this dude that's been trying to get wit' me. Met him at Danger a few weeks ago," she said, scrolling through her phone's directory, locating his number. "And he's been calling me ever since. I've been hung up wit' Steve's broke ass so I couldn't get back, but today, ladies," Alizé announced, punching in his number, "is his lucky day."

She waited a moment. The phone rang twice, and then on the third ring, it was picked up.

"Hello. This Mike? This is Alizé," she purred, winking at her girls. "Alizé. I met you at Danger a little while ago."

The girls snickered because they knew the guy didn't remember her.

"Naw, I'm the one with the fat ass and big lips," Alizé said, giving the girls a confident smile. "Yeah, I thought you'd remember. And yeah, I know you been dyin' to get wit' me," Alizé said, flipping back her hair as if she was a supermodel. "Well, how about next week? Yeah, yeah." She nodded her head. "I don't know, how about going some-where nice to eat? Havin' some drinks afterward, you know. Yeah . . . cool . . . cool. All right, baby. Yeah . . . yeah . . . can't wait to see you, either." Alizé disconnected the call, then stared down her girls.

"Now, watch your girl get treated the way she's supposed to."

SEVEN

LIVVY shouldered her bag, closed her locker, and turned the combination on it. It was the end of another long day, and there was nothing more that she wanted to do than just get away from that hospital.

It was a shame, because it wasn't that she didn't like her work. It was just the limited responsibility, the fact that she knew she could do a lot more, but wasn't allowed to because of her level of education.

Livvy thought about what had happened earlier. Lucy Kolson, a middle-aged woman with gastrointestinal problems, was in room 324. When Livvy walked in there to check on her, Lucy told her that one of her IV bags had run out.

"Not a problem," Livvy said, disconnecting the old bag from the tubing, taking it from the stand, and tossing the empty plastic bag in the trash. She went into the cabinet, found another bag, checked the label to make sure it was the same solution, and went about connecting it to Mrs. Kolson's tubing.

Livvy smiled as she was doing this. There were only a couple of things that she was allowed to do that made her feel like she was really important, and this was one of them. But just when she was about to connect the tube, a nurse walked into the room.

"What are you doing?" she demanded. It was Jennifer something or other. She had one of those long Polish names that Livvy didn't even think about trying to pronounce. She had only been there a few days, and this was Livvy's first time working with her.

"I'm changing Mrs. Kolson's IV," Livvy said. "It was empty."

"And who told you to do that?" Nurse Jennifer said, rushing over to Mrs. Kolson's bedside, checking her arm where the IV entered her vein, as if Livvy was trying to shoot her up with heroin.

"The bag was empty. She needed a new one," Livvy explained.

"You should've called me instead of trying to do it yourself."

"What do you mean, *trying*? I did do it myself, and I've done it a thousand times before, so what's the big deal?"

Jennifer didn't respond right away but looked down into Mrs. Kolson's face, now looking slightly distressed.

"Excuse us for a minute, Lucy, okay?" Jennifer said, speaking to the fifty-two-year-old woman like she was a child.

Jennifer grabbed Livvy by the elbow and led her into the hallway.

"Listen," Jennifer scolded, her face starting to turn a pale shade of red. "I don't care how many times you changed bags in the past, and I don't care if the other nurses let you perform open heart surgery on these patients, when you work with *me*, you perform only the duties that are in your job description."

"But that *is* in my job description," Livvy said, pleading her case.

"Look, I'm the nurse. You're the nurse's assistant. It would make my job a lot easier if you just do what you're supposed to do and assist me. Okay?"

Livvy didn't respond, but it wouldn't have made a difference if she had. Jennifer turned away from her and looked as though she was about to walk off, but then she turned her pink face back, and waving a finger up in Livvy's face threatened, "And if you ever question my responsibility in front of a patient again, I'll have you written up." She strode off.

Written up, Livvy thought now, leaving the locker room. That woman was lucky Livvy was in control of her emotions and her actions, because if she wasn't, if she was to let that project girl in her out, she would've been whupping the poor girl's ass in front of that patient instead of just questioning her.

Livvy walked slowly down the hall, every other fluorescent light above her turned off, dimming the place for the night shift and sleeping patients. She told herself to forget what had happened earlier. Don't complain, don't try and fight it, she told herself, because there was nothing she could do. Jennifer was right, regardless of how much Livvy hated to admit it. She was the assistant, and her job was to assist. There was no way around that.

But wait. Livvy stopped, seeing something out the corner of her eye. She turned her head to the right and focused on something posted on the bulletin board. It was a long page, a lot of fine print running down the entire sheet, but on the top, and this was what caught her eye, were the words "Hospital-Based Nursing Scholarship."

Livvy stepped over to the board and quickly scanned the page, taking in the details. The hospital was offering a two-year scholarship for an associate's degree in nursing. Only hospital employees were eligible. Applicants had to work in a patient care field (Livvy did), and they had to have a high school diploma, or equivalency, which she had, and she was thankful now that she had gone back to get her GED. The applicants also had to write a three- to five-page essay about why they wanted to become a nurse.

She could do that, Livvy thought, feeling the excitement build in her. She could write the essay, win the scholarship, and become a nurse, and never have to put up with the crap she'd been dealing with ever again.

Livvy looked up and down the hall, and when she saw that no one was around, tore down the notice and stuffed it in her purse. With this new information, she practically skipped out of the hospital, thinking that everything was going to change for her.

When Livvy got home, she was still excited about the scholarship, but as she walked in the door to her apartment, one thing dominated her thoughts: Carlos. She walked to the phone, picked it up, and started scrolling through the previous call directory, looking for his number, praying that he had called.

The phone emitted tiny beeps as she rolled through all the numbers, but no Carlos. Livvy started to dial his number, but stopped herself and placed the phone back into the cradle.

She looked over her shoulder, then walked back toward the girls' room. Livvy knocked softly on the door. When there was no answer, she gently pushed the door open, only to find that her daughters weren't there.

Good, Livvy thought, as she made her way back to the phone with quicker steps than she had left it. She knew the girls had to have heard her that night having sex with Carlos, even though that morning, they acted as if nothing had happened. At least Hennesey did. Over breakfast, Alizé kept on giving her mother looks as though she had been betrayed.

Yeah, she had told the girl that she would give Carlos his walking papers that night, but when the man walked through the door, Livvy could feel her body temperature rise, and when he said nothing, just wrapped his arms around her, pressed his body into hers, slid his hands down over her behind, she thought she would fall out right then.

Whatever fight she had had in her disappeared, along with the idea of painting the town. All she wanted was him, was him inside her, and he had to have known that because he took her hand and led Livvy into her bedroom. The only words they spoke that entire night were in the fit of passion. She moaned and grunted how much she loved him, and to never leave her, and he told her that he loved her too and that he never would stay away for as long as he had. But his promises sounded hollow; she could detect the insincerity in his words. He couldn't hide the fact that he was lying to her, no matter how good he made her feel.

After they had finished, when he carefully pulled himself from her bed, Livvy was half asleep. He kissed her passionately on the lips, something that felt like a dream, and then he left. The next morning, even though Alizé was giving her that evil stare at breakfast, Livvy didn't care, because of how good she felt.

But the other night, Alizé walked in and caught Livvy on the phone, practically begging to see Carlos again after he had not called back as he promised. She'd tried to lower her voice, but she knew Ally had heard her, and that was embarrassing.

The girl just shook her head, and she knew what was in her daughter's mind. *What a poor desperate woman my mother is*, she was probably thinking. And now, standing with the phone in her hand, about to dial Carlos's number, Livvy realized that maybe Ally was right.

Livvy put the phone down. "I'm not going to call you," she said aloud, trying to strengthen herself.

She looked over at the clock. It was just five minutes to nine. It was still early, and Livvy needed to unwind. She headed upstairs to the fifteenth floor and knocked on Sharika's door.

"Thought you had packed up and moved away, I ain't seen you in so long," Sharika said, letting Livvy in.

HALF AN HOUR later, Livvy was well into the unwinding process. She had kicked off her shoes, was sitting on the floor, and was working on her second big glass of wine.

Sharika was on her third glass, but her head wasn't probably feeling nearly as good as Livvy's because the girl was a natural drinker. Livvy had known her best friend practically her entire life. She was the one person, it seemed, whom she could rely on for everything. Sharika was there to rush Livvy to the hospital when she was pregnant, and should anything ever happen to Livvy, she entrusted Sharika to care for her daughters.

"You just got to position him right in your head then," Sharika said. They were talking about Carlos, and Livvy knew she could always count on good advice from her girl. They were the same age, but Sharika didn't have any kids, had never gotten pregnant, and to Livvy's knowledge, never got played by any man who didn't live to regret it.

"And what I mean by that is, if all he wants to do is come over and screw, then fine, sistah. Get yo' fuck on! But when you doin' it, save all that 'I love you' stuff for someone who really matters. You don't have to love a man to sleep with him. What's the problem?"

"The problem is," Livvy said, looking down at her glass, feeling shame, "I do love him."

"Damn, girl. Then you should probably just leave him alone."

"But he loves me too."

"And how you know that?"

"He told me."

"That's it?"

"We been together for years, Sharika."

"Then you should know where you stand right now. You shouldn't have these questions, shouldn't have to be chasin' him around like you doin'." Sharika scooted across the rug a little closer to Livvy. "And the worst thing is, you said your daughters are starting to see what's going on. You don't want them to see their mother actin' a fool, jumping through hoops for no man that's not even interested, do you? You gonna make them think it's okay for men to treat them like that too."

"No." Livvy shook her head, trying not to imagine that happening. "I can't have that."

"Then no matter how much it hurts, let him go."

"But . . ."

"But what?"

"But then I'll have nobody."

Sharika blew out a sigh, shaking her head. "Livvy, you're a gorgeous woman. Just go out and get you a new man. A real man this time."

"That's the problem," Livvy said, taking another sip from her wine glass. "There are no real men out there our age. They're married, in jail, gay, or just losers."

"Then date someone not our age, silly," Sharika responded.

"I don't have time to be teaching no young boy new tricks, Sharika."

"I'm not saying date a younger man. Date an older one."

"Un-uh," Livvy said, screwing her face up, as if she just got a whiff of something horrible.

"I'm not talking about ninety year olds. Just older, distinguished gentlemen. Don't you know the deal with them, girl?" Sharika looked at her as if this should be material that all women were familiar with.

"No, and that's maybe because I never wanted to date anyone's grandfather."

"Well, let me explain. A lot of these older, divorced, or widowed men would love to have a beautiful younger woman on their arm, but they know in order for that to happen, there has to be a trade. They come off a little money, and we give them a little time. Everybody gets exactly what they want."

"I can't take no money from no man," Livvy protested.

"Bill collectors still calling?"

"Never stop."

"And if there was a man that was willing to help you out in exchange for a little time with you, you wouldn't go with that?"

Livvy didn't answer.

"Livvy, deal is, either you use, or you get used. It can never be fair and square across the board. And the problem is, all your life you been getting used. For all the love that you been giving out, all you been getting back is pain. You thirty-three years old now. It's time to dash that dream and get real with what's goin' on. You feel me on this one?"

"You ain't never lied to me before," Livvy said, quickly examining her life's past and realizing what Sharika said was true.

"Good, then. Tomorrow night, you get off work and put something nice and tight on. We gonna go lounge hoppin', find you a distinguished gentleman who has a little something to offer."

EIGHT

ON THE DAY of Rafe's meeting with his parole officer, he looked a bit more presentable than he had after getting out of prison. After awaking from a long, restful night's sleep, Rafe had walked downstairs to talk to his aunt.

"You think you can do something with my hair?" he asked her. "Don't want to look crazy when I go see this man."

"Of course, baby." His Aunt Dorothy got a few things from the bathroom, set the hair oil and combs on the table, then pulled a chair out and sat down in it. Rafe knew to sit on the floor in front of her, in between her knees.

She parted and oiled his hair, then braided it in tight, neat cornrows.

"Just like when I baby-sat you as a little one," she smiled, giving Rafe a hand mirror to look into. She also gave him a button-down, collared shirt. One of her late husband's.

RAFE stepped into the diner, a bell ringing to announce his entrance. There was a long dining counter on one side of the restaurant, a row of booths on the other. Practically all the stools at the counter were taken, people hunched over their plates, busily shoveling food into their mouths. Two sets of couples sat at two different booths. Then Rafe's eyes caught sight of a slightly overweight, haggard-looking white man. The man caught Rafe's glance, and with a look, let him know that he was the man Rafe was looking for.

"Sit down," Mr. Dotson said after Rafe walked up to his table.

Rafe did as he was told, looking at the cup of coffee and plate with a crust of apple pie on it, sitting in front of the man. But what most held Rafe's attention was the folder the man was looking in. Rafe was sure it had all of his information in it: where he grew up, birthdate, mother's and father's names, all that stuff. When Dotson looked up at him again, Rafe felt naked.

"Would offer you something to eat, but this is only gonna take a minute, so . . . ," Dotson said, still flipping pages through Rafe's file. "They let you out in three of a five for good behavior. Even though you didn't test positive for them, you got busted selling drugs, so you're gonna be tested every month. You get caught using or dealing again, you go back and finish your five. Got that?" Dotson looked up from the file, grabbed his coffee cup, and took a sip.

"Yeah, I got it," Rafe said, taking in the beat-up-looking man. He looked at the tired tweed sport jacket he was wearing, the sweater vest and shirt under that. His hair was short, graying, messy. He had wrinkles under his eyes and dirt under his nails. Rafe wanted to see this guy as few times as possible.

"You got somewhere to stay?" Dotson said, not bothering to look at Rafe this time.

"Yeah."

"Write it down," the man said, pulling a small pad and pencil from out of his inside breast pocket and pushing them across the table. "Phone number too, if you got one."

Rafe wrote down the address. "I don't know the phone number, yet."

"Give it to me next time," Dotson said. "You got three weeks to find employment. Got any idea of where you're going to be working?"

"Un-uh," Rafe said, giving Dotson back the pad and pencil. "I was hoping that maybe you might know of somebody or something I could do."

Dotson sat his cup down, and gave Rafe a long look without saying a word or sacrificing what he was thinking. Then he said, "As a matter of fact, I do know of something. Says in the file that you took some automotive repair courses while inside."

"Yeah, I did," Rafe said, proudly. "I got really good too."

"Well, there's this exotic car dealership. You know, Porsches, Ferraris, things like that, about twenty minutes from here. I happen to know that they're looking for a mechanic. You think you could work on cars like that?"

"Yeah, yeah." Rafe tried not to sound too excited. It wasn't the fact that he'd be working on Porsches that got him going, although that didn't hurt. It was just the fact that he'd be working.

Dotson went into his pocket again, pulled out a number of small, folded pieces of paper, and finally found the one he was looking for, passed it to Rafe.

"You know where that is?"

"No. But I could find it."

"Don't worry about it. They're looking for someone immediately, so I'll just take you over there." Dotson fingered a few bills out of his wallet and tossed them on the table.

"When?" Rafe asked.

"Now," Dotson said, standing from the table. "That's what immediately means. C'mon."

Dotson's old Ford LTD pulled up in front of a building with huge storefront windows and shiny, expensive European cars sitting behind them. Rafe looked up at the building. Mirror Motors read the sign that stretched out over the sidewalk.

"All right, good luck," Dotson said, the car still running.

"Aren't you coming in, or something?" Rafe asked, turning to him.

"I'm not the one that's trying to get a job. Now go on in there. You got nothing to worry about. I told you they're looking to fill the position. Now go, and give me a call by next week."

Rafe reluctantly got out of the car, and after it pulled away, he felt helpless, clueless, and questioned if he should even go inside the store. Then he realized he had nothing else. This was his only lead, so he might as well make an attempt, even if they did laugh him right back out onto the street.

Rafe walked into the dealership and in between all the beautiful cars, saw men in expensive suits, some showing the cars off, others nodding enthusiastically at all the features being shown to them.

For what seemed a full minute, Rafe stood practically in the middle of the showroom, between a black Lamborghini Diablo and a champagne-colored convertible Jag. He stood there, looking around, not knowing what or whom to ask for, when he felt a tap on his shoulder.

He jumped, spun around to find a petite, beautiful blonde woman in front of him, with a jacket and matching skirt on.

"May I help you with something, sir?" she asked, smiling, and to Rafe, she seemed pretty sincere.

"Yeah, I uh . . . I uh," he said, nervously. And when he sensed that he would have continued problems getting the words out, he reached into his pocket and retrieved the little scrap of paper, handed it to the woman. "I was supposed to come here about a job as a mechanic. Mr. Dotson brought me here."

She took the paper, didn't even look at it, and said, "Oh, yes. Here for the repair position. Come this way, sir."

Rafe followed her, feeling guilty about glancing down at the woman's behind, almost feeling as though he was doing something illegal. He pulled his eyes away and quickly stared up at the ceiling. She turned and said, "Right in there, sir. Just have a seat, and the manager will be in with you shortly," and disappeared without a sound.

Rafe took the seat opposite the desk in the small, windowless office. His palms were sweating, and rubbing them together in attempt to rub the sweat away only made them sweat more. *What the hell was he doing here?* he thought. Yeah, he knew how to work on cars, and he was good—he ain't lied about that—but they were VW Beetles, Chevy Camaros, and Ford Mustangs. Old ones at that. Why did he think he could work on cars that he knew cost up to, and over, a hundred grand?

He was losing his damn mind if he thought they'd hire him, and now Rafe was starting to get angry with Dotson's old, worn-out ass for even bringing him here. He wondered if this was some game that was being played on him. Make him look like a fool for the hell of it.

Rafe needed to be at some warehouse somewhere, interviewing for a job lifting boxes. Something that he knew he could get, because they wouldn't be asking him a million questions about what makes a million-dollar-car run.

Yeah, that's what he would do. He would get real and get out of there. He stood and was turning toward the door, when he was met by a fit older man with slicked back black hair, wearing a suit. He looked a lot like the former LA Lakers coach, Pat Riley.

"Takin' off?" the man asked, with a thick Italian accent.

"Naw, naw," Rafe slowly sat back down. "I was just about to go to the bathroom, but I don't have to go no more."

"You sure?"

"Yeah. Sure."

"Okay." The man walked behind his desk and took a seat. There was a *Car & Driver* magazine there, which he removed and slid into a drawer, then rested his folded hands atop the desk.

"So you're here for the mechanic's position?"

"Yeah." Rafe didn't feel right about this whole setup.

"You know how to fix cars?"

"Yeah, some of them, but I don't know about cars like you got out there," Rafe said, turning to look out the door, toward the showroom.

"They're cars, like all cars. They got four wheels, one steering wheel, and an engine that makes them go. Just like women, once you fuck one, you know how to fuck 'em all. Don't matter that one cost you ten dollars to take her out to dinner and the other cost you a hundred and ten. They all got the same equipment."

Rafe didn't know if he should smile at the remark, but the man wasn't smiling, so he didn't.

"So you want this job, or what?"

"Yeah, but—"

"But nothin'. What you don't know, we'll teach you. Are you a good mechanic?"

"Yeah," Rafe confirmed.

"You on time, don't play games, don't bullshit?"

"I'm on time, and no, I don't play games."

"Okay then." The man stood up, walked around to the front of the desk, and extended his hand. "You got the job."

Rafe couldn't believe what he was hearing, and now he knew this wasn't right. "What do you mean, I got the job?"

"That's what I mean. You want it or not? Because if you do, you not shakin' my hand is saying something entirely different."

Rafe quickly placed his hand in the man's and shook. "But I don't even know your name. You don't know mine."

"My name is Mr. Sillva, and you are Raphiel Collins, otherwise known as Rafe," Mr. Sillva said, walking toward the door.

Rafe stood there dumbfounded.

"Raphiel," Mr. Sillva said, standing just outside the door. "You were in prison, right?"

"Yeah," Rafe said, still not believing any of this.

"Well, I was too. I know what it was like to be where you are. Somebody gave me a second chance, and now somebody's giving you one. Stop questioning things. Just take it, and be happy that it's being extended to you, okay?"

The man was right.

"Okay, Mr. Sillva. Thank you."

"Good. Brandy will be back in to settle the particulars, and we'll see you in a couple of days. Good?"

"Good," Rafe smiled. Real good.

NINE

THE FOLLOWING evening, Livvy and Sharika hooked up as planned.

"I don't know about this," Livvy said, pausing in front of the door to the New Raven Lounge.

"What do you mean, you don't know about this?" Sharika mimicked, standing behind her, wearing a shiny gold, silky-looking dress, that hung just above her knees. "You look fine."

Livvy looked down at herself. She remembered looking in the mirror for the thousandth time before they left, and there she thought she looked okay, wearing the red dress she'd had on the other night—the dress that was supposed to have seen the town with Carlos, when all it saw was her bedroom floor. But now, looking at herself, at her matching red shoes that all of a sudden felt two sizes too small, and feeling the makeup on her face that felt way too heavy, she didn't feel attractive enough to walk through those doors.

"I don't feel right," she said to Sharika. "I feel slutty."

"Good. That's the idea," Sharika laughed, pushing her in. "Get more attention that way."

They paid the huge round man at the door the five dollar cover and walked into the dimly lit lounge. The place was carpeted and mirrored from floor to ceiling, in the old seventies style. Even the weight-bearing pillars that held the ceiling over their heads had little squared pieces of mirror glued to them.

There were three bars in this room—two on either side of the lounge and one huge U-shaped bar in the middle. Men and women dressed in nice suits and dresses sat and stood at those bars, and in chairs lining the lounge's walls, laughing and conversing.

Livvy walked behind Sharika through the lounge, feeling somewhat overwhelmed, but also slightly intoxicated from the excitement around her.

"What do you think!" Sharika asked, her mouth right up to Livvy's ear, because of the loud James Brown song that was playing.

"Lots of people!" Livvy said, loudly.

Sharika said something back to her, which Livvy didn't hear, and then Sharika grabbed her hand and quickly pulled her across the room.

They ended up at the big bar in the center of the lounge. "Quick, sit there!" Sharika plopped her bottom down on a stool, yanking Livvy down on the one next to her.

"These are the best seats in the place," Sharika said. "Now all we have to do is wait."

"Why don't we at least get something to drink?" Livvy raised a hand, trying to get the bartender's attention. Sharika quickly grabbed her hand and forced it down.

"You really haven't been out in a while. We don't have to do that."

"Why not?"

"Give it a minute, would you?"

Livvy turned her attention to the TVs that hung in the corners of the bar. She saw Jordan in his blue Wizard's uniform, dunking on his old Chicago team, but before she could see what the score was, the bartender was standing in front of her and Sharika.

"The gentleman across the bar wants to know what the ladies will be drinking."

"See, I told you," Sharika said out the side of her mouth, nudging Livvy with her elbow.

"Which gentleman is that?" Livvy asked, speaking sideways back to Sharika.

"It doesn't matter, girl. Whoever it is ain't askin' you to have his baby. He just trying to buy you a drink. Absolut and cranberry for both of us, thank you," Sharika ordered.

Livvy watched which way the bartender walked to get payment for the drinks.

"Don't look over there!"

"Why not?" Livvy said, quickly turning away.

"Don't want him to think that this doesn't happen to you all the time."

"Well it doesn't."

"There's a time to acknowledge him, and now ain't it."

The bartender brought the drinks over to them, set them on napkins, placed two tiny straws in each of them, then walked away.

Sharika picked up her glass, took a sip, then looked across the bar. She nudged Livvy again.

"Now you can look."

A man across the bar lifted his glass and smiled at the two women.

"My goodness," Sharika said. "He's hideous, and big as a baby hippo."

"Ooh, you're right," Livvy said, shielding one side of her face with her hand as she pulled her drink to her lips with the other.

"But since you took a sip of the drink he bought you already, you know you're going to have to sleep with him. Rules of the game."

"He's going to have to catch my ass first," Livvy said.

TEN

WADE WILLIAMS was pretty pissed off as he made his way home. He had followed the little old lady and her son up and down that car lot for what seemed like an hour and a half, waiting for her to decide which one she liked.

"Well, does this one have the antenna that pops up and down when you turn on the car?" the little old lady asked.

"No ma'am," Wade explained, walking toward the back of the car. "As you can see, the antenna is always up. It's a fixed antenna," he said, smiling, but grinding his teeth at the same time.

"And this car," she said, sitting in a Ford Thunderbird. "It doesn't have a handle over the driver's side window I can grab onto," she said, reaching a shaking, arthritic hand up to the place where she wished the handle would've been.

"Well, ma'am, I believe the carmaker expects both your hands to be on the steering wheel at all times. That's why there isn't a handle there."

"There are handles over all the other windows."

Wade looked at her son for help, but the middle-aged, clean-cut man just gave him a look that said, *You're trying to sell her the car, not me*.

"They have handles because they aren't near the driver's seat, Ma'am," Wade explained patiently.

"Well, I don't like the no handle thing. What else have you got?"

The only reason Wade persevered was that he knew this woman had money, could tell by her clothes, by the way those veiny little clawlike hands held onto her bag. The clothes she was wearing were a horribly colored rainbow of sherbet pastels. She looked as though she had been dipped in Easter egg dye, but Wade knew those clothes were expensive. If there was nothing else a used car salesman knew, he knew how to spot a person with money, and she was one.

The blue-haired lady finally settled on a late model Mercury Marquis. He finally had her sitting in front of his desk. Her body was so little that she was swallowed up by the chair. She looked like she was 12 years old instead of 112, which was how old Wade figured her decrepit butt to be.

"So, I've been back to my manager, and this was the final number he said we could do." Wade jotted it on a scrap of paper, and pushed it over to her across the desk, looking intently at her. Of course, there was no going back to the manager. The damn manager had left for the night, and even if it was noon, the whole "going back to the manager" thing was nothing more than Wade taking a leak, standing around, whistling "Dixie" in the break room for five minutes, or just walking around the corner, and hanging out for a bit.

The little old lady looked down at the price and gasped as though it wasn't numbers that were written on the page but a threat on her life. She adjusted her glasses as though maybe they were to blame. Then she passed the page to her son.

"Do you see that, Abner?"

Poor guy, Wade thought. *Fellow's name is Abner. He has to hate his mother for that.*

"Looks pretty fair to me, Mother," Abner said.

"It's a great price, Ma'am. We're only making a five hundred dollar profit."

"Then maybe you ought to have a talk with Mercury for charging so much for their cars. I can remember when brand-new cars cost only two thousand dollars."

"With all due respect, Ma'am, that had to be a long time ago."

"I know it was a long time ago!" the lady snapped at Wade. "I was there! But it still doesn't matter. A car is a car, and to ask a poor little old lady for this much money is robbery. Let's go, Abner," she said, standing. Abner stood, and took his mother's arm. "My house didn't cost this much," she said, turning to Wade just long enough to throw back the words and give him a dirty look.

Wade parked his Lincoln Town Car in front of the house. He'd spent two and a half hours with that woman, and what had come of it? Nothing. Nada. Zip! He'd watched as a black man and woman, obvi-

ously married, walked onto the lot, their eyes big, looking at cars. He
watched as an older, distinguished white fellow wearing a suit stepped
into the showroom and overheard him saying he was looking for a nice
midrange sedan. In both situations, they'd gone to other salespeople.
The couple to Janet, the guy to Rob, and both of them had made sales
while Wade was toiling with the little old lady from hell.

He jumped out of his car, his pride and joy, and looked it over.
There was a smudge on the hood, so he pulled his handkerchief out
and wiped it away. That was the first thing that had brought a smile to
his face all day. What a shame, he thought.

Wade skipped up the two stairs that put him on the walkway to the
house. He bypassed the stairs to the front door, because he didn't walk
through the front door to enter the house. He took the side, just like
the other two boarders.

Forty-eight years old and living in a single room. Paying some
woman $125 a week for a room no bigger than the room he had grow-
ing up as a child. If he had known what his future was going to look
like as a child, he probably would've done everything to change it or
wouldn't have stuck around long enough to see it.

It was quite pathetic, Wade thought, climbing the stairs to the second floor. He walked into the hallway, checked the mail on the table,
but there was nothing there for him. Hardly ever was. He made his car
payment right there at the dealership, and, well, he didn't have a
house, and since he was trying to save all of his money, he didn't do the
credit card thing, so he really had no bills.

He passed by Fredrick's room, stopped briefly in front of it and
thought about knocking but decided not to. The old man would want
to talk, want to sit around, and listen to more of his classic jazz records,
and yes, Wade was old, but not that damn old. And besides, he wanted
to get out tonight, see what was happening out there, maybe pick up
on something nice to look at.

It had been only a couple of weeks since Wade had had his last
piece, but it was something that was bought. And not with dinner and
a couple of drinks—actually paid for. She was a hooker. He'd met her
at a lounge, bought her a drink, and tried to strike up conversation, but
she'd stopped him.

"Thanks for the drink, but you don't have to do all that talkin'. We
both know what you want," she said, pulling the toothpick out of her
drink. A cherry had been impaled on the end of it. She sensually encir-

cled the small ball with her tongue, then pulled it off into her mouth with her teeth. "Seventy-five dollars will get you the works."

Wade thought about walking off, but it had been more than a month since he had felt the inside of anything other than his fist. He looked over his shoulder, as if someone was listening, waiting for his response. Then he looked over the woman again. "Okay. Let's do it."

He was tired of all that. It was time to find a good woman, settle down. He didn't mean get married, though. Just settle down. Start a relationship.

Wade stepped into his room. It was cluttered, but then again, what could someone expect. Everything that would've been in his house was in that room. It included his kitchen (microwave and tiny fridge), his office (desk and computer), and his entertainment room (TV, VCR, and stereo).

He took off his shirt, stood in the mirror, and gave himself a once-over. Not bad for an old pimp, Wade thought to himself. His wavy hair was graying, but he still had most of it, outside of what was slowly disappearing from his front hairline. He kept his face cleanly shaved, and now as he rubbed fingers across his square jaw, he debated shaving again today. It would wait until tomorrow, he decided. Wade stood back some in the mirror, in his wife-beater tank top, and didn't even have to pull in his gut. His two hundred sit-ups every night handled that for him, and his arms and shoulders had a decent amount of definition, thanks to his fifty nightly pull-ups.

He went to his closet, pulled the plastic off a laundered shirt, and put it on. He began to button it up, then stopped, and took it off. He pulled the tank top up over his head, put the shirt back on, and left the top two buttons undone. He would show a little chest tonight, he thought.

He went over to his dresser, opened up the jewelry box, and pulled out his gold herringbone chain, with the gold Mercedes Benz symbol on it, and threw it around his neck.

He stepped back in front of the mirror, throwing on a lightweight trench and Dobbs hat, then pulled the belt on the coat tight, his chest still exposed. "Time for some action," he said, pointing a finger at his reflection. Wade was about to turn and go, but he didn't. He just stared at himself for a moment. Did he actually look as ridiculous as he thought he did? Should he feel ashamed of himself for being where he was at this point in his life? Did he actually think any decent woman would want to be with an old guy who owned nothing but a five-year-old car?

He looked himself deeply in the eyes. Degrading himself wouldn't do him any good, so why do it?

"Bah," he said, smiling. "Whatever." He had never intended on growing up to be the old guy at the club, but that's what he was. Somebody had to do it, so he might as well be the best he could possibly be at it.

ELEVEN

IT WASN'T quite a dozen, but almost that many men had rolled up on Livvy since she had been at the lounge, and at least six of those men had offered to buy her a drink. She had to start refusing them after the third, because the room was starting to spin, and all the men were beginning to look a little more like Denzel with each moment that passed. She didn't want to make a mistake, give some man she thought looked like Michael Jordan her number, only to find when he showed up at her door that he actually looked like Michael Jackson. Because she really wasn't into white men.

Livvy danced four times, got groped three of those, twice from in front and once from behind. That particular man kept bumping into her, pushing himself into her behind. He was so aroused that she could feel him through both of their clothes and thought that any minute he was going to tear right through those purple slacks he was wearing and just poke her right up the butt. After he had done it for the third or fourth time, Livvy turned around, slapped the crap out of him, and stood there a moment, daring him to say something.

When she got back to her seat, Sharika had almost fallen off her stool she was laughing so hard.

"What's yo' damn problem?" Livvy demanded, sitting down, sucking down the last of her drink.

"You smacked the shit out of that man, and all he was doing was dancing with you."

"Hell, if we didn't have any clothes on, that would've been fuckin'."

"Whatever, girl. Yo' ass just old."

"No," Livvy said. "I just can't get off on the idea of having sex on a dance floor in front of a hundred people. Besides, if you didn't say that he was okay to dance with, he wouldn't have gotten slapped."

All night, Sharika had been either giving the "okay" or the "no-go" to the guys who walked up on Livvy. She also kept pointing out all the older men with younger women.

"See, there's another one." Sharika had discreetly pointed to a graying, wrinkled man with his arm around a woman who looked less than half his age.

"What? The man hangs out with his daughter. So what?"

"That ain't his daughter. That's his woman."

"Hell, naw. She looks like she just left home, and he looks like he's about to be put in one."

"I told you what the deal was, girl," Sharika said, taking a sip from her zinfandel. "Just watch him." And sure enough, that hand that was around the young woman's back slid down to her waist and then rested on her butt.

"Told you!" Sharika laughed, as though she had just won a million dollars.

Then she pointed out another old guy with square glasses so thick and cloudy they looked like two tiny TV screens. He had a goatee and enough gold around his neck to purchase a house with. A beautiful woman with a great body walked beside him. Livvy didn't know if she was there as his partner or as his geriatric nurse, but either way, she was there.

"Because they're taking care of these women" was Sharika's explanation. "I'm tellin' you."

Sharika told Livvy what to look for and what to watch out for in the men who came up to her.

"You already gave me too much info as it is. I'm half drunk, and you trying to read me the book on dating. Just shake or nod your head for yes or no if someone comes up to me," Livvy said, feeling as though her head was about to explode if she was given any more rules to remember.

"Fine."

The first guy who came up to Livvy shouldn't have been at this lounge. He was way too fine. Somewhere, some movie had probably had to stop production, because they were missing their leading man, Livvy thought. She had seen him start toward her from the other side of the room, and she had to cover her mouth as he approached because she thought she may have been drooling.

After he asked her if she'd like to dance, Livvy casually looked

toward Sharika, and the crazy woman was frantically shaking her head.
She must've gotten her signals backward. Livvy widened her eyes as if
to ask her again. Sharika shook her head harder this time.

After he walked away, Sharika explained. "He was too fine, Livvy.
That man got five other women at home. Three of them pregnant, one
his wife, and the other got a gun. You're better off without him."

She was probably right, Livvy thought.

Another man was too young, Sharika decided, because he looked
under forty-five. One of the older guys was wearing worn-out shoes, so
even though he flashed a wad of money and bought them both drinks,
he didn't really have any money, Sharika said. If he did, he would've
bought a new pair of loafers. Another guy had the tan line of a wedding
ring around his finger. Instant disqualification.

It had been one very long and intense education that Livvy was sick
of receiving.

"I'm ready to get out of here, girl. Grab your stuff, and let's go,"
Livvy sighed.

"But we only been here for . . . ," she paused to look at her watch,
" . . . three hours."

"That's three hours too long," Livvy said, walking toward the door.

"But what if the next man is perfect? What if he's the one?" Sharika
demanded, following her.

"Then if he's the one, I'll meet him somehow anyway. Ain't that
what they say?" Livvy said, both of them stepping out into the spring
night air.

"If that were true, then both of us would've met him by now."

"Got that right," Livvy said, jumping into the passenger side of
Sharika's car.

IT WAS 11:30 P.M., and as Wade drove his car down Stoney Island
Avenue, he knew the parking lot would be packed. But what could he
do? He was already there, and just as he thought, there was nothing
doin'.

He rolled through anyway, just to see if there was a spot that someone had missed, and as he made his second turn through the lot, he saw
a little car with its reverse lights on, pulling out of a space. "Good," he
thought. He was right near the car, but backed up some to let it out.

The car didn't back out though, just sat there, its white reverse lights still on, not doing anything. Wade turned his head, looking around the lot to see if anyone else was coming out or even if anyone was walking from the lounge to get in their car, but there was no one. He looked back at the car, then tapped his horn twice, letting them know that he was wondering what they were going to do.

The car didn't budge. *What the hell is going on?* Wade thought, trying to see what fool was driving. But then he decided that he should just find a spot on the street, because one never knew what crazy gun-toting types were out here.

He placed the car in drive and started to pull off, when the little car in front of him quickly backed up, blocking his way.

Wade honked his horn again. The two people in the front seats of the car looked as though they were arguing. *Fine*, he thought, *I'll just back up*. But when he looked over his shoulder, there was a car behind him. He threw his car in reverse and honked his horn, but the car just honked back at him, since there was another car behind that one as well.

Wade looked into the car in front of him again, and now it looked as if the two were fighting, taking weak swipes at each other. He didn't care about that. They could fight all they wanted to at home or any-where else, Wade thought, but they just had to let him out.

He placed his car in park and opened his door. He stood for a moment, making sure this was what he wanted to do, then moved.

As he walked toward the car, he saw both people stop fighting, and the person in the passenger side ducked down below the window.

As he walked up to the car, the passenger side window lowered. He stopped five feet in front of the door and bent down to see the driver's face.

"What is the problem? I'm trying to park, so either you're leaving or pull in so *I* can leave."

"I'm sorry, sir," the smiling, apologetic woman said from the driver's seat. "But we're having a little problem."

"And . . . ," Wade said, his patience being tested.

"Well, I saw what a handsome man you were out of my rearview mirror when you pulled up behind us, and I brought my friend out to have a nice time and meet a nice man, but none of that happened."

Wade was flattered by the compliment and even managed to crack a smile, but still wondered where all this was going. "And . . . ," he said again.

"And before we left, I told her that the next guy she met may have been the one for her, and I think I was right," Sharika said.

"And where is your friend?" Wade asked.

"Sir, I'd like for you to meet Livvy Rodgers."

Nothing happened.

"Livvy, sit up, and meet this nice man," Sharika said, scolding her like a child.

Slowly, the top of Livvy's hair could be seen over the surface of the door, then her forehead, and finally her entire face. She wore an extremely embarrassed look, but she managed a smile.

"Hi," she said shyly, waving. "I'm Livvy."

She was more than Livvy, Wade thought to himself as he stepped toward the car. She was beautiful.

TWELVE

THINGS COULDN'T have been going better, Rafe thought as he got ready for his second full day of work. It was almost like a dream. Here he was just getting out of prison, not even a full week had passed, and he had a decent place to stay, in a very nice neighborhood, thanks to his Aunt Dorothy, and a really good job, thanks to Mr. Sillva. Mr. Sillva was giving out second chances, and man, that was what Rafe needed more than anything.

Rafe spat toothpaste into the sink, cupped his hands under the running water, and rinsed. He looked in the mirror and was pleased with himself. His aunt did a wonderful job on his braids, but after he got his hair and beard lined up at the barber shop, the "do" looked much tighter. He flexed his tattoo-covered biceps in the mirror, and they hardened into stone at his command, along with the well-developed pecs. The one benefit of jail time, Rafe thought. You work out 'til you fall out. He slipped on the white T-shirt that contrasted greatly against his dark brown skin and smiled, his teeth appearing almost as white as his shirt. Yes, he was happy.

He grabbed his toiletry bag and left the washroom that he shared with the two other boarders but hadn't met yet. While he was getting dressed, he felt energy running through him, and he knew it was an eagerness to get back to his new job. He thought about yesterday, his first full day. After filing all the tax paperwork and other employment forms, Mr. Sillva showed him the locker room.

"Number 412," the man said, stopping in front of that locker. "This is yours from now on. Get a lock from home or buy one from the store, and keep it on here. Okay?"

"Yeah," Rafe said, feeling more and more like this place would soon feel like a home away from home.

"And here's a little something for you," Mr. Sillva said, stepping out from behind another locker door, and tossing Rafe a package wrapped in plain brown paper.

"What is it?" Rafe said, looking at the package.

"Open it up and see."

Rafe tore the paper away to find a red mechanic's oversuit. He held it by the shoulders and let it unfold in front of him. It had two yellow stripes going down either side and the Ferrari logo on the right breast pocket, his name embroidered on the left.

"I didn't know what you wanted to be known as around here, but we're all family, so I just had them stitch *Rafe* on the suit," Mr. Sillva said.

Rafe smiled at seeing his name. "Thanks, Mr. Sillva. Rafe is perfect."

"Good, but from now on, my name is Tommy."

That day he met the other mechanics. There were four of them, and now Rafe stood in the mirror, trying to remember their names. Julio, Paul, Randle, and . . . he couldn't remember the last name, but it didn't matter, because he would see them all today, and that made him feel good. He felt as if he belonged to something, that he was important, even though he was just turning a wrench, changing oil, repairing brakes. He still felt more important now than he had ever felt before.

The guys there had shown him around the repair area. Rafe told them that he knew only so much, but they didn't look down at him or see him as a burden, someone who would slow their progress. They said they were there to help, and if he had any questions, don't hesitate to ask. He wouldn't.

Upon arriving to work that day, he saw Julio in the locker room slipping on his oversuit.

"*Que pasa*, Rafe?"

"Nothin', Julio. What's up?" Rafe said, opening his locker.

"Nothin' here too, man," he said in his thick Hispanic accent. "Just one more day workin' on hundred thousand dollar cars. I hate my job," he said, smiling sarcastically, pulling his long hair together, wrapping a rubber band around it.

"See you out there, man."

"Yeah, see you," Rafe said, pulling out his suit and slipping it on over his jeans and T-shirt. He went out into the service area and saw that the guys already were doing work on a Porsche 911 and a Mercedes SL500. It was only seven in the morning, and the dealership didn't open until nine, so the guys had the music pumping, Biggy Smalls rappin' about how he was Goin' back to Cali.

Rafe liked this place more and more every day.

By ten minutes 'til noon, Rafe had mostly watched as the other guys worked on cars, and as they worked, they would tell him to pay close attention to this, or step in and give that a try. But in between observing, Rafe also changed the exhaust on a Saab 9-3, replaced the ball joints on an Audi A4, and took a spin in a BMW 840.

"The guy says there's something shaking in the dash of his Beemer, but he can only hear it when he drives it. So what do I do?" Rafe asked Paul, a country-fed, freckled-faced white boy.

"Take that fucker for a spin, man. And hold up, I'm going too."

Rafe and Paul had the rare two-door-coupe BMW sailing down side streets at ninety miles per hour. When they got back, Rafe pulled the dash and found a quarter that was bouncing around in there.

"Found it!" Rafe yelled across the service area to Paul, holding up the coin.

"See. You never would've known if we didn't take that baby out."

It was five minutes 'til noon, and Rafe was on his back under a car, checking for a leak. He glanced at his watch because his stomach was growling. Sure enough, it was just about lunchtime. He was looking forward to that, because all the guys said they were going out to a pizza place a block from the dealership that made the best Chicago deep dish.

Rafe was almost tasting it when he felt someone kicking the sole of one of his boots.

"Yeah," Rafe said, clicking off the light he was holding under the car.

"Roll out from under there," Rafe heard Mr. Sillva tell him.

Rafe came out from under the car. "What's up, Tommy?"

"Got a surprise for you. The owner wants to meet you."

"Oh, okay." Rafe looked down at his greasy hands, feeling the gunk that must've been on his face. He didn't want to be shaking hands with some rich old white man looking like a grease monkey.

"Can I wash my hands first?"

"Don't worry about it, Rafe. The owner doesn't think you're performing surgery back here. You're fixin' cars. You supposed to be dirty, and he knows that. C'mon."

Rafe followed Tommy out of the service area, down a number of hallways, and past countless office doors.

Tommy stopped in front of one of them, a plain door, no name on it.

"How you feel?" Tommy asked.

"Fine," Rafe said, swallowing hard, not feeling as fine as he said.

"Well, just relax," Tommy said, slapping his shoulder. "The owner is a regular guy, just like you. He understands where you're coming from, and that's why I think he allowed you to join our little team. So just remember that, okay."

"Yeah, okay," Rafe said.

Tommy opened the door, and Rafe stepped into the large, finely decorated office, then turned around when the door was pulled closed on him. He turned back around to face the desk, and the tall executive chair that was facing the wall, making it impossible to see who, if anybody, was sitting in it.

Rafe stood there wringing his hands together, feeling nervous, not knowing whether to speak or just stand there. The high-backed chair started to swivel. Rafe quickly straightened himself in preparation to meet his boss, but when the man behind the chair was completely facing him, Rafe couldn't believe who he was looking at.

The brown face, the deep-set eyes, the manicured mustache and goatee, and the tightly braided hair snapped Rafe back to three years ago.

"FUCK MAN, we gotta do something," Rafe remembered Smoke saying as flashing red and blue lights invaded the back window of the '75 Cadillac. Rafe looked over his shoulder, saw two police cruisers behind them, saw another one speeding up on the other side of the street, whipping a U-turn to join the others.

"Give me the stuff," Rafe said to Smoke, holding out his hands.

"What?" Smoke said, frantically, his hands on the steering wheel.

"Give me the stuff! Don't make sense both of us gettin' caught and going up."

"Hell naw, Rafe. Fuck that! I ain't lettin'—"

"Smoke! Give me the shit!" Rafe whipped his head around to see officers cautiously approaching either side of the car, their guns slowly being drawn.

"I ain't got no record. For me, this only enough for a minor possession charge. I'll get probation. They get you for this, you going away for ten to fifteen. Now c'mon."

"But you my brother. I ain't lettin' you go down for this alone. We're in this together. We go down together," Smoke said. But Rafe grabbed the shoulder bag out of the back seat before Smoke could reach it. He quickly pulled out the small amout of weed they had left from the day's sell and shoved it in his pockets.

"What are you doing!" Smoke said, his eyes wide.

"Just be cool. I'll handle this," Rafe told him, catching sight of the officer just outside the car door. He looked as casual as he could until one of the cops tapped on the car window with the barrel of his gun.

The cop was a black man, name was Bryant, and he hated Rafe and Rafe hated him. He was an Uncle Tom officer if there ever was one, beating down brothas with his nightstick harder than any white cop dared.

When Rafe rolled down the window, the black officer pointed the gun in at Rafe, even though his hands were already in the air. Countless times, he and his white partner had stopped him and Smoke, hoping to catch them with something. He'd finally gotten lucky and seemed to know it.

"Get yo' black ass out the car, slimy nigga," Bryant said. "Something's telling me this is your lucky night."

It was only two dime bags of weed. The public defender said it would be nothing, simple possession, no intent to distribute. They would hold Rafe 'til his court date, then slap him on the wrist with probation.

But when that court date arrived and Rafe stood there in front of the judge listening to the charges being read off, he thought he had to have been hearing things.

He saw the white man in the suit read something from a clipboard. Rafe heard his name, then heard the words "possession of cocaine." He heard the words "with intent to distribute." Then heard something about "five-year sentence."

He felt light-headed, felt the room whirling around him. He quickly looked to the Asian female public defender beside him.

"Don't worry. They've obviously made a mistake," she said. "We'll get this cleared up."

But Rafe knew that wouldn't happen when he caught sight of Bryant, there in the back of the room, smiling an evil, wide grin, bobbing his head, mouthing the words, "Gotcha, nigga."

As Rafe was being dragged out of the courtroom in handcuffs, the last thing he saw was Smoke rushing toward him, as if to rescue him, climbing over courtroom seats, yelling, tears in his eyes, "I'm gonna get you out of this. Don't you worry. I'm gonna get you out of this!"

RAFE'S EYES refocused on Samuel, the man in front of him, the man everyone had called Smoke. He had earned the nickname because of the weed he had sold and had later convinced Rafe to start selling when he was seventeen. Smoke was smiling, getting up from behind the huge desk, walking over toward Rafe, his arms extended.

Rafe took a step back, but Smoke took him in a brotherly hug anyway, rocking him side to side for a moment. Then he leaned away from him, looking him over fondly, as if they were high school buddies meeting at their twentieth reunion.

"How you doin', brotha?" Smoke said, a huge smile on his face. "It's been a long time. I missed you, man."

Rafe didn't say a word, still shocked to see him here, shocked that he was his employer.

Smoke let go of Rafe, stepped back.

"So one day you just decided to fall off the face of the earth, huh?" Smoke said.

Still Rafe said nothing.

"I mean, we was talking every day. We was mounting your defense. I had lawyers on retainer and shit. We was gonna get you out, and you just stop calling, stop taking my calls. I spent thousands of dollars tryin' to get you out, and nothin'."

"You want your money back, Smoke?"

"Naw, naw," Smoke quickly said, sounding almost apologetic. "It ain't about the money. I told you I'd get you out of there, and that's what I was trying to do. I didn't know what happened to you. Didn't know if you was dead or what." He was silent, as if giving Rafe a moment to respond to any of what he said. Rafe didn't.

"I was worried about you," Smoke said, the look on his face now expressing that sentiment. "I thought we were brothers. That's what we said, right?"

"Yeah," Rafe said, sounding now as though that had been a mistake.

"So why ain't you never call back?" Smoke asked, concern on his face. "Was it about Eric?"

Eric's face flashed across Rafe's mind, causing a quick pain in his heart. "Yeah. That's it, but I don't want to talk about Eric. I'm here, and that's all that matters."

"Yeah, yeah. That's right." Smoke brightened. "That is all that matters. That reminds me. Got something for you." He raced around his desk, going in his drawer, and handing an envelope to Rafe. "Go ahead. Open that it."

Rafe looked at Smoke strangely, turning the big, oddly shaped envelope over in his hands to see his name scribbled across the back. It looked like the handwriting of a third grader.

"Open it, man!" Smoke said, with ever building excitement.

Rafe tore open the envelope to find a greeting card enclosed. There was a cartoon hippopotamus on the front wearing a cap and gown with a diploma in its right hoof. On the cover it read, *After four years of being away* . . . Rafe opened the card, where it continued . . . *all you have to look forward to is hard work. Happy graduation.* Glad to have you out, *brotha*, was scribbled in the same handwriting as his name on the envelope. When Rafe looked up at Smoke, he was chuckling.

"I know you ain't graduate from college or nothing, but they don't make no 'Congratulations for getting out of the joint' cards. Besides, that shit was kinda funny, hunh?"

"Yeah. That was real funny, Smoke," Rafe agreed, handing the card back.

"Naw, naw. You keep it. Besides, I got a bunch of other stuff for you—your birthday, Christmas gifts, Halloween candy. All that shit. You ain't think I forgot about my brother, did you?" Smoke threw an arm around Rafe's neck and pushed him toward the door.

"Naw. How could I have thought that, Smoke?"

"That's right. Now let me show you around."

Rafe let Smoke show him around the dealership. He took Rafe across the showroom floor, through the parts department, through the service area, the break room, locker room, and storage room. He wore slacks and a collared shirt, so unlike the jeans and tees that he and Rafe used to always wear. He was very businesslike, seeming to have the sincere respect of all the people who worked for him there.

"I owe a lot of this to you, Rafe," Smoke said, as they stood in front of a brand-new 7 series BMW on the showroom floor. "After you cut connections, I had to do something with all that energy I had trying to get you out. I knew I wanted it to be legit and something that you could benefit from when your time was over. This is what turned out."

Rafe looked up at Smoke, not knowing how to take what the man had said. He didn't know whether to believe him, but then he asked himself, Why wouldn't he? Why was he being cold to the man who was once his best friend, the man who tried so hard to get him out of prison? Did he deserve this treatment? Rafe didn't know, didn't feel like trying to find the answer that very moment, so he looked back down at the car in front of him.

"Like that?" Smoke smiled. "Let's go for a spin."

Smoke drove the car fifteen miles per hour slower than the passing traffic around him, as Rafe looked out at the street in front of him, a blank expression on his face.

"So what you think of my establishment? Nice setup, hunh?" Smoke smiled at Rafe again.

"How did I end up here?" was all Rafe could say, not turning to look at Smoke. "How did you get to my parole officer?"

The smile on Smoke's face disappeared. "Why you gotta even ask that? Can't you just be glad that you *are* here?"

"So you ain't answering questions," Rafe threw back. "Fine. Just pull the car over, and let me out."

"All right, all right," Smoke said. "You weren't stayin' in contact with me, but it's not like I didn't know where you were, what you were doin' every day of the week. I probably knew when you were getting out before you did."

"How?" Rafe said.

"The guards. You know how little the state pays them to be locked up with dangerous types like you," Smoke said, smiling.

"And my parole officer."

"What about him?"

"How did you get him to send me here?"

"Damn," Smoke blew, throwing his hands up. "I got to spell it out for you? How you think?"

Rafe knew it was money. "You said you were clean, said the place was all legit."

"It is, but I still know how to get shit done."

Rafe shook his head.

"What's up with you, man? Don't be mad. I get you a job, show you around my place, and you actin' like I'm doin' you harm."

"Can't do me no more harm than you've already done," Rafe said.

Smoke hit the brakes. The car screeched to a halt. Smoke turned to

Rafe, sadness on his face. "I ain't want to give you those drugs. All that you did for me in the past. You were the only family I had. I ain't want you to go down. I did everything I could to get you out, but you acting like I didn't even care."

Rafe threw a hand over his face, exhaled, and told himself to take some steps back. Smoke was right. Rafe woke up this morning happy that he had a job, a new lease on life, and it was all because of Smoke, and he's treating him like this. But he knew what the reason for this treatment was. The lease wasn't exactly new. It was given to him by the same man who got him caught up in the business that had him going to jail in the first place. But that was all in the past now, wasn't it?

"All right. Okay, Smoke. You're right. You've been being nothing but cool to me, and I'm giving you a hard way to go. I just got some shit on my mind that I gotta get right, and then I should be straight. All right?" Rafe did his best to conjure up a smile.

"Well, I got something that might just help you."

THIRTEEN

SMOKE pulled up to Rafe's once worn-looking wood-framed house but it was now covered with brown aluminum siding. There were small, neatly trimmed shrubs in front of the house and along the walkway leading up to it. New window fixtures were in place. Even the banisters that enclosed the porch were new.

Smoke looked over his shoulder as he parallel-parked the BMW. "Got to be very careful," he said. "Don't want to hit your old man's Cadillac."

Rafe turned his head and looked out the back window. His old man didn't have a Cadillac. Always said that he wanted one, but . . . and then Rafe saw the 2001 STS parked behind him.

"Where did he get that?" Rafe demanded, turning to Smoke. Smoke was smiling, pulling his key from the ignition. "Why don't you ask him?" He got out of the car. Rafe was afraid to step into that house, afraid to find out what was really going on, but he pushed the door open and got out the car anyway.

Up on the porch, Rafe stood to the side while Smoke rang the doorbell. After a moment, Rafe heard the locks on the door being turned. He stepped further aside so he wouldn't be seen.

"Hey, Smoke. How's it going? Didn't expect to see you this week," Rafe heard his father say, sounding as though he and Smoke were old friends, fishing buddies.

"Yeah, well, Pops," Smoke said, "I have a surprise for you and Ma that I wanted to bring by."

Hold it, Rafe thought. Had he just heard Smoke refer to his parents as Ma and Pops, like Rafe always had? What the hell was going on?

"Well, c'mon in," Rafe heard his father say, then saw the door open, saw his old man's hand holding it there for Smoke. "The little woman is in the kitchen. Just have a seat, and I'll get her."

Rafe didn't budge, just stood outside, still trying to understand why Smoke had called his parents what he had. Smoke stuck his head out the door. "C'mon in, brotha," he said with a genuine smile. "Everything's going to be fine."

Rafe stepped into the house, was going to find out just what the hell was going on, when he was halted by everything around him. The house had changed. Yes, structurally it was the same. The shape of the living room wasn't different. The kitchen door was still at the back of the room. The stairs leading up to the second floor, where his and Eric's bedroom was, were still back near the dining room. But that's where it all ended.

None of the the plastic-covered, flower-print-upholstered furniture was there anymore. It had been replaced with fine Italian leather sofas and a chair. The ancient floor model RCA Colortron, with its mammoth wooden shell, wasn't there either. In its place stood an entertainment center. On the shelves were a 36-inch flat screen Sony and full Bose audio system with surround sound, as well as countless CDs and DVDs.

Rafe spun in a circle, his head feeling light, looking at the floor, the expensive deep-pile carpet that covered it. He saw the window treatments, the gold metal, and glass end and coffee tables. There was no way that his parents could afford this stuff. There was just no way.

Rafe turned to Smoke, having an idea where all this stuff had come from, but not wanting to find out for sure.

"Let's go," Rafe said. He headed toward the door, opened it, and was almost out of it when he heard his mother's voice. "Hey, Smoke," she said, and in it was none of the anger, the malice that Rafe had heard in her voice the last time she'd spoken to him.

"He said he got a surprise for us, baby," Rafe's father said, his voice filled with an almost childlike excitement.

Rafe stood outside the door now. He wanted to run away from there, actually wanted to just disappear into thin air. But he just stood there.

"So what you got for us?" Rafe's mother asked. She gave Smoke a hug, then looked over her shoulder, catching sight of someone just outside her front door.

"Who is that?" she called.

Rafe froze.

"That's the surprise I brought for you, Ma," Rafe heard Smoke say, his voice cheerful. "Come in, man."

Rafe still stood there, his body feeling leaden with anxiety, his head racing as he thought about what he would do, what he would say if his mother found out it was him standing there. He couldn't allow that. He couldn't speak to them now, especially after seeing how they responded to Smoke. They were allowing Smoke to refer to them as though *he* were their new son, the one who had replaced Rafe. He had to leave because he knew if he confronted them, he would have nothing but hateful words for them.

Rafe turned, and was ready to bolt when he heard, "C'mon, don't leave, Rafe. Give it a chance."

Hearing his name, Rafe stopped his forward movement and stood on the porch, knowing that now his mother knew who was out there.

"Who did you say?" Rafe's mother said, slowly stepping toward the door.

"Raphiel. Your son." Smoke's voice sounded even cheerier now. "Ma, Pops, your son is home now." Smoke walked up between the two, placed his arms around each of their shoulders, and said, "Now we're a family again. Finally."

Rafe opened the screen door and stepped into the house. He saw the surprised and anguished looks on both his mother's and father's faces. His mother took a step back, bumping into Smoke, as if she was seeing a ghost.

Reading the expression on her face, Rafe asked, "What's wrong? You aren't happy to see your son?"

She said nothing, so Rafe looked to his father. "How about you, Pops? You got anything more to say to me now that I'm in your house, and you can't just hang up the phone on me like you did when I was in prison?" Rafe's voice shook with emotion because of all the times that he tried to reach out to his parents, and was ignored.

"Son," his father said, carefully extending a hand, as if to calm a rabid dog about to attack. "Now you have to understand. We were—"

"You were what!" Rafe yelled, slamming the inside door as hard as he could. "What were you so damn busy doing that you couldn't come to see me, couldn't write me back, couldn't even take my fucking calls!"

"Don't you use that language in my house, son," his father scolded.

"Or what, Pops? What the fuck are you gonna do? You gonna put me out your house? You gonna fuckin' disown me? Too late for that. You been doin' that for the past two years."

"Raphiel," Rafe heard his mother say. "How else were we expected to react? We were grieving for our son."

"And what about me?" Rafe said, looking up at his mother, a tear spilling down his cheek. "Don't you think I was grieving for my brother? Don't you think I was dying just like you were because he was killed? You two had each other, but who the hell did I have to help me get through Eric being killed? I was relying on the two of you, but I had no one. No goddamn body!" Rafe yelled. "Because you didn't want to see me."

"Because it was your fault," Rafe's father exclaimed, stepping forward in front of Rafe's mother. "You were out there slingin' that shit, wearin' those fancy clothes, comin' in here with fistfuls of dollars, and your little brother was taking all that in, wanting to be just like his big brother Rafe. If you had never started doing that, your brother would still be alive. We'd all still be a family. But we aren't. And there ain't nobody to blame for that but you."

Rafe shook his head and started to chuckle sadly. "You blame me for Eric's death because I was slingin', making that money . . ." He chuckled again, raising a finger to wipe the tear from his face. "But where did all this stuff come from Pops?" Rafe said. "You win the lottery or something? You win some kind of lawsuit? Where you get the money to afford all this fine-ass furniture and that Cadillac outside, Pops?"

His father didn't say anything.

"What! Cat got your fucking tongue, Dad?" Rafe said, taking steps up to his father, then walking past him over to the entertainment center, thumbing through the extensive collection of DVDs.

"You talkin' about the fistfuls of money I influenced Eric with, but what about you, Pops? You knew where I got that money. You knew who I was hanging wit' to get that money. But now I get out of prison, and I come over here, and Smoke calling you Pops, calling her Ma. You talking to Smoke like he's your new son. Ma is over here giving him hugs and shit, callin' him baby and shit, and I'm thinkin' the only reason that ya'll so happy to see him is because he paid for all this. That motherfucker," Rafe said, stabbing a finger in Smoke's direction, "bought you all this shit."

"Hey, hey," Smoke cautioned. "We're all family here. No need to talk like that."

"Shut the fuck up, Smoke," Rafe yelled, then turned his attention back to his parents. "Am I right about that, Pops? Is he giving ya'll money?"

His father didn't say, just dropped his head low.

"Ma, what is it? Are you takin' money from this man, or what?" Rafe demanded, extending a stiff arm in Smoke's direction, jabbing a finger at him.

"Yes," Rafe's mother answered shamelessly. "But it ain't the same money. Smoke is clean now, and what were we supposed to do!" she spat, trying to step toward Rafe, but held back by his father. "You were in jail. Eric was dead. We didn't have anything. We had no money. We had nothing. And then Smoke was good enough to come along and tell us how sorry he was that Eric got killed and that you were in prison. He said he wanted to help us, because he was your friend, and because of what had happened to Eric. Were we supposed to turn him down?"

Rafe looked at his mother, shaking his head at how disgusted he was with this entire situation.

"Answer me, Raphiel," she said, still pulling to get loose from his father's grasp. "He was offering us money that we desperately needed, but we were just supposed to tell him no? I wasn't going to do that. We had nothing else. Both my sons were gone, but at least I'd have money," she said, tears running down both her cheeks. "It couldn't compare to getting my sons back, Raphiel, but it was something. God-dammit, it was something," she said, turning and falling into her husband's embrace.

Rafe could no longer bear to look at her. He hated her, hated them both right now for how they had treated him, and for taking Smoke's money, even though they'd condemned Rafe for working for it so many years ago. It was different money, his mother claimed now, but she was taking it from the same man.

Rafe scanned the room again, took in all the things that Smoke's money had bought them, then looked at his parents. They had not changed. They were the same two people they were when they lived in the badly furnished, paint-chipped house from years ago, and he wondered if they thought selling the memory of his little brother was worth an Italian sofa.

"Good-bye," Rafe said, and he knew those would be the last words he would ever speak to his parents.

"MAN, I'M really sorry, Rafe. If I knew it was going to go down like that, I would've never brought you over there," Smoke apologized to

Rafe. They were parked in front of Rafe's house, the car running. Smoke had made several attempts to speak to Rafe on the way there, but Rafe didn't respond until now.

"What are you doing calling my parents that?" Rafe said, finally turning to look at Smoke.

"Remember when we shorties, when my folks would be gone for days, sometimes even weeks? When they wouldn't leave no food in the crib. Remember that?"

"Yeah."

"Remember when you told me to come to your house, when you let me eat there, and then your folks let me sleep there with you and Eric? They asked me once what was going on at home, and when I didn't want to tell them, remember what they said to me?"

"Yeah, I remember," Rafe said, nodding his head.

"They said, don't worry about it, Samuel. Whatever's going on, it'll be okay, but 'til then, you can stay with us. They didn't have to do that, but they did. They was more mother and father to me than my own folks was. My people didn't care about me, but your folks did!" Smoke said, emotion in his voice. "You was my brother, and that meant your family was my family. So when you went away, when little Eric got killed, what the hell else was you expecting me to do?"

Rafe didn't say anything, just turned away, looked out his window.

"Look at me, motherfucker!" Smoke said, snatching Rafe by his shirt, forcing him to pay him attention.

"They gave to me when I was down, when I had nothing, so I was doing the same for them. They treated me like I was they family, so now I'm treating them like they mine."

Rafe just stared at Smoke, not speaking a word.

"What?" Smoke said.

"You done now?"

"What you mean?"

"You don't got to give to them no more. Their son is out. Their *real* son." That remark seemed to hurt Smoke. It was intentional. "So you can just keep your money from now on."

Smoke shook his head. "I can't do that, brotha. They need that shit, man. I been giving them money for two years now. They depend on that now."

"You said you owe me. Pay me back by stopping what you're doing," Rafe said.

"Tell them to tell me they don't want it no more. Then I'll stop."

Rafe looked at Smoke, hatred starting to grow inside him for the man. "Whatever," Rafe said, jumping out of the car.

"Rafe," Smoke called out of his window. "Don't be like this, man. You know how long I been waiting for this day?" He stepped just outside his car, so Rafe could hear him as he continued distancing himself from Smoke.

"I'm only doin' it for you, man," Smoke yelled. "I love you. Believe that!"

FOURTEEN

HENNESEY told herself she would check out the two children's books the little girl just handed her, and when she was done, if the guy at the back of the library was still staring at her, she would say something to him. Exactly what she would say, she wasn't sure. Maybe something like, "Hey weirdo? Would you mind keeping your eyes on what you're reading, or getting the hell out of here?" Or maybe she'd just go over to the dozing gray-haired security guard and tell him to put the thug who kept peering over his book at her out on the street.

She assumed he was a thug with his hair all braided up like that. He had a hardened look about himself, like he could've killed a man, knocked off a bank, or spent years in jail. Henny laughed to herself, thinking that it was probably all three.

She stamped the two checkout cards with the return dates and slipped them back into the little girl's books. She handed them to her and said, "You enjoy those now, okay?"

The little girl took the books and smiled back up at Henny. "Okay," and Henny couldn't help but see herself in that girl.

Now Henny would see what was going on with this man. She pretended to be busy behind the counter, and then all of a sudden, she quickly looked up, directly at him. Just as she had thought: he was gazing at her again, but he quickly ducked behind the big book he was reading, hiding his face.

Henny laughed again to herself, thinking no man is strong enough to look directly into the eyes of Hennesey Rodgers and not be changed, not be seduced, not be transformed into the whimpering, slobbering puppy dog that he truly is. *He wants me is what it really is,* Henny thought to herself. But then again, who the hell was she fooling? Was there ever a man who truly wanted her for more than getting an inside shot at her sister, Alizé? No.

Henny was the smart one, the one who wore glasses, sweatshirts, and jeans. Ally was the seductive one, the one who traipsed about in high heels and thongs. That guy was probably staring at her because she had something in her teeth, or maybe her hair was sticking up, making her look like a cockatoo.

Who knew, and what difference did it make anyway? He was a thug, and that definitely wasn't Henny's type. But he was kind of cute, she told herself, sneaking a peek at him now as he went about writing something on some paper.

Just forget about it, and do your work. You have your entire life to think about some man, she told herself. She'd shifted her thoughts to the stack of books in front of her when her sister walked in.

"What's up, bookworm?" Alizé said, flopping her purse on the checkout desk. She was popping gum in her mouth, and her hair was all done up, wrapped and curled and spritzed in some way that led Henny to believe that she had just left the salon. She was wearing low-cut jeans that damn near exposed her ass crack and another one of those shirts that exposed her pierced navel.

"Came to check out a much-needed book on fashion, Ally?" Henny said, smiling.

"Cute, sis, but the only help I need would be from a book about how to stop being so damn fine." Ally chuckled and did a little dance, ending it with a spin. "You like my hair? Just got it done."

Henny gave it a quick look to see if it had changed any from a moment ago. "It's interesting. That's all I can give you," she said looking back at the library's computer screen.

"Whatever. Why don't you check out, or punch out, or whatever you do around here, and let's go get something to eat and see a movie."

"You know I don't get off for another three hours, Ally."

"So. Leave now. You always talking about how you want us to spend more quality time together. Here's your chance."

"I got to work," Henny said, stamping some recently returned books, and placing them in a stack to get reshelved.

"You trippin'. You up in here makin' probably four dollars an hour, when you about to go away to school in less than a month. Quit this job, and let's hang. Stop being such a stick up the butt. Damn, you only got one life. Have fun with it."

Maybe she was right, Henny thought. Not about quitting the job, of course—she had two more weeks here, and she wouldn't abandon old

Mrs. Pembleton like that. But maybe she was right about having more fun, about living life more fully, and the first thing that popped into her head was the man who had been eyeing her. As she had so many times before, Ally must've been reading her twin sister's mind, because just at that moment, she heard Ally say, "Oooooooh, giiiirrrrlllllll," turning around to face Henny, and sliding halfway down the front of the check-out counter, as if her knees were weak from what her eyes just beheld.

"Who is that fine-ass nigga over there?"

"Who?" Henny said, playing dumb. "What fine-ass nigga are you talking about?" she asked, trying to mimic her sister's speech, but the words sounded stilted, awkward coming out of her own mouth.

"That nigga back there." Ally tilted her head in the man's direction.

"I don't know who he is. Why would I know who he is?" Henny felt both intimidated and defensive.

"That's right. Please forgive me. Forgot who I was talkin' to. Fine-ass man sittin' around, probably been here for hours, and why would I think my sister would know who he is. But don't worry because I'm about to find out." Ally dug into her purse, quickly pulled out a compact mirror, popped it open, checked her face and hair, smacked her lips, then shut the compact. "How I look?"

"What are you going to do?" Henny asked, feeling very threatened now but not understanding why.

"What you think I'm about to do? 'Bout to go over there and take care of my business. Now how I look?"

"Fine," Henny said, halfheartedly.

"I know that. Just wanted to hear you say it." Ally smiled, confidently turned around, and swished her round ass down across the library floor, through the tables, and toward the man who had been eyeing Henny for the past hour.

Ally was strutting confidently on her high heels as if she didn't have to second-guess a single thing in the world, and all Henny could think was, *Fall, fall Ally.* She wanted Ally to have a misstep, get her feet all tangled up in those heels, and land right at the feet of that man. Then she'd be so embarrassed that all she could do was crawl away. But that didn't happen. Ally didn't fall, and Henny watched as she spoke to the man, as the man spoke back to her. She saw Ally pull out a chair, sit in it, and scoot up, almost in between the man's knees. She saw the man laugh a little, saw her sister laugh a lot, flirtatiously place a hand on his knee, and then Henny had to turn away.

Although this wasn't Henny's man, she still felt slighted now that Ally was over there talking to him. Things never changed, she thought, and remembered the countless little boyfriends she thought she really liked and thought really liked her. But then she would walk down one of the dark hallways of their building, and find them kissing Ally, or the elevator doors would open in front of her, and she'd find Ally and one of the boys on the elevator floor, her sister's shirt pulled open. And how could she forget, last year, when Ally was screwing one of those boys right on the living room couch.

That was Henny's last boyfriend, and when she saw that, it almost didn't even register. She simply walked past them to her room and said in an unaffected voice, "If you get stains on that couch, Mama's going to kill you."

It was what she'd grown to expect regarding Alizé, but now, for some reason, she truly felt betrayed.

Henny didn't know how much time had passed—five, maybe ten minutes—but when she looked up again, Ally was standing in front of her, gasping for air, as if she had run around the perimeter of the library, before making her way back to that very spot.

"So how'd it go?" Henny asked, but she didn't have to, judging by the huge smile on Ally's face.

"The boy is fine, and I'm feelin' his ass tonight, sis," she said, waving a torn piece of paper with the guy's number scribbled on it. "You slipped on this one, Henny," Ally said, grabbing her purse off the counter. "See you later," she said, and then clip-clopped her butt up out of there.

She was right, Henny thought. She did slip on this one. But it would've only been for a minute. She was just about to go over there before Ally came in, but now . . . Yeah, she'd slipped. But once again, Ally made sure that she fell. Henny banged angrily at the keys of the computer, and this time when she looked up, the man was standing at the counter in front of her. Henny stumbled back, almost fell, but regained her balance before that happened.

"May I help you?" she asked, composing herself, pushing her glasses back up on her nose.

The man said nothing, just smiled, and Henny hated herself more because he was a lot cuter than she originally thought. But *cute* really wasn't even the word. Maybe handsome? No, something deeper. Something very close to beautiful. It was in his eyes, something so deep that Henny couldn't put it in words.

"It was you I really wanted to talk to," he finally said.

Right, Henny thought. What bullshit. He was just saying that so he could bed both me *and* my sister. But she wasn't like that, even though she felt a little better after hearing this.

"Then why—," Henny began to ask, but stopped herself.

The man paused, as if waiting for her to say more. But when she didn't, the man said, "Why what?"

"Nothing."

The man looked around the room, up at the ceiling, as if something there was grabbing his attention, then looked back at Hennesey. "I just came in here because I was really feeling down about something, something to do with my parents."

Don't know why he's telling me that, Henny thought to herself, but felt enough concern to ask, "They're all right, aren't they?"

"Yeah, they're fine. But I used to spend a lot of time in the library where I used to live. I would go there when I felt down, or just to get away, and that's why I came this time. But when I saw you, thought you were . . . you know . . . beautiful. That's why I kept staring at you. It's not because I'm crazy or nothing. I know you was thinkin' that, wasn't you?" he asked.

"Of course, not," Henny smiled.

"Of course, you was." He smiled too. "Thing was, I didn't have the nerve to approach you, and when I kept lookin' at you, you didn't seem like you was interested so—"

"—so you decide to get with my sister," Henny finished.

"I mean, she's cute too, but different from you."

"How, different?" Henny asked, really intrigued to know this man's take.

"Not pure like you. Not true like you."

Henny didn't know what to say. It wasn't exactly poetry, not a lyric from a Vandross song, but it had to have been the most beautiful, most sincere-sounding thing anyone had ever said to her. She couldn't speak after that. Her breath just simply seemed to disappear.

"So what if I tear this up?" he said, holding up what had to be the piece of paper with her sister's cell phone number on it. "And tell your sister that I want to talk to you instead?"

Henny wanted that, wanted to tell him that he had a deal. Call her now, hell you can use the library's phone, just dial 9 and then the number, she thought, but said, "Don't do that. If it was me you really wanted to talk to, you would've gotten up from behind that book you were hiding in and walked up here and spoken to me. That's the man's responsibility, isn't it?"

He smiled. "And that's what I'm talking about. There's the difference. You waiting for me to do the man thing, and your sister stepping up on me like she the man and damn near taking my phone number from me. And you know that's what she did, right. She talked it out of me."

"Whatever, man. Lying to me already, and I don't even know your name."

"It's not important. Tell me this, though. What if it don't work out with me and your sister? What then?"

"You don't have to worry about that," Henny said. "I have never heard any of her men say it hasn't worked out with her. Haven't heard any of my men, for that matter, say that. So you should be fine."

"I'll be fine when you decide to give me a play."

She tried to hide her smile, but she couldn't help it, and even though she felt her cheeks warming, she hoped the blush didn't show. "Whatever," she said coolly, acting as though none of his words affected her.

He stood there staring at her, watching her smile, 'til it faded from her face.

"I'm serious, Henny," and she looked surprised at hearing him speak her name. "Your sister told me," he said, reading the questioning expression. "I'm supposed to go out with your sister tonight, but you say don't, and I'll stay at home."

He looked sincere, Henny thought, but it wasn't her place to sabotage any of Ally's business, even though the girl had done it to her a zillion times.

"No, do your thing. You made plans with my sister. You should keep them."

"All right then," he said, looking disappointed. "I hope you don't mind if I keep coming up here, though. I like the books. And I promise I won't stare at you like that no more."

"I don't mind," she said, and actually, she was looking forward to it.

He turned to leave, but before he walked out the door, Henny called to him.

"You never did tell me your name."

"It's Raphiel, but everyone calls me Rafe."

FIFTEEN

ALLY was excited about seeing the man she'd met in the library earlier today, but when he called her this evening, he kept asking her if she was sure she still wanted to go out.

"Yeah, I'm sure, and why you keep askin' me that?"

"I don't know. Just wanted to make sure that you did, but if you don't, it's okay."

"I do, all right? Now what do you want to do?"

"I don't know. Maybe we can go to the movies, get something to eat, you know."

Yeah, Ally knew. It was always the first thing that brothas with no money suggested, but she wasn't going to have another Steve encounter—Burger King, then to the dollar flick. Ally wasn't trying to make this guy her boyfriend; she was just looking for a little fun, so she said, "How about we skip all that. Give me your address, and I'll come over there. We can watch TV and order some food. How's that?"

"Yeah, okay," she heard Rafe say.

On the train, then bus ride to his house, Ally kept wondering if he would be good or not. There wasn't even a question whether she would have sex with him. She knew she would after they had exchanged their first few words.

Since she'd given Steve the ax, she'd been dry, and it'd been driving her crazy. She had made a date with the baller she called a few days ago, but that wasn't for another couple of days, and Ally just didn't feel like waiting that long.

When she finally got to Rafe's house, she thought she had made a mistake about him being poor, judging by the huge house she was looking up at and the nice neighborhood it was located in. She went around to the side door as Rafe had told her to and rang one of the

three doorbells—the one with a piece of tape over it, with his name
written on it. Then she realized that her first impression was right. He
lived in a boarding house.

Rafe answered the door and immediately scanned her up and down.

He likes what he sees, Ally said to herself, allowing him to rest his
eyes on each sensual part of her body he desired.

She wasn't sure, but it felt like it had only been fifteen minutes that
she had been up in Rafe's room before they were rolling around on the
floor, their lips pressed together, Ally reaching down his pants, him
reaching up her shirt. It took some maneuvering on her part, though.

Rafe didn't really seem into it when she'd first gotten there. He
seemed standoffish, like he really didn't want her there. But Ally knew
that wasn't the case, or he wouldn't have agreed to her coming over.
He was just shy, she told herself, and she just had to loosen him up
some. So while they were watching TV, Ally scooted very close to him.
He moved away from her a little, but he was pressed up against the wall
behind his bed, and there was no place to go. She placed her hand on
his knee, then slowly slid it up to in between his legs. She felt that his
body was tense.

"Just relax," she whispered in his ear and kissed him there. That
didn't help, but the more she rubbed him, the more he seemed to
loosen, and when she raised her face to kiss him, she didn't have to ini-
tiate, for he threw his lips onto hers as if he couldn't control his
actions. After a short while of kissing, Ally rolled on top of him, straddled him, and kissed him some more. She grabbed the bottom of his T-
shirt, pulled it off him, and tossed it across the room.

The muscles in his shoulders and chest rippled with his movement,
and Ally placed a palm on his abs as he tried to reach up to undo her
bra, felt how tight and hard they were. Tattoos were painted all across
his arms and torso. She would ask him about those after they were
done, she told herself, but at that moment, she wanted him to see her,
see what he was getting.

She reached around herself and undid her bra. She let the straps
hang open for a moment, then reached up under the cups of her bra
and covered her breasts with her hands, wiggled 'til the bra fell away.
She was teasing him, and he looked up at her with lustful eyes. It was
working. He was becoming more excited, and if she wasn't certain by
the ever increasing hunger in his eyes, there was no denying the hard-
ening that was taking place between his legs.

She gyrated a bit on top of him, causing him to close his eyes momentarily and let out a moan. Then he looked up, wrapped his hands around her wrists, and pulled her hands away to reveal her breasts.

When he saw them, he let out a gasp, and Ally lowered herself some, 'til they hung in his face. She felt him wrap his mouth around one of them, his hand around the other, and squeeze and suck her at the same time.

This excited her more than she anticipated. She felt herself getting wet, and when he reached around with his free hand and started massaging that place just between her legs, she felt that she would topple over, her head was feeling so light.

Ally quickly raised herself up, her breast coming out of Rafe's mouth, and she frantically went at the snaps of her jeans. She pushed them down as far as she could while still straddling Rafe, then rolled over onto her back, kicked her legs in the air, and slid the jeans and panties off, leaving herself totally naked.

When she rolled back onto her knees, she noticed that Rafe wasn't moving fast enough. He still had his pants on, was slowly fidgeting with the buttons as though he was wondering if he could screw through his jeans. So she helped him. She undid the buttons, the zipper, and yanked the things off of him, exposing the part of him that was obviously very happy to see her.

"You got something?" Ally said, her breath coming fast.

"What?"

"Never mind. I do." She reached up to the bed, grabbing her purse, sinking her hand into it, and grabbing a rubber. It was a Magnum, and she was happy, because he definitely seemed large enough to fill it. She stuck it into his hand.

He held it for a moment, as if he had no clue as to what to do with it.

"You gonna put it on?"

"Yeah, yeah." He sounded more hesitant than Ally thought he should've.

When he finally got the thing on and slid all the way down, Ally crawled over to him, placed herself back on top of him, grabbed him, and was readying to slip him into her when she heard Rafe say, "Hold it."

"I am holding it," Ally said, anticipating feeling him inside her. "And I'm about to ride it."

"No. I want you to stop," Ally heard Rafe say.

"What did you say?"

"I said I want you to stop. Maybe we shouldn't do this."

"What the fuck are you talking about? What do you mean, maybe we shouldn't do this?"

"It's not a good idea," Rafe said, trying to squirm his way from under Ally, but she wouldn't let him go.

"And why not?"

"Because I shouldn't be with you."

"Hold it, hold it," Ally said, shaking her head in disbelief. "You weren't saying that when I walked up to you, when you were looking all down my shirt, undressing me with your eyes."

"Look. I'm sorry, but . . ."

"But, what! You all of a sudden gay now or something?"

"No, I'm not gay now," Rafe said, taking offense to the comment. "I like your sister. I should've said something to her, but I didn't."

Ally couldn't believe her ears. Here she was, butt-ass naked, straddling some nigga, his dick in her hand, about to slide down it, and he says to stop.

"So you trying to tell me you don't want this?"

"It ain't right," Rafe said.

"I just want to be totally fucking clear on this. You sayin' that you don't want to fuck. I got your hard-ass dick in my hand, but you sayin' you don't want to do nothin' with it."

Rafe didn't say anything this time, just sadly shook his head.

"I drag my ass all the way down here on the bus and the train, and now you flakin' like some little tease."

"I told you, I'm sorry."

"Oh, you damn right you sorry," Ally said, raising up off Rafe's hips. "You had the chance to get all this," Ally said, cupping both her breasts, then sliding her hands down the length of her curvaceous body, letting them rest on her hips. "And then you say that you can't. You sorry as hell or stupid as hell? Saying you don't want this, because you like my fucking sister? Nobody likes my sister. Everybody likes me," Ally said, picking her clothes from the floor.

"I do," Rafe said, slipping into his jeans.

"Well, then your sorry ass can have *her* sorry ass. I don't give a fuck." Ally pulled her top over her head. "But when you see that you made a

mistake and realize how much you want me, don't come dragging your
stupid ass over here, sayin' that you want another chance at it. You get
only one chance at this pussy. You fuck it up, you done," Ally said,
opening the door to his room.

"Well, I'll remember that," Rafe said, not seeming to care that he
was passing up the opportunity of a lifetime.

He's a fool, Ally thought to herself, as she took the long bus ride
back home. She felt herself tingling from the anticipation of having
that man, felt her legs trembling just a little still and she commanded
them to stop, slapping both her palms down hard on her knees.

"I like your sister," Ally remembered him saying, and she would've
laughed out loud remembering that if it hadn't been so damn sad. How
in the hell could he have liked Henny over her? The girl had nothing
going for herself. She didn't know how to dress, didn't worry about getting her nails done, did her own hair at home, and all that consisted of
was brushing that mop back into a ponytail and wrapping a rubber
band around it.

Ally, on the other hand, paid meticulous attention to what she wore
each day, making sure that her clothes fit her body just right, showed
just the right amount of cleavage or midriff, depending on how daring
she felt that day. Her hands and feet were done at least once every two
weeks, and her hair was never out of place. Everything that she did,
every minor detail she looked after in order to make herself irresistible
to men, and this Rafe says he wants Henny instead. It wasn't fair, it just
wasn't fair, Ally thought.

Henny had enough going for her, with all her good grades, and her
scholarships, all the people who loved her so much, in comparison to
the people who thought Alizé was evil. She didn't need anything else.
It was the reason that Ally took all of Henny's boyfriends. There was
just no other way she could compare to her sister. There was no other
way she could prove to herself that she was valued just as much as Hennesey was other than to take what her sister had, and she was always
able to do that. Until now.

Ally looked out onto the dark streets that passed her by, almost
wanting to cry, wondering to herself if everything that people said
about her was true. Maybe she wasn't worth a damn. Maybe she really
was just a slut, and if she didn't have her good looks, she wouldn't have
a damn thing. It's what her own mother had come close to saying so

many times, so how could it be false? But no, Ally thought, catching her reflection in the bus window. She was more than that, and just because this man didn't want her didn't mean she was worthless. There were always other men, and always other opportunities to prove that she was just as good as her sister. All she had to do was find them.

SIXTEEN

TONIGHT LIVVY would be going on a date with the man she had met two nights ago in the parking lot of the New Raven Lounge. She was really looking forward to it, so all during work, Livvy told herself she would have a smooth day. No mishaps, no arguments with the nurses, and she would get out on schedule so she would have plenty of time to prepare for her date with Wade. The day didn't go that way. Livvy made three mistakes that she got reprimanded for. She got her head bitten off twice by two different nurses because she wasn't paying close enough attention to what she was doing, and then was late getting off by forty-five minutes because the nurse's assistant who was supposed to relieve her came in late.

It was the day from hell, and Livvy told herself that there was just no way that she could continue going through this for too much longer. She thought about the essay she was going to write, and it lightened her mood. But it also bothered her, because she knew she hadn't written more than a grocery list in almost fifteen years. She wouldn't let that worry her now, though, she thought. She had a date to get ready for, and she wouldn't allow the day's events to stop her from having a good time tonight.

After Livvy had gotten dressed, she stood in the mirror, applied her lipstick, then looked herself over. She had done her hair differently, in a kind of straight style that hung down around her face. It made her look slightly seductive. She looked over the dress she had just bought. It was red with white flowers, and it made her look thinner. At least she hoped it did.

Livvy didn't know why she was concentrating so much on this date. She hardly knew this man and had spoken to him only a few times on the phone, yet the butterflies were flapping around frantically in her stomach at the thought of how the night would go.

She wasn't actually expecting this date to turn into a marriage. All she was hoping for was a man who truly cared about her. A man who thought about her needs, cared about her feelings, about what she liked, and expressed his feelings back to her.

She missed having that so much so that she dealt with what little Carlos was willing to throw her way. She still loved Carlos, but she needed to free herself from him, and Livvy was hoping that this man, Wade, would give her that strength.

Livvy grabbed her purse and keys and was walking to the door when the phone rang. She looked back, the open door in her hand, and thought of not answering it, knowing that it was for one of the girls, most likely Ally. But she let the door fall closed and went to pick it up anyway.

"Hello," she said.

"Hey, baby. I'm coming over to see you tonight, so look good for me, okay."

It was Carlos, and something in Livvy was both delighted to hear his voice and furious. She didn't speak for a moment, telling herself to be strong, because even though she was angry at him for not returning any of her last four phone calls, she still wanted to see him. She could feel her body preparing itself for him at that moment. She shook free of the lustful lock her body temporarily had on her, and said, "Don't bother, because I won't be here."

"What do you mean? Where you goin'?"

"Out, Carlos."

"But I want to see you."

"How about the four times I called you, wanting to see you? Didn't make a difference then. But now that you want to see me, I should jump at the chance, right?" Livvy said, her voice firm.

"Baby, I've been busy with the business and all. You know how that keeps me tied up. But the first chance I got to get away, which is now, I called you. C'mon, cancel whatever little plans you got tonight. I'll swing by, and we can do what we were supposed to do last time. Night on the town, baby. Best restaurant. Drinks after that, then you and me. What do you say?" His voice sounded as sweet and convincing as ever. As he spoke, the events of his planned night with Livvy unfolded in her mind, and for a brief moment, she wondered just how mad Wade would be if she called him and canceled. Then she caught herself. She was falling back into the same trap that she had a thousand times in the past, and although it felt like the hardest thing she had ever done, she said, "No, Carlos. I won't cancel my little plans. I'm going out, so I'll talk to you later."

She hung up the phone and felt powerful. She wasn't sure, but she thought she might just finally be able to get rid of this man.

That night, Wade was a total gentleman. Each time she got in and out of his beautiful car, he opened the door for her and closed it behind her.

"Is everything okay? You all right?" he seemed to ask her a thousand times that night, and she never tired of it.

The restaurant was at the top of the John Hancock Building, ninety something floors up in the sky, and Livvy could see all of Chicago spread out before her. She looked out at the millions of lights sparkling like diamonds cast on the city's streets. It was breathtaking. The live jazz trio played soft music as Livvy and Wade toasted their new friendship.

Afterward, they went to a small hole-in-the-wall blues spot Wade said he frequented every now and then. The music was so loud that Livvy could barely hear a word he said when he tried to speak to her. He had to yell in her ear when he asked, "You having a good time?"

"I'm having a great time!" she yelled back, and it was the truth. The place was packed with people drinking, laughing, and clapping to the music that the band of old, suited black men played. The large black woman who sang was covered with sweat, and there was so much emotion in her voice, in the words, in her movement, that Livvy had to stop herself from crying right there. It was like sensory overload. She was having such a wonderful time that she had forgotten about all that had happened earlier today, about her financial situation, and about how Carlos had mistreated her for all those years. Livvy just gave herself over to this place, to this woman singing about how her man had mistreated her, and how *finally she was able to see the light, see what was right, and in his shadow she would no longer dwell, but tell him to kiss her ass, and go to hell.*

Livvy laughed out loud and wiped tears from her eyes at the same time, and feeling Wade next to her, she turned to him, threw her arm around his neck, pulled him in, and gave him a big kiss on the cheek.

That was an hour ago, and now, strolling down Columbus Drive, pulling off her sweater, Livvy glanced over at Buckingham Fountain and saw the color of the lights changing under the water that sprayed up some thirty feet into the air.

Wade spread the blanket he had pulled from his car out on the grass facing the calm waters of the lakefront. There they sat, Livvy staring out at the water that seemed to go on forever and Wade lying on his side, curled around her.

"What's on your mind? You've been quiet," Wade asked.

Livvy came out of her trance, and apologized. "It's just that I've had such a wonderful time tonight—I mean, I'm *having* such a wonderful time. I don't think I've ever had this much fun," she admitted.

"That's really nice of you to say," Wade smiled.

"No, I mean it." Livvy turned to him, a serious expression on her face. "There's like an entire world out there that's going on, where people have fun, and don't worry about . . ." she cut herself off, about to talk about her desperate financial situation. " . . . where they don't worry about anything. They just enjoy life, enjoy their work, enjoy everything they do." Livvy lowered her head. "It's just not that way for me."

Wade didn't say anything to her at first, just gazed at her, again noticing how beautiful she was. Then he said, "Well, change it."

Livvy looked up at him and laughed sweetly. "It's not that simple."

"And why not? Why not? What's the biggest thing that's bothering you now?"

"I guess what I do for a living, being a nurse's assistant," Livvy said, a tinge of shame in her voice.

"And what do you want to do?"

"I want to be a nurse," she said, brightening some.

"Then go for it. Just like that."

"Well, there is this essay contest that I'm going to enter. And if I win, I get a full scholarship to nursing school."

"Now see, there you go." Wade gave Livvy's shoulder a confident squeeze. "That's a start. But what if you don't win, Livvy?"

Livvy looked taken aback, overwhelmed. "I don't know."

"Why don't you? Just because you don't win the scholarship, does your dream to be a nurse change?"

"No," she said.

"Then why should your plans? You want to be a nurse, then you plan to go to nursing school. You get the free ride, great. But if you don't, then you go anyway."

Livvy never thought about that, never really thought it was possible, and actually still didn't think it was. "But how can I afford . . ."

"Livvy, there are grants and loans all over the place for people like you who want to go back to school."

"But my daughters—"

"Your daughters are grown women. You said they'll be eighteen any month now," Wade said, resting a reassuring hand on top of her hand. "You've sacrificed and raised your children. You've given to them, and now is the time to give something back to yourself. I don't know exactly what that's going to take, but you find out, and you make it work. Okay?"

"Okay," Livvy said, feeling as though she had a new outlook on life.

THE SHINY Lincoln Town Car pulled up in front of Livvy's building and parked for a moment.

"I hope you had an okay time," Wade said.

"Don't act like you don't know," Livvy said, taking his hand. "I already told you I think I had the best time of my life."

"Oh, yeah, you did say that, didn't you?" Wade smiled, leaning in closer toward her.

"Yeah, I did," Livvy said, doing the same, their lips almost touching. "I want to thank you for everything tonight. All you've done and all you've said. You've given me so much to think about."

"And, I hope, so much to do."

"Yeah, that too," Livvy said, leaning in to kiss him. They kissed for only a moment, his kiss, soft, sweet, and lingering. Then he gently pulled away.

"I really hope I'll be seeing you again, Miss Livvy."

"You can count on it, Mister Wade." And with that, Livvy backed out of the car, closed the door, and waved as he pulled away. She was absolutely bubbling inside, and she wished the girls had been looking down from their window to see Livvy getting out that man's car. She had wished they had been around to see how their mother was getting treated all night long.

When Livvy walked into her apartment, the girls were still up watching MTV. Livvy closed the door behind her. Henny looked up, and said, "Mama, you look happy."

"I am happy, baby." Livvy walked over to the sofa and sat down on the edge of it, next to Henny.

"You had a good night?"

"Oh, wonderful night."

"What did you do?" Henny said, excitedly. Ally just laid across the love seat, looking very uninterested, flipping channels.

"We did everything. Had dinner at the John Hancock Building, heard some blues, went to the lakefront. He's such a wonderful man."

"Well, who is he, Mama? Tell me," Henny practically bounced up and down on the sofa.

"No, not yet. You'll get to meet him. You'll both get to meet him."

"So he took you out, hunh, Mama," Ally said, still flipping through the channels, not looking at her mother.

"That's right, he did."

Ally turned to look at Livvy. "So what did he want from you?"

"What do you mean, what did he want from me?"

"You know what I mean. When Carlos takes you out, he always want something. More times than not, you always give it to him, even if he don't take you out."

"Ally, you need to shut up," Henny said.

"I don't need to do nothin'."

Livvy did everything within her power to keep from pulling herself from that sofa, walking across that room, and smacking the taste out of her daughter's mouth. She swallowed hard, the anger going down with it, and then she calmly said, "He didn't ask for anything. He just took me out to have a good time. He's not like Carlos. And you might as well forget Carlos's name because I have. This new man is special, and I think this might be the beginning of something good."

"That's wonderful, Mama," Henny said, smoothing a hand across her mother's back.

"Well, before you go forgettin' Carlos's name, he called twice tonight," Ally said, spite in her voice.

LIVVY didn't know what was wrong with Alizé or her relationship with her. She acted as though she wanted Livvy to get rid of Carlos, and she knew how much Livvy desperately wanted to. So why did she scoff at the possibility of Livvy's finding someone new, someone nice? And why did she go and tell Livvy that Carlos had called? She had to have known Livvy was weak. Ally wasn't a child, and Livvy knew she had been around men, knew she knew the effect they could have on a woman, the effect that Carlos had on her. She knew that it would take a willpower that Livvy didn't possess to stop herself from calling him back. She knew that even though Livvy had had a wonderful time with Wade, it wasn't so easy to erase Carlos from her life.

Livvy knew that it would be wrong to call him back, knew that he would want to come over there and slide up in her, use her body 'til he was satisfied, and then leave. But the thought of even just that was too much for her.

NOW THAT Carlos was lowering his body onto hers, spreading her legs, and entering her, she knew that she was wrong to have called him back, but she was so glad that she had.

SEVENTEEN

TONIGHT WAS Ally's date with the so-called baller she had called back, and she was thankful. She should never have given that fool Rafe the time of day. Knowing he didn't have any money should've alerted her to the fact that he didn't have no sense either.

"Motherfucker turning me down, like I'm just any ole piece of ass," Ally complained to her girls, Sasha, JJ, and Lisa.

"Maybe you are just any ole piece of ass, and don't know it yet," JJ said, sticking a barbecue sauce–covered fry in her mouth. They were all at Lenny's B-B-Q, carry-out, picking over rib tips and sipping pops.

"He was broke as hell, and I should've known better," Ally said, pacing about in front of the girls.

"Damn, Ally, this is really bothering you, ain't it, girl?" Sasha said. "Just relax. Ain't no big deal."

"It's like lack of money is the same as lack of oxygen for these fools. It causes brain damage." Ally spun a finger at the side of her head. "I can't believe he played me. And for my nerd-ass sister at that."

"Henny's cool," Sasha said. "Why can't she have a man feel her too?"

"Because she got everything else," Ally spat.

"Aw, poor Ally," JJ cooed in her big baby voice. "She's upset because one man out of the thousands that she threw ass at didn't want it. You having a hard time getting dick, baby? Come to mama, and I'll make sure you never want that nasty thing again."

"It's all good though," Ally said, ignoring JJ's teasing. "I'm gettin' wit' dude tonight, and he gonna take me out, wine and dine me and thangs, and then if he lucky, I'll give him some."

"And then if you lucky, he might take some and not turn your ass down like yo' boy just did."

All the girls started laughing.

* * *

DUDE'S NAME was Rick, and he drove a phat-ass black Lincoln Navigator, with black tinted windows and shiny chrome wheels. When Ally stepped up into the truck, he had a DVD playing on a tiny screen that popped up out of his car stereo. It was *Set It Off*, one of Ally's favorite movies, and Jada Pinkett, Vivica Fox, and Queen Latifah were in the middle of yankin' down a bank. They had their wigs and dark glasses on, waving their guns, threatening to shoot anyone who blinked.

Now this is more like it, Ally thought as she pulled the truck door closed behind her.

"Damn, you lookin' fine as hell tonight, girl," Rick said, reaching down while he was driving, grabbing one of Ally's calves. "Thick!"

She had decided to wear a skirt that fell just below her knees. She let Rick have his feel, let him run his hand up the side of her thigh before he pulled it away. Maybe that would loosen a little more of that change from his wallet when it was time to spend, she thought.

Rick wheeled the big truck coolly down streets and around curves, spinning the wheel with one finger sometimes as he glanced over at the tiny DVD screen. He was a decent-looking guy, brown skin, baseball cap, so Ally didn't know what his hair was looking like. He was bigger than average, but she didn't know if it was muscle or fat because he wore a huge Chicago Bears football jersey.

"You know how long I been tryin' to get wit' you, girl?" Rick said, throwing a glance her way, then looking back at the road.

"I know, baby. I had a lot goin' on. But that don't make no difference, because you wit' me now." Ally placed a hand on his knee.

"I never had to call no woman more than once. I call them, and we do our thing. But you . . ." He left the sentence hanging there, as though he was searching for the words to finish it.

"I know, I know," she said smiling, sweet, and stupid. "I don't know what I was thinkin'."

"Damn right."

Ally grabbed his hand from the armrest and squeezed it. "You think you can forget about that, and we can just start this over from right here?"

He gave it a second, looked like he was putting some serious thought into it, and Ally thought, if this fool doesn't respond in two more seconds, I'm going to really tell him what he can do with his Navigator and his funky attitude.

"Yeah, it's cool," Rick finally said, turning around, smiling, showing his silver-capped tooth.

THEY DID dinner just like Ally had asked, but it wasn't no five-star spot downtown. There were no waiters in white waistcoats, or French-speaking hosts who pulled her chair out for her and commented about how fine her dinner selection was. It was a soul food restaurant on the South Side. But the food was real good, and although there were some ghetto-lookin' folks there, nobody decided to start shootin', and that was always a good thing.

After that, they went to a comedy club. South Side again, but Ally decided not to complain. To her surprise, she was having a fairly good time, and this Rick guy didn't turn out to be as much of an asshole as she'd thought he most definitely was at first. He was kinda funny after he loosened up, and for a minute the thought that this guy might be someone she could chill with flashed through her mind, but then she stopped that nonsense immediately. She'd just gotten out of a relationship, so why go get all chained into another one, when there were a million other men out there after a woman like her?

After the hour-and-a-half show at the comedy spot, Rick had really loosened up with the help of about four drinks. His eyelids hung low, and he was smiling as he wobbled out to the truck beside Ally.

"You all right?" Ally tried to steady him by holding his arm.

"Yeah, I'm cool. But why don't you drive." He dipped a hand into his jeans pocket and fished out the keys, handing them to her.

"Cool," Ally said, excited, because she'd never driven a Navigator before.

They were on the highway, and Ally was being a good girl, driving with hands at ten and two o'clock like she was taught in driver's ed.

"Girl, what are you doing?" Rick said, turning his spinning head toward Ally. "This is a Lincoln. Punch this bitch so we can get to the hotel before next year!"

That was all Ally needed to hear. She punched the gas, and the truck took off, pressing both of them back into their seats.

"Whoooooo!" Ally cried out, feeling the force of the huge truck.

"Now that's what I'm talkin' about!" Rick said.

ALLY knew she heard Rick say hotel, but what they were walking toward, with a plastic key in their hand, was a motel room. Funny what a big difference one little letter M could make, Ally thought. She had had a good time tonight, though, and now it was time to finish things off right. As long as this place provided privacy and a bed, she'd be all good.

Ally figured that she would make out all right tonight. She noticed the first time that Rick had stepped out the truck that he had a little bulge up front, so she guessed that he was packin'. She just hoped that he knew how to use it, because up until this moment, as Rick slipped the key into the door, and they stepped in to see the huge king-size bed awaiting them, Ally hadn't realized just how sexually frustrated she was.

Rick walked over to the nightstand and started emptying his pockets of all the crap that he was carrying, shedding all the jewelry he was wearing. He took off his baseball cap, tossed it over toward a chair sitting in the corner, then flopped backward onto the bed, his arms spread out.

Ally saw him there and got even more excited. She thought he was about to start undressing, pulling down his jeans or something, but he didn't move. Oh, no, this nigga is not about to fall asleep, Ally thought, while I'm over here about to explode.

She went to him, hiked her skirt up, straddled him, and bent over him, kissing him on the lips. His breath smelled strongly of alcohol, so she pulled a stick of gum from her blouse pocket, unwrapped it, and stuffed it into his mouth.

"Eat this," she said.

She kissed him again, and said, "I know you ain't falling asleep on me before you get this, are you?"

"Aw naw, hell naw," Rick muttered, his eyes mere slits now.

Ally stepped back, making sure that he was watching, and started doing her striptease, slowly unbuttoning her blouse, dropping it to the floor, then bending over and rolling the waist of her skirt down over her round behind. After she was done, she stood in front of the half-conscious Rick, wearing nothing but high heels and her pink thong. The man should've been losing his mind at this point, attacking her like a crazed rapist, Ally thought, but he just lay there, teetering on the edge of passing out.

"Don't you want to take off your clothes?" Ally asked with attitude.

Rick made the effort, fumbling with the buttons, but he was moving too slowly for Ally, so she helped him. She went to her purse, came back with a condom, and held it out to him.

"Put it on for me, baby," Rick said, lifting his head, his speech slurred.

Shit, Ally thought, starting to get pissed, but thinking, whatever it takes for me to get off and be done with this fool so I can go home.

Ally grabbed Rick's penis with one hand and used the other to tear open the condom package with her teeth. She tried rolling down the condom onto him, but he wasn't there yet, so she started tugging on him, trying to get him stiff enough so the thing would work.

It took a moment, but he was there, and she quickly covered him, not wanting to lose her opportunity. She couldn't believe how wet her body was when she positioned herself over him. When she finally slid down on him, she thought she would cry at how good it felt.

She would take it slow, she thought, as she closed her eyes and started to gyrate on top of him. She didn't hear any response from him, but that made no difference to Ally. She was moving into her own little world, where all that mattered was her satisfaction, nothing else. Side to side she was moving, and in tiny circles, feeling every part of him inside her, as she licked her lips, and pinched her hard nipples between her thumbs and forefingers.

This had to have been the best piece she's ever had, she was thinking, as she started to ride him even faster. Had to have been, had to be, she thought in her head, and then she felt that feeling coming. Somewhere from far away, but it was definitely coming, and coming strongly. It would be huge, and she tried to hold it off, knowing that that would only intensify this feeling, but she couldn't. It took over her body, demanded that she succumb to it, and nothing was going to stop this from happening, but . . . she heard Rick start to moan loudly.

"It's . . . it's . . . ," he said.

Those words snatched Ally from out of her world.

"I'm . . . I'm . . ."

"No!" Ally cried, her eyes still shut, trying to find her way back, trying to force the orgasm to come faster because she knew he threatened it coming at all.

"I'm coming!" Rick cried, his body stiffening.

"Don't you fucking do it!"

"Aaaagghhhhhh!" Rick yelled.

"NO!" Ally yelled, looking down at Rick, her eyes wide, an unbelieving glare on her face. But it was too late. She felt him thrusting deeper into her, letting his load loose into the little latex pouch. Oh, how good it felt for him, she thought angrily. She could see it in the contortions he made with his face. But that feeling that she had, the one that had taken over her body, was gone—so far gone, she didn't even have enough memory of it to pull herself off him and masturbate to climax.

Ally just sat there on top of Rick, feeling his organ shrivel inside her 'til she heard him snoring, and she could no longer feel a thing.

Ally pulled herself off him, leaving him there, and took a long, hot shower. She thought more than once of trying to satisfy herself, but she knew that would never compare to the feeling that she came so close to experiencing, so she left it alone.

She toweled herself off and, still pissed, she got dressed. She wouldn't even wake his tired ass. She kept money in her purse for instances just like this, just in case she needed to take a cab home because some dude was a punk in bed, and she couldn't stand to look at him anymore, even on the ride back to her house.

Dressed and ready to go, Ally grabbed her purse and then stood over Rick's drunk ass one more time. He was gone for sure. Passed out. She grabbed his hand, raised it, and let it fall. If his chest wasn't rising and lowering and that stench of alcohol wasn't blowing out his nose and mouth, she would've thought he was dead.

She was angry as hell at him for wasting her time, and knew she would never speak to his ass again, but she wished there was more she could do. He got his, but he left her dry, and more frustrated than when she came out tonight.

Fuck it, she thought, turning around to go, but not before she caught sight of everything he had dumped out on the nightstand. Platinum necklace, bracelet, watch, and ring. A wallet that was sitting open, showing at least a half a dozen credit cards, and then there was the money clip. A shiny, curved piece of metal, with a huge dollar sign on it. It looked stressed at the bend from holding such a tight, fat wad of money. There had to have been at least a grand there, Ally thought, glaring at the bills.

She looked over at Rick, who was still sleeping heavily. She looked back at the money, then reached out for it. This'll make things even for my wasted time, she thought.

But then Rick rustled. Ally froze, her hand still outstretched, quickly looking at Rick. He fell silent, but it spooked Ally enough that she pulled her hand back without the money and slipped out the room.

EIGHTEEN

RAFE waited 'til the last moment before getting out of bed and rushing to get ready for work. He told himself that he was not going in today because he was feeling strange about Smoke giving his parents money. He didn't know why that was. There was nothing saying that Smoke couldn't do that. It was his money, so it was his decision. And Smoke was right. Rafe's folks cared for him as if he was their own. Smoke was over at his house so much, he almost couldn't remember him not being there. So why was Rafe trippin'?

When Rafe finally did get to work, he was happy to find out that Smoke wasn't coming in today.

After work, Rafe took off his jumper, hung it in his locker, and was out of there, not waiting to talk to any of the guys as they made their way to the locker room. No need getting to know them any better, Rafe thought, as he stepped out of the showroom into the late afternoon sunlight. He probably wouldn't be there much longer, something told him.

It was Rafe's day to see his parole officer again, and it couldn't have come at a better time, he thought. He had spoken to him earlier, and they were to meet at the same greasy spoon restaurant.

Rafe walked in, and as before, when he looked toward the table where he and Dotson had sat, there the man was again.

It was cake this time that he had eaten. Chocolate, Rafe concluded, from the dark brown crumbs on the plate and the smudges of chocolate frosting on his fork.

"Sit down," Dotson said. He closed the cover on his *National Inquirer* and pushed it aside. He picked up his coffee, took a sip, put it down. "I would offer you something, but . . ."

"I know," Rafe said, "this is only gonna take a minute."

"Right. Now how's everything going? You stayin' out of trouble?"

"Yeah."

"And the job at the dealership. How's that coming along?"

"Well, that's what I really want to talk to you about." Rafe squirmed some in his chair.

"Shoot," Dotson said.

Rafe didn't know just how to put things, so he came out and said, "I ain't going back."

"What are you talking about?" The expression on Dotson's face changed to something more serious.

"The person I got arrested with three years ago owns that spot. I'm working for him, and that's the last person I should be coming in contact with, right?" Rafe asked, panic in his voice. "Ain't that violating my parole? Can't I be thrown back in jail for that?"

"Now, hold on. Just hold it a minute," Dotson said, trying to calm him. "This is your job, and you should feel damn lucky to have it. And who's to know you're working for him, unless you go getting stupid and telling someone?"

"I know, but—"

"But nothing." Dotson cut Rafe off. "This is an opportunity that a lot of guys comin' out don't get. They're sweeping up trash or bagging groceries next to sixteen year olds. You got a great job because you know somebody. That's a good thing," Dotson said, pushing his index finger down into the table in front of Rafe as if his point was right there, plain to see.

Rafe looked around, over both shoulders, then scooted up on the table, closer to Dotson. "Look, I know Smoke came to you. I know you took money, but that's none of my business. I won't tell nobody," he said, in a hushed voice. "I just got to get out of there or—"

"What! What are you talking about, taking money?" Dotson said, his whisper loud enough to be a shout. "I don't know what the hell you're talking about, and if you repeat that shit, you don't have to worry about who you work for landing you back in the joint. I'll personally drag your black ass there. You got me?"

Rafe didn't speak, feeling trapped, helpless.

"Hey, fucker." Dotson reached across the table, grabbing Rafe's shirt and shaking him. "I said, did you get me?"

"Yeah, I got you." Rafe felt defeated, his voice low. "I'm sure I was wrong about what I just said."

"Damn right, you were. Now the only thing you're gonna do is continue takin' your ass over there to work, because you're smart enough to know that's the best thing for you. Right?"

"Yeah," Rafe answered.

"Good, now get out of here," Dotson told him, throwing a finger toward the door, reaching across the table, and reopening his *National Enquirer*.

The man was dirty, and he didn't want anyone finding out, Rafe thought, as he walked away from the dingy little diner.

Rafe stopped at a couple of automotive repair places on his way home, Car-X and Midas, asking if they had any positions open. Neither place did, but even if they had, he didn't know if he could've taken them without running the risk of pissing off Dotson, having him trumping up some violation to land him back in the joint. He didn't know how much Smoke had paid the man, but Dotson sure acted as though he would do anything to make sure Smoke was happy, and that meant keeping Rafe right there at the dealership.

RAFE ended up at the library again. He needed to be somewhere he could relax and let some of the stress from his crappy day leave him. And, well, he was also hoping to see that girl, Alizé's sister. He had a hard time trying to remember her name, but he knew it was an alcohol just like her sister's. Tequila, or Martell, something like that. Anyway, he was disappointed to see that she wasn't at the counter when he walked in, so he just walked over to what he now regarded as his table and started thumbing through the books that someone had left there.

"So how long have you been studying astrophysics?" He heard a voice ask him, and when he looked over his shoulder, it was Hennesey. The name came back to him upon seeing her lovely face.

"Well, you know," Rafe said, "I mess around with it when I'm bored or nothing's on TV."

"Oh, I see. So you come up here a lot, hunh?" Henny said, resting her hands on the back of the chair next to his, leaning against it.

"Yeah, I told you this was my spot. But I'm not gonna even try to front and say that I wasn't hoping to see you."

"And why is that?"

"Because I'm still hopin' to get with you. You know nothing has changed with us." Rafe placed his hand on top of one of hers.

"I didn't know there was anything about us *to* change. Never even knew there was an us," Henny said, pulling her hand away.

"C'mon. I told you it was you that I really wanted to talk to, and besides, didn't your sister tell you what happened between us the other night?"

"My sister is a private person about her affairs. She's discreet during and discreet after. She kisses, but doesn't tell."

"She didn't say anything to you because there was nothing to say. Nothing happened. Not saying that nothing could've, and you knowing your sister, I'm sure you know what I'm talkin' about. But I didn't do anything, because I didn't want to mess up my chances with you."

Henny gave Rafe a look, like she was trying to decide if he was being honest with her, then said, "You messed that up the minute you decided to go out with her. Enjoy your reading, Raphiel," she said, and walked away.

Well, at least she remembered my name, Rafe thought.

Three hours later, after the sun had gone down, Rafe stood behind a tree, pitching little rocks he had gathered off the ground at another nearby tree. He was waiting for nine o'clock. During their conversation, Hennesey had told him that she worked 'til closing.

So here he was, waiting outside like a purse snatcher for his next victim. He didn't know what, but there was something about this girl that kept drawing him back to her.

Rafe's attention was caught by the sound of someone walking out the library's door. He glanced around the tree and saw that it was her. He hid himself and waited for her to pass. Then when she was just two steps past him, he stepped out and said, "Hey!"

Hennesey jumped and screamed, startled.

"Hey, hey," he said, holding both his hands up in front of him, stepping a few paces back. "It's me. It's me, okay?"

Hennesey looked at him, her hand over her pounding chest, trying to slow down her breathing. "Are you crazy, jumping out at me like that?" she said. She looked at where he had come from, then back at him oddly. "Hold it. What were you doing? Were you, like, waiting for me to get off or something?"

"Now, don't go gettin' the wrong idea," Rafe said, knowing exactly where her head was going. "Ain't nobody stalking you or nothing. I just wanted to talk to you again, and I didn't want to go bothering you at work like no pest, all right. So don't go gettin' ahead of yourself."

She gave him another once-over. "A girl has to be careful. Never know what crazies are out here lurking."

"What you doin' walking the streets this late at night by yourself then?" Rafe asked.

"Because my Benz is in the shop, and my chauffeur took the night off. Why you think?"

"Well, I'm going your way. I can protect you," Rafe said, smiling.

Henny cracked a smile too, and said, "All right. C'mon."

RAFE walked Henny all the way home. That's what she said people called her—Henny. That was cool. Anything was better than Hennesey, he supposed.

"Was it rough, growing up with a name like that?" Rafe asked on their trip toward her place.

"It wasn't as a kid, because most kids don't know about liquor. But now people are like, 'Ooh, Hennesey, that's my favorite.' Or, 'Hennesey, can I get a taste. I'd love to dip a cigar in you and smoke it.' Crap like that," Henny said. "But it's the name my mama gave me, so I love it. End of story."

"So, why should I call you Henny, if you don't want to call me Rafe," he said, kicking a can that was lying in the middle of the sidewalk.

"I didn't say you should call me Henny. I just said that's what *people* call me. You can call me what you like," she said, stepping in front of Rafe and playfully kicking the can herself.

"I'll call you Henny like everyone else then. But I bet you're sure smooth over ice," Rafe joked, and took off running, as Henny chased after him, trying to swat at him.

ON THAT long walk home, they had talked about everything. Henny said she was going to be a doctor as she had always wanted to be. Rafe felt inferior for a quick moment, but it passed when she said that anyone could do it. "Most doctors are C students. People think that you have to be an Einstein or something. But you don't. All you have to do is study."

"That's cool," Rafe said, impressed with her intelligence and her modesty.

"Where you going to school?"

"University of Illinois. Got a scholarship," Henny said, as they stopped at an intersection, the light turning red.

"Downtown campus?"

"No, Champaign, Urbana," Henny said. "It's . . ."

"I know where it is," Rafe said, trying not sound as disappointed as he felt.

They walked across the parking lot, Henny's huge building standing over them. They walked up to the building and stepped up onto the stairs.

"So this is where you live, huh?" Rafe said, standing two steps below her.

"Yeah, and it only took us an hour to get here," Henny said.

There was a long awkward moment, then Rafe said, "So, you inviting me up?"

"Why, so you can say goodnight to my sister?"

"Oh, okay, good one. Good one. I guess I deserved that."

"You most definitely did," she said laughing, then said, "I'll see you later."

"Wait, wait a minute," Rafe said, climbing a stair to put him one below her, making them the same height. "Can't I get a handshake, maybe a hug goodnight?"

Henny gave Rafe a long look, then she leaned forward into him and wrapped her arms around him. He embraced her, and he had to have sworn it was the sweetest, softest hug he had ever received. He told himself to let go of her after a moment, but his arms wouldn't move, and then he decided he wouldn't pull away until he felt her hold on him start to loosen. It was another few seconds before any other movement was made, and then he felt her whispering in his ear.

"That was very nice of you to walk me home. Thank you," she said, sweetly, then gave him a soft kiss on the side of his face.

Rafe didn't know what to say, and after stumbling across several bad possibilities in his head, he decided that there was just nothing that should be said. He watched as she disappeared into the doors and around the corner, and after a moment of letting the good feeling sink in, he left.

NINETEEN

ALL THE WAY home from work, Livvy kept thinking about what Wade had told her the night they had gone out.

"What if you don't win the essay contest, Livvy?" he'd asked her, and she felt her very foundation shaking. The only thing she knew for sure was that if she didn't win, she would be stuck at that job she was hating more and more every day.

"Then you plan to go to nursing school anyway," was his answer, and he was right. But that meant making changes, huge changes, changes that would affect everyone. But like Wade had said, her daughters would be eighteen in less than a month, legal adults, and it was now time for Livvy to start taking care of her own life.

Livvy was exhausted when she got off the elevator from another hard day at work. She turned the key to her apartment and opened the door to find Alizé lounging on the sofa, her feet kicked up on the coffee table, the place a mess. It was the last thing Livvy needed to see, but it let her know that what Wade was saying was right and all the decisions she felt guilty about making were right as well.

"Get your damn feet off that table, and turn off that TV," Livvy snapped, slamming the door behind her.

"If I was Henny, you wouldn't be telling me to turn off the damn TV," Ally said, slowly pulling her feet from off the table.

"If you were Henny, I would know that you were watching TV to relax, because you'd worked all day, like I do, instead of sitting on your ass."

Ally didn't move fast enough, so Livvy clicked off the TV as she walked past it into the kitchen. She stood there in the midst of all the left-out food containers, the dirty pots and pans that Ally must've used to cook her dinner, and Livvy just wanted to cry.

"Get in here," she demanded, trying not to scream at her daughter.

"What?" Ally called from the sofa, sounding as if she was being needlessly bothered.

"I said, get in here!" and this time Livvy did scream.

Ally appeared in the doorway, looking less than enthused.

"Look at this mess," Livvy said, waving a hand over the destruction that had been done to her kitchen. "You did this?"

"Yeah," Ally agreed.

"Then get in here and clean it up."

Ally sighed like she had a million better things to do, but walked past Livvy and started stacking dirty dishes under some running water.

"I don't know what to do with you, child. I go to work every day, provide for you, and look how you thank me. Your entire life, all I've done has been for you, and you can't even keep the damn house clean. Just once, why can't I come in here and see that you've cleaned up? You know after a long day I don't want to come in here and see no mess, but that don't even matter to you. All I've tried to do was bring you up the right way, give you all I could, and—"

Ally turned around, dish suds climbing up her forearms. "Why you sayin' me—me—me, like you haven't done the same, if not more, for Henny. You actin' like I'm the only one around here that you had to raise," Ally charged.

"At least Henny's doing something with her life. She's working. She's going to college. What are you gonna do?"

Ally had turned back around, was halfheartedly scrubbing dishes. She didn't answer her mother.

"Alizé, I said, What do you plan on doing with yourself at the end of this summer?"

"I don't know," Ally shrugged, not turning around. "Ain't gave it much thought."

"Well, you need to start thinking, because you never know when things might change."

"Whatever," Ally muttered.

"What did you say to me?" Livvy demanded, taking a step toward her daughter.

"Nothing," Ally said, still not facing her mother.

Livvy was angry, angry as hell. She just stood there, staring at Ally standing at that sink, wearing tight thigh-high shorts and a cut-off T-shirt.

"And you need to lose some weight off that ass off yours," she said, just because she was angry with Ally.

"Men like this ass of mine," Ally smirked, seeming to simply dismiss her mother's comment.

"You need to be going running with Henny every morning. Lose some damn weight."

"Can we just stop talking about Henny for one minute?" Ally said, finally turning to look at her mother. "All right, I know she's great. I know everybody should be just like her, but I'm me, and maybe one day, you can try accepting that." Ally held her stare on her mother, then finally turned away when Livvy was silent.

She was probably right, Livvy thought, but this definitely wasn't the damn day.

"I get any calls?" Livvy said, looking in the fridge for something light to eat. Either her daughter didn't hear her, or she was ignoring her again.

"I said, did I get any calls?"

"Somebody named Wade called a million damn times."

"Anybody else?" Livvy said, pulling out a plate of pasta.

"No, Carlos didn't call," and then mumbled, "You know he ain't callin' for at least a week after he fuck you."

Livvy froze. She was right behind Ally so she knew it was meant for her to hear it. But Livvy just stood there, holding the glass plate in her angrily trembling hands, trying to summon all her strength not to turn around and break the thing over Alizé's ungrateful head.

The front door opened, and Henny walked in, and with that, Livvy calmed some, telling herself that there was no need to stoop to Alizé's level. Everything would be straightened out right now.

"Hey, Mama. How was work?" Henny asked, giving Livvy a kiss as she came out of the kitchen.

"The usual, baby. But that's going to change. Ally, come out here," Livvy called in a very businesslike voice.

Ally came into the living room.

"Girls, have a seat. I have something to tell you."

Henny and Ally sat down, looked at each other as if the other had done something terribly wrong.

"What's going on, Ma?" Henny asked.

Livvy stood in front of her daughters, took a deep breath in, and let it go. "I hate my job. I'm a smart woman and should be doing more than what I am. So I'm entering this essay contest. I have to write about why a hospital employee wants to be a nurse, and if I win, they'll give me a full scholarship to their nursing school. I'll be able to do what I always wanted to do with my life."

"Mama!" Henny bounced up from the sofa, giving Livvy a huge hug. "That's great! That's great!" she said, calming herself enough to sit back down. "I'm so excited for you."

"Thank you, baby. But I'm going to need your help. You good at writing essays?"

"The best, Mama. Don't you worry about a thing."

Ally just looked away, her face in her hand, as if her mother had told them nothing more than what she was cooking for dinner tomorrow.

"But there's something else. There's no guarantee that I'll win. I could lose."

"Yeah, you could," Ally finally chimed in.

Livvy acknowledged her comment, but moved on. "So I have to prepare for that. Even if I do lose, I'm going to nursing school anyway, but I can't do that working full time, so I'm going to cut my hours in half."

The smile still remained on Henny's face, but on Ally's face now was concern.

"You can barely afford the bills and rent here now. How we gonna make it on you workin' part time?" Ally asked.

"Well, first off, Alizé, we ain't never been makin' it. It's been me, making it for *you*. Second, you're absolutely right. I can't afford to live here once I cut my hours, so when Henny leaves for school, I'll be moving to a one bedroom. I can afford that."

"A one bedroom." Ally looked alarmed. She stood up. "Where am I gonna sleep?"

"Well," Livvy said, seeming not that bothered at all about the dilemma. "There's always the sofa, and later on, if it's ever in the budget, we may be able to buy you a let-out bed, and that may be a little more comfortable. Or . . . ," Livvy said, and this caught Ally's attention, ". . . you may want to do something real crazy, like becoming responsible, getting a job, and finding your own place. Which I think is best, because one day, woman, you're going to have to start acting like one and make a way for yourself, and stop expecting me to carry you."

Livvy said all this while smiling very sweetly, feeling very good about herself, experiencing only the slightest bit of guilt.

"Any questions, ladies?"

"I'm so proud of you, Mama," Henny said.

Ally just got up and headed for her room.

Livvy watched as her daughter stormed out of the room, and a look of sadness all of a sudden covered her face. Henny stood, walked over to her mother, and gave her a hug.

"Mama, don't worry. It's the right thing. It's time for her to be pushed out of the nest. The baby birds have to learn how to fly some time."

"I know, but . . . ," Livvy tried to say.

"But nothing," Henny said, squeezing her harder. "I'm so proud of you. So proud."

When Henny walked into their bedroom, Ally was pacing the floor.

"Ain't sleepin' on no let-out bed."

"Then you got to do what Mama said and get a job," Henny said, sitting on the edge of Ally's twin bed.

"And do what? Flip burgers. 'Welcome to McDonald's: how may I help you?' I ain't qualified to do that shit. Besides, this body wasn't made for no nine to five. I ain't built that way."

"Then maybe you ought to think about rebuilding," Henny said, chuckling some.

Ally stopped just in front of her sister. "Hell wit' you, Henny."

"Well, you got to do something, and do it fast. Summer's almost over. So what's it going to be?"

"I don't know. But I'll think of something. Bet that," Ally said, her mind already starting to work.

TWENTY

WADE pulled the Town Car in front of his house, or rather the house that he was renting a room in. He had just come from getting the car washed, and they did a decent job, but as he got out and took another walk around, he noticed a dull spot on his rear tire. He quickly opened his trunk, pulled out the bottle of Liquid Black Tire Shine, and squirted the gray area away, making it a shiny black.

His car really didn't need a wash. He could've gone another day, hell, maybe two. But sitting around his room wouldn't clear his mind of the woman he couldn't stop thinking about.

He didn't know what the deal with her was. He'd taken her out, shown her a good time. No spending limits, no time constraints. He took her to the nicer spots, even though, when he picked her up, he saw that she lived in the projects. Wade didn't know exactly what she was accustomed to, but he was sure if he had just driven her around the corner to the chicken shack and ordered a three-piece dinner, she'd have been just as satisfied.

But he didn't do that, thinking that she would be worth the invest-ment. And when Wade spent money, that's how he had to view every-thing: as an investment. Every spare cent he made was put into his savings account so one day he could buy a house. He was tired of living in that one cramped room. But what other choice did he have, know-ing how horrible his credit looked? With marks like that on his credit report, the only place that would rent to him would be somewhere deep in the 'hood, overrun by rats and roaches. A place he knew his car would be stolen only minutes after his stepping out of it, if they didn't jack him while he was trying to park. And there was just no way he was trying to part with his car. No way.

So he rented from the nice lady who said she didn't bother about credit reports and things like that. She judged a man by the vibe she got from him, and she said she had gotten a great one from Wade. Paying her the four hundred dollars a month allowed him to stay in a beautiful neighborhood and save a decent amount of money to buy that house he always wanted. And then maybe, if he were lucky, that special woman would come along. It was the other reason he was sacrificing now, because when she finally did make herself known, Wade wanted somewhere nice that he could invite her to. And when their relationship finally got to the point where they decided to live together, he didn't want there to be any talk about apartment living. He wanted to have a home so they could live the way he always wanted to live with that special person.

The sad thing was, he thought that special person could've been Livvy, but after he showed her the town, opened up to her, and now after he had called her a thousand times, she didn't even have the courtesy to call him back—even to say go to hell. Maybe he was too old for her, he thought. But of course he was too old for her. This was a convenience situation. He knew a woman like her was looking for a man to help her out financially, and he was sure she knew what he was looking for as well. But maybe she already had a sugar daddy. Wasn't that what they called guys like him nowadays, sugar daddies? Whatever. He wouldn't waste any more time thinking about it.

Wade dropped the bottle of tire shine back in his trunk and slammed it shut. When he looked up, he saw a young man walking up the steps and heading toward the side door of the house. He recognized him as the guy who had moved in a couple of weeks ago. Wade made sure his car was locked, then went after the man, trying to catch up to him.

By the time he caught up, he was at the door to his room, about to stick the key in. Wade walked up behind him.

"How's it going?" Wade said to the man's back.

Rafe didn't completely turn around, just looked over his shoulder, nodded his head. "Whassup," he said coolly, then went back to putting his key in the lock.

"So you're the new guy here?"

"Yeah, guess so."

"How you liking the accommodations?"

"Keeps the rain off my head," Rafe said. He stood there a moment, hunched over the lock. Then when Wade didn't walk away, Rafe turned around.

"Can I help you with somethin', man?"

"Yeah. I'm Wade. Wade Williams," he said, extending a hand.

Rafe looked down at it for a moment, as if examining it to make sure it was clean, then shook it.

"I'm sorry," Wade said. "Didn't catch your name."

"That's because I ain't thrown it."

"Oh, okay. Well, the old guy next door, Fredrick, has been asking about you. See, normally the woman downstairs doesn't rent to anyone under fifty years old, so old Fredrick was wondering—"

"It really ain't none of your business, but Dorothy is my aunt. Does that answer the question?"

"Sure, sure. I'll let you get back to your business." Wade turned around and headed toward his room, and only then did Rafe go back to trying to open his door. But just before he could walk in, Wade was behind him again.

"You know, I got a bottle of something in my room and a couple of glasses. You cool with having a shot or two with an old man?"

Rafe looked down at the lock, which he was having trouble with anyway, then back at the man. "What the hell. Why not?"

HALF OF the cognac was gone and both men were feeling quite relaxed when Rafe picked the bottle up and read the label aloud.

"Hennessy. I know a girl wit' that name."

"You do?" Wade took another sip from his glass. "What kind of woman would name her daughter after a bottle of liquor?"

"That ain't the worst of it. She got a twin sister named Alizé."

"What kind of woman would name her daughter after a bottle of cheap-ass liquor?" Wade said, and both men started to laugh. They both emptied their glasses, and Rafe poured them another generous shot, their fourth.

"I don't know what kinda woman, but she has to be fine, because her daughter sure is," Rafe said, setting the bottle down. He brought his glass to his nose, and sniffed. "But she ain't interested in me. And even if she was, once she finds out . . ." Rafe stopped himself and brought the glass to his lips, resting it there for a moment.

"That you did time, she really won't be interested," Wade finished for him.

Rafe brought the glass away from his mouth, looking at Wade oddly.

"That's what you were gonna say, right?"

"But . . . how you know?"

"Your arms," Wade said, pointing to the tattoos running down the length of Rafe's biceps and forearms. "Some of those are jail tats. My half-brother's been in and out a zillion times. That's how I know." Wade pulled his eyes from Rafe and took a drink of his liquor.

There was an awkward silence, but Wade broke it by saying, "It's nothing to be ashamed of. Things happen. I mean, you didn't kill anyone, did you?"

"Naw," Rafe said, setting down his glass, rubbing both his palms over the tattoos on the opposite biceps. "Caught sellin' weed. You know how it is."

"Yeah. I think most brothas know how it is. It's no more dangerous than cigarettes or this shit we drinkin' right here, but for weed, they'll throw a man in prison. Doesn't make much sense to me."

"I don't even think about it no more," Rafe said, his head hanging low. "Just try to forget about it, but I don't want the secret coming back, biting me in the ass."

"Then just tell her."

Rafe gave Wade a look suggesting he was crazy.

"Is she a good woman?"

"From the little I know about her, she's a damn good woman."

"Then she'll understand. But wait a little while, and tell her when the time is right. That's not the type of thing you want to tell her after your second date."

"Guess you're right," Rafe agreed. "What about you? You look like a smooth old pimp. How come they ain't lined up, bangin' at your door right now?"

"Ah," Wade blew, setting his glass down. "I'm just like you. Got my eye on one, trying to close the deal, but seems she's got other plans. Called her a few times after taking her out once, and she hasn't called back."

"So. Call her ass back again," Rafe said.

"Obviously she's not interested."

"Did you pay for the date?"

"Yeah."

"Dinner, drinks, someplace after that?" Rafe asked.

"Yeah."

"Then call her back. She owes you another date just because you spent all that money. Ain't nothin' free around here," Rafe said, getting pumped up. He raised his glass to Wade. "She at least owe you a little action after all that. Know what I'm sayin'!"

"Yeah. Hell yeah!" Wade said, getting equally excited, raising his glass to Rafe's.

"Us men got to stick together and watch out for each other. Right?"

"That's right!" Wade barked enthusiastically.

"Then let's drink to that."

"All right!" Wade said, and they both tossed back their drinks. They finished at the same time, and slammed their glasses onto the table in unison, making one loud clop as both hit. They smiled at each other in silence for a moment, then Rafe said, "It was good meeting you, Wade. And by the way, people call me Rafe." He extended his hand to Wade. Wade took it, and gave it a hearty shake.

"Okay, Rafe."

Rafe stood, turned to leave, but stopped and said, "Now call that woman, and get what's coming to you."

WADE was happy that he had met Rafe, glad that he had taken his advice, because two hours later, he had Livvy in the passenger seat of his car. They were heading north to get ice cream at Ben & Jerry's and then take a walk around the Lincoln Park Zoo.

When he called, Livvy picked up the phone, and after hearing her sweet voice, Wade was paralyzed. He wanted to talk to her, but felt he should hang up for fear he was pestering the woman.

"Hello," she said, for the second time.

"Hello," he finally answered.

"Is this Wade?" she asked, and that made him feel a little better, knowing that she at least remembered his voice and his name.

"It is," he said.

"I'm sorry I haven't called you back," she said, "but I've been so busy with . . ." and he didn't know if he should believe whatever she was about to say or not. But when she was finished giving her explanation and suggested that they do something, he rushed right over to get her.

At Ben & Jerry's, Wade bought Livvy a double scoop of pralines and cream and chocolate fudge brownie, and himself two scoops of strawberry.

As they walked across the street toward the zoo, Livvy said, "So I'm doing what you told me."

"What's that?" Wade said, licking his ice cream.

"I'm making plans to go to nursing school, whether I win the scholarship or not," Livvy said, smiling.

"That's great, Livvy. That's terrific!"

They walked around some more and ended up on Wade's blanket again, stretched out in front of the pond on the farm section of the zoo, watching as chickens and roosters poked and pecked about on the grass in front of them.

Wade's head was in Livvy's lap and she was running her fingers through his hair as she gazed off into the sky.

"Easy there. Old man's already receding. You don't want to pull out all my hair and have me walk around bald do you?"

"Stop it," Livvy said, tapping him on his forehead. "You aren't receding. And just how old are you?"

"I don't want to say."

"Why not?"

"Because I don't want the cops coming to arrest me for child molestation."

"Oh, so I'm a child now," Livvy said, laughing. "Just tell me, old man."

"I'm forty-eight," Wade said, expecting her to lift his head out of her lap and break for the gate, hurdling a couple of pigs and a cow in her hurry to get out of there.

"So. You're fifteen years older than me. So what?" Livvy said, not blinking an eye. "We're both adults. And besides, I like older men. They've accomplished things. They're successful," she said, caressing the side of his face. "That's why I'm trying to better myself, make more money, so I can bring something to the table. I want a man who makes some nice money, so why shouldn't I too? You know?" Livvy looked down into Wade's eyes.

Wade nodded, gazing up into Livvy's beautiful face.

"So don't worry about the age thing. It took you those years to become the success you are. Owning a car dealership doesn't happen overnight," Livvy said, smiling even brighter down into Wade's face.

"Yeah, guess you're right," Wade said, feeling uncomfortable. He had told her that lie on their first date because he guessed that's what she wanted to hear, what all women wanted to hear. She kept commenting on the beautiful car he had, how nicely he dressed, and how high a position she assumed he had at work. What else was he supposed to tell her?

"So you never told me what kind of cars you sell. Lincolns, right?" Livvy asked now.

"Yeah, those and some others, but I don't want to talk about business now. You said you have daughters?" Wade said, changing the subject. "What are their names?"

Livvy smiled, thinking about her girls. "The oldest is named Hennesey."

"Hold it," Wade said, sitting up. "Hennesey?"

"Yeah."

"And don't tell me that you have twins, and the other one's name is Alizé?"

"Yeah, how did you know that?" Livvy said, looking at him suspiciously.

Wade laughed. "I just met a fella by the name of Rafe today. You know him?"

"No. Why?"

Wade thought for a moment, then said, "It's not important. He's a good kid, and hopefully, if things work out, one day you'll meet him."

"And that's it?"

"It's really not important," Wade said, letting his head fall back into Livvy's lap. "How about instead we talk about how beautiful you are to me?"

"Oh, all right," Livvy said, feigning disappointment. "If we have to," and she bent down and gave Wade a kiss on his lips.

TWENTY-ONE

THE NEXT morning, Rafe didn't lie in bed, dreading the fact he had to go to work. It was something he had to do, at least for right now, until he found a way to get himself out of there.

When he got to work, he went about the routine of getting dressed and only saying a few words to the guys. He didn't want them trying to pry into his business.

Rafe didn't know if Smoke was there today or not and didn't really care. He would do his job, the job he was so lucky to have, as Dotson told him, collect his check, and be out. He'd treat Smoke like he did all the other people who worked there. He would pretend nothing had happened between them over the last couple of days, pretend they had no history at all, because something deep inside his gut, he didn't know exactly what, was telling him it was best that way.

Late that morning, Smoke appeared behind Rafe. "C'mon, let's take a ride."

"Don't want to. Got work to do," Rafe said, turning the bolt on the exhaust of a vintage Jaguar raised up above him.

"Don't have no choice."

"Or else what?" Rafe said.

"There is no 'or else.' You my boy, but I'm still your boss, and I'll tell you when you have work and when you don't. Now, c'mon," and Smoke turned to walk out the service area.

Rafe tossed the wrench toward the tool box, picked up a rag to wipe his hands with, and followed Smoke.

SMOKE had them in a different car now—a Mercedes S500. It was gold, with smoked-out windows. Smoke's window was cracked so he could look out the top of it as he slowly cruised down the street. He rolled them through their old neighborhood, past the spots they used to sell at before Rafe got sent up.

As they continued to drive, looking at the old run-down buildings, the familiar stores that had long ago been boarded up, Smoke would say, "Remember that?" Or "Remember this?" Or "Remember over there where you beat that kid down, because he was talkin' about your mama?" Images of those times found their way into Rafe's head, and though he tried his hardest to fight them, push them away, they played out anyway.

Smoke drove by all the places he and Rafe used to visit as kids. The places they used to ride their bikes to when they were in grade school, Smoke balancing Rafe on his handle bars the time Rafe's bike was broken. Half the time, the bike would swerve this way and that, and ultimately, Rafe would always get dumped off onto the sidewalk or grass. But he never minded, because Smoke always tried his hardest to keep the bike straight.

Rafe wanted to crack a smile, even laugh, as he saw the faded image of the two boys on their bikes, racing down the street, both their front teeth missing, as they smiled wide, the wind whipping them in their faces, but he fought against it.

Smoke slowed the car some, powering his window down so Rafe could see out of it, at the rundown house across the street.

"Whose house is that, Rafe?" Smoke said, a smile spreading across his lips.

Rafe didn't turn around.

"C'mon, man. Just look at it."

Rafe turned to see the house. He knew who it used to belong to, knew the significance it held for both of them, but he didn't speak a word of that.

"Whose house?" Smoke asked again.

Silence.

"It's Tanya Jackson's house," Smoke answered for him. "The girl wit' the big-ass tits and fat ass that was fuckin' everybody. 'Member her, Rafe? She took us down in her basement, did us both on that nasty-ass mattress layin' on the floor. We was both virgins. Didn't know what the fuck to do. Both of us nutted in less than thirty seconds combined." Smoke laughed so hard he had to hold his stomach against the pain. Even Rafe could no longer hold his smile. "And then her ole man came down the stairs and we took off running wit' our pants around our ankles 'cause your ass was moaning so loud."

"That wasn't me moanin', that was . . . ," Rafe said, enthusiastically chiming in, then caught himself, remembering that that was all in the past, that times had changed.

Smoke looked at Rafe, the wide smile still hanging on his face, as if waiting for Rafe to continue so they could keep on joking and reminiscing. Rafe just sat quietly, Smoke's smile slowly disappearing from his face.

"Fuck is your problem, Rafe?" Smoke wondered, turning to him.

"Don't know what you mean," Rafe said, his face turned toward his window—not looking out, just trying to avoid Smoke.

"You actin' like you don't want to be brothers no more. Actin' like you don't want to work for me. That's what I mean."

"It ain't that I *don't* want to work for you anymore. I can't. I'm tryin' to keep my ass out of prison, and you want me to hang around you. You the nigga that got me there in the first place. The one that got me started sellin' drugs. How can it be good, me hangin' wit' you again, working for you again?"

"Because I'm paid as hell," Smoke said, cutting off the car, turning in his seat to face Rafe. "And the beauty of it is, the shit's all legal, baby."

Rafe gave Smoke a scrutinizing look, staring deep into his black eyes. "Is it really, Smoke?"

"What the fuck you talkin' about?" Smoke sounded as though he was hurt by Rafe's accusation.

"You know what I'm talkin' about. Is it really legal, or is this just some front for your real business?"

"I'm clean, man," Smoke said with a straight face. "I gave all that up. You was my boy, my brother. And the day the cops dragged you out of that courtroom, man, I lost a part of myself. I told myself then that if those drugs could do something so terrible as take my brother away, then I ain't want nothing to do with them anymore."

Rafe looked over at Smoke, still not knowing what to think, what to believe.

"Ain't you got nothing to say?" Smoke said.

"Naw, nothin'," Rafe said, looking away.

"You know you actin' like a little bitch."

"Then I'll be that."

"Fine. Fine then, Rafe," Smoke said, throwing up his hands. "Be that then, but all this nonsense is making me hungry. We gettin' something to eat."

Smoke drove them a block off Roosevelt Street, near the South Loop. He stopped the car at a little Polish sausage stand where they once used to eat. Smoke jumped out the car. "Get out. We eatin'."

"Ain't hungry."

"Get out anyway. I want the company."

Rafe got out, walked up to the stand they used to ride their bikes to to buy sausages and cans of pop, which they would eat as they rode back home. Rafe remembered loving those sausages. They were so good, with all those grilled onions and peppers, and they smelled even more delicious now. There was a huge grill in plain sight, and at least a dozen of the dogs sizzled there, covered with onions and peppers.

"Two of those for me, extra onions," Smoke told the man in the paper hat and white apron. "Two for him and two cans of grape pop."

"I told you I ain't hungry," Rafe protested, but his stomach said something entirely different. It moaned loudly, reacting to the scent he was breathing in.

"Oh, you ain't hungry, huh? You don't have to eat 'em, but I'm buying 'em anyway."

They sat at a wooden table. Smoke was devouring his first dog, ketchup and mustard all over the sides of his mouth. He had opened the foil packages of the other two dogs and set them in front of Rafe.

"I know you said you ain't hungry, but I'm gonna just open these and set them there, so you won't have to go through the trouble, just in case you change your mind. All right?"

Rafe didn't say anything.

"These is damn good, man. I'm tellin' you, you don't know what you missing."

But Rafe did, and he could smell them, almost taste them, and he was so hungry that he could've damn near eaten the foil the dogs were wrapped in along with the dogs themselves. He couldn't fight the urge any longer. He quickly picked one up, took a huge bite out of it, then set it back down.

Smoke laughed, his mouth still full. "Now that's what I'm talkin' 'bout."

They drove around some more, Smoke taking them who knew where, but Rafe felt a lot better now that he had something in his stomach. He sat there in the passenger seat, rubbing a hand over his belly, still tasting the sausages.

Smoke caught sight of this. "They was good, weren't they?"

"They were all right," Rafe said, coolly.

"Aw man, they were the shit. You know it," Smoke said, giving Rafe a hard nudge with his shoulder. "You wouldn't be rubbin' your stomach, suckin' your teeth, tryin' to still taste them if they weren't."

Rafe smiled and conceded. "All right. Yeah, they were good as hell. Almost forgot how good."

"I know, I know," Smoke said, bobbing his head.

When they stopped again, Harriet Tubman Elementary School was sitting in Smoke's front windshield.

"Damn, man," Rafe said, the sight taking him back, as he stepped out of the car.

"Memories like a motherfucker, hunh," Smoke said, getting out as well.

This was where they met. It was the beginning of sixth grade, and Rafe was new. Now they walked across the small lot the school sat on and ended up behind the building, both staring at one particular area of its brick surface.

"Remember this?" Smoke asked, and there was no way Rafe could forget it. It was after school his second day there, and five boys had him backed up against a wall, a floor tile cutter to his eye. They wanted his brand-new Nike gym shoes and the knock-off Members Only jacket his parents couldn't afford but bought him anyway.

"I thought I was gonna die that day, or at least be blinded for the rest of my life, until you showed up."

"Yeah, I saw what was going on and rushed over here," Smoke remembered. He had noticed the new kid only once, but Smoke himself had been the new kid only a year ago and understood what it was like, how the other boys had been plotting to get him all day. Smoke was smaller than those kids, but even in sixth grade, he had a reputation for being a crazy little nigga. He spent more time in detention than in class. People weren't necessarily scared of him, just uncertain, and Smoke knew that a little uncertainty could carry him a long way.

"I been lookin' all over for you, man," the young Smoke had said, walking coolly through the crowd of boys, casually pushing aside the hand of the boy who held the cutter to Rafe's eye. He threw his arm around Rafe and walked him away from there, as if none of the other boys even existed. He stopped for a moment, looked over his shoulder at the boys, and gave them a menacing look. Smoke saw something in each of those boys weaken just a little. He smiled to himself and continued walking off with Rafe.

"You saved my ass that day," Rafe said. "I'll never forget that."

"Is that why you saved mine the day we got popped?" Smoke asked.

"Maybe. I don't really know," Rafe said, being honest.

They walked over to the play lot. Smoke stepped away from Rafe, his head down, looking for something on the ground. Rafe just stood there watching him. Smoke looked as if as he had dropped a contact.

"What you lookin' for?"

"Don't act like you don't know."

"I don't."

"You just tryin' to get out of it, 'cause you scared. You was always too slow."

And then it came back to Rafe, just as Smoke said, "Here it is. Right here."

Rafe walked over to him, saw a long, narrow crack in the pavement.

"Startin' mark, baby," Smoke said, smiling slyly, nodding his head. "From here to the monkey bars and back, nigga. You ain't that old that you forgot."

"Naw, Smoke," Rafe said, turning Smoke's invitation to an old-fashioned footrace down.

"Chicken, hunh."

"Naw, it's just that, last time I checked, I used to always whup that ass, and I was leading."

"Then you need to check again, 'cause last time I checked, we was tied. That was like fifteen years ago, but I'm sure my memory is servin' me correctly. So what you say, boy?" Smoke bent to one knee and tied his shoes in double knots like they did when they were kids. "Got it in you?"

"Fuck it. Let's roll."

They lined up, both crouching low, in starting stance. Then Smoke called out, "On your mark . . . get set . . . go!"

Both men shot off the mark, hammering down the pavement toward the monkey bars. Smoke had gotten the best of Rafe from the jump, and it seemed as if he would pull ahead, but around the turn and just past the monkey bars, Rafe caught up to him. As they sped toward the finish, they were virtually even. Rafe looked out the corner of his eye, saw Smoke looking back at him. He couldn't shake him, nor could Smoke pass Rafe. But then with just another twenty feet to go, Rafe saw Smoke dropping back just inches. This was when Rafe gave it all he had. Smoke bumped him, briefly trying to find any way he could to beat Rafe to the finish, but Rafe was too strong and blew over the line fractions of a second before Smoke did.

Afterward, they hunched forward, breathing hard, their hands gripping their knees.

"It's them polishes, man. If it wasn't for them . . . ," Smoke said, huffing, ". . . I woulda had your ass."

"Whatever . . . man," Rafe said, slowly walking over to the swings and sitting himself down in one.

Smoke did the same, both men sitting quietly.

"I ain't lying, man. The business is really doin' well, and I want you in on it, Rafe. Want you to be my right-hand man, just like it used to be," Smoke said, not looking at Rafe, but wistfully out at the school grounds in front of him.

"You said it's all on the up and up?" Rafe asked.

"I told you that. What I got to do to make you believe that?"

Rafe didn't answer, just thought about the possibility that Smoke was telling the truth. If he was, almost instantly Rafe could have a better life: no more living in the rented room, no more taking buses, no more feeling like he was a loser.

"Damn, man. I just offered you a partnership, and you ain't sayin' nothing," Smoke said, twisting his swing to face Rafe.

"Yeah . . . I mean . . . I guess I'll take it," Rafe said, knowing he could always back out if the arrangement wasn't truly as Smoke described it. "What am I supposed to be doin'?"

"Shit. Whatever you want. You like working on the cars. Be chief mechanic. You want to sit behind a desk? Do that. You want to put on a suit, shoot some game, and try to sell? Do that. I don't care, man. I just want my brother back. Don't want to lose you again. Cool?" Smoke said, standing from his swing, opening his arms for a hug.

Rafe stood, walked into the man's embrace. Hugged him back.

"All right, cool. We'll see what happens."

"Good. Good!" Rafe could hear the happiness in his voice. "You made the right decision, man," Smoke said, still hugging him. "Because I'd die before I'd let anyone break us up again."

TWENTY-TWO

OVER THE past couple of days, Ally had been doing some serious thinking. Her mother was going to put her ass out in little to no time at all, because she sure as hell wasn't sleepin' on nobody's damn couch. Ally knew she had to make some money in a hurry.

She thought about the possibilities that were available to her and could come up with nothing beyond the average, work-your-ass-off-for-minimum-wage gigs. She wasn't about to call fools up at dinnertime, trying to sell them cable or cheap long distance. She wasn't going to stand around in a mall, smiling ear to ear and spraying folks with a funky-smelling perfume tester either. And she sure as hell wasn't ringing up nobody's groceries at the local grocery store.

That work was far beneath her, and her image would be torn to shreds if she was ever spotted doing some shit like that. It took her all night lying in bed, her mind wavering between just what she would do for money and the fact that she was still horny as all get out. Ally's hand moved down under her blanket, snaking down the center of her belly and in between her legs. She touched herself, let out a long, cleansing sigh, and thought back to the other night when she was riding Rick. If only he hadn't passed out, not lettin' her get hers, she wouldn't have to be . . . and then she stopped. She had it! It came to her like that. She shot up in bed, feeling as though not only did a light bulb appear above her head, but it glowed brightly, then exploded with the brilliant idea she had. She knew exactly what she was going to do.

The next day, she called her girls. "We got to have an emergency meeting," she said to JJ.

"A meeting? What, are we in a club now?"

"Just be home around four."

Ally called Lisa, told her to meet her at JJ's too, and then she had to run a little errand.

Ally walked up the rickety stairs of a worn-down building on the rough side of town. She passed a few people standing on the stairs on the way up. Painfully skinny guys huddled around a single glass pipe, as if they were worshiping it, praying for the next hit of crack. Then she came upon a woman, her dirty blonde hair matted down across her head, dark circles around her eyes. She held one end of a belt in her teeth, tightening the thing around her arm, a syringe and a tiny vial at her side. Ally had to step over her, because she was stretched out across one of the stairs and didn't seem as though she was going to move, didn't seem as if she was able.

When Ally made it to the third floor, she walked down a long hall-way to a single door with a small, narrow, sliding door peephole at eye level.

She knocked three times, a pause between the first and second knock, and an even longer pause between the second and third. Moments later, the tiny sliding door opened to expose two wide brown eyes. They darted around, then settled on Ally.

"What you want?" the muffled voice said.

"T-mac," Ally said.

"Who are you?"

"Tell him, Alizé wants to see him."

The narrow door slid shut. Ally heard movement, and then it faded out of earshot. A minute after that, the door slid open again, familiar eyes looking out this time, and then it slid shut once more.

Ally could hear the locks on the other side of the door being undone. Then it opened to reveal a bony, brown-skinned, buck-tooth brotha, wearing thick eyeglasses, a T-shirt, underpants, and an open bathrobe.

"Alizé, Alizé," he said, opening his arms for a hug. "You finally decide to come visit the candy man for some sweets?"

"Yeah, but not for me."

"For who then?" T-mac said, gazing at Ally's body through the thick lenses.

"Can't say, but so you know up front, I can't pay you now."

"Aw, baby," T-mac said, lowering and shaking his head, as if he had just heard news of someone passing away. "I'm sorry. So sorry. No pay, no play."

"I'm good for it. I promise," Ally begged.

"When?"

"No longer than a week. Ten days tops."

T-mac looked as though he was giving it thought, then smiled and said, "All right. This one time. But if you can't get the money up, you know what I want instead."

"What?"

"Pussy!" T-mac grinned.

"I'll have your money, T."

"C'mon in," he said, stepping aside. "And tell me what you need."

AT 4:30 P.M., all the girls were assembled and again they were drinking. Since Ally called the meeting, she had to bring the liquor: two bottles of strawberry Arbor Mist. She poured the glasses and brought them out to the girls. Ally stood in front of JJ, Sasha, and Lisa and told them how her mother was going to put her out on the street.

"You know, this place is big enough for you to stay here," JJ said.

"Thanks," Ally said. "But the idea of waking up with your face in between my legs just doesn't sit right with me."

"Forget you, ungrateful ho," JJ said.

She told them how she needed to make some money fast and that she wasn't going to take the normal route.

"Then how?" Lisa said. "You ain't talkin' about sellin' your ass still, are you? Because if you are, I'm out of here."

"No, no," Ally said. "But close. Remember the date I was supposed to have wit' that so-called baller?"

Everyone nodded.

"Well, he took me out like I wanted, showed me a good time, and so I decided I would give him some. We got naked, I was ridin' it, and the shit was good. I mean I was feelin' it, until his ass came, passed out, leaving me empty."

"Damn!" JJ said. "I can remember from my dick days that there wasn't nothin' worse than that."

"Tell me about it," Ally said. "But like I said, dude had loot. He had taken it all out, laid it across the nightstand before we got undressed. It just kinda slapped me in the face after I got dressed and was about to leave. Jewelry, credit cards, and his clip. He had to have about a grand in it. So I reached over—"

"Giiiiiirrrrrrrrllllllllllll! No you didn't," Sasha gasped, covering her mouth with her hand. "Let me see it! Let me count it."

"Good fa you, Ally!" JJ said, shooting up from the sofa, stabbing a finger at her. "Now niggas know they got to pay when they come weak. Literally!"

"Oh, my god," Lisa said. "You robbed a balla'."

"No. I didn't, but I could've. He was out cold, and I was standing right over all his loot," Ally said, crouching over JJ's coffee table, extending a hand as if she was still in the moment. "I coulda grabbed all of it, and he woulda never seen me again. One night's work, and I would've been a grand richer. See what I'm sayin'?"

The girls all looked at each other. Huge, sly smiles spread across Sasha's and JJ's lips, but by the time Lisa caught on, she said, "Ohhhhh, no. If you're thinking what I think you're thinking. Oh, no. Hell no. That's crazy."

"Sounds like fun to me," JJ said.

"And profitable," Sasha said.

"How about suicidal?" Lisa asked, giving them all questioning looks. "How we going to do that without them knowing who we are? What if we rob them, then see them again? We're dead."

"She got a point, Ally," JJ said.

"Not a problem. We wear wigs, colored contacts, glasses, and stuff."

"Ooh, we get to dress up. That might be fun," Sasha said.

Lisa just gave Sasha a sideways look and shook her head. "Well, how are we supposed to get them unconscious? Knock them over the heads with pillows, or sit there and wait 'til they drink themselves silly? And won't they expect the same from us?"

"She got another point," JJ said.

"I already thought of that," Ally said, confidently. "While they're not watching, we slip something in their drinks. In about ten to twelve minutes, they'll be out for the count, and they won't wake up for at least an hour. And by that time, we'll be long gone."

"And what is this *stuff*, and how do you know it'll work?" Lisa said, skepticism thick in her voice.

"Because someone I trust told me it will. And anyway, I'm gonna find out for sure very soon," Ally said, glancing over at Sasha.

"When?" Lisa said.

And Alizé knew she couldn't have planned it any better when she saw Sasha's eyes roll to the back of her head, saw the cup jump from her hand, and watched as the petite woman dropped to the floor, a drunken smile on her face.

"Now," Ally said.

JJ and Lisa were still facing Ally when they heard the thud behind them. JJ spun around, saw Sasha sprawled out across the floor, and screamed at the top of her lungs, racing over to her. It was the first time Ally had heard JJ sound like a woman.

Lisa turned from Sasha back to Ally. "You didn't slip some of that to her?" Lisa asked, looking like she knew full well that she had.

"Yup," Ally said, looking down at her watch. "Eleven minutes, exactly. Told you it would work. Try wakin' her up."

JJ was down on her knees, smacking Sasha lightly, but she didn't respond, made no movement at all. JJ turned to Ally, murder in her eyes. "I'm gonna kill you!"

Ally ran behind the sofa, and Lisa got in front of JJ, holding her off, or at least trying to.

"What you doin' using my baby as a guinea pig?" JJ said, clawing and fighting to get at Ally.

"I just gave her a little. She's only gonna be out for like five or ten minutes," Ally said, dodging and weaving around behind the sofa. "I wanted to prove to ya'll that it'll work. Just watch and see. I'm tellin' you."

While Sasha was out cold, the girls stood over her, her head in JJ's lap, JJ looking like a worried mother, wondering if her child would pull through her serious battle with a deadly disease. They talked over whether they would pursue Ally's idea.

"I was game before you pulled this shit," JJ said, smoothing her hand over Sasha's wavy hair. "But now I don't know."

"C'mon, JJ. This shouldn't change anything. It's a good plan. Fast money, and you can get back at all the men in the world for turning you into the evil bitch you are. Just think of these fools as your mama's boyfriend."

"Yeah, I wouldn't mind that," JJ said, still looking worried. "But I'm only down if Sasha is."

"Fair enough," Ally said, turning to Lisa. "You?"

"Ain't no way," Lisa said, shaking her head. "I'd have to be in a serious pinch to participate in some craziness like this."

"C'mon, Lisa. You my girl," Ally cajoled, wrapping her arm around Lisa's shoulder. "It wouldn't be the same without you. I told you. It's fast money and practically foolproof. Just roll one night."

"No way," Lisa said, pushing Ally's hand from off her shoulder. "I'm strapped. I need money just like everybody else, but I don't need it that damn bad. Ya'll roll without me."

"Suit yaself," Ally said, and just then, Sasha started to come to. She batted her eyes a number of times, then looked up in JJ's face.

"Baby, you okay?" JJ said, caressing her face.

"Yeah," Sasha said, her voice groggy, wiping her eyes. "When do we start? I got a perfect wig for the first night."

Ally smiled, and JJ started laughing out loud, bent down, kissed Sasha on the lips, and said, "Well, I guess it's on!"

The three girls hugged each other, leaving Lisa just outside of their embrace, shaking her head.

TWENTY-THREE

THINGS WERE going good with Wade, Livvy thought, stepping in from shopping. She had been speaking to him for the past three days over the phone, and they had gotten a lot closer in a much shorter time than she ever imagined.

Their last two conversations had started late at night, after 11 P.M., and ran into the morning hours, Livvy lying in bed, cuddling her pillow, a candle lit on her nightstand. Those talks reminded her of when she was in high school, before she got pregnant. They were playful conversations, "What are you wearing?" conversations, and they spoke of what turned each of them on, how old they were when they lost their virginity, and what they each considered romance.

"Have you ever been in love?" Wade asked her.

"Yeah. Twice."

"With whom?"

"The father of my children, and . . ." Livvy stopped herself, about to tell him that she had also loved a man named Carlos, but the fact was, she was still in love with him. And yes, because of Wade, that feeling was slowly fading, but she didn't want to risk his possibly hearing in her voice how much she still cared for Carlos when she said his name.

"You were saying," Wade prompted.

"And someone else," Livvy finished, "but it didn't work out. It was a bad situation."

"Oh, I see," Wade said, sounding as though he knew there was more than what she was telling him.

The subject all of a sudden turned to sex. Wade told her how physically attracted he was to her. He told her that he had struggled on their dates not to touch her soft body, not to wrap his arms around her, yank her in, and give her a big fat kiss each time he picked her up.

"Why?"

"Because I didn't want to seem frantic. I didn't want to move too soon."

"Well, next time, if you feel that way, you can do those things."

"Really," Wade said. "What else can I do?"

"I don't know. What do you think you'd want to do?" Livvy said, giggling shyly.

"As much as you would allow," Wade chuckled.

"So I guess it would really depend on the mood, how we both feel. If we think it's right. But I'm sure we'll both know when that is. And just so you know, I feel the same way you do."

They made plans for the following night—tonight—and Livvy had a sneaking suspicion about how the night would end. That was the reason that she was just walking in from Victoria's Secret.

She was running a little late. Wade said he would call to let her know what the plans would be, so as soon as she walked in the door, she went to the phone without setting her bags down. Livvy picked it up, ready to call him, but she heard no dial tone.

She pressed the talk button a number of times, but still nothing. She checked the cord in the back of the base of the phone, then followed it to the wall, where it was plugged in. She took out the plug and clicked it back into the wall, then tried the phone again. Nothing.

"It's shut off," Alizé said, walking past her mother. "You must ain't pay the bill."

Livvy looked up at Ally as she walked into the kitchen, sensing that for some reason, the girl got pleasure from delivering this news. Livvy thought about the last notice she'd gotten from Ameritech, the third notice, the one in the pink envelope. She was waiting until payday next week and didn't think they'd cut her off so fast.

Damn, she thought, getting up from the floor. She wouldn't have the money to pay them for a week, when she could pay all the other bills that were past due too. But she wouldn't worry about that now. What she needed to do was call Wade.

Livvy looked over at her daughter, who was standing beside the open refrigerator door, picking grapes from a bunch, and popping them into her mouth.

"Alizé, I need to use your cell phone."

Alizé ate one last grape, then closed the fridge. "Hennesey's so perfect, why don't you use hers?"

"Because you know Henny don't have no cell phone. Now go get it. I ain't playin' with you."

Ally poked her lip out and stomped in the direction of her room, returning a moment later with the tiny cell phone, and held it out for her mother to take.

"Maybe you should get yourself one," Ally retorted as her mother took the phone.

"I can't keep the house phone on. How am I supposed to be able to afford one of these," Livvy said. "Don't know where *you* got it from."

"Men like the ass you said I should lose," Ally said, turning her back to her mother, and swished her butt into the kitchen.

Livvy dialed and after only one ring, Wade picked up.

"Hey, I was getting worried. We still on for tonight?"

"Yeah, yeah. I've just been a little caught up is all, but we're still on."

"I don't recognize this number," Wade said. "Where you calling from?"

"Oh," Livvy said, glancing up at Ally who was looking her dead in the face. "I was doing some shopping, and I'm still out, so I'm using my daughter's cell phone."

Ally shook her head at her mother, a disgusted look on her face.

"Should we push it back an hour?" Wade asked.

"Could we do that?"

"Not a problem. It won't mess anything up. But I just want to tell you I got something special planned." Livvy could hear the excitement in his voice through the phone.

"I'm sure you do. See you later." She disconnected the call. Ally walked over to her and took the phone. Not a word was said, but by the way her daughter took the phone from her, Livvy knew the tension between them was getting a bit out of hand and something would have to be done about it. Soon.

TWENTY-FOUR

WADE had a good day today. With no little old blue-haired ladies to deal with, he'd sold three cars, and for a nice amount over what the dealership paid for them, making him a decent little piece of change.

It was a sleazy gig, but he was good at what he did, better than anyone else there, including the owner. He could've done *his* job, run this place, Wade thought.

And if someone were to ask Livvy, he was doing just that—running the place, owning it even. He laughed at himself for telling that lie and wondered what had driven him to do such a thing. Livvy seemed like such a nice person, but he would never know the extent of it, because if he got too much closer to her, she would ultimately find out that he wasn't really the owner of this dealership but just a peon salesman. If he wanted to keep seeing Livvy, this would always have to be his little secret.

The extra money he made today would come in handy, because his last couple of conversations with Livvy had been quite steamy. They had him feeling like a teenager, up until all hours of the night, sittin' on bone for much of the time they were talking.

Toward the end of their last conversation, she had said some things that had Wade believing that she could've actually been thinking about giving him some sex. She said something about the chances depending on how they both felt, something about the timing and the mood being right.

When Wade heard that, it gave him an idea. This morning, before he went in to work, he called a few of the nicer, moderately priced hotels downtown.

"We have a nice restaurant on the third floor with a huge bar and pleasant lighting," the receptionist at the Omni on Michigan Avenue told him, and he knew this was where Oprah had all her guests stay for the show. Wade didn't know if this fact would get him anywhere, but he would make sure this tidbit of information came up. He booked the room.

On the way home from work, he started to ask himself why he was going through all this trouble for this woman. Was it just to get some sex? That couldn't have been the case, because the room alone cost $225. And for that price, he could've had two hookers, decent-looking ones, scrubbing his back, toweling him off, boning him well, then putting him to bed. But he realized now that he didn't want to have sex with just any woman anymore. He wanted that person to matter to him, and this Livvy did.

When the person on the phone said what the room cost, it didn't make one bit of difference, because Wade enjoyed impressing Livvy. It made her face light up, made her smile, and it made him feel like a bigger man than he was used to feeling.

Besides all this, he just really liked her. Maybe something might actually come of this, Wade thought, after he had gotten off the phone, confirming his plans with Livvy. Maybe it wasn't just a convenience situation. Who knows? Maybe there could be a future for us, Wade thought.

TWENTY-FIVE

"So I think he's going to make a play for it tonight," Livvy told Sharika. Livvy had gotten dressed in a classy, simple, black calf-length summer dress and high heels. She had just finished her hair, but she had to run up and talk to her girl before she left.

"You think so?" Sharika said.

"We talked a little about it, and that's what I'm feeling. What should I do?"

"Give it to him, girl!" Sharika advised, looking at her as if any fool should've known the answer to that question. "Give it to him good. And don't worry. He won't last nothing but a minute. Then when you're done, tell him that you been having problems makin' the bills and could he help you out."

"Won't nobody be lyin'," Livvy said. "They cut my phone off today."

"There you go. Tell him that if he wasn't in your life, you wouldn't care how long your phone was off, but the idea of not speaking to him every day would just kill you, drive you to tears, girl, so he has to pay for you to get it back on. How does that sound?" Sharika looked proud of herself.

"Yeah, I'll say something like that," Livvy said, smiling. Then all of a sudden the smile disappeared.

"What's wrong?"

"You really think I should?"

"Have sex? It's a means to an end," Sharika said, placing a hand on her shoulder. "Do what you gotta do."

"No. I'm actually very attracted to him. If the sex happens, then it happens. I'm talking about asking him for money. It feels like this relationship could be something more than . . ."

"Oh, no, you don't," Sharika said, throwing her hands in the air, walking away from Livvy. "Don't you go turning this into your search for love again, girl. That's not why I dragged your ass out the house, for you to go replacing your crush on Carlos with a crush on another guy that's gonna put you in an emotional straight jacket, have you going crazy over him."

Sharika walked back up to Livvy and put herself right in her face. "You have to set the boundaries. You have to place demands on this relationship, let this man know that you all have a mutual agreement: you will spend your time on him if he spends his money on you."

"I know." Livvy made a face that implied that Sharika's words were soiling her. "But that just seems so . . . so . . . professional."

"Look, Livvy," Sharika advised, still looking intently into her eyes. "I'm not saying that you can't have fun with this man. I'm not even saying that you can't develop some feelings. But keep them in check. You ain't tryin' to find a father for your children. They grown. You ain't tryin' to find a man to marry. You just need one that'll help make life a little easier, and if you play your cards right, you got that right in front of you. Okay?" Sharika grabbed her by both shoulders and gave her a little shake.

"Yeah," Livvy said, uncertainty in her voice.

"Go out there, have a great time, give him the best you got, but one thing."

"What?"

"Don't go down on him the first night. Yes, he has to pay for it, but we don't want him to think you're a ho."

"Thanks a lot, Sharika."

WADE looked handsome when he picked Livvy up an hour later, and as always, he was a perfect gentleman. He took her to dinner downtown at the Omni hotel—"Where Oprah put up all her guests," Wade let her know. Of course, Livvy knew that, because at the end of the show, the announcer always said just that, but Livvy acted as though she was surprised anyway.

Afterward, he took her up to a beautiful suite, where they got comfortable, had a few more drinks. With the lights low, the music soft, and the alcohol working on her, she couldn't help but feel more attracted to him than ever before.

Wade turned to see her gazing. "What?"

"I don't know," Livvy said. "I don't want you to think the wrong thing about me, but I just really need to kiss you right now. Can I do that?"

Wade didn't even take the time to answer her, just grabbed her face in his palms, and started kissing her gently, deeply.

LIVVY didn't know what the hell Sharika was talking about when she'd said he'd last only a minute, because the old man had damn near wore her out.

An hour or so later, he was lying there next to her breathing heavily, the sheet pulled up just below his waist, his body covered with sweat, as hers was. He turned to her, smiling. Livvy smiled back, and then he grabbed her hand, brought it to his lips and kissed each and every finger, then let it rest on his muscular chest.

Forty-eight and still in great shape, Livvy thought as she rubbed her fingers over his torso.

They had been finished for all of only a minute or so, and Livvy wished that this moment could go on forever. It was nice to just lie there with him, share his space; this was as meaningful to her as the sex they had spent the last hour having. Livvy liked that she didn't feel worried that Wade might bolt up, jump into his slacks, and race out like Carlos always did. She felt very comfortable with this man, felt that the sex meant a lot more to the both of them than just sex and that there could really be something there for the two of them if she played her cards right.

Livvy felt Wade kissing her fingers again, and she was becoming aroused, felt her body starting to tingle. No, no, she told herself. Got to set boundaries, Sharika said. Got to place demands. Because Sharika, who never got dogged in a relationship, Sharika who never got her heart broken, had told Livvy—who was always getting dissed, who was always crying over some fool—that this was what she should do. So she had to do it. Right? "No romance without finance," she said to herself, drawing strength from the old song. If she let Wade roll up in her again, regardless of how much she wanted just that, he would think that he could get it anytime he wanted, without having to give anything for it. No romance without finance, Livvy said to herself.

Wade rolled over to her, still smiling, and said, "That was wonderful."

"I know. I thought so too," Livvy said, trying to return the smile, but feeling that her face wasn't doing what her mind told it to. She must've been right, because Wade's eyebrows furrowed and the smile left his face, as if he sensed something was wrong.

"Is everything okay, baby?"

"Yeah," Livvy lied. "I mean, no."

"What is it?" he asked, scooting closer to her, wrapping an arm around her.

Why does he have to be so damn caring? Livvy thought. But she continued with what she had to do. "Well, when I said that I was calling from my daughter's cell phone, I was. But when I said that I was still out, I lied."

"I see," Wade said, looking concerned.

"See, I was at home. But when I tried to call you, my phone had been turned off. And well . . . I was wondering . . ." As Livvy spoke, she was still questioning why she was going through with this, because at that moment, she felt lower than she ever had in her entire life. But she continued anyway, trusting what her girl had told her. "Since I don't get paid until next week, maybe . . . I don't know . . . maybe you could pay it for me?" And there it was. It was out there, and if Wade jumped out of bed, threw his things on, and raced out, leaving the door open behind him, she wouldn't have been surprised.

Wade looked at Livvy at first as though he was lost, as though he didn't fully understand what she was talking about. But then Livvy said, "What do you think?" and he snapped out of it, his demeanor all of a sudden changing to something very businesslike.

"Oh, yeah," he said, quickly, jumping out of bed. "Of course," he said, reaching for his pants on the dresser, digging into the back pocket for his wallet.

"I mean, you don't have to do it right now," Livvy said, raising up, reaching out her hand, as if to beckon him back to bed.

"No, no. No problem. I know how things can get." He sounded slightly disappointed. "How much do you need?" he asked, thumbing through his money.

Part of Livvy wanted to tell him to forget about it, but since she had gotten this far, she said in a tiny voice, "A hundred and nineteen dollars. It'll take a hundred and nineteen to turn it back on."

"Okay," Wade said, and he fingered out five twenties. "I only have a hundred," he said, handing it over to her. "But they have a teller machine downstairs in the lobby. I'll just go down there and—"

"Wade, don't."

"It's not a problem. I'll just slip these on—" But Livvy reached out from the bed, took the pants from him, and placed them on the floor on her side of the bed.

"Just come back to bed. Okay?"

Wade gave her a lost look, as if he really didn't know what she wanted of him and didn't know to trust it, even if she told him.

"Just come back to bed," Livvy urged, giving him a little smile. He did, and Livvy put the money on the nightstand on her side of the bed, truly feeling like a lady of the night now. He lay down beside her, his back to her, and Livvy wrapped her arms around him, pulling herself as close as she could to him. He didn't speak, and neither did Livvy. She just lay there, feeling his heart beating through his warm skin, and hoped that she hadn't just done irreparable damage to something that could've really been good.

TWENTY-SIX

RAFE stood by the tree outside the library again, but this time he wasn't hiding. He stood out in plain view for Henny to see him when she left. When she stepped out the door, he noticed he was the first thing her eyes looked toward, and when she saw him, she started to smile.

"Is this going to be a regular thing, you meeting me out here like this?" Henny smiled.

Rafe smiled back at her. "Yeah, but only because you want it to be."

"What are you talking about?"

"I saw you looking over at this tree, hoping that I would be standing right here. And when you saw that I was, you started cheesin'. Don't try and play me, girl," Rafe said.

"All right, I'm busted. So what? What's my punishment?"

Rafe grabbed her hand. "You have to come with me."

THEY ENDED up in Hyde Park on the huge square rocks bordering the lake. The stars were out, and miles away, the lights of the downtown skyline sparkled against the calm Lake Michigan waters.

"I used to come here a lot when I was a kid, and just look up at those buildings, and think that one day I would live in one of them," Rafe said wistfully, his body leaning against one of the large rocks.

"What did you want to be?" Henny asked him. She was sitting very close to him, allowing Rafe to rest one of his arms across her thigh.

"I don't know. Anything more than just an auto mechanic, I guess." Rafe glanced at Henny for a moment, then looked back out over the water.

"You said that where you lived before, you spent a lot of time in the library. Was that in college?"

Rafe didn't answer her, didn't look at her. He thought about what the old guy, Wade, had told him—to wait a while before telling her about his jail time. But Rafe didn't want to lie to her, didn't want this relationship to start off that way. He just hoped that she wouldn't judge him by his past alone.

"It wasn't college, Henny," he said, and then turned to her. "I was mixed up in the wrong things when I was younger, with the wrong people. I spent three years in jail for being involved with this guy who sold drugs, for selling drugs myself." Rafe tried to look at Henny but turned away again, not wanting to see her expression. "I was young, stupid. Just wanted to make money, and this guy who got me into it, I rolled with him, didn't question nothing he said, because he was my best friend. He said we weren't doing nothing wrong. Said the people came to him askin' for it. That he ain't try to push it on them, ain't make nobody take it. And he said that even if they didn't get it from us, they would just get it from somebody else, so why not make the money. I knew it was bullshit. But we were poor coming up, and it seemed the only way, so I did it. But some bad things happened, like me being thrown in jail. I knew I never should've done it then."

"You said things. What else?" Henny asked, softly.

"After I was in, my little brother got killed."

Rafe heard Henny gasp, and when he turned toward her, her hand was covering her mouth, shock in her eyes.

"I don't know who did it," Rafe said. "The cops said he was just walking home one day from school and got hit by stray gunfire. I know that ain't all there was to it, because he wasn't even near school, off up in the far West Side, where he knew he ain't have no business." Rafe dragged a hand down the length of his face, pulled at his chin. "I just know that if I wasn't in prison, I would've been there to stop what happened. He looked up to me, and I wasn't there. So I'm responsible for his death."

"Raphiel," Henny said, sliding down from the rock, putting herself right in front of him. "There was nothing you could do from behind bars. It wasn't your fault. You can't control what—"

"Don't, Henny," Rafe pleaded.

"But—"

"Please, just don't. It is the way it is. I've already accepted it," Rafe said, surprised at how strong he was being. "But I'll understand if you want me to take you home, if you don't want to see me no more."

Henny moved closer to Rafe and wrapped her arms around his neck. "I want to be here with you more now. You didn't have to tell me those things, but you were honest with me, and that means so much. I know you aren't the same person that you were then."

"How do you know that?" Rafe asked.

Henny looked up into his eyes, bringing her face very close to his. "Because I couldn't feel this way about you if you were." She raised herself up on her toes to touch her lips to his. He was hesitant at first, but then he wrapped his arms around her, pulled her into him, and passionately kissed her back.

THE NEXT DAY, Rafe was back at the job, working in his usual capacity as a normal mechanic.

Smoke had pulled him aside first thing in the morning.

"So, you want me to make the announcement now or what?"

"What announcement?"

"That you're gonna be head mechanic from now on. That if any of the mechanics have any questions or problems, they should come to you."

Rafe was silent.

"So, what? You still got a problem with this?" Smoke said.

"Naw, man," Rafe lied.

"Well, just let me know when you decide," Smoke said as he walked off.

For the rest of the day Rafe had been doing nothing but thinking about if he should take Smoke up on his offer. Problem was, Rafe knew Smoke had a tendency to lie. He remembered Smoke telling him that his mother was really his sister and that his father was really his uncle because he was ashamed that the drunken, disorderly pair were his parents.

He also remembered when Smoke told him that he was moving to Florida when his parents really had to move to public housing because they had been thrown out of their house. He lied for as long as he could get away with it, and confessed only when he was caught.

But, then again, Smoke had never lied to Rafe about business. Never. And that was why now, at closing time, Rafe was marching toward Smoke's office, duplicate work orders from the service department in his hand.

As Rafe knocked on the door, he couldn't deny how things would change for the better if he did take the job. He thought about the money he would make, the things he could buy with it—a car, maybe one of the shiny, exotic numbers he always saw as he walked through the showroom for work. He wouldn't have to take the bus to the library to see Henny anymore, and Rafe could just imagine the look on her face the first time she saw his new ride. Eventually, he would even be able to move out of his aunt's place, get something of his own.

Rafe knocked again on Smoke's office door as a smile slowly stretched across his face.

When Smoke didn't answer after Rafe's second knock, he turned the knob and pushed the door open to see if Smoke was in, but he wasn't. Rafe stepped in to drop the duplicate papers on his desk. He set the copies down, then just stood over the big oak desk, admiring it and the leather executive chair behind it. If Rafe took the job, would he get a desk and chair like that? Of course not. He'd be chief mechanic. They don't need desks. But what if Rafe said he wanted one anyway? And an office too, just like this one? Smoke wouldn't turn him down. Hell no! They were brothers, right?

Yeah, Rafe would have a desk just like Smoke's, and now Rafe wanted to know how it would feel to be sitting behind it. He walked around the desk, pulled out the chair, and slid down into it.

Perfect fit. Immediately Rafe felt like an important person. He felt he had decisions to make, procedures to put in place, felt like he could greatly impact the course of someone's life with just the swipe of a pen.

He slid open one of the drawers, looking for a pen or pencil to hold, furthering his little fantasy.

In the open drawer, he saw a pen, pulled it out, and pretended as though he was signing some important bill into law. He scribbled his name in the air in front of him with the pen. That's how he would sign the orders in the service department once he was in charge as head mechanic, he thought to himself, smiling. Maybe he would change his signature just a little bit. Something a bit fancier.

Rafe opened one of the side drawers, looking for a piece of paper to practice on. Nothing. He shut it and opened another. Nothing but two volumes of the Yellow Pages. He pulled open the last drawer and at the bottom of it, Rafe saw a narrow wooden box. He halted, his eyes fixed there, not knowing what to think.

He would've thought nothing of it had he not seen that box before.

He knew it well. It was the box Smoke had always kept his personal stash in. Rafe wanted to close the drawer back, act as though he had never seen what he had, but he continued eyeing it, knowing what was probably inside.

He pulled the box out and set it in front of him. He looked down at it as if it would open up itself, reveal its own contents to him. He didn't want to find out what was in there, because if he was correct in his suspicion, that meant that Smoke was still using drugs, had lied to him. And if he lied to him about continuing to use, then he'd probably lied about selling the drugs too, and Rafe didn't want to find that out.

Rafe felt as though his entire bright future was disappearing right before him.

But what if he didn't look in the box? What if he just slid the drawer shut and forgot about it?

Rafe put the box back, pushed the drawer closed, and let out a sigh of relief, telling himself he'd done the right thing. But he knew deep down he hadn't. He knew he had to find out what was in that box, and now he was yanking open the drawer, dipping his hands into it, fishing out the box, and flipping open the cover.

There it was, just like Rafe was afraid of: three joints, a lighter, and a quarter bag of weed. And there was more, something Rafe hadn't expected: a vial half full with a white powdery substance. Cocaine, no doubt.

Smoke had not only lied to Rafe about quitting drugs, but had moved up to coke. If Smoke had lied about this, what else was he telling stories about? Everything, Rafe thought. If Smoke truly was still dealing, then Rafe was in jeopardy of being thrown back in prison for just being in this room. This outraged him. He had to know for sure. Had to know so he could take proof back to Dotson, or whoever had the power to get him out of here, so he wouldn't get slapped with more time when he was innocent.

Rafe spun around in the chair, not bothering to put the uncovered box of drugs back in the drawer. He quickly took in the room. There were cardboard boxes stacked in a corner. He raced over there, started ripping at the tape, tearing at their flaps, opening them up, only to find auto parts wrapped in plastic.

Rafe headed toward Smoke's closet door, threw it open, pushed the garments on hangers aside, scanned the floor, and found nothing. He cleared the top shelf, sweeping off everything that was on it. Nothing.

Rafe hurried over to the tall wall cabinets. They were locked. So he went to the boxes of auto parts that he had torn open and pulled out what looked like a jack handle, a flat head on one end.

He shoved the flat end of the bar in between the narrow space where the doors of the cabinet came together. He pulled and pried with all he had until he heard a splintering sound. The lock ripped away from the wood, and the doors popped open. He threw the bar aside, flung the doors back, and gasped at what he saw: at least twenty large plastic bags, filled fat with cocaine, sat neatly atop one another like small, fluffed pillows.

Fuck! Rafe thought. He was in trouble—and much more trouble than he had actually known, because he hadn't heard the office door open behind him during all the racket he was making opening the cabinet. He wasn't aware of the huge man creeping into the room behind him either, bending down, retrieving the discarded jack handle off the floor, and stepping toward him.

"Fuck!" Rafe said again, this time aloud. "I gotta do something." That's when he turned around and caught sight of the man in the room. He also caught sight of the metal bar slicing down through the air at him, and then there was blackness.

WHEN RAFE came to, his head was killing him. He brought a weak arm up to his skull to feel a large, pulsating bump there. As his eyes started to open slowly, he didn't know where he was, only knew that he was moving.

Rafe heard someone's voice echo through his brain. "He's waking up, boss."

"Don't worry about him, just keep driving," and that was Smoke's voice. Rafe knew that.

Rafe's eyes opened more, focused, and he realized he was in the back seat of a car. He saw Smoke turn, look over his seat at him, concern in his eyes.

"You okay? How's your head?"

"I saw what you had in your office."

"I know, I know. When my man saw you snooping around in my office, all he could think of to do was take you out. He's kinda like that. When he's uncertain about something, first thing pop into his head is just to smash it. But he's sorry about it, ain't you, Trunk?"

"Yeah, I'm sorry, boss," the big man said, looking up into the rearview at Rafe, not really sounding very sorry at all.

"We call him Trunk, by the way, because he as big as a damn tree trunk. Ain't he," Smoke said.

"You said you'd stopped selling. You said the business was legitimate. You lied, Smoke," Rafe said, trying to pull himself up in the back seat.

"Well, it was only a half lie, because the business is legit, but yeah, I am still slangin' on occasion. What's the fucking big deal though? Ain't like we ain't did it before."

"You selling coke now," Rafe said. "And ain't no we to it. I'm out of this shit. I don't know you no more, man," Rafe said, glancing out the window. "So you might as well pull over right now and let me out."

"Rafe. No, man," Smoke said. "You're back now. We ain't never breaking up again. You said that."

"I didn't say that."

"Well I'm sayin' it!" Smoke said, raising his voice.

"Fuck that!" Rafe said, grabbing hold of the front seat, and pulling himself up. "Let me the fuck out. Now!"

"All right, all right, brotha. No need to get your braids all frizzled and shit," Smoke said, calming now, a smile actually on his face. "I'll let you out of here. But first I got a suprise for you. And if you still think you can walk away from all I'm offering you, then you're free to go."

TEN MINUTES later, Trunk pulled the Mercedes into a vast, vacant parking lot by a huge warehouse. The three men jumped out and started walking, Trunk walking very close to Rafe, their shoulders almost touching, keeping Rafe from taking off.

"Where you taking me?" Rafe asked.

"Aw, I'll show you when we get there," Smoke said, waving the question off. "It's a surprise. You'll get a kick out of it though. Something I promised you."

They walked into the open warehouse, then down a long corridor. They headed down to the fourth door on the right, then stopped in front of it. Trunk pulled a key from his pocket and slid it into a door that looked just like all the other doors that lined both sides of the hallway. He didn't open it, but looked at Smoke, as if for permission. Smoke held up a finger, gesturing for him to wait a moment.

"You know," Smoke said, an almost giddy expression on his face,

"I've been waiting three years for this moment, and I can't believe it's about to happen. I'm just so happy, man. So happy." It was apparent by the way he was almost shaking with joy. "And like I said, if you want to walk away from me and everything else, you can. But after you leave this room, I sincerely think there's no way that you'll be able to."

Rafe didn't know what the hell Smoke was talking about, didn't know what to think, but he would be lying if he didn't admit to himself that he was scared, almost frightened, by the dark tone all of this had.

Trunk stepped away from the door, allowing Smoke access. Smoke turned the key, pushed the door open, and stood to the side. He extended an arm out, as if he were a doorman, welcoming Rafe into some exclusive hotel.

"Ain't you gonna go in, brotha?" Smoke said.

Rafe didn't budge, afraid of what he might see. Then without notice, he was pushed through the door by Trunk, who had been standing behind him. When Rafe stumbled into the tiny room, he was confronted by a black man with bulging, frightened eyes. Rafe didn't know what the hell was going on at first, but then he saw that the man's ankles were tied to the chair he was sitting in, his hands tied behind his back. Tape was wrapped thick and tight around his head to muffle his loud moaning.

It appeared as though he had been there for a little while, had been struggling for some time, judging by the thick coat of sweat that covered his face and had poured down over the front of his T-shirt in a large dark V. His eyes ballooned when he saw the men enter, and he started struggling with his restraints, started rocking back and forth, looking as though he was trying to topple the chair to free himself.

"Calm yo' motherfuckin' ass down, bitch!" Smoke yelled, and then in a very calm voice asked Rafe, "Know who that is?"

Rafe had no clue. He felt Smoke's arm around his shoulder. "C'mon, remember back, Rafe," he said in the same soft voice. "It'll come back to you."

Rafe tried his best to recall this man, but half his face was covered with tape, and Rafe was sure last time he saw him—if ever—his eyes weren't damn near popping out of his head with terror.

"I said, sit yo' ass still!" Smoke yelled again. "Trunk, give him some more phone numbers to think about." And at Smoke's request, Trunk walked across the room, grabbed the thick Ameritech Yellow Pages off the table, and with all his force, slammed it across the aging black man's head.

The man's neck snapped, almost seemed to break, and then his head whirled lazily about his neck twice before it slumped onto his chest.

"Now concentrate, Rafe. You'll get it," Smoke said.

Rafe looked at the man again, at his soaking T-shirt, at his blue trousers, his shiny black shoes, then he quickly looked across the room to see the man's shirt, hanging on the back of another chair. The shirt had stripes and a badge on it. He was a policeman—the policeman who had busted Rafe and Smoke, who had lied to put Rafe behind bars. Rafe gasped loudly, taking a frightened step back.

"Ah, I knew you'd get it, Rafe," Smoke said, leaving Rafe's side, and walking over toward the terrified cop, who had regained consciousness. "You didn't think I'd let this motherfucker get away with hemming you up like that, did you? Hell, naw," Smoke said, standing behind the cop, both his hands on his shoulders. "The things I do for you, and you said you didn't want anything to do with me anymore." Smoke smiled.

Rafe didn't say a word, couldn't. Just stood there, a stupid, disbelieving look on his face.

"I told you I'd handle this. Told you that. We brothers, baby, and that's why the day this nigga decided that he was gonna frame you with that coke, get you locked up, was the day he decided he was going to die. He just didn't know it yet. Did ya' nigga? Diiiiiid yaaaaaaa? No, you didn't," Smoke said, speaking in the cop's ear, in a playful goo-goo, ga-ga, baby voice.

"But it was," Smoke said, walking toward Trunk, pulling out a pair of gloves, and slipping them on. "I woulda got the cracker too, but his ass got himself killed before I could do the honors. Lucky bastard." Smoke held out his gloved hand, and Trunk, who was now wearing gloves as well, reached behind him, and pulled out a gun from the small of his back, placed it in Smoke's hand.

"Now I got this motherfucker for you, Rafe, because he took three years of your life. This bastard is old as hell. Probably going to retire in a few years anyway, so you might as well make it an early one."

Smoke held out the gun for Rafe to take.

Rafe couldn't move, couldn't speak, because he couldn't believe what Smoke was asking him to do. When words finally did come, he said, "I'm not doing it."

"Well, see Rafe. It's not just about wanting this motherfucker dead. I mean, there is that." Smoke moved closer to Rafe and presented him with the weapon again. "But there's also the little issue of me being able to trust that you ain't gonna go running to the cops about my side business."

"I wouldn't go to them. I hate them as much as you do. You know I'd never do that to you."

"Yeah," Smoke said, chuckling some. "You right. I know you won't, after I get this little bit of insurance. You feel me? Now take the gun and do this motherfucker, Rafe, so we can go get some lunch."

Rafe hated the cop, always had, but he couldn't kill the man.

"I ain't taking that gun. Forget it. You want him dead, do it yourself!"

"Fine. You right," Smoke said, and before Rafe knew it, Smoke had tossed the gun at him. Reflexes had Rafe catching the weapon, had him holding it in his hand, and then all of a sudden, Rafe felt as though he had been run into by a freight train. Trunk had run up behind him, wrapped both his hands around the hand that Rafe was using to hold the gun. Rafe started to struggle to get his hand from around the weapon, but Trunk's grip on his hands was too tight.

"What the fuck are you doing! Smoke, what's he doing?" Rafe cried, trying to get a look at Smoke and fight his way free of Trunk at the same time.

"He's doin' what he got to do, since you won't," Rafe heard Smoke say over the commotion, as he felt Trunk dragging him over closer toward the bound officer. Trunk raised Rafe's arms up toward the cop's head.

"No! No!" Rafe yelled. "Don't do this, Smoke! Don't make me do this!"

Rafe tried to do everything in his power—kicking the big man, ramming his body into him—to get away, but he was like a stone wall. Rafe tried to free his finger from the trigger, but Trunk had one of his thick fingers jammed in the trigger's ring up to the first knuckle, stopping Rafe from pulling his out. Rafe felt him starting to press down, trying to force him to pull the trigger, to kill this man, who was now moaning so loud Rafe thought he would go deaf by the sound of his muffled screams.

"Please. Please, don't!" Rafe yelled again, still fighting with all he had to keep his finger from being forced to pull that trigger, but he was getting weak, and he knew he couldn't hold back too much longer, and then Rafe heard the explosion, heard the sound of something thick and wet splatter against the wall. Trunk released Rafe. His body slumped to

the ground, the gun still in his hand, and when Rafe raised his tear-
streaked face up, he saw that half the officer's skull had been blown
from his head.

Smoke stood in the corner of the room, an odd smug look on his
face. "So, like I said, you can walk away if you want to now, but I would
strongly advise against it."

TWENTY-SEVEN

ALLY, JJ, and Sasha had planned how everything was supposed to take place in order for these robberies to come off successfully. Ally had already taken care of the drugs, and each of them was supposed to carry some, so whoever had the best opportunity to slip the powder into the victims' drinks would. They would always have to wear wigs, plenty of makeup, sunglasses, and colored contacts, just in case the glasses had to come off. They could never use each other's real names and never speak about where they lived or anything in that area.

The most important rule was that since there were only three of them, they could take on only two guys at a time—just in case something went wrong and, God forbid, they had to fight their way out of there.

They all agreed that they would target clubs only on the opposite side of town, places more than thirty miles from where they lived, because even though they were wearing disguises, they didn't need anyone recognizing them on the street. In the clubs, to keep things at a fast pace, the three of them decided that they would go their own way, looking for potential victims. If any of them found what she thought was a sure thing, she would go back to a previously chosen spot and wait until the others noticed her, then proceed from there.

The morning of their first hit, Ally was looking over her outfit when her cell phone rang.

"Hello."

"Ally, it's Lisa."

"Don't try and talk me out of this. We've already decided. Just because—"

"That's not why I'm calling," Lisa said. "I want back in."

"What are you talking about?"

"Meet me downstairs. I'm outside, in front of your place."

Ally threw on her shoes and went down to meet Lisa. When she approached her, she looked shaken, frightened, as if someone was after her. She told Ally that someone had broken into her place last night. She'd heard something break, woken up, and heard someone moving around inside her room. Her son was with her in bed, so she knew it couldn't have been him.

"I couldn't reach the phone, so I just lay there, covering my son's mouth so he wouldn't cry or make no noise." Lisa started to cry. "I watched that man move back and forth outside my bedroom door . . . and Ally . . . I was so scared. I thought I was going to die. I thought my baby was going to die. And I promised that if I got out of that alive, I was going to get me and my son out of there as fast as I could. I just can't take being in that place no more," she sobbed, brushing tears from her face.

"He get anything?" Ally asked, comforting her friend, smoothing a hand across her back.

"TV, stereo. It ain't important, long as he ain't hurt me and my son."

Ally looked at Lisa for a long moment. "I still don't think you should get back in, Lisa."

"Why? What are you talking about?"

"It's something you didn't want to do at first, so you shouldn't do it now. Yeah, you should get out that place, but maybe you need to find a different way."

"There is no different way," Lisa said, frantically. "I need to get out now! If you don't want me in, then just come out and say it, but don't be making no excuses."

"All right then," Ally said, gesturing for Lisa to follow her up to her building. "Let me fill you in on everything you have to know for tonight."

AT 10 P.M., the girls stepped inside a darkened club, lights flashing and music blaring over the voices of hundreds of people dancing, laughing, and talking. They huddled just inside the door, nervous and uncertain. They all wore wigs; JJ and Lisa's were black and short, Ally and Sasha's long and brown. Their faces were heavy with makeup, and dark glasses hid their eyes, themselves disguised with colored contacts.

Ally noticed that Sasha was looking over her shoulders and jumped when someone brushed past her.

"What's wrong with you!" Ally had to shout in order for Sasha to hear her over the music.

"I'm okay, I'm okay," she said, but she wasn't, and Ally knew it.

She grabbed Sasha by the arm. "Come with me," she said, leading her through the crowd of dancing people, toward the restrooms. JJ and Lisa followed them.

As soon as they got inside the ladies' room, JJ said, "Why you draggin'—"

"Hold it," Ally said, and pushed open the doors on the four stalls to make sure that no one else was there. When Ally gave her the okay, JJ continued. "Why you draggin' my girl in here like she stole something?"

"Why don't you ask her?" Ally said, looking over at Sasha who appeared shaken, sweat accumulating on her upper lip.

"What's wrong, baby?" JJ asked, placing a gentle hand on her face.

"Nothing. I'm okay."

"She's not ready for this," Ally said, pacing away from them toward the sinks.

"I told you, I'm fine. My nerves were getting to me just a little, that's all."

"Dammit!" Ally slammed her purse down near the sink. "I told her back at your place that if she wasn't feelin' this, then she should just stay home. Now we gotta give the whole thing up."

"Fuck that," Lisa said. "Sasha can just catch a cab back, and we can do what we gotta do."

"I told you, I'm fine!" Sasha said, raising her voice, pulling away from JJ. "I can be a little fucking nervous at first. But let me tell you, when it's time to throw down, I'ma be straight."

"You better be," Ally said.

FORTY-FIVE minutes of dancing and getting groped, of smiling, drinking, listening to the game of weak wannabe playas, and trying to screen for the perfect victims was starting to wear the girls down. Remarks from guys like, "Naw, we don't gotta get a room. I got my own place." Or, "We can just go out to my car," or, "It's me and my three boys. You said you got three friends," were all cause for instant disqualification. Ally knew the strict rules that they set had to be followed if they didn't want to get their asses hurt or even killed doing this thing.

Ally bumped into Lisa on her way to the restroom. "What's up? Anything?" she asked.

"Ain't nothing. I almost had a couple, but they were just too damn big, and I ain't tryin' to take no chances, things get out of hand."

Suddenly she and Lisa were grabbed. They turned around to see JJ.

"Look, over there!" JJ shouted over the music, tilting her head in the direction of the spot they'd chosen to stand if they found the right guys. Sasha was leaning up against the bar, two men on either side of her, their arms around her, both of them whispering in her ears.

Sasha caught the girls' glances and nodded her head as if to say that these were the lucky guys for the night.

JJ and Lisa walked over and took Sasha's place, and Sasha told the men she had to go to the restroom with her other girlfriend.

"See? What did I tell you?" Sasha said, a little too excited for Ally. "See all the jewelry they wearin'?"

"I see it, but do they have any money?"

"Girl," Sasha said, holding onto Ally, as if she felt weak in the knees, "they must be tryin' to see who dick is bigger, 'cause they both whipped out they rolls, tryin' to be the first to buy me a drink, and them rolls look like they was too big to fit back in their pockets."

"All right, then," Ally said.

"So I did good?" Sasha asked.

"Yeah, you did good. But don't let it go to your head, 'cause it's just startin'."

TWO HOURS later, a couple of four packs of coolers, a six pack of MGD, a fifth of Remy, and one of Quervo were stacked on the dresser of a Red Roof Inn motel. The TV was turned to a porn flick one of the two guys had ordered. The music on the clock radio was turned all the way up, its tiny speaker shooting out nothing but distortion, but it was enough for Sasha and JJ to do their little routine to.

Pete and Cool—those were the guys' names—were both clutching beers in one hand, plastic cups filled halfway with liquor in the other, yelling at the top of their lungs as Sasha, stripped naked from the waist down, gyrated in the middle of the floor. JJ, naked from the waist up, kissed and sucked Sasha's toes, working her way up her right leg, baby-kissing her thigh, and slipping her finger up between her legs.

"Goddamn!" Pete yelled, setting his cup down, digging into his pocket, pulling out the thick wad of cash he had, peeling the rubber band from around it, tossing tens and twenties down at the two girls.

Ally, who was sitting on the arm of Cool's chair, shot a look at Lisa, who was sitting next to Pete, when the man set his cup down. This was her cue to slip him the drug. But when Lisa went for the little plastic pouch in her bra, he wrapped his arm around her waist, grabbed his cup, and took a huge gulp from it.

"You want another drink, baby?" Ally asked, trying to pull the cup from Cool's hand, even though it wasn't near empty.

"Naw. Don't want you to go nowhere." Cool fondled Ally's left breast. "Matter of fact," he said, setting down his cup and grabbing Ally by the waist, pulling her in front of him. "I wanna see that fat ass of yours," and he turned her around so that her back faced him. He started unfastening the tight-fitting polyester pants that clung to Ally's hips.

"But don't you want something else to drink first?" Ally asked, motioning for Lisa to go for his cup.

"Fuck the drink," the man replied, quickly peeling down her pants to her knees. "Damn!" he said, giving her behind a slap that stung. "Look at this ass, boy!" he yelled over to Pete. "Now give me a lap dance. And I want it to be the best one I ever had."

Ally halted a moment, wondering what the hell she was doing in this position. Was the money even worth it? She shot a glance at JJ, who seemed as though she was trying with her eyes to tell her to just go along, everything would work out, and then she heard JJ say, "Yeah, girl. Show that nigga what you got. Show him what you got, girl! You know how you do," she urged, trying to pull Ally into the moment.

Ally heard JJ shouting at her and thought that either she could quit now, walk away with nothing, or commit totally, do this thing the right way, and take these two sorry bastards for everything they had. Unless she wanted to live with her mother the rest of her life, there was no other way.

As Ally looked over her shoulder at the cheesing motherfucker who had ripped down her pants, something inside her clicked, and then she said, "Oh, is that what you want?" giving her own ass a harder, louder smack than the one she had gotten a moment ago. "You want this ass?"

"Hell yeah!" he yelled, reaching out for it.

"You got it, motherfucker," and Ally started bouncing her behind on the stiffness under his jeans. She heard him moan, felt him grabbing her, felt his hands going under her shirt, squeezing her breasts, but she kept on, ignoring him.

"Like that?" she cried. "Like that shit?"

"Yeah."

"Well let me hear it, motherfucker!" she yelled.

"I like this shit!" he yelled.

"Want this pussy?"

"Fuck, yeah!"

"He wants this pussy, girl," Ally yelled to Lisa, who was riding Pete the same way Ally was doing Cool.

"Well, I wanna give it to 'em," Lisa called back.

Ally rose up off the man and told them, "Lay your asses on the floor and take off your pants."

"On the floor?" Pete said.

"On the floor!" Ally yelled, then said to JJ, looking her intently in the eyes. "And get us something to drink, 'cause I want us all to be right for this."

She was sure JJ got the message. JJ went to the dresser and as Ally and Lisa were dancing over the two physically excited men, she saw JJ go into the waist of her pants while she poured the drinks. Ally looked back over a second later, saw JJ shaking the cups in her hand, making sure that the powder couldn't be seen floating on the top of the alcohol.

JJ passed the cups to Ally and Lisa, Lisa looking to Ally for instruction. Ally took off her bra, threw it across the room, kneeled down over the man, and took one of her breasts in her hand. "Wanna suck it?"

Cool nodded his head frantically, a silly grin on his face. Then Ally commanded, "Open your mouth and take a drink." Cool opened his mouth wide, Pete doing the same for Lisa, as both girls started pouring the drinks into the men's mouths.

"Now I can give you a taste of me," Ally said, lowering her breast over the man, placing herself into his mouth, allowing him to suck and lick her nipple.

"Drink some more," Ally urged.

"Yeah, we want you nice and fucked up," Lisa said to Pete, and they poured the rest of the liquor into the men's mouths, some spilling over the sides of their faces.

"Here, get me some more," Ally said, holding up her cup, but when JJ came to take it, Pete said, "I don't want no more to drink. I want some pussy." He grabbed Lisa and hoisted her up onto the bed. Ally whipped her head around to see Lisa being tossed about, the man forcing her legs open with his arms.

"Hold it!" Ally shouted, trying to get over there, but was grabbed by the arm.

"Don't worry about them," Pete told her, standing and pushing Ally down to her knees. "You need to worry about this right here." He had his stiff penis in his fist, shoving it in her face.

"Here, let me jerk that thing for you," JJ offered, trying to come to Ally's rescue.

Sasha was trying to distract Pete from attempting to slide himself into Lisa, who was struggling as much as she could to get away from the man.

Both men pushed the other girls off, Cool saying, "Ain't said shit about jerkin'. I want this bitch's fat lips on my shit," and then he grabbed Ally by her hair, forced her face in between his legs, the tip of his organ pushing into her cheek and then into one of her tightly shut eyes.

"I said suck it, bitch!" Cool commanded, and then all of a sudden, Ally felt the grip on her hair loosen.

"What the fuck is happening to me?" she heard him say. A second later, the man's hand fell away altogether. Ally felt a whoosh of air and then heard a thud as the man dropped to the ground.

"What the fu—", Pete said, turning, seeing what happened to his friend, still holding Lisa's legs open. Then he too started to waver and lost consciousness, flopping over, his half-naked body falling in between Lisa's open thighs.

The girls said nothing. Their mouths hung open, eyes wide, bodies frozen. The blaring of the distorted music from the radio played, and the faint sound of voices moaning in sexual pleasure from the TV was all that was heard.

Another moment of silence and stillness passed. Then finally Sasha said, "What we do now?"

"We grab they shit and go," JJ advised, and the girls did just that.

AFTER THE hour-long cab ride back to JJ's spot, the makeup rubbed off, the wigs thrown aside, and the money counted and split, the girls joked and drank wine coolers, celebrating their first night's take.

"Almost eight hundred dollars apiece," Lisa said, holding her stack of cash. "They had more than three grand between them. What kind of fool walks around with that kinda money?"

"Fools who wanna lose it," JJ answered, holding each individual bill up to the light to make sure she could see its watermark.

Sasha fanned herself with the splayed dollar bills in her hand. "This'll buy some nice clothes."

"And some nice Vickie's underwear," JJ said, leaning over and kissing Sasha on the lips.

"And we got to get at least a grand for all this jewelry once we pawn it," Ally said, sliding the platinum rings, bracelets, and necklaces into a plastic bag. "But what was up wit' that nasty-ass show on the floor, JJ? I almost gagged when I saw ya'll rollin' around like that."

"Naw, baby. What you almost gagged on was that nigga's dick! Did ya'll see the look on Ally's face when he was poking her in the eye with that nasty thing? You are so lucky that stuff worked when it did," JJ said, laughing, along with Lisa and Sasha. "Or you would've been doin' the chicken head for sure."

"No," Ally said, waving a finger. "Alizé don't suck no dick. I woulda bit that bitch off before I stuck that thing in my mouth. Trust me."

"Whatever," Sasha said, and the girls' laughing died down as they all looked down at the money they now held.

"Tonight was a good night," Ally said. "Is everyone still cool with doin' this?"

"Yeah," JJ said.

"But how long we gonna keep it up?" Sasha asked.

"Until we don't want to no more," Ally said, looking to Lisa.

"Cool wit' me," Lisa replied.

"You sure?" Ally looked her intently in the eyes.

"I said, it's cool."

"All right. Then let's lay low for a few days and hit it again next week."

TWENTY-EIGHT

THE NEXT day, Rafe didn't go to work. He lay in bed wondering what to do. The phone rang several times before he turned the thing off, and he knew it was probably Smoke.

How could he have done this to him? Rafe wondered. They used to be best friends. As a kid, Smoke ate in Rafe's house, food that his mother had prepared for them. At night, he stayed there. Rafe never knew that Smoke had the capacity to do something like this. Had his parents, his mother, ever been in harm's way? Had he?

An image of the screaming policeman flashed in Rafe's head. He saw the man's sweat-covered face, his bulging eyes. Rafe felt the gun heavy in his hand, felt Trunk pull the trigger, and then heard the explosion.

Rafe shut his eyes against what was playing out in his head, not wanting to see the event unfold yet again. It kept him up all night, the scene constantly behind his closed eyes.

Smoke had told Rafe he didn't know what to do when he was carted off. He said it was the worst three years of his life without his so-called brother. He even told him that he loved him, that he would do anything, even die before he let them get broken up again, but he said nothing about killing. Had Smoke been that attached to Rafe? Had his issues with his parents' abandoning him for weeks at a time manifested into this? Was that why he was going through all this just to keep Rafe around? Rafe didn't know. But something had to be done. He had to find a way out of this before it got any worse.

Rafe thought about calling Dotson, but knew Smoke had his parole officer in his back pocket. If anything, calling him would do more harm than good.

The idea of going to the police crossed his mind several times, but the man Rafe killed, or was forced to kill, last night was an officer, and Smoke had Rafe's prints all over the gun. He couldn't go to the cops.

He was trapped. There was no place he could go, no one he could run to and tell, so he just lay in bed the entire day, trying to figure out why all of this was happening to him, and wondering if he would ever find his way out.

AT 9 P.M., Rafe was waiting outside the public library again. During the day, thinking about Henny was the only thing that kept him from going crazy, and as he waited for her, he tried to put out of his mind what he had done, tried not to think about the little droplets of dried blood still on his palms by the time he had gotten back to his place.

Rafe looked down at the back of his hands, still seeing the tiny red drops, even though he had long ago washed them off. He tried to tell himself to look normal when Henny came out the door, but when she walked up to him, she immediately knew something was wrong.

"Are you okay, Raphiel?" she asked, touching the side of his face.

He took her hand and caressed it in his. "Yeah, I'm fine. Just got some stuff on my mind. But I'll be fine in a little while." He did his best to put a smile on his face, then said, "Now where you wanna go?"

"I don't feel like hanging out tonight."

Rafe thought he would lose what little grip he had on his sanity if he were forced to be alone again to fight with his conscience. Then Henny said, "Can we just go back to your place."

"Are you sure?"

"Yeah."

THE CLOUDS opened up, and it started to pour just before Rafe and Henny made it into the house, drenching them both. He gave Henny one of his T-shirts and a pair of sweatpants to change into, and he did the same.

Half an hour later, soft music playing that Henny had turned on and a candle burning that Rafe had lit, Henny pulled herself off Rafe's bed. She walked over to the chair he was sitting in and stood behind him. He was staring at the rain as it crashed into the window and ran smoothly down the pane.

Henny gently placed her hands on his shoulders. "Raphiel, what's bothering you? You've been sitting here staring out at the rain since we got here."

He turned to her, sadness written all over his face. "It's nothing."

"Don't tell me that. You may not think so, but I know when there's something wrong with you. Now tell me. Please."

Rafe looked at her, wished that he could let her know everything that happened, and she could take him in her arms and tell him it would all be okay. But he couldn't, and the pain showed on his face as he turned away.

Henny took his face in her hand and turned him to face her. "C'mon, baby. It can't be that bad. Nothing is ever that bad."

Rafe looked up at her, this sweet, innocent girl, and again he thought of telling her. But why would he do that? To drag her into this mess so his cowardly ass wouldn't have to face it alone? Didn't he know that getting her mixed up in this, getting her involved with Smoke, even indirectly, could ruin her life?

"You got to go," Rafe told her softly, his voice unsure.

"What?" Henny leaned closer in to him.

"I said you should go."

"No. I want you to tell me what's wrong. I want to be here with you."

"Why?" Rafe raised his voice some, shooting up from the chair, pacing away from her. "Why you want to be with me?"

"Because . . . I like you. Because we have fun together."

"It's not worth it just to have fun."

"What's not worth it, Raphiel?" Henny asked, standing too, putting herself in front of him. "Would you just tell me?"

"Ruining your life. There are things you don't know about me, Henny."

"But you told me everything last night, and I still want to be with you. Nothing could be that bad."

Rafe walked over to the edge of his bed, lowered himself on to it, then let his face fall into his hands. "The man I was mixed up with . . . ," Rafe said through his hands.

"Yes. Your best friend," Henny encouraged him, standing over him, rubbing a hand over his hair.

"He made me do something bad, and . . . and . . ." Rafe started to cry. He tried to hide the tears with his hands, but Henny knelt in front of him, bringing his face up, and kissing them away ". . . and I don't know what's going to happen," Rafe finished.

"It's going to be all right, baby," Henny soothed him, still kissing his wet cheeks.

"No, no, no." Rafe shook his head.

"It will. I'm telling you it will. You just have to trust me." Henny grabbed his face with both her hands, holding him still. She looked into his eyes, then gave him a long, soft kiss.

"Do you believe me?" she asked, pulling away from him.

Rafe didn't answer, just lowered his head.

Henny kissed him again. "Do you believe me?"

"I want to, but things never work out for me. They just don't."

Henny reached down and started to lift up Rafe's T-shirt. He raised his arms, allowing her to lift it over his head.

"You don't have to do this."

"I know," she said. "I want to."

THE NEXT morning brought a cloudless sky with it, and when Rafe rolled over in bed and saw Henny's smiling face, he felt as though what she said last night could actually come true, that everything could be all right.

They had made love, and Rafe felt as if it had all been a dream. He remembered holding her tightly, hearing her calling out his name, and him questioning whether he loved this girl. Could it be just gratitude for being there for him when there was no one else, and for believing in him when it seemed no one had ever before?

Rafe moved in close to Henny, leaned in, and kissed her on the lips. She smiled again. He smiled as well, wanting to ask her something.

"What?" Henny said, reading the expression.

"You okay . . . from last night?"

"Yeah. I told you before we did it that it was what I wanted."

"I mean, physically. You know it's been a long time for me," Rafe said, brushing a strand of hair out of her face.

"Yes," Henny smiled. "You're a big boy, but I think I'll be able to walk again. Thanks for your concern."

"Stop it. You know I ain't mean it like that. I was just thinking about you."

"Yeah, I know. You're thinking about a lot, aren't you?" she asked, and Rafe knew she was referring to what he had started telling her last night.

"Forget about that. It was nothing."

"Whether it was or it wasn't," Henny said, raising herself up on one elbow, "I was thinking that maybe if you want to get away, you can come down with me to school when I go. You know, help me move, and if you want to, stay a little while. I have two weeks before school actually starts."

"You'd want that?" Rafe sounded surprised. "To see me after you leave?"

"Yeah. What did you think—that I just slept with you because I thought I'd never see you again? No, no, buddy. Now that you got the goods, I don't just *want* to see you after I leave, I *expect* to."

"But ain't there nothing there but smart people with Porsches and loads of money that their parents give them to go to school with?"

"Yeah, there are those people, but there are also people like me. I don't have a Porsche."

"But you're smart."

"So?" Henny said.

"You wouldn't rather be with somebody smart like you? Somebody with money, somebody . . . ," Rafe said, looking away from Henny, ". . . who wouldn't embarrass you?"

"Raphiel," Henny said, rolling on top of Rafe. "You're smart. You don't embarrass me. And who gives a damn about money? I want you, okay? Now think about it. And your answer better be yes."

"I'll think about it," Rafe said. "Now I should be gettin' you home before your moms thinks I kidnapped you."

"Can we do dinner next time? My treat."

Rafe was about to say yes, excited that she would want to take him out and pay his way, but then he stopped himself. If he were one of her soon-to-be-doctor friends, would she think she had to pay for him? Rafe told himself that she'd offered because she didn't think he could afford to take her out. But he could.

"Yeah, we can do dinner. But it's my treat, okay?"

"You sure?"

"Positive."

WHEN HENNY walked into her room later on that day, Alizé quickly hid something under her mattress.

"What was that?" Henny asked.

"Just a little something I'm saving up for."

"For what?"

"Something for Mama."

"I thought you all were mortal enemies. The last person I thought you'd be trying to buy something for would be her."

"She's always workin' so hard, and I need to let her know how much I appreciate all that she's done for me, even though she kickin' me out. What you think she'd like?"

"I don't know. Maybe you should ask her," Henny said, sitting down next to her sister. "Can I tell you something, though?"

"Yeah, like where your ass was last night."

"I'll tell you that, but I want to know something first."

"Shoot."

"The boy you met in the library that day. The one you went out with. Did you like him?"

"The one wit' the braids, and the tattoos. Naw." Ally waved the entire idea off. "After a minute of being on that date with him, I knew I shouldn't have been there. Why? You like him, don't you?"

Henny started smiling and blushing at the same time. "I think it's more than that. You wouldn't be mad if I told you that I'm falling for him?"

"Girl," Ally said, hugging her sister, "I'm happy for you, sis."

Henny leaned away from her sister, looking as though she was questioning what she was about to say next. "If I tell you something, you have to promise not to tell nobody, especially Mama. You promise?"

"Girl, just tell me, and stop acting like a child."

"Naw, I'm serious, Ally. Do you promise?"

"Yeah, I promise." Ally crossed her finger over her heart. "Hope to die, stick a needle in my eye. Satisfied?"

"He spent three years in prison for selling weed. You think I'm crazy if I keep seeing him?"

"Is he still sellin'?"

"No."

"You think he's a good guy, and you say you really like him, right?"

"*Really* like him," Henny smiled.

"Then just go with it, Hennesey. You ain't getting married. What's the worst that could happen?"

"You're right," Henny said, giving Ally another hug. "What *is* the worst that could happen?"

TWENTY-NINE

THAT NIGHT Livvy had Wade over. She felt terrible about having asked him for the money to turn her phone back on, and it had taken her three days to finally get him over so she could apologize to him and, she hoped, put their relationship back on the right track.

She had made him dinner. Porterhouse steak, mashed potatoes, gravy, corn, apple pie and ice cream for dessert. But when she tried making conversation, he responded with one-word answers and when she asked him how his food was, he only nodded his head, looking at her for a moment, saying, "It's good," then lowering his face back into his plate and sticking another piece of meat into his mouth.

After dinner, they moved over to the couch in the living room. Livvy brought out the essay that she and Henny had been working on, her entry in the contest for the nursing scholarship, and read it aloud to Wade. She was very proud as she read it, glancing up at him every few moments to get his reaction as she read from the page. He looked thoughtful, as though he was being touched by every word she spoke, and when Livvy was finished, she said, "The end."

"That was good, Livvy. It was really good," Wade said, not standing and giving her the hug she knew she would've gotten had she not blown it with him the other night.

"It's almost done," she said. "Just a couple more touches, and it'll be finished."

"I'm sure it'll be even better then," he said, instead of saying something like, "Wonderful! I want you to read it again to me when you're finished." That led Livvy to believe that maybe he wouldn't be around to hear the final version.

It was after midnight now, and the room was almost totally dark save for the light that came off the TV. They had been sitting in silence, both staring at the television for over an hour and a half, Livvy going over and over in her head what she should say to this man. Unable to come up with any great speech that would remedy all her problems, she simply said, "Wade, I'm sorry."

"For what?" He turned to her, a fake look of surprise on his face, as if he had no idea of what she was talking about.

"For asking you for that money. I had no right."

Wade just gave her a long, questioning look.

"What?" Livvy asked.

"We both know that's not true. We're adults, Livvy, and me being a much older adult than you, I believe we both know what's going on."

"What's going on, Wade? Tell me," Livvy urged, sliding closer to him on the couch. Wade got up, stood over her.

"This is an arrangement, Livvy. I think we both knew that going into this thing. Why else would a beautiful young woman be seeing an old guy like me?"

"Because I'm attracted to a guy like you," Livvy said, grabbing the hand that hung by his side. "And you're not old."

"In a relationship like this, there are conditions that must be met in order to keep it going. I expect certain things from you, namely sex and your time, and in return for that, from me, you expect money."

Livvy couldn't believe what she had just heard, because even though he accurately summed up the situation, it made her seem like nothing more than a pay-for-hire prostitute. She wanted to rise from that couch and slap the smug look off his face, but he was right. She wished he hadn't been, but he was, and Livvy wondered why she ever listened to her big-mouthed friend, Sharika.

"I see." Livvy sounded hurt. "So since it took me giving you sex in order to keep this relationship going, if I hadn't given it to you when I did, if it had been months, then you just would've stopped seeing me?"

Wade looked away from her, giving it thought, then told her, "No. It really wouldn't have mattered, because I was really starting to like you. And that was where the problem was, Livvy." Wade lowered himself back down to the sofa. "I thought what was going on between us could've been turning into more than just a damn arrangement. And then after we made love, you asked me for that money. That let me know where we really stood, that I was a fool to think any more of this."

"But you're not, Wade. I knew I shouldn't have asked you for that money right up to the point that I did."

"Then why did you do it?"

Livvy shook her head, not wanting to sound stupid, but said, "My crazy friend told me to. I should've never listened to her, but then again, she's the one that dragged me out in the first place, the one that saw you and forced me to introduce myself. Wade," Livvy said, moving as close to the man as she could, without actually sitting on top of him. "I'm sorry that this happened. I have to tell you that when I first went out with you, it was partly with the intentions of finding someone to help me out, but now that I've gotten to know you, I really like you, and I want this to be something special."

"You mean that?"

"Yeah, that's why as soon as I get paid, I'm giving you your money back."

"Did you really need that money?"

"Of course. I wouldn't have asked for it if I didn't."

"Then I don't want it back."

"But—"

"No," Wade said, firmly. "It's not about sex for money or money for sex. It's about me wanting to help you. You need help, and I'm in a position to do that. Let me."

"But, Wade—." Livvy tried to interrupt again.

"Livvy, It's done, and that's all to it. I'm sure there's going to be a time when I need something from you, and I'm hoping you'll be there for me."

"Of course," Livvy said. "That's what real relationships are about."

"So is that what this is now? A real relationship?"

"Is that what you want it to be?"

"Absolutely," Wade smiled.

"Then that's what it is," Livvy said, smiling back, and started to move in to kiss him when she heard the fridge open and close. When she turned around, Livvy saw Alizé walking out of the kitchen, wearing nothing but tiny panties and a thin tank top, the dark area around her nipples showing through the almost transparent fabric.

Ally, a can of grape pop in her hand, looked up at her mother and was shocked to see a man peer out from behind her mother's body. Immediately, with her arms and hands, Ally tried to cover all her scantily dressed parts as she sidestepped toward her bedroom.

"Sorry, Mama. I didn't know you still had company," Ally apologized, disappearing down the hall and into her bedroom.

Wade laughed. "One of your daughters?"

"Yeah," Livvy said, still looking in the direction Ally had walked away in. "And I told that girl a million times about walking around here naked." Livvy moved back toward Wade. "Now where were we?"

"I really should be going."

"Are you sure?"

"Yeah," he said, standing, pulling Livvy up with him, and hugging her. "Work in the morning."

"Okay, but next time we're hanging out at your place. I bet you got a big, beautiful kitchen, and I'm going to cook you dinner. Maybe we can even make a weekend of it. Do some things downtown again, and then I'll pamper you at your house all weekend. How does that sound?"

"Sounds good. I'm not sure when I'll be able to get the time off, though," Wade said, uncertainty in his voice. "But we'll make it happen. Let's talk about it more tomorrow."

"Okay, baby." They kissed, and Livvy let him out the door. She watched out the peephole until she saw him get on the elevator and the doors closed. She turned around, a smile on her face, happy that their misunderstanding was behind them.

A moment later, Ally peeked out, wearing one of Henny's college sweatshirts and a pair of sweatpants.

Immediately the smile on Livvy's face disappeared, turning into a frown.

"Mama," Ally said, walking a little farther out into the room. "I heard the front door close. You still got company?"

"What were you doing?" Livvy said, anger in her voice.

Ally looked as if she had no idea what her mother was talking about. "What do you mean?"

"What were you doing coming out here with no clothes on?"

"I was thirsty. I was getting a pop, but I ain't know you still had company."

"You're lying!" Livvy said, raising her voice, storming over to Ally. "You just heard the door close, and you knew now that my company left. When you came out before, had you heard the door close?"

"No, but—"

"But what?" Livvy grabbed Ally by the arm. "But you decided to come out here with your ass hanging out—see-through shirt and everything—and flash the man that I'm seeing? For what, Alizé? For what?"

"I don't know what you're talkin' about."

"Why did you come out here like that when you knew he was still here?" Livvy said, raising her voice even louder, shaking Ally for the answer. "You wanna fuck him?"

"What!" Ally was shocked.

"You wanna fuck him like all the other men I hear you be fuckin'?"

"What other men?" Ally asked, but her mother ignored her.

"You the one that said that men like your ass. You thinking he's going to like it too?"

Ally yanked away from her mother, something between shock and deep hurt on her face. "I told you, I ain't know you still had company, and when I saw him, I apologized. I don't want your man. Why would you even say that?" Ally was on the verge of tears.

"Because all you ever do is take, take, take. You criticize me for the man I had, and now you try to ruin things for me with the man I got. I'll be glad when your ass is gone." And Livvy immediately knew that this was the worst thing she had ever said to her daughter.

Ally looked more hurt by this than any slap that Livvy had ever given her, and a single tear rolled down her face. It looked as though there was something she wanted to say. But then she changed her mind, turned around, and ran back into her room.

Livvy thought about running in after her, apologizing, telling Ally that she hadn't meant what she'd said, but she couldn't, because that just wasn't true.

THIRTY

THE NEXT day at work, Wade was pretty much worthless. He spoke to customers, answered their questions, but if they seemed as though they were on the fence as to whether they wanted to buy, he didn't go in for the kill as he normally would've, closing the deal. There was too much on his mind.

He was happy that he cleared things up with Livvy, but there was also a downside to that. Because they were in a "real relationship" now, as she put it, he knew there was no way that he could continue to lie to her about his financial situation. He would have to tell her there was no huge home, that he didn't own a Lincoln dealership.

Livvy probably envisioned herself moving into his place, living there, walking across his marble floors, under his crystal chandeliers that hung from fifty-foot ceilings. She had mentioned them spending a weekend together, maybe doing some things downtown again.

Wade got out of his car in front of the house, and wondered if she knew how much "doing things downtown" cost for just one night, not to mention an entire weekend. But as he climbed the stairs to his floor and glimpsed the mail on the table in the hall to find he had only one piece, he asked himself, Was she to blame for thinking those things? After all, he drove around in his shiny Lincoln for the sole reason of making women think he had that kind of money. When Livvy asked what he did, his silly ass had lied to her, saying he had a job that would make anyone believe he had truckloads of cash. And when he took her out, it wasn't to Old Country Buffet, where they could've eaten all the food they wanted for $6.95. No, he had to take her ninety-some odd floors into the sky and serve her steak and lobster.

Fuck, Wade thought morosely, closing his room door behind him. He was knee deep in it now.

HALF AN HOUR later, Wade's head was spinning. He was sitting across from the kid, Rafe, from down the hall again. Just after he had come in and taken off his jacket, there was a knock on the door. Wade opened it to find Rafe standing there, looking kind-of lost, his hands behind his back.

"Hey, what's going on?" Wade asked.

"I, uh . . . I ain't go to work today. I wasn't doin' nothing, and just wanted to know if you were cool to talk about some things?" He pulled his hands from behind his back and was holding a bottle of Hennessy. "Drinks on me this time," he said, managing a smile.

An hour later, the bottle was more than half empty, and even though the kid had come to talk, he hadn't been sayin' much, had just been listening to Wade spill his guts.

"So, guess what. You'll never believe this," Wade said smiling, gesturing with his glass.

"What?" Rafe said, sitting slumped forward in his chair, his eyelids hanging low from all the alcohol he consumed.

"You ready for this?"

"I'll be ready when you finally tell me." Rafe casually took another sip of his drink.

"Your girlfriend is the daughter of the woman I'm dating."

"You're bullshittin'." Rafe sat up straighter, opening his eyes wider.

"Naw, ain't shittin' you, man. Your girl's name is Hennesey, right? Just like this fine liquor here?" Wade said, holding up his glass.

"That's her."

"Got a sister named Alizé, who got a big fine behind on her and perky tits," Wade said, his speech beginning to slur.

Rafe looked at Wade oddly. "How you—"

"She walked out in her panties while I was there. I tried not to look, I swear I did. But I couldn't help myself," Wade said, laughing.

"Oh, I know what you mean," Rafe said, laughing too. "I had me a peek. How are things workin' with you and her mother?"

"Aw, man," Wade said, taking another tiny sip of his liquor. "It's a long story, Rafe. I fucked up and lied to her, told her I'm makin' all this money, and now I don't know what to do now that it's time to prove it. Hate that I started it all, but the fact is," Wade said, tapping Rafe on the arm, as if what he was about to say demanded an extra little bit more of his attention, "regardless how sweet, these women are all about money. Everyone knows what draws a man to a woman is beauty and sexual appeal. What draws women to men is money and power, status, success. You know what I'm saying?"

And Rafe did know. He had heard this all his years coming up, if not from Smoke, then from every other man he knew.

"I mean, bless her heart. Livvy ain't really got a pot to piss in, and even she's talking about she wants a man that makes a lot of money. What you think a woman who's really doin' something, like a lawyer or a doctor, wants? A billionaire, I bet."

Maybe because he knew that Henny was going to school to be a doctor, Rafe put his glass down, leaned in, and paid more attention to the older brotha.

"You sayin' that just because a woman is makin' money, if she a doctor or something, she couldn't get with a brotha who's an electrician?" Rafe asked, mentioning a job that he felt was comparable to his.

"It's okay if it's the other way around, but for the woman to be making that much more money, have that much more education, it would be hard. Women like to show things off. They want to be proud of their man. 'Oh, my man does this,'" Wade said, doing his impression of a woman. "'My man does that, or he drives this kind of car.' Why you think I drive that Lincoln out there? Women like nice cars."

Wade swallowed down the last of what was in his glass, then grabbed the bottle, and poured himself another shot, then started to pour Rafe one.

"Naw, I'm cool," Rafe said, looking as though he was deep in thought.

"Why you asking these questions? You got a good woman. Doesn't seem like she'd be caught up in all that."

"Yeah. You're right," Rafe said, more to himself than to Wade. He thought so too. He just hoped the fact that he was an ex-con, poor as hell, and didn't have a pot or a plastic bottle to piss in wouldn't start to matter.

THIRTY-ONE

ALLY sat on the couch drinking a grape pop, the same kind of pop she walked into the kitchen to get the other night when she was thirsty, wearing panties and a "damn see-through shirt." That was the way her mother put it.

Ally flipped the channel to BET, and on the screen, the little computer-generated sistah with attitude, Cita, danced all about and gave her opinion, with a little ghetto flavor, about the topic of the day.

Normally Ally would've been up, dancing around, mimicking Cita's moves, laughing at her wisecracks, but Ally was in a funk today and pissed off that she'd let her mother put her there. Her mother had more or less called her a ho and then had the damn nerve to say that she was tryin' to take her man. That old ass relic? Ally didn't think so.

If she wasn't hurting so badly at that moment, so near the verge of crying, Ally would've laughed in her mother's face, but there really wasn't anything funny about any of it.

Ally wasn't trying to get with that old dude, and she was sure that if her mother really sat down and took a moment to think about it, she would've realized the same thing. So it had to have been her feelings for this Wade character clouding her judgment. She must've really liked him so much that she feared even her own daughter was trying to take him from her. Or maybe it wasn't even him in particular, Ally thought, taking a sip from the can of pop. Her mother had been dogged by so many men in just the time that Ally had been around, she was sure that it had to have a negative effect on her. Ally's father had gotten her mother pregnant, and then he took off. There's no telling how badly all the boys that came before him must've treated her, and now, of course, there was Carlos.

Ally figured him to be the worst of all, catching her mother when she was most vulnerable, and regardless of how many times her mother said she'd get rid of him, regardless how many times she tried, he keep showin' his slimy, smiling ass up at their door, wanting only one thing.

Her mother needed to be away from that man once and for all. If he hadn't treated her so badly, hadn't had her questioning her worth, maybe she wouldn't have gone off on Ally last night for making a mistake as simple as not putting on something before going to the fridge.

Or maybe she wouldn't have said that awful thing to her, about not being able to wait until she left. That had hurt her feelings more than she was sure her mother could've ever known. She wasn't kicking Henny out of the house, and Ally wondered that if her perfect sister weren't going off to college, would her mother be so quick to improve her life. She didn't think so. But that was just the double standard that Ally had learned to live with.

Ally sat up on the sofa and was about to flip the channel when there was a knock at the door. Ally looked over her shoulder, then stretched back out across the couch and ignored it. She had too much on her mind right now to bother with anyone who ain't had the sense enough to call first before they came over.

The knock came again, harder this time.

"Who the fuck is it?" Ally finally called out, annoyed.

No answer.

Ally blew a frustrated sigh and pulled herself from the sofa, carrying her can of pop with her. When she got to the door, she didn't even bother to look out the peephole, because regardless who it was, they would all get the same funky reception.

Ally pulled the door open and saw Carlos standing in the doorway, wearing slacks, an open sports jacket, a nice button-down shirt, a slimy smile on his face. He held something behind his back, which Ally believed to be flowers or something, considering she hadn't seen his ass in a little bit and figured he was over here with a bouquet tryin' to suck up.

"Yeah," Ally said, coolly, leaning on the open door.

"Hey Alizé," Carlos said, talking to her like she was a child, when he was only thirty-four years old himself. "How you been doing?"

Ally didn't respond, just stood there shaking her head.

"Mama ain't home."

"When does she get back? She hasn't been returning any of my phone calls."

"She don't get off work for another four hours, but it wouldn't make no difference if she walked in the door right now, 'cause it seems like she finally got yo' number."

"Alizé, what are you talking about?" Carlos smiled uncomfortably now.

"Ain't seen you in a couple of weeks, and that means that she obviously ain't fallin' for that nonsense you be tellin' her no more. 'I'ma take you out and show you the town,' when all you tryin' to do is crawl your sorry butt up in here and get you some pussy."

"Really," Carlos said, a confident air about him now. "And what do you think about that?"

"I think Mama stupid. If she down for fuckin', cool. Then just fuck and be done with it. But to let you make her think it's more than that just so you can get yo' thang off," Ally said, quickly glancing down just below his waist, "is just stupid."

"So you think your mother is stupid for dealin' with me, hunh?"

"What I just say?"

"And what do *you* think of me?" Carlos looked very relaxed now.

"What you mean? I don't think nothing."

"Seems that ain't necessarily true," Carlos said, looking down at her baby-size see-through T-shirt. Ally followed his eyes to see that her nipples were growing and starting to softly protrude through the thin fabric of the shirt. She took a long swallow of her pop and pretended like it wasn't happening.

Carlos took a single step closer. "Can I touch one?" he asked, his voice low and heavy, one of his hands already appearing from behind his back.

Ally looked at him for a moment, saw him lustfully taking in her breasts, scanning down, devouring her entire body with his eyes. Sorry-ass motherfucker, she thought. Then a thought popped into her head. "I don't care."

With that, Carlos slid a warm hand under the T-shirt and cupped one of her breasts. He kneaded it around in his hands like dough, then pulled back, focusing on her hardened nipple.

He was far past excited, Ally knew, saw him pressing forcefully at the slacks he was wearing. Carlos raised her shirt with the one hand, lowered his face, and locked his lips around her breast. Ally was hardly aroused, but she moaned in fake pleasure anyway.

Carlos dropped the dozen roses he had been carrying right there in the hallway and used his other hand to grope her other breast, as he went back and forth between the two, coating them with his saliva. Ally quickly grew sick of this, and pushed Carlos down by his shoulders, onto his knees.

His hands slid off her breasts, down her waist, grabbed handfuls of her round behind, his face landing just below her waist. He pressed his face into the panty-covered V her legs and pelvis formed, and then started breathing in deeply, rubbing his face across it frantically, as if he was trying to wipe something clean from his nose.

Ally wrapped both hands around the back of Carlos's head and pushed him in even further. He grabbed even tighter to her ass, and she felt his wet, hot tongue flittering around her inner thighs. She felt it latch on to one of the sides of her panties, pull it aside. She felt as his tongue busily worked just on the outside of her, brushing over her pubic hair, and then with a quick side movement of his head and a push forward, his tongue was inside her. Ally jerked abruptly, feeling the quick sliver of wet warmth slip into her, and again the sensation registered nothing more than faint nausea.

She stood there in the doorway, looking down the hallway, this man down on his knees, feverishly sucking and slurping as if there was a lollipop shoved up her pussy. He was in plain view for anyone who happened to be walking down the hallway to see.

She grabbed a handful of Carlos's curly black hair, peeled his face from in between her legs, and asked, "You want some of this?"

"You know I do," he said, his mouth and cheeks covered with shiny fluid.

Inside her bedroom, Ally peeled off her T-shirt and panties, then walked over to the bed, climbed on the edge of it, and lay on her belly, her knees tucked under her, her ass hiked up in the air.

She looked over her shoulder, saw Carlos undressing so quickly that he almost tripped and fell over as he tried to step out of his slacks.

"Come over here, and show me what you got," she teased.

They fucked for something like twenty minutes, but Ally didn't know. She wasn't paying any attention, because there was nothing that was making her. She rode him hard, screwed him so hard he was crying like a baby, like a punk. He was saying how much he loved it while she was on top of him, and when he was on top of her, he was saying shit like, "Whose pussy is this? This my pussy!" Ally didn't even answer him, trying her hardest not to laugh in his face, because she was being tickled to death with that feather dick of his.

When they were done, Ally walked Carlos to the door, and opened it for him. He stepped out, then turned toward her.

"That was wonderful. When can we do it again?" he asked, still looking slightly out of breath, his hair disheveled.

Ally could no longer hold her laughter in and started to giggle.

"What?" Carlos said, smiling uncomfortably.

"You sorry-ass, limp-dick motherfucker. I don't know why my mother was so sprung over you. She must've just felt sorry for your ass, because I know I was closer to fallin' asleep than having an orgasm."

"But—"

"But nothin'. From now on, you gonna stay away from my mother. She's far too good a woman, and she deserves so much more than your sorry ass. So don't come back around here. And if you do, I'll go to the police and scream rape," Ally said, seriously. "'Cause, you know I'm still a minor."

"But—"

"Goodbye, motherfucker!" Ally slammed the door in Carlos's face, hoping that that would be the end of him.

THIRTY-TWO

RAFE, awakened by the telephone, rolled over in bed, slung an arm toward his nightstand, and fumbled blindly for the phone. He brought it to his face, pressed Talk, and then said, "Hello," in a groggy voice.

"Wake up, sleeping prince," Rafe heard Smoke say on the other end. Rafe groaned sadly.

"Wake up, wake up, and turn on channel 5. There's something you gotta see."

Rafe didn't move, and Smoke must've sensed that for he yelled loudly into the phone, "Get up, nigga, and turn on the tube. Now!"

Rafe rolled out of bed, clicked on the TV, and settled back onto the edge of the bed. When the TV came on, Rafe saw a blonde female news anchor talking, the picture of a black man in a police officer's uniform behind her, the word MISSING in capital red letters printed under him.

"He's an ugly somethin', isn't he? Or should I say *was?*" Smoke, chuckled on the other end of the phone.

"They . . . they find him?" Rafe asked, his voice unsteady, feeling a fearful tremor race though his body, thinking that the police could've been on their way to lock him up that very minute.

"They ain't find him, and they ain't gonna, because when I tell Trunk to get rid of somebody, he *really* gets rid of them. But you need to get your ass in here. You know you still have a job you have to come to, and if you don't want to take my word for it, I'm sure Dotson will tell you the same thing."

And there it was. Rafe knew that Smoke had a direct line to Dotson, but he just didn't know how taut that line was.

"So did you go to him? Tell him what happened?" Smoke asked.

"I ain't tell no one."

"Really? You sure about that? Because you know just because there ain't no body doesn't mean the cops can't get a tip on where to find the gun that killed one of their fellow pigs. So you certain you ain't tell nobody a thing."

"You'd already know, since you and Dotson so tight."

"That's right. I would. And it's a good thing you know that. Now you had a long enough vacation. Think it's time you come back to work." And before Rafe could say a single word, Smoke had hung up the phone.

ONCE HE got to work, Rafe put on his uniform and went straight to the cars, not stopping at Smoke's office. It would be best to avoid the man. Near lunchtime, there came a tap on Rafe's shoulder, and as he pulled himself from under the hood of a 3 series Beemer, he saw that it wasn't Smoke himself but one of Rafe's coworkers.

"The man wants to see you," he said. Then he turned and left.

Rafe wiped his hands on a rag and headed for Smoke's office. Once he got there, he knocked on the door.

"*Entrez*," he heard Smoke say from behind the door.

Rafe opened the door and took one step into the office.

"Damn," Smoke said, out the side of his mouth, a cigar stuck in the other side. "You look angrier than a mug."

He picked a set of keys off the desk and pitched them to Rafe. "Black convertible Jag out back. Take it for a spin, make sure it's running perfect. Wash it, shine it up real nice, then let me know when you're done." After giving his instructions, Smoke spun around in his executive chair, turning his back to Rafe. A moment passed. Not hearing the door close, Smoke swiveled back around to find Rafe still in the doorway, the same angry glare on his face.

Smoke pulled the cigar from his lips. "I don't have to say pretty please, 'cause it ain't no request. Now make this easy on both of us, and wash the car, man."

WHEN RAFE came back two and a half hours later, Smoke grabbed the keys from him and led him outside.

They stepped out, and Rafe stood aside as Smoke took a walk around the car. "You shined this bad boy up good. Drives okay?" Smoke asked. "Everything's cool wit' it?"

"Yeah, did a diagnostic on it. Everything checks out," Rafe confirmed, all the words in a monotone.

"Cool," Smoke said, throwing the keys in Rafe's direction. They hit him in the stomach and fell to the ground.

"We out. You driving."

They ended up at a nice Italian restaurant on the West Side, very near the dealership. There was no one there but the staff and the owner, who greeted Smoke personally at the door. They didn't open until hours later, but he let Smoke in and made sure he was treated like close family.

Smoke was deep into his spaghetti and meatballs a moment after it arrived, while Rafe sat there, his place clear before him, staring past Smoke.

"Sure you ain't want nothing to eat?" Smoke said, twirling a thick band of spaghetti noodles around his fork.

Rafe didn't say a word.

Smoke stuck the food in his mouth, then pushed the plate aside, pulled the napkin from his lap, and wiped his mouth. "You got to excuse me, but I was hungry as hell." He tossed the cloth napkin aside and leaned over the table some. "That shit had to happen, Rafe."

Rafe turned his stare on Smoke, anger smoldering in his eyes.

"I killed him! That ain't have to happen," Rafe said in a hushed voice, looking side to side, making sure he couldn't be overheard. "Did you fucking have to make me kill him?"

"Rafe, you ain't kill nobody. Trunk did. You ain't pull the trigger, and if that black bastard was alive today and not in little pieces floating in the water somewhere, he'd say the same thing. You ain't wanna do it, and you ain't done it. I just needed to make it seem as though you did. That's all," Smoke said.

"But why?"

Smoke rolled his eyes, blew out a long, exasperated sigh as if Rafe should've known everything he was about to disclose to him. "You know how much money this car business generates alone? And we ain't even factoring in the money I make on . . . well, you know. My other business. Something happens to me, what happens to it all? The businesses, the loot. What? Let the goverment take it? I don't think so," Smoke said, gesturing with a toothpick he pulled from his lips. "Everything you did for me, everything we been through, all the times when we were shorties and talked about how we weren't forever gonna be poor, that's why I did what I did. That's why I'm forcing your ass to stay around, because one of these days, I'm hopin' that it's gonna come to your dumb ass, and you gonna realize just how good you got it, brother."

"That won't ever happen. Just let me out now."

"Can't do that, man."

"You keep saying how tight we used to be, how we brothers. All that shit from the other week, takin' me back around the crib, bringing up all that shit from the past, all of that. Just bullshit, right?"

"Rafe, c'mon, man. You know better than that."

"Then let me out."

"Brotha Rafe—"

"Let me out, Smoke. If I mean all that to you, then let me the fuck out."

Smoke gave Rafe a long look, shaking his head sadly, as though he was about to say something he'd regret. "All right, look. Roll wit' me, just for a little while. A month. See if you feelin' the game again, like I know you gonna. But if you don't, the door is open. You can just walk on out."

It wasn't exactly what Rafe wanted to hear, but it was better than nothing.

"I ain't killin' nobody, ain't roughin' nobody up, ain't doing nothing illegal."

"Naw, man. Just hang out wit' me. Help me spend some of this money that I got. Shit, have a good time. You been locked up for the past three years. You should be jumpin' at the chance. You fuckin' earned it."

Smoke dug in his pocket, flipped off a couple of fifties from his roll, and threw them on the table. He grabbed a breadstick, popped it in his mouth, then said, "Let's roll. Got somethin' for ya'."

THAT SOMETHING that Smoke had for Rafe was the Jag they were whipping around in.

"I ain't takin' this, Smoke," Rafe had told him.

"You'd be crazy not to. It's clean, Rafe. I wouldn't give you no shit that's been chopped on. It's straight from the Jag dealer on Fulton, not even my store. Bought it outright." Smoke went into the glove box and pulled out an envelope. "Here's the sticker, the receipt, and registration. Had it made out to you, title should be here in a couple of weeks, in your name. Cops can stop you all they want. You more legit than they are in this car, Rafe. Just take the motherfucker."

"I said I ain't. You can keep me working for you, but you can't make me take no car, so keep it."

LATER THAT night, when Rafe knocked on Henny's door, he kinda wished he had taken the car, because he was half an hour late. The buses never seemed to come on time. He should've taken a cab. He could've afforded one, because before Rafe left for the day, Smoke had handed him four fifty-dollar bills.

"Take it. I know you ain't got a lot of loot. Think of it as an advance on your next check," Smoke said.

Rafe wanted to turn it down, but Smoke was right. He had little to nothing, and this money would allow him to take Henny somewhere other than Wendy's for dinner.

After work, Rafe had walked around downtown, peering in the windows of restaurants he thought looked nice. He stepped in one, a place called Ten, and asked if they had a reservation open for eight o'clock. They did. He booked it.

When Henny's door finally opened, Rafe said. "Sorry, I'm late, the bus—"

"It's okay." She looked him over. "You look very sharp," she said, but Rafe figured she was saying that just to be nice. He had on the best clothes that hung in his closet: tan khaki pants and a cheap rayon shirt. He probably looked presentable if he was lucky, but definitely not sharp.

"Are you ready to go?" she said, pulling back from the hug she had just given him.

"Yeah. I'm good."

"Hold it," Rafe heard a voice saying from inside the apartment. "I want to meet this man you been spending all your time with, Henny."

"Mama, we ain't got time. We're late already," Henny called over her shoulder while grabbing Rafe's hand, as if she was running from something.

"I'm sure he has time to meet your mother."

Rafe leaned in past the doorway to see Livvy and nodded his head, saying, "Yeah, I do." He looked at Henny with mild concern, wondering why she was trying to whisk him out of there so quickly.

Henny's mother was fine for an older woman, Rafe thought as he walked through the living room, toward the dining room table where she was sitting.

She was smiling at first, but he noticed that as he walked closer to her, the smile started to fade. She looked at his braided hair, his cool swagger, which he had to admit had been practiced to make him look hard when he was a youngster, but now had just become a part of him. She noticed the Timberland boots and rested her stare on his outstretched arm, on the tattoos spilling out from under his sleeve, down his arm.

"Good to meet you, Miss Rodgers."

Livvy stood and took his hand, allowing hers to be shaken.

"So Henny hasn't told me anything about you."

Rafe shot a quick eye at Henny. She looked uncomfortable, as if she was holding her breath, counting the moments 'til she could breathe again.

"Where you from?" Livvy asked.

"I'm from here," Rafe answered.

"How old are you?"

"Twenty-six. Just turned it not long ago."

"Well, you know Henny's only seventeen," Livvy said, gauging Rafe's reaction.

"But I'll be eighteen in two weeks, Mama."

Livvy cut her eyes at Henny, then focused back on Rafe. "You been to college?"

"No," Rafe said, feeling ashamed, but refusing to lower his head.

"Henny's about to go off to medical school."

"It's pre-med, Mama," Henny corrected.

"Her ex-boyfriend is down there. He's in med school now."

"That's nice," Rafe said, trying his best to smile at the woman, not knowing if that intention was making its way to his face.

"So if you didn't go to school, what do you do?"

"Mama, we really got to go," Henny said, pulling Rafe by the hand toward the door. But as she was spinning him around, Rafe caught sight of someone stepping into the room. It was Henny's sister, Alizé, and before Rafe was pulled all the way out of the apartment, he noticed the long, jealous stare she gave him.

Rafe walked with Henny, hand in hand, toward the bus stop, trying to put behind him the interrogation Henny's mother had just put him through. When they got there, he saw a taxi rolling toward them, threw up his arm, and flagged it down.

"What are you doing?" Henny said. "Aren't we taking the bus?"

"Naw. We're gonna be late for our reservation."

When the cab stopped in front of the restaurant and the driver turned to look over the seat to tell them how much the fare was, Henny dug into her purse.

"How much do you need?"

Rafe took mild offense to her attempting to pay and went into his pocket to retrieve his wallet.

"I told you I was taking you out. Okay?"

They got out of the cab and walked through the doors of the restaurant. Rafe heard Henny gasp behind him at how beautiful the place was. Long white curtains hung from the towering ceiling all the way to the floor. White tableclothes covered all the tables, single candles sitting atop them. Men in suits and women in dresses talked, ate, and laughed, as the hostess showed Henny and Rafe to their table.

"Enjoy your dinner," the smiling hostess said after she had seated them and given them their menus.

"Thank you," Rafe said. He looked across the table at Henny and caught the look of mild shock on her face as she looked around the huge, elegantly decorated room.

"You like it?" He was hoping she was impressed.

"It's beautiful," Henny said, turning to him, almost breathless.

"Go ahead, open your menu. Order anything you want," Rafe said, certain that the $175 left in his pocket would cover it.

Henny lifted her menu, and Rafe did the same. He was carefully looking over the selections, narrowing down his choices, when he heard Henny speak.

"Rafe," she whispered loudly, peeking over her menu, as if they were a fraud, on the verge of being found out. "What are we doing here? You can't afford this."

This was the wrong thing to have said to Rafe at that moment, for he had been trying to hold in all his anger at what her mother had said to him, how she had looked him over as if he wasn't good enough for her daughter. And now, for Henny to tell him what he could and couldn't afford, like she actually knew . . . he could no longer contain himself.

"How you know what I can afford?" he spat over his menu.

Henny leaned back, slightly shocked at his outburst. "No offense, but you're an auto mechanic, and you just started at that."

"Oh, I see. So is that why you yanked me out of your apartment when your mother asked what I did for a living?"

"No. It was because we were late, and it was none of her business."

"I see," Rafe said. "And why didn't you tell me about your medical school ex-boyfriend?"

"Because, quite frankly, Raphiel, that was none of *your* business."

Now Rafe jerked back.

"That man means nothing to me," she went on. "He's down there, but I don't know where. I haven't spoken to him since he left a year ago. And besides, I didn't care about him the way I care about you. That's why I want to know how you can afford this on the money you make and why you would even think you had to take me someplace like this."

Rafe leaned in a little across the table: "Because you're a fancy-ass woman, and you expect it."

"That's not true. You don't have to take me to places like this. I care about you. Not where we eat."

"Yeah," Rafe said, not believing a word she said. "But if I had money to afford this kind of stuff when you first met me, would you be complaining that you ended up here?"

"But you didn't!" Henny said, raising her voice, then looking around to make sure no one had heard her.

"But I got the money now."

"Then tell me how."

Rafe thought for a moment, then thought better against it. "I get paid like everybody else."

"But enough to afford this?"

"I make money, and that's all you need to know."

"I don't think so," Henny said, pulling the napkin from out of her lap and standing up. "I think you need to be taking me home."

Rafe looked up at her, wanting to stop her, to stop this, tell her to sit down so they could rewind, work this out, but he simply said, "Fine. Let's go."

He hailed another cab back to Henny's place. When the taxi pulled up in front of her building, Henny jumped out, slammed the door harder than she had to, and headed for the steps to the front door. Rafe watched her as she went, telling himself that this was going to happen anyway. Eventually she would've gotten sick of his being poor, of his having nothing, and no education, and then she would've left him. Tonight, things had just gotten sped along a little.

THIRTY-THREE

TWO NIGHTS later, Ally was at a club that was far too packed for her taste. It took her much longer than she had hoped, pushing and shoving her way through bunches of people, just to get seen and approached by men. She didn't know how JJ, Sasha, and Lisa were making out, but after an hour, Ally finally had some man drooling over her, buying her drinks, and telling her just how much money he made, how much he was carrying in his pocket at that moment, and how much he would sure love to take her home with him.

"I don't go home with men the same night I meet them," Ally said, cutting her eyes, as if he said something that had greatly offended her. "But I don't mind hotels," she threw in.

The man beside her was a rough-looking character, wearing slacks and just a button-down vest over his bare torso, countless gold chains of varying lengths looped around his neck. He smiled. "Cool."

"One more thing," Ally said.

The man's smile shrunk a little.

"You got a boy? 'Cause I got three friends with me, and I don't think you could handle us all."

He smiled even wider this time, nodding his head. "Yeah, my boy is out there somewhere. I'll go find him. We'll get your girls and be out. Don't go nowhere."

Ally nodded, not looking up at the man, just swallowing the last of her drink through her straw. After that, she spun on her stool and looked out over the bobbing and swaying sea of heads moving to the deafening music that shook the walls of the huge club.

Ally didn't see any of her girls and was starting to get frustrated because she really wasn't in the mood for this tonight. She wanted to grab her gang, get those guys back to the hotel, jack them quickly, and be out. If she could help it, she wouldn't have to participate in any of the nonsense that took place the last time. It was way too much work for the amount of money they had each gotten out of it.

Suddenly, Ally was grabbed by her upper arm, and then she heard a man's voice say into her ear, "What are you doing here?"

She quickly turned to see who this was, grabbing her like he owned her. When she looked into his face, she saw that it was what's his name . . . Rafe. The punk who had passed her up for her sister.

Ally looked at Rafe, dropped her eyes down to the hand that was still wrapped around her arm. "Do you mind? You lost the chance to get your feel the day you punked on me."

Rafe released his grip on her.

"But you can always buy me a drink."

"You didn't answer my question. What are you doing here?" Rafe asked the question as if there was life-and-death importance in it.

"What are *you* doin' here? Steppin' out on my sister already?"

"I'm here with a friend," Rafe said, looking over his shoulder. "But that's none of your business."

"Well, I'm just chillin'."

"And what about the guy you been sittin' here talking to all night?"

"Why you wanna know?"

"Because he looks like bad news. I heard some things about him. He's into some shit you don't want to get involved in," Rafe told her.

"Why, because he look like he got money? He does," Ally said. "He got lots of it, and if that's the kind of shit you talkin' about, that's *exactly* what I want to get involved in." Ally spun around on her stool, turning her back to Rafe.

Rafe grabbed Ally again, spinning her back.

"What did I tell you about that?" Ally said, looking angrily up at Rafe.

"Look, just grab your things, and I'll put you in a cab home." Rafe reached for Ally's purse off the bar, but she snatched it out of his hand and slapped it down back on the bar.

"I ain't gettin' in no damn cab. Don't need no ride nowhere, because I'm leaving with that dude." Ally knew this would piss Rafe off.

"Listen, you Henny's sister, and I don't want nothin' to happen to you. Now I don't know what you're up to, but just come home with me."

"I don't think my sister is going to like that. And if you don't get away from me now, I'm gonna tell her that I seen you here and you couldn't keep your hands off of me."

"Then you do that, but I'm gettin' you out of here," Rafe said. He was about to pull her from her seat when the man Ally was with came back, his boy with him. They stood on either side of Rafe.

"Yo' baby," he said to Ally. "Is there a problem?" Both men looked at Rafe, studied his hand on Ally's arm.

"Naw, baby," Ally said, sliding off the bar stool, and placing herself next to the man. "Just one more nigga thinkin' he stand a chance, tryin' to holla'. Like I said," Ally said, turning to Rafe. "I already got plans for tonight."

"Look," Rafe said, trying to pull Ally to his side. "Just come with me, please."

"Yo, potna," the man with the vest said, reaching over, grabbing Rafe's arm and yanking it off of Ally. "I think she said she don't want to come with you. You understand that, or do I got to make you understand?"

Rafe looked at the man, felt the grip he had on his arm. He sized him up quickly. He could take him, could flip his big ass, have him on the floor, his foot dug into his throat before he knew it, but Rafe backed off.

"Naw, I understand, man. My fault," and he backed up, giving Ally one more cautionary look. She turned away from him, whispering something in the man's ear, then laughing with him.

IT TOOK another half an hour, but Ally found JJ, Sasha, and Lisa, and they all left in the guy's Infiniti. The hit went off just as smoothly as Ally was hoping. As soon as they walked into the hotel room, the guy—Mason was his name—told Lisa to make them all some drinks. She did as she was told, returned, giving the men their glasses of gin and O.J., which they threw back. Approximately ten minutes later, both men were soundly sleeping, and the girls went about the task of taking anything and everything of value from them.

On their way home, they stopped off at an all-night pawnshop and sold all the jewelry they'd taken. After getting back to JJ's place, they split a little more than sixteen hundred dollars among them.

The motherfucker lied, Ally thought. He didn't have as much money on him as he said. The girls were disappointed, but it was another four hundred in each of their pockets, and they all agreed that next time they would just have to do a better job at picking the right hit.

THIRTY-FOUR

OVER THE past week, Rafe had been hanging with Smoke outside the dealership, because he had no choice. One day after he was finished with work, Smoke came to him and said, "Go home, change into something nice, and be ready in a couple of hours."

"Why?" Rafe wondered. "My job is to fix cars around here. Why does that require me going home and changing clothes?"

"Because I said it does. I told you, I just want you to hang with me for a little while. See how shit is. You never know. You might like it."

When Smoke came to pick Rafe up, they would hit clubs, sit around, drink, have a good time, nothing more than that. Afterward, Smoke would drop Rafe off at his place, and that would be it.

"We had a good time tonight, didn't we?" Smoke said, turning to Rafe from the driver's seat, smiling, after one of the nights they had hung out.

"Yeah, it was cool." Rafe couldn't deny it.

"Ain't nothin' like the VIP section, hunh?"

Rafe agreed, thinking about all the beautiful women walking around, catering to Smoke's every desire.

"So this is your spot?" Smoke tilted his head toward the house Rafe lived in. "A single room up there?"

"Yeah, this is home," Rafe said, turning to look at the place as well.

"You can do better, man. I got property. Lakefront. It's phat to death, and I—"

"I ain't takin' it, Smoke," Rafe said, stopping him. "I ain't take your car. I sure as hell ain't taking no crib."

"I still think you crazy for that, Rafe. But it's cool. You know where the keys are, where the car's parked. Whenever you ready for it, it's yours."

He would never be ready for it, Rafe thought, getting out of Smoke's car, and heading up to his room. But he didn't know then what he would see the following night.

THAT NEXT evening, Rafe picked up the phone at least half a dozen times to call Henny at work, tell her that he was wrong about what happened while they were at dinner. It had been a week since he had spoken to her. He wanted to explain to her that he was scared that she'd lose interest in him, scared that he couldn't compare to the men she would meet down at that school—educated men with money and a future. That wasn't him, and Rafe was sure that she would come to realize that sooner or later and leave him. He wanted to tell her how much that would kill him, because no one had ever cared for him the way she had.

Rafe held the phone to his ear, poised to dial Henny's work number again, but after a moment, he lowered it back into its cradle. He would just go there, he thought. What he had to say to her, he needed to tell her in person.

He was a little late getting there because of the bus again, but he was hoping that she hadn't left yet. Rafe quickly turned the corner onto the street the library was on. But then he halted and stepped back behind that corner, peering around it.

What he saw was Henny walking out of the library and toward a man leaning against the hood of his car. It was a huge brand-new Cadillac, and Rafe hated to admit it, but the man was handsome, well dressed, totally out of his league. Henny walked over to him. The man extended his arms and gave her a hug. He kissed her on the side of the face, smiled, and opened the passenger side door for her.

Rafe felt his insides burning, felt a jealous wave pass over him, and thought about racing over there, throwing punches at that man, whoever he was, beating him unrecognizable. But why would he do that? The man hadn't knocked Hennesey over the head. He wasn't dragging her screaming into the back of his car. She hugged that man, let him kiss her, got in voluntarily because she wanted to.

Rafe watched as the man strode back around his car, got in, and drove off with Rafe's woman.

So Rafe was right, he thought to himself now. She did want a man with money and nice things, and he thought back to what Wade had

told him about why he drove around in a Lincoln. The best woman
Rafe had ever had, and he was about to lose her because he didn't have
the things it took to impress her, to keep her interested. That shit
wasn't going to happen, he told himself. He turned around and headed
back to catch the bus, knowing it would be for the last time.

THE FOLLOWING night, Rafe was sitting with Smoke and Trunk at a
rounded booth in the corner of a club called SoulSmack. The table was
covered with glasses of liquor, dense smoke hanging over their heads
from Smoke's cigar. Another on a list of many nameless, beautiful
women was pushed up against Smoke, her hand dipping below the surface of the table and in between his legs.

"So how you liking that ride?" Smoke leaned over and whispered
into Rafe's ear. "Saw you take the Jag out for lunch. What changed
your mind?"

"You said it was mine whenever I was ready for it, right?" Rafe said
back out the corner of his mouth.

"Yeah."

"Then let's just say I was ready for it, and leave it at that."

"Cool, baby." Smoke turned away from Rafe, when his attention
was caught by someone walking through the front door and heading
toward the men's room.

Smoke leaned over, whispered something to Trunk, then excused
himself with a smile. "Got to got take a leak, baby. Be right back," he
said to the woman next to him.

Trunk steadily watched Smoke as he went.

"So, what did you say your name was again?" Smoke's girl for the
night asked.

"Didn't say," Rafe answered, paying no attention to her, but focusing
on the men's room door. It had been only a few moments since both
men disappeared into the restroom, but something was telling Rafe
that not everything was right.

He scooted across the vinyl bench, wiggling out from under the
table, and stood.

Trunk looked up at Rafe. "Where you think you goin'?"

"It ain't none of your damn business where I'm goin'," Rafe said,
turning and walking in the direction Smoke had gone in.

The music was blasting throughout the club, but as Rafe neared the men's room door, he heard muffled yelling. It was a man's voice, then Smoke's voice over his. "Fuck that! I told you that if you ever did it again then I would—" Rafe heard Smoke threatening just before he burst through the door to find a man looking frightened to death, backed up into a urinal, his slacks undone, a dark urine stain stretching down the front of his pants.

Smoke stood in front of him, holding a gun high in the air and pointing it downward at the man, as if he was going to shoot him on top of the head.

"Please, please!" the man begged, tears in his eyes, his palms raised. "I won't ever—"

"Fuck that, motherfucker!" Rafe heard Smoke say, and before he knew it, Rafe was lunging forward, wrapping his arms around Smoke, because he knew Smoke was about to pull the trigger, kill this man right there in front of him.

Rafe got his arms around Smoke, pulling the gun down before it discharged. Smoke spun on Rafe, not looking into his face, just sliding the barrel of the gun in between Rafe's ribs. Rafe thought he was going to die that very moment.

"Smoke! It's me!" Rafe yelled, holding him tighter, bracing himself for the explosion he thought he would feel. Smoke looked into his eyes, and still Rafe waited to feel the bullet tearing through him, until the expression on Smoke's face changed from deathly to familiar. He almost smiled.

"Fuck you doin' in here, Rafe?" Smoke asked, still not pulling the gun from out of Rafe's gut.

"Don't do it, Smoke. Don't do it, man. It ain't worth it," Rafe said.

"Listen to him," the crying man said, his hands still up, now backed all the way up into the urinal, his behind dipped into the bowl of water.

"Shut the fuck up, bitch!" Smoke raised the gun over Rafe's shoulder, pointing it at the man. "You stoppin' me from taking care of my business," Smoke said, directing his attention to Rafe. "You don't even know what's goin' on, and you stoppin' me."

"You said no more crazy shit was gonna happen if I hung out with you, Smoke, remember? You promised. Just let this shit ride." Rafe tried to convince Smoke, looking deeply into his eyes. Smoke was glaring at the man, then looking back at Rafe, as if he was weighing what was more important to him—his word to Rafe or seeing this man dead.

"Whatever the fuck he did, Smoke, you lettin' him live will prove you to be a much stronger man than if you kill him. Just let him walk, dog. Let him walk."

Smoke was eyeing the man, then looked back into Rafe's face, and all of a sudden, he lowered the gun and started to smile. "You right, Rafe. Damn right."

Rafe heard the man on the urinal sigh loudly.

"Yo' ass was saved today by my boy," Smoke said, sliding his gun back into the waist of his pants. He then walked over to the man. "Thank him for that shit."

"What?" the man said, wide-eyed.

"I said, thank my man for saving your sorry-ass life!" Smoke looked as though he was about to reach for the gun again.

"Thank you, thank you," the man said, quickly looking Rafe directly in the face. He was terrified and sincerely grateful. Rafe could see that plainly on his face, knew that whatever had gotten the man here to begin with, he would never involve himself in again.

After that, Rafe and Smoke stayed at the club for only a half an hour longer. When they got outside, Trunk grabbed Rafe by the arm.

"Yo' dude. I gotta talk to you."

"Talk to me about what?" Rafe said, allowing himself to be held.

"Just step over here. It's something that got to be said."

Smoke stopped a few paces in front of them, looking back. Rafe shot him a questioning glance.

"Go ahead," Smoke said, reading the situation. "I'll be in the car."

Trunk pulled Rafe aside and directed him just behind the club, into a trash- and dumpster-lined alley.

"What's up?" Rafe asked, looking up at Trunk, standing wide and heavy in front of him.

"You interrupted Smoke's business," Trunk finally said. "That shit had to get taken care of and you—"

"Me and Smoke cleared that up, all right?" Rafe said, turning to walk away from Trunk, but was grabbed, practically lifted off the ground, and put back in his place.

"Like I was sayin'," Trunk continued, "you fucked that up. Don't ever do that again," he said, pointing a thick, iron bar-like finger in Rafe's face. "'Cause whether you like it or not, business always get done."

"*You* done?"

"Not quite," Trunk said, and before Rafe knew it, he had been drilled to the gut with two powerful punches, and then a fist tore across his face, sending him flying back into the trash and boxes lining the wall of the club. He thrashed around on his back, peering out of the debris, trying to make sure Trunk wasn't still coming for him to finish him off. He wasn't there anymore.

Rafe relaxed a little, feeling the pain in his stomach and against his jaw. Okay, he had been punished for butting in, but at least he had saved that man's life, he thought, as he tried to clear away some of the boxes surrounding him. He pushed away most of them, then felt his hand being stopped by something warm and heavy, its surface feeling strangely like skin.

Rafe pushed away a large piece of cardboard and found himself staring into the wide, dead eyes of a man. Terror was frozen on his face, his mouth wide open, as if caught in mid-scream, just before a bullet burned through his forehead.

Rafe shot back from the dead man, swallowing his own scream that he felt trying to come out. His heart beat wildly, as he realized that this was the man from the bathroom, the man that Smoke was going to kill. And just like Trunk had just told him, "Business always gets done."

ON THE WAY home, Rafe rode in the back while Smoke sat up front in the passenger seat. Not a word was said the entire trip to Rafe's house, until Trunk pulled the car over to let Rafe out. Rafe pushed the door open, was about to get out, when he heard Smoke say, "It's just how it is, Rafe, my man. Getting here is the easy part. Stayin' is what's rough, and you don't stay by lettin' people shit on you and get away with it."

Rafe got out of the car without responding, but before he closed the door, Smoke said, "Take your usual couple of days off to get your head straight. I know you will. But don't be disappearing on me, because you know, you still my man. See you at work."

Rafe slammed the door and stalked off.

THIRTY-FIVE

THE NEXT time Rafe showed up at the library, he wasn't late. He sat in the Jag, parked out in front with the top down. *Let that other fool show up again and see what he gets*, Rafe thought to himself.

He looked at the dash clock. It was a minute past nine, and he expected Henny to be walking out any minute.

She stepped out a moment later. She saw the car out the corner of her eye as she walked past it but dismissed it, not turning her head far enough to see the driver.

"So what, Henny?" Rafe used the windshield to pull himself up, yelling over it. "You don't even see me no more, hunh!"

Henny spun around, startled. When she realized it was Rafe, she looked in disbelief at him, at the expensive, brand-new car he was standing up in.

"Just walk right past me, because you don't need me no more, that it?"

"What are you talking about? You the one who stopped calling me! And whose car is that?" Henny demanded, walking toward it.

"Whose do you think it is? It's mine."

"What are you doing with it?"

"Seems if I wanted to keep dealing with you, I needed it."

"What are you talking about?" Henny looked bewildered. "I been calling you like crazy, and you ain't return none of my calls."

"Who is he?"

"Who are you talking about?

"Don't lie to me," Rafe said, jumping over the door of the Jaguar, placing himself in front of Henny.

"Who the fuck is he!" he repeated, grabbing her forcefully.

"I don't know who the hell you're talking about!"

"The motherfucker who picked you up the other night. You fucking him?" Rafe felt a jealous anger burning inside him that he never thought he could feel toward this woman.

"What do you think?" Henny said with attitude, swatting Rafe's hands off her.

"I don't know. That's why you need to be telling me."

"If you don't know, maybe you need to think about it more, and when you come up with the right answer, let me know." She turned and started walking away but didn't get more than a couple of steps before Rafe had his hands on her, whirling her around to question her.

"I said, tell me!" he yelled.

"Why! You take me to a restaurant I know you can't afford, and because I care for you, tell you that you don't have to do all that for me, you start trippin'. I haven't spoken to you in a week. I thought we were over. Why should I tell you anything?"

"Because I need to know what's going on in my camp. If you still down or not."

Henny glared pathetically at Rafe for a moment, then said, "So I'm in your camp now. I see. Well if that's what this is all about, then maybe it *should* be over. Goodbye, Raphiel." She turned to go.

Rafe watched her, thought of just letting her carry her ass on out of his life, be done with her. But he couldn't because he . . . because he . . . "I love you," he mumbled, his head down. The words were barely audible, but Henny heard them, stopped and turned around, walked back toward him.

"What did you say?"

"I said, I love you," he said, looking up at her. "That's why I need to know."

IT TURNED out the guy who picked Henny up was named Carlos. He was Henny's mom's ex-boyfriend. He was coming around, trying to do nice things—like picking Henny up from work, without her knowing—to try and squirm his way back into her mom's life.

It was half an hour later, and Henny and Rafe were parked at Forty-Seventh Street, off Lake Shore Drive. They sat on the hood of the car, looking out at the water.

"So why didn't you call me back?"

"I didn't want to give you the chance to tell me that I wasn't good enough for you, that I ain't make enough money," Rafe explained.

"I told you that wasn't important."

"Your mother seems to think it is."

"My mother doesn't make decisions for me. *I* decide who I want to be with, and that person is you." Henny scooted a little closer, looping her hand through his arm. "And this car. You somehow got it to impress me?"

"Yeah."

"But how?"

"The guy I work for, the one that I got in trouble with, bought it for me."

"Is it—"

"It ain't stolen. All the paperwork is in the glove box. I didn't take it when he first tried to give it to me, but when I saw that man picking you up in his car, saw you hugging him, I thought I needed it. I ain't want to lose you. I love you, Henny," and he wrapped his arm around her, pulling her closer to him and kissing her on her forehead.

"I love you too. You know that, don't you?" Henny looked up into his eyes.

"I didn't know until this minute, but I was hoping you did," he said, smiling a little.

"So you know you can't keep the car. You said this guy was bad news, right?"

"Worse than you can imagine. I don't know what happened. He changed from when we were kids. Or maybe he didn't change at all. Maybe it was me. I just didn't know how bad he was then. Every day that goes by, I get deeper and deeper in with him, with the bad things that he does."

"Then just leave, baby," Henny said, turning to Rafe, deep concern in her eyes.

"I told you, I can't. He got stuff on me. If I stopped doing what he said, he could use that and have me back in jail. I don't know what to do," Rafe said, desperately.

"Come with me."

"What do you mean, come with you?"

"Leave with me when I leave for school. Pack up your stuff and move down with me."

"I don't understand." Rafe looked baffled.

"You have to get away. He'll never find you down there. He'll never think to look. Since he's doing illegal stuff, he probably won't go through the trouble of calling the police on you, taking the risk of their checking him out in the process."

"But what would I do down there? You'd be busy going to school, being with your friends," and now Rafe started to think about what her mother said about her ex-boyfriend. A look of sadness appeared on his face.

"I'd be with you," Henny said, taking his arm in hers, stroking it. "And you can get a job in an auto shop, and next semester you can start taking classes too."

"Henny, I don't know if I'm smart enough," Rafe said, apprehension in his voice.

"You're smart enough. I know you are. C'mon, baby. It'll be you and me."

Rafe shook his head, looking burdened with doubt.

"I'll have my own place. And at night, I can cook for you, and in the morning you can cook for me. That is, if you know how to cook," Henny joked.

"Hey. I make good eggs."

"Then come with me, baby."

"But Henny—"

"You said you loved me, didn't you?"

"Yeah."

"Then that's all that matters," she said, kissing him softly on the corner of his lips. "Please, baby. At least give us a chance."

"Okay," Rafe said, feeling that she was right. "Okay. I'll go."

THIRTY-SIX

ANOTHER NIGHT came, and another hit had to be made, so the girls ended up at a huge club in the western suburbs. Lisa had found a couple of guys who seemed suitable, but Ally didn't trust something about them. They were laughing, joking, flashing money, throwing it at the bartender, as if their cash was nothing but useless scraps of paper. Something about their behavior made Ally restless. They seemed too volatile. Something about them gave Ally a bad feeling.

"They have to be better than the guys you all picked last time," Lisa told the other girls when Ally pulled them all into the ladies' room to discuss their plans.

"It's just the two of them. They ain't got no boys here that's gonna follow them, or none waiting back at the room?" Ally asked, concerned.

"Naw, I told them we only gonna do the two," Lisa said.

"I still don't like 'em."

"Don't nobody want you to marry them, girl," JJ said. "They got money, and that's what we want."

Everyone else agreed, leaving Ally no choice but to go along as well.

AT THE motel room, Ally felt that she may have misjudged these guys. Things were chill. They weren't grabbing or pawing at any of them. JJ and Sasha didn't even have to put on the show. The men—Black and Tan, they said to call them, "Just like the scotch," because one was a light-skinned brother, the other dark—were comfortably drinking, listening to music, and allowing the girls to do the same thing as they walked around half-naked, occasionally sitting in the men's laps, rubbing their hands over their heads, treating them adoringly.

Ally was sitting in Black's lap, her tongue in his ear, when his cell phone started ringing. He dug into his pocket, pulled the phone out, flipped it open, and smiling, placed it to his other ear.

This had been the third or fourth call that he had received since they had gotten to the room. He laughed on this call, like he had on the others.

"Aw, yeah, yeah, that's cool. That'll work," he said. Ally could hear the sound of a man's voice squawking loudly out of the tiny flip phone but could not make out what he was saying.

"Whatever, just chillin' . . . Right, just like we planned . . . Okay. Yeah, yeah, do that. Bet . . . Peace," he said, flipping the phone closed and stuffing it back into his pocket.

"Who was that?" Ally whispered in Black's ear. She was unsettled by what she had just heard.

"Wasn't nobody, baby," Black responded, a smile still on his face, straight white teeth showing. "Just business," he said. "Just business. Now give me a drink of that."

Ally held the cup of Jack and Coke, the cup that JJ had just given her, laced with drugs, up to Black's lips. He took three swallows, then eyed Ally slyly, seductively. Ally glared at him suspiciously, then quickly smiled back, hoping that she didn't have anything to worry about. Black placed his hand over the hand Ally was holding the cup with, moved the cup back to his mouth and drank some more.

Fifteen minutes later, the girls had just about finished redressing. The music was turned off, and they were now all about business. Both men were passed out, one across the bed, the other slumped across the arm of the recliner in the corner of the room.

Lisa smacked Tan lightly on the cheek a few times to make sure that he was definitely out cold. When he didn't respond, she said, "What did I tell you, Ally. Can I pick these fools or what?"

"Whatever. Just grab they shit and let's go." Ally pulled on her left boot and zipped it up to her calf.

"Sasha, you got him covered over there, baby?" JJ asked, watching Sasha go through Black's pockets.

"I'm fine, baby. It's like searching for buried treasure," she said, raising up one of his pants legs, reaching into his sock, pulling out another wad of money, and then holding it up, gleefully. "See what I mean."

"We almost out of here?" Ally asked JJ, still feeling uneasy.

"Yeah. We getting there. But these fools are loaded, and I got to go to the bathroom, so just chill, all right?" JJ grabbed her bag and went into the bathroom, closing the door behind her.

Ally watched as both Lisa and Sasha continued to strip both men of whatever they had of value and set it down beside them. Both piles were beginning to add up to a nice amount, Ally thought. They would dump it all into a plastic bag—money, jewelry, credit cards, everything—tie it in a knot, and when they got back to JJ's, they would divide it four ways. They'd pawn off what wasn't cash, then divide that too.

Maybe Ally was just being paranoid about tonight. She was glad that her girls had outvoted her and gone ahead with this hit, because they would've lost out on a basketful of cash if they had listened to her.

"We just about done, ya'll?" Ally asked the girls.

"Yeah," Lisa said, "and we hit the mother lode tonight."

Ally smiled, telling herself that after tonight, she should have enough to get her own place and even lay down a couple of months in advance. Everything might just be all right from now on.

She glanced toward the motel room door. Had she seen a flash of red on the door handle? That couldn't have been, Ally thought, as she focused intently on the two little darkened squares beneath the handle, one red, one green, informing the key card holder if the key was working or not.

No, Ally thought. She hadn't seen a flash of red, because if she had, that would've meant that somebody was trying to get in, and . . . another flash of light. This time, it was green, and now she knew for sure someone was trying to come in. Ally saw the door handle turning, and she pulled herself off the chair, telling herself to run to the door. She didn't know what she would do once she got there, but she knew she had to go. But before she could even stand all the way to her feet, the door opened and a man burst in, a bottle of liquor in his hand, a huge grin on his face.

Sasha and Lisa spun around, shocked to see this smiling man in the doorway, yelling, "Let's get the party started!"

It took him only a second to realize what was happening. His eyes took everything in: his boys out cold, their valuables pulled out and resting beside what looked like their dead bodies, and the three woman, dressed like prostitutes, standing over them.

"What the fuck?" The man dropped the bottle, where it exploded on the cement patio walkway just outside the door. "What the fuck did you do to my boys?" he yelled, racing into the room. Ally put it together then. The last person Black spoke to on the phone must've been this fool. He must've told him to come by and get in on the party.

The big man rushed over to Tan, who was on the bed. He swept Sasha aside, sending her falling to the floor and crashing into a nearby wall. He grabbed Tan by his shirt, shook him frantically, Tan's head wobbling and spinning about on his neck, but he would not wake up. He let the drugged man fall back to the bed, then rushed over to Black, grabbing him the same way. Black's body was limp, and lifeless looking as well, and when he released Black, he turned to Lisa, a crazed look on his face. "You kill my boys, just to take they money?"

Lisa stood trembling, frightened before him, trying to open her mouth, but unable to form words.

"I said, did you fuckin' kill my boys!" The man, this time yelling, reached behind him, grabbing something from the waist of his jeans.

Ally didn't have to see what it was to know. She ran at the man and was only two steps from him when she saw the gun emerge from behind him. He tried to level the weapon on Lisa, but Ally swatted at his arm, hitting him on the wrist, knocking the gun away from him, where it slid across the room, stopping against the wall.

The man whipped around, swung out at Ally, and caught her hard across the face with the back of his hand. She spun on her feet, spiraling clumsily down to the floor.

He then grabbed Lisa by the arm, yanked her into him, and was rearing back with his fist to hit her when Sasha ran at him from behind, leaped on his back, and began to scratch wildly at his face. She dug into his skin, opening up narrow, bloody slices from his cheeks to his temples.

The man yelled out in pain, forced his body backward, slamming himself and Sasha into a wall, smashing her against it. When he pulled himself away, she fell to the floor, where he threw himself on top of her, straddled her, and started pummeling her with hard blows to her face.

In the bathroom, JJ was on the toilet thinking about just what she would do with all the money they took in tonight, how exactly she would spend it, and just how her and Sasha would celebrate. Maybe a bath for two in Kristall champagne, or a trip to the islands. It really didn't matter, JJ thought, smiling. Whatever she wanted. Whatever it took to make her happy, JJ would do. Poor girl had been through so much, all JJ wanted to do was see her smile and hear her laugh.

JJ finished peeing, raised herself from the seat, and was about to wipe, when she heard a loud thud in the bedroom. She quickly wiped herself, yanked up her pants, and called, "What the fuck was that?"

Then she heard a man's voice. "You kill my boys just to take they money?"

Something had gone wrong, seriously fucking wrong, she thought, pacing in a tiny circle around the bathroom floor. She heard the man repeat the question again, this time yelling, and JJ pressed herself up to the door, her heart pounding, her mind racing over just what she should do.

There was more commotion. JJ heard something against the wall the bathroom door was on and still she had no idea of what to do—until she heard the noise that had her whipping open the door, no longer thinking, just knowing that she had to react.

The sound was Sasha screaming out in pain, and when JJ came out that door, she saw a man straddled on top of her, raining down angry blows onto her face.

"No!" JJ cried out, throwing herself onto the man's back. She was bigger than all the other girls but not big enough. The man slung back an arm, forcefully throwing her off him. JJ stumbled backward, her arms pinwheeling, 'til she fell against a wall. She looked up and saw Lisa and Ally trying to pull the man from Sasha, but having no success.

She quickly looked around the room for something to hit him with, and she saw the gun lying there on the floor near her. She stretched out for it, grabbed it, and then went at him again.

"Get off her, motherfucker!" JJ said, holding the gun outstretched in both her hands.

He continued to attack Sasha, ignoring JJ 'til he heard the click of the gun cocking. He halted in midmotion, another punch about to hammer down on the badly beaten girl.

Lisa and Ally slowly backed away from the man as JJ took a single step forward.

"Now get the fuck up off of my girl, bitch!" JJ ordered.

The man stood, turned himself to JJ, his palms raised, shoulder level.

Ally and Lisa quickly went to help Sasha, and when they stood her up, JJ saw that both her eyes had been blackened and swollen shut. The area over her cheekbones was ballooned, and colored purple. Her lower lip was split deeply down the middle, her entire face smeared and splattered with a layer of blood.

When JJ had cocked back the hammer of the gun, she had not

intended on shooting this guy. She had just wanted to scare him, to stop him from beating Sasha, but she hadn't yet seen what he had done to her face. JJ hadn't seen the pain he had put her through, and the place he had most certainly taken Sasha back to, when she was getting the shit kicked out of her by her ex-boyfriend.

JJ hadn't known all that when she had cocked the gun, but now she did, and she decided that he had to die. He definitely had to die.

Ally must've read that on her face, JJ thought, because she hurried over to JJ. "Don't do it, girl," she pleaded. "Don't do it. Just let it be. Let this shit be."

"Can't," JJ heard herself saying, seeing the gun ahead of her, pointed at the man, the thing shaking wildly in her sweaty grip. "See what he did to my baby," JJ said, tears spilling from her eyes. "See what that motherfucker did."

"I know, but she'll heal. You kill this motherfucker, and he dead for good."

"I know. That's how I want him." JJ shot a quick glance at Ally, then focused back on her target.

"And then you go to jail, and you can't be with ya girl no more. Think about that. She needs you. Needs you now more than ever. Don't do this shit."

Ally was right, and JJ knew it. She couldn't take the chance at being put away, pulled from Sasha's side just because she wanted to see this asshole dead. No, she couldn't do that exactly, but she could see him hurt very badly, JJ thought, as she walked toward him, lowering the gun to her side. When she came within an arm's length of him, with all her force, in a wide arching motion, she threw her arms around, forcing the barrel of the gun, and its sharp site at the tip, to tear into the man's face. It cut into his cheek, opening up a jagged gash across the thin cuts already there.

The man let out a high-pitched cry and fell to his knees, covering the wound with his hands, as if trying to close it somehow.

JJ rushed at him, kicked him in the chest with the flat of her foot, pushing him over. She quickly changed her grip on the gun, holding it now by the front end with both fists, exposing the butt of the weapon. She threw herself onto the man, straddled him as he had Sasha, and started pistol-whipping him. He tried throwing his arms up wildly to protect his face, but JJ was crazed, working maniacally on him, feeling his facial bones give under the pressure of the gun she sent crashing down on him. Then before she knew it, she was being dragged off him.

"C'mon. We gotta get out of here. We gotta go!" she heard Lisa and Ally's voices say. She felt Ally grab the gun from her, and she and Lisa start to pull her away. JJ would've fought harder to stay there, to continue to beat that man, but she was exhausted from all she had given him already.

TWO HOURS after they had gotten home, after JJ had done her best to clean up Sasha's face, given her some painkillers, and put her to bed, she walked out into the living room where Lisa and Ally were.

"How's she doing?" Ally asked.

"She's gonna live. It ain't like she ain't been through it before, but . . ." JJ stopped, looked as though she was suppressing tears, choking on sobs that were trying to come out. "She shouldn't have had to have gone through this shit again," JJ said, pulling herself together.

"I know," Lisa said, resting a comforting hand on JJ's shoulder. "But next time we'll be safer."

JJ looked up. "Won't be no next time. I ain't takin' no chance on this happening again. We out."

"But JJ, we ran out of there without the cash. We ain't got shit to show for tonight, except the fact that we got beat down," Lisa said.

"Then maybe you should've thought to grab the money," JJ shot back.

"My hands was filled with you."

"What the fuck you tryin' to say?" JJ stood up.

Lisa stood up right along with her.

Ally stood up too and pushed herself between the two, spreading them apart with her arms. "Hey, hey. We already been through enough tonight with that crazy motherfucker back at the motel. We don't got to start here."

JJ and Lisa slowly sat back down.

"JJ, if you out, then you just out," Ally said, still standing. "And I feel you. I don't think this is worth it anymore either."

"Good," JJ said, standing back up. "I'm gonna check back on Sasha." She turned to walk toward the bedroom. "Ya'll can stay if you want to. If not, lock the door when you leave."

Ally sat back down and felt Lisa's eyes heavy on her.

"What?" Ally wanted to know.

"Don't punk out on me now. One more hit, Ally, and I'll have enough to get me and my son up out the 'hood and into somewhere decent. Just one more good one. Don't punk, girl," Lisa said, grabbing Ally's hand, as if to give her strength.

"I ain't punkin'," Ally said, snatching her hand away. "I'm tryin' to get my own place too. But you see what happened to Sasha in there," Ally whispered. "I ain't tryin' to have that happen to me."

"We just got to be more careful next time," Lisa said, desperation in her voice.

"I don't know, Lisa," Ally said, shaking her head.

"Just think about it, all right. Because if we don't get that money, I'ma still be in the 'hood, and your ass gonna be sleeping on a let-out couch in your mama's living room. So think about it, okay?"

"Yeah. I'll think about it."

THIRTY-SEVEN

THE NEXT day, Livvy was looking over her essay. Henny had helped her with it, as she said she would, and as Livvy read over it for the hundredth time, she felt that it was good, damn good.

She got up from her bed, went to put the pages back into her dresser drawer, but stopped after sliding it halfway open. She thought she needed a better place to put it. She didn't know why she thought this, but something told her that if Ally got her hands on this essay, she wouldn't have had a problem setting the thing on fire, thinking that this was the catalyst for putting her mother on a new path. Livvy couldn't have that, because she needed to turn the essay in in a couple of days.

Livvy turned around, looking about the room for a good hiding place, but realized that no place was safe. She walked out of her room and into the living room, her eyes still looking for a place she could hide her essay. She looked about the kitchen, thought about hiding it under the fridge, on top of a cabinet, rolled up and slid into the cardboard paper towel tube, but none seemed right to her. Ally spent too much time in the kitchen eating for Livvy to feel safe about that place.

She walked out into the living room again, glanced at the cushions of the couch where Ally spent so much time lounging. Livvy thought about folding her work into an envelope, placing it under the TV, the one thing that occupied most of Ally's time, then smartly thought better of it.

Livvy turned in a complete circle, about ready to give up, when her eyes passed the leaning stacks of old magazines, piled up on the shelves and on the floor in front of the book shelves. That was it, she thought, stepping quickly over to them, bending over, and pulling one randomly from out of the toppled stacks.

It was an *Ebony*, a handsome, smiling, S-curled Billy Dee Williams on the cover.

Livvy let the pages fall open, and there between an ad for Murry's Pomade and an ad for the new 1988 Pontiac Firebird Trans-Am, Livvy gently tucked the essay. She closed the magazine and slid it back into the stack, four magazines from the top. It was perfect, she thought, a triumphant smile on her face. If there was one thing that she knew Ally never did, it was read.

Livvy then went into her closet, pulled out a jacket, threw it on, and grabbed her purse and keys, because she had something very important to do on this day off.

Every since Hennesey's date had come by to pick her up, Livvy had been bothered by his appearance, by the way he spoke, by the way his hair was braided up, by the tattoos on his arms—everything about the man.

No, she didn't know him, and who knew, she thought, walking out of her apartment, locking the door behind her, he may have been a good man. But he definitely wasn't good enough for her college-bound daughter.

That night after Henny had pulled him out of the apartment before Livvy could get any info out of him, Livvy turned to look over at Ally, who had just stepped out of her room. She had a jealous look on her face, but that was nothing new for Ally. She was always jealous of her sister. What concerned Livvy was what else was in that stare. Familiarity.

"You met him before?" Livvy asked.

"Hunh?" Ally answered, snapping out of whatever trance she was in.

"I said, have you met him before?" Livvy asked the question more slowly. "What's his deal?"

"What do you mean?" Ally answered, playing dumb.

"Am I not speaking English to you, girl? What's up with Henny's new boyfriend? What do you know about him?"

"I don't know nothin' about him, Mama," Ally said, but she was lying, and Livvy knew that, because the girl was looking down at her toes, had been doing that since she was two years old.

"You're lying. Does he sell drugs, has he murdered anybody, married, got any kids?" Livvy rattled off.

"I don't know," Ally said again, this time looking her mother in the eyes.

"Then what does he do? Where does he work?"

"Don't know that either."

"Where does he live then?" Livvy asked, and then Ally lowered her eyes to her toes again.

So today, Livvy would use her day off to find out what this man was really about. She got in her car, the address Ally had reluctantly given her the other night, on a scrap of paper on her dash. Livvy would've called information first, got his phone number and called to make sure he was there before she dropped in on him, but Ally didn't know his last name, and she couldn't get the number without it. She started the car, threw it in gear, and headed toward his house.

Livvy pulled up in front of a rather large brown brick house in Beverly. She checked the address twice, then a third time, thinking that a boy who looked like the character Henny had dragged out of her place couldn't have come from somewhere this nice.

Livvy grabbed her purse, climbed out of the little car, and walked toward the house. Standing in front of the door, after she had rung the doorbell, she wondered if she was making a mistake. Was she wrong to come here with the intention of telling this man what she knew he wouldn't want to hear without Henny knowing? She wondered, but it was only for a moment, because she knew what would be in store for her daughter if she continued to see this guy: a life of hardship, broken promises, and then, most likely, desertion. Henny would've probably abandoned everything for that man, to wake up one morning to find him gone, and her left with a couple of kids, and the memory of what she could've been. Livvy wasn't going to allow that to happen.

Livvy saw a figure behind the smoked glass of the big front door window, and then the door opened up to reveal a large smiling woman wearing one of the worst wigs she had ever seen. This must be the thug's mother, Livvy thought.

"Hi. Can I help you?" Thug-mama said.

"Hi there. Is Rafe home?" Livvy said, speaking his name as though it wasn't a part of the English language.

"I don't know, but you'll have to go to the side entrance," wig-wearing-Thug-mama said, leaning out the door and pointing a flabby arm in that direction. "The bell has his name on it."

"Thanks." Livvy headed down the stairs and over toward the side door.

When she got there, she saw three bells and knew she should've asked what Rafe's last name was. *What the hell kind of name is Rafe, anyway?* she thought.

Livvy looked at the three bells. One had no name on it at all. Under the other bell, an old, yellowed strip of paper had the name James scribbled across it in shaky, faded ink. The last bell belonged to Collins. This name was written on a fresh strip of paper in hard, dark, thick letters.

For no reason other than intuition, she pushed the last bell.

Moments later, Livvy heard bolts turning from behind the door. It opened, and there stood Rafe, his hair pulled out of the braids, all over his head, in long, crinkled strands, wearing baggy jeans and a wifebeater T-shirt.

The boy didn't look as shocked to see Livvy as she thought he would. In fact, he looked surpassingly calm.

"How you doin', Ms. Rodgers?" he said, pushing the door open and holding it for her. "Come in."

LIVVY followed the thug up two flights of stairs, her eyes taking in everything around her, and she realized that this wasn't Rafe's house. This had to be a boarding house where he was renting a room. What a shame. A grown man living in a single room. Where the hell did he go wrong? Livvy wondered. And why would any woman, especially her own daughter, be interested in such a loser? She finally made it up the stairs, Rafe already down the hallway, sticking a key into his door. Livvy walked past a table standing in the hallway, the only piece of furniture there. It had a number of pieces of mail on it, which she quickly glanced at, and then did a double-take. She thought the name on one of those letters said—

"Ms. Rodgers," Rafe said, standing at his open door. Livvy pulled herself away from what she was looking at and walked into Rafe's room.

Rafe grabbed his bathrobe off a hook and threw it on over his T-shirt. It didn't make him look any more presentable, as he probably thought it did.

"Sorry," Rafe said, trying to smooth down the thick mane with both his hands, as if he knew she was paying particular attention to it. "It's been one of those weeks." He smiled sheepishly at Livvy.

"What do you do, Rafe?"

"I fix cars. I mean," he said, catching himself. "I'm an auto technician, at Mirror Motors."

"That's nice. But I'm gonna get right to it," Livvy said. "And I really don't want you to interrupt me, because what I got to say isn't open for discussion. Okay?"

Rafe nodded.

"My daughter is the best thing about my life. Unlike me, she's very smart, has been since she was a baby. I always knew she would do well. When she got older, unlike her sister, she didn't get all boy crazy, because she knew boys had nothing to do with being successful in life.

"If she continues on the path she's on, she's going to do very well for herself. She's going to become a doctor, make good money, and hopefully find a good man, get married, have some children. Now I'm not saying you ain't a good man. I'm just sayin' you're not the *right* man. Henny is going to be very educated, and something tells me that you're not. And that doesn't work. It just doesn't. Because somewhere down the line, she's gonna resent you for what you didn't do, and haven't accomplished, and you're gonna resent her for what she has. It would just never work between the two of you, so I want you to stop seeing her. Just let her go on with her life, and you go on with yours. It'll be better that way."

Rafe stared at Livvy, then said, "Can I speak now?"

Livvy nodded.

"How do you know it'll never work? How do you know it'll be better if I just left her alone? You don't know nothin' about me."

"You said you didn't go to college. What were you doing from the time you left high school 'til now?"

Rafe wanted to lie, but he couldn't to this woman. He felt doing that would shame himself for needing to hide his past, especially considering the things she had just said about him.

Rafe decided to sidestep the question. "I did some things."

"What things, if not college? Did you just work? The military? The Peace Corps? What?"

Rafe looked sadly in Livvy's eyes, trying his best to be strong and tell the truth.

As if she could read what was in his mind, she whispered, "Please don't tell me you were you in prison?"

Rafe just dropped his head.

"Answer the question," Livvy demanded. "I'm gonna find out from Hennesey anyway."

"Yeah. I was," Rafe said, holding his head as high as he could.

"There," Livvy said. "Well, I know that about you now, and that's more than enough to know that it'll never work."

THIRTY-EIGHT

LATER THAT night, Rafe and Henny sat in his car, parked out in front of her building. He had picked her up after work and taken her home, even though she said she felt like celebrating him going down to school with her.

"What's wrong? You haven't said anything all night," Henny said, staring at the side of his face.

Rafe didn't respond, just kept looking out the windshield, because he didn't want to say what he knew he had to, what he had been convinced to tell her.

"Ain't nothin'," Rafe said, under his voice, his eyes still pointed forward.

"Raphiel. Raphiel, look at me," Henny said, when he continued not to acknowledge her. Rafe reluctantly turned his face toward her.

"You got to be open with me. Now just tell me. We can't be living together down at school, and you start acting like—"

Rafe cut her off, not knowing any other way to tell her. "I'm not going with you to school."

Henny fell silent, unable to voice words for a moment, then asked quietly, "What do you mean you're not going to school with me? We just decided that you were."

"Well, I'm not now," Rafe said, his tone filled with anger. He didn't mean to be cross with Henny. It wasn't her fault.

"You would just get in the way," Henny's mother had said to him. "I've been speaking to Henny's ex-boyfriend down there, and he's looking forward to her coming. He wants to get back together. So it's best you just leave her alone, because how could you compare to him?"

Rafe balled his hands into tight fists and shut his eyes, trying to suppress those words from echoing in his head. "I'm sorry," he said. "But I just can't go, so you might as well just get on out. Leave."

"But Raphiel," Henny pleaded.

"And I don't think that we should see each other anymore."

The look on Henny's face changed from sadness to anger. "What the hell is going on with you!"

"Nothin'," Rafe said casually, turning away from her as if none of this meant anything to him, when actually it was killing him inside.

Henny grabbed his shirt at the shoulder, pulling at him to make him turn around. "No. That's bullshit. You just don't change your mind like that. Something happened, and I want you to tell me what."

Rafe looked at her, an apathetic expression on his face at first. Then all of a sudden he looked as though he was in as much pain as she was. He started to shake his head.

"Raphiel, please tell me. Just tell me."

THE ELEVATOR couldn't go up to her floor quick enough, and Henny couldn't burst into the apartment fast enough to curse her mother out.

The tears Henny cried hadn't mattered—these being the same tears that stung her face now. Rafe wouldn't listen, just kept pulling away from her, kept telling her she had to go, and kept trying to push her out the car. What did her mother say to him? she kept asking herself. It had to have been very bad, she thought, as Raphiel got out the car, came around to her side, opened the door, and pulled her out. It had to have been so bad.

"I'm sorry," he said, and he was hiding his face. She couldn't see the tears but heard them in his voice, and she knew he was crying too.

He quickly jumped back into the car and sped off, Henny running behind him a number of yards, her arm outstretched, as if trying to grab onto some piece of him.

Now the elevator doors opened, and Henny practically ran out of them, thrust the key into the lock on her apartment door, opened it, then furiously slammed it shut.

Livvy had been sitting on the sofa, peacefully watching TV, but jumped, whipping her head in the direction of the door. "What is your problem slamming the door like that?"

Henny stood just inside the apartment, her chest heaving, fists at her sides, an angry scowl on her face. "How dare you, Mama!"

"Child, what are you talking about?" Livvy said, looking at Henny as if she had lost her mind.

"You went to Rafe's house, didn't you?"

"I don't know what you're talking about."

"Don't play that shit with me," Henny threw back.

"What?" Livvy said, shocked.

"I said, don't play that shit!" Henny raised her voice, taking steps forward. "You went to his house to tell him not to see me anymore, that me and David were going to get back together, when I can't remember the last time I even spoke to him. How could you have done that?" Henny said, the tears spilling quickly from her eyes again.

"Baby," Livvy said, rising slowly from the sofa. "It would never work—"

"How would you know!" Henny yelled.

"Because I been through it," Livvy said, speaking in a soothing voice. "I've been where you are, and I know what you're thinking: that you love this boy, and you two will be together forever, happily ever after. But sweetheart, it don't work that way. It's hard enough being two people that got everything in common, but you got nothing."

"You don't know that," Henny said.

"You're going to college. He's been to jail. Don't sound like a lot in common to me."

"How did you find that out?" Henny gasped, looking toward her bedroom, knowing that Ally had to have betrayed her trust, told their mother about his prison time, even though her sister promised that she wouldn't.

"It doesn't matter how I found out."

"I don't care what you think, Mama. I love him, and he's coming down to school with me, whether you like it or not!" Henny stormed away and headed toward her bedroom so she could take care of business with her sister. Before she was able to take two steps, she was grabbed by the arm and spun around to face her mother.

"I don't know who you think you're talking to, young lady, but I am still your mother. And it does matter what I think. If I say he's not going to school with you, then he's not."

Henny snatched her arm out of her mother's grasp. "I'll be eighteen by the time I leave, and I'm going on scholarship money. You ain't payin' for none of it, so you can talk all you want, but it don't mean a thing."

Her mother was stunned, and Henny could see it on her face, but she didn't care. She deserved to be hurt right now.

"Hennesey, baby," Livvy said, taking a milder approach, grabbing her softly by both shoulders. "You've come all this way. You've done so well up to this point. Why throw it away now on some worthless man who can't do anything for you?"

"He's not worthless," Henny defended.

"He is, Henny. He'll never amount to anything. I know them when I see them."

"How? Because that's all you ever get involved with?" Henny said, hearing more than enough of what her mother had to say. She was taking this too far. "I'm sorry that every man you ever chose to be with was a loser," Henny continued, holding nothing back. "Including our father. Who knows why you always end up with that type. Maybe you just like getting fucked around by these men. But whatever the case, I'm thinking before you start trying to make decisions on how I run my life, maybe you need to get your own shit straight."

The last word wasn't even completely out of Henny's mouth before Livvy hit her across the face with a hard, loud smack that seemed to echo throughout the entire room.

It burned like hell, and Henny knew as she stood there defiantly, staring hatefully into her mother's eyes, her face was probably already turning red.

Her mother didn't do anything, just stared back, matching her daughter's stillness, her silence, and Henny knew their conversation was over. She walked past her mother, opened the front door, and said, looking back, "I'm still seeing him, and there's nothing you can do about it." Then she slammed the door behind her as hard as she could.

THIRTY-NINE

THE NEXT day at work, Livvy tried busying herself with her responsibilities, but she couldn't keep her mind on what she was doing. She thought about the argument she had last night with Henny, how it ended, her hand across her daughter's face. She had never hit her before, never had to, but now . . . Livvy looked at the palm of her hand, still thought she felt the stinging there, still saw the reaction on her little girl's face after the assault.

Henny had to know what she was doing was a mistake, Livvy thought. And she would do whatever it took to make her aware of this, short of hitting her again. Livvy just hoped that she would have another opportunity, hoped that Henny wouldn't entirely shut herself off to her mother, never want to speak to her again.

Livvy was in the employee locker room now, and she was going for her jacket and purse. It was only a little after four, but she had told her supervisor that she wasn't feeling well and had to go home sick. It was a lie, but only partly. She was ill, but not physically. It was the stress of everything that was happening recently—of her having to argue with her daughter, her having to go to that boy Rafe's place and tell him never to see Henny again. And then it was the stress of looking down on that table in the hallway of that boarding house, and seeing that envelope.

At first she just thought her eyes were playing tricks on her, but then she took a closer look and saw the name on the letter definitely said Wade Williams.

After Rafe's and her discussion ended, she said, "I'll walk myself to the door." She figured he wasn't going to offer anyway, and she wanted to get another look at that letter. It ended up in her purse, and since then she had looked at it a thousand times and called Wade at home twice. Both times she'd gotten his voice mail, but didn't leave messages, because she really didn't know what to say. This was something that she needed to discuss with him face to face.

Only now, sitting in the locker room, her jacket on, her purse slung over her shoulder, did she sit down, the letter in her hand, and decide to tear it open. It was a phone bill. All the time she was carrying it with her, she was thinking that maybe there was just a mix-up over at Ameritech, or maybe there was more than one Wade Williams. There had to be. It wasn't the most common name, but it was common enough.

When Livvy pulled the billing statement from the envelope, saw the record of calls on the page, there was no longer any question as to who this Wade Williams was. She saw her phone number on that page at least a dozen times. She looked at the "minutes per call" column to the right, and saw how long he had been on the phone with her. There was the two-hour conversation that one night when she had her candles burning, and there was the one-minute conversation that Saturday morning when he had called just to say that he was thinking about her. How sweet, Livvy had thought at the time. But now . . .

Every single time she'd spoken to him on the phone, when she thought he was standing in his ten-room home, complete with huge kitchen, family room, master bedroom, and three bathrooms, he was living in someone else's home, renting a room, just like that loser Rafe. Only difference was, Rafe was still a kid, while Wade was almost fifty, and at least Henny *knew* how her man was living. Only now did Livvy have a clue as to what was going on with Wade, because that motherfucker on countless occasions had sat there and lied to her face about where he was living. Then she started thinking that if he lied about where he lived, then he probably lied about a lot more: who he really was, what he did for a living, what he was making.

Livvy stormed out of the locker room, the billing statement crumpled in her fist, as she made her way to the employee break room and the phone that allowed her to make outside calls.

She had to talk to him, had to confirm all the lies she believed to be true. She grabbed the phone off the wall, put it to her ear, and was about to punch in his number when she realized her finger was trembling. Livvy thought she had finally found the right one, found someone who was paid. But those weren't even the real reasons she liked him so much. It was because he was honest, caring, and affectionate, or at least she thought he was. Livvy knew that if she made this call, all the lies would be confirmed and the relationship would be over. Once again, she'd be alone.

She thought of slipping that phone right back into its cradle and pretending she had never found that envelope, let everything fall into place however it would. Sure, she would always be looking at him oddly, waiting for the truth to come out his mouth, questioning everything else he said. But at least she'd still have a man. At least she wouldn't be alone.

She held the phone tightly in one sweat-covered hand, the finger of the other still poised to punch the buttons. She just couldn't let him get away with lying to her like that, without at least letting him know that she caught up to his slithery ass.

She dialed the number. His voice mail picked up again. She slammed the phone down, angry that she could not release her fury on him that moment. He was probably still at work, she thought. Then she looked down at the phone bill again.

Livvy picked up the phone and started dialing random numbers. After hearing a few random voice mails, some unanswered rings, and the voice of an old man, wondering how he and Ace Hardware could help her today, she finally heard a woman ask, "Tanner Lincoln Mercury, how may I help you?"

"Hi," Livvy said. "Does Wade Williams work there?"

"Yes, he does. Would you like for me to connect you?"

"Uh, no. Can you tell me how late he'll be there tonight?"

"Just a minute," the woman said, and a moment later, "nine o'clock."

"And your address?" Livvy took down the location the woman gave, and said, "Thank you very much."

Livvy found the dealership half an hour later, parked her car, and entered the showroom, looking around for Wade. She saw no sight of him, but after wandering around on the showroom floor for a few minutes, a large white fellow wearing a sport jacket and slacks approached her.

"Can I help you, miss?"

"Yes, I'm looking for Wade Williams. Is he available?"

"Hold on. Let me check, okay," the man said. He turned and walked toward an office some fifty feet away, just off the showroom floor. He knocked on the door, stuck his head in, and afterward, walked back over to Livvy. "He's in with a couple of customers, but he's finishing up. Would you like to wait?"

"Most definitely," Livvy said. Then thought to herself, *Most mother-fucking definitely!* "And could you tell me what position Mr. Williams holds here?"

"He's one of our preowned automobile associates."

"Ah, I see," Livvy said, a fake smile glued to her face, while she felt herself burning from another lie he had told her. He said he was a dealership owner, when this fool was nothing but a used car salesman.

"Would you like anything to drink?" the man asked. "Water, pop, coffee?"

"No thank you," Livvy said, trying to smile. He smiled back, and turned to walk away, when Livvy stopped him.

"Is the coffee hot?"

"Piping," the big man said.

"Okay. Give me the biggest cup you have."

"How would you like it?"

"Doesn't matter," Livvy said, but when the man gave her an odd look, she said, "Oh, black. Black is fine."

The man came back with a big container of black coffee and handed it to Livvy.

"Everything fine?" the man said.

Livvy noticed the steam rising off the liquid. "Everything is perfect."

Livvy watched the man walk off and disappear down a hall. She waited a couple of moments and then started across the showroom floor, stepping between a Mercury Marquis and a Lincoln LS. She stopped just in front of the office Wade and his customers were in.

Holding the still steaming cup of coffee in her left hand, she grabbed the doorknob with her right and asked herself if she was doing the right thing. No, it wasn't necessarily right, she decided, but it *felt* right, and that was all that mattered.

Livvy turned the knob and threw the door open. It banged hard against the back of the office wall, startling the young husband and wife sitting before Wade's desk, as well as Wade himself.

When he saw Livvy standing there, he looked as though his mind could not comprehend what his eyes were seeing. He shot up from behind his desk, and said in a shaky voice, "Livvy. What are you doing here?"

"What am *I* doing here?" Livvy said, anger heavy in her voice.

"Yes, that's what I said. What are you doing here?"

"Well, I wanted to talk to you about something, so I went to your house and you weren't there."

"What do you mean, you went to my house?"

"I went to your house, or, I'm sorry, I mean, your room, and you weren't there."

Wade was starting to look sick.

"But don't worry. I did pick up your mail," Livvy said, reaching into her jacket pocket with her free hand, and bringing out the wrinkled phone bill and dropping it down on his desk as proof that she really had been there.

Wade's eyes widened at the sight of the bill, his name and address at the top. He gave Livvy a sorrow-filled look, then turned to his customers, smiling sheepishly in their faces.

"I'm sorry folks," Wade said, walking around the desk, trying to do damage control. "There's been a little misunderstanding," he said, extending an arm, touching Livvy on the shoulder. "But if you just give me five minutes," he said to the baffled-looking couple, "I'll be right back, and we can have you sign the papers, and be off in your car."

Wade tried to direct Livvy out the door, but Livvy pulled away from him.

"No, you won't be right back, and there hasn't been a goddamn misunderstanding!"

"Livvy, I wish you wouldn't say that," Wade whispered, as if his customers, not a foot away from him, couldn't hear him.

"And I wish you wouldn't have lied to me, motherfucker."

"Let's just step outside. We can talk about this," Wade said, trying to calm Livvy down.

"We can't talk about this, Wade. Ever again," Livvy said, then with her right hand, she reared back, slapped Wade across the face as hard as she could. It was a good one, landed flatly, and she knew it pained him, but he played it off as though it hadn't even happened. Then he looked Livvy in the eyes and said in a calm voice, "Now Livvy, why don't you just cool off."

"No," Livvy shot back. "Why don't *you* just cool off," and then she threw the twenty ounces of steaming coffee at him. She knew it wasn't as hot as it was when it was first given to her, but he still yelled out when it splashed across his face and chest. She knew it just stung him more than horribly burned him, but that would be more than enough.

As he frantically tried to wipe the hot liquid from his face with his hands and the end of his necktie, Livvy looked at the shocked couple still sitting in their chairs, clutching the arms like they were on a high-speed roller coaster.

"If you haven't bought that car from this man yet, don't. He's a lying son of a bitch. And if he lied to me, then he probably lied to you too."

"Livvy," Wade said, able to open his eyes now.

"Go to hell, Wade," Livvy said, then quickly walked out of his office, picking up speed, and running out of the showroom and over to her car. She got in, sat there a moment, and wanted to laugh at how funny Wade had looked, swatting at his face like he was being overrun by a swarm of killer bees, but she couldn't. The urge to cry was just too powerful, and the thought of how once again she had been played for a fool did nothing but make the urge more intense.

She let the tears fall, not even bothering to wipe them away. She cried all the way home, all the way up to her apartment, and even when she felt she wanted to stop, she couldn't. The tears just kept coming, even after she had gotten home, and she knew it wasn't just because her heart had been broken, but also because of the fear of being alone again. The pain that would come from knowing that no one loved her, no one cared.

Livvy couldn't deal with that again, just couldn't, and especially now. She shot a glance at the phone and thought a moment about calling Carlos, but she couldn't. She had finally gotten over him, and she knew that he wanted her only when it was convenient for him. But Livvy also remembered some of the times they had shared, and she felt herself standing from the sofa, taking a step in the direction of the phone. She thought about all the times they had made love, the last time in particular. How wonderful it was, how he told her that he truly loved her and that he never wanted them to be apart.

Livvy was standing just in front of the phone now, looking down at it, telling herself she shouldn't call Carlos. But he had been calling her so much lately. After all they had been through, she could've at least had the decency to have called him back. She would do that now. That's all she would be doing, calling him back.

Livvy picked up the phone, dialed his number, wiping tears from her eyes and cheeks, trying to pull herself together. The phone rang three times, and she prayed that he'd pick up, swearing that if he did, all she would do was talk to him, all she would do was explain how she was feeling, what she was going through. Maybe she would even tell him about Wade. Maybe Carlos could give her some advice about men. Who knows, maybe they could become just good friends.

The phone rang a fourth time.

THE WAY Carlos made love to her this time was so good that Wade was fast becoming a memory.

Livvy was lying on her belly, Carlos was spent, lying heavy on top of her, blowing soft, cool air into her ear. "Was it good for you, Mommy?"

"Ah, *si, Papi,*" Livvy said, smiling, her body still shaking from the huge orgasm she had just experienced.

Carlos raised himself up, allowing Livvy to roll over on her back. He lay his slick, sweat-covered body back on top of hers, and kissed her deeply. He pulled back from her and said, "I thought you had forgotten about me. Thought you didn't love me no more."

"I thought you had forgotten about me."

"Never," Carlos said, sounding very committed. "You'll always be my woman. I will always love you."

And those were the exact words Livvy needed to hear at that moment. She wrapped her arms around Carlos's bare body, clasping her hands together, closing her eyes, and never wanting to let go.

It was after 11 P.M., and she was hungry, but she wouldn't eat. She didn't want to interrupt this for anything. The place could've been on fire, and she would've preferred to lie there and risk getting burned. She decided they would just lie in bed, make love some more, and in the morning, Livvy could call in, say she was sicker than she'd thought. She'd make them a huge breakfast, and they'd lounge around in bathrobes and make love some more. It would be perfect, she thought, and then she heard the tiny, electronic sound of "London Bridge" being played. It was Carlos's cell phone.

She felt him stir above her, but she tightened her embrace.

"Don't get that."

"Baby . . ."

"Let it ring," Livvy pleaded, holding him even tighter.

"Can't," he said, tearing himself from her, leaping out of bed, and grabbing the phone off the dresser, where it was prominently displayed, as if he had expected it to ring.

"Carlos," he answered. "Yes . . . yes . . . okay. Be there in half an hour," he said, then clicked off.

When he looked back to Livvy, she was sitting up in bed cross-legged, shaking her head.

"Don't say it," she said.

"I got to go, baby. Business," he explained, slipping on his pants.

"At almost midnight? What kind of fucking business is that?" Livvy said, knowing she shouldn't have been going there, but she couldn't help herself.

"Livvy," Carlos said, leaning into her, buttoning his shirt with one hand, caressing her face with the other. "You will not do this. Business happens when business wants. I cannot argue with that." He stepped into his shoes without even putting on his socks, just stuffed them into his pants pockets.

He leaned back over the bed toward her, "Now give me a kiss good-bye."

She gave him a long hateful look.

"C'mon, now."

She did as she was told, and then he was gone, leaving Livvy lying in bed, the sweat from his body not even dry on her skin yet, the phantom feeling of him inside her still present.

"Business," Livvy huffed, just after she heard Carlos walk out the front door. She knew it wasn't any fucking business. It was some other woman. She just knew it, and at first she told herself that she had no right to get angry, but then thought why didn't she? She was the woman who was there for him when he had nothing. She was the one who held his hand through every endeavor, celebrated with him during his first triumphs, and comforted him during his many failures. She was the woman who made that man strong, and now, just because he was successful, did that mean that she had to take his treating her like nothing? Did she have to lie there while he used her as a stress reliever, a toy for his pleasure, and then say nothing when he decided to roll out on her not even five minutes after getting his thang off?

Hell naw, Livvy thought, jumping out of bed and quickly throwing on some sweats. She was used by Wade, but she'd gotten back at his ass today, and she would do the same thing with Carlos.

FORTY

BY THE time Livvy jumped off the elevator and ran outside, she saw Carlos's car just pulling out of the parking lot. She got in her car and followed him, making sure to keep a good distance behind him so he wouldn't spot her.

She didn't have to drive for long. It was just a few blocks before he had stopped in front of an old frame house, looking as though it would topple to the ground any day.

Livvy stopped abruptly, still a number of car lengths behind him. She didn't know what he was doing, whether he was onto her, but she pulled in between two cars that were parallel parked on the street and waited.

She saw the brake lights of his car flash, then the white reverse lights quickly blink, and she knew he had put the car in park. Livvy continued to wait intently, her eyes going back and forth between the car and the house it was sitting in front of.

She had an idea why he was there, but she was hoping that she was wrong. Livvy was praying that it was truly business. Hoping that some man would walk out of that house wearing a suit, carrying a briefcase, and roll out huge architectural plans of some structure he wanted built, and that would be the end of that.

But Livvy was pretty sure she was just dreaming, and that was confirmed when the front door of that crumbling house opened, and out walked a beautiful woman about ten years younger than Livvy. She wore a tight-fitting dress, her long, loosely curled hair flowing down over her shoulders and back.

It wasn't like Livvy was telling herself to do it, more like her body had just taken over her mind. She pulled the car out of the parking space and just sat there in the middle of the street, still a good distance away from Carlos and the woman now walking to his car.

As she sat there, tears started to fall down her face for the second time today. It wasn't even because he was with another woman. There had been rumors that he had been cheating on her for years, and she'd always known it might have been true. It was more the fact that he had just left her. That he had just climbed out of her bed after lying with her, making love to her, blowing in her ear, and telling her that she would always be his woman, that he would always love her. Then the first phone call he got, he was up and running. Running just down the fucking street. The dog didn't even have the decency to shit outside his own backyard.

Livvy felt her foot lying heavy on the gas pedal, heard the engine revving, low and then high, each time she applied pressure. She knew that any other day, seeing what she was seeing, she would've felt like cursing the man out, like going off on him like never before. But after today and all the shit with Wade—tonight, Livvy felt like killing Carlos.

The woman got into the passenger side of the car and closed the door, and that was when Livvy threw the car in drive, punched the gas, and took off.

It didn't happen in slow motion as she always heard it did. It all occurred in the blink of an eye. One moment she felt the force of the car speeding off, throwing her back into her seat. Then she saw Carlos's car become bigger and bigger in her windshield, and then the impact. It was as if she had hit a brick wall. She was jolted forward. She heard the deafening crumpling of metal. The seat belt yanked her back, and then for the slightest minute, she didn't know where she was.

Everything came back to her, though, when she saw Carlos stepping out of his car, looking as if he was ready to murder whoever it was who had rear-ended him.

Livvy quickly undid her seat belt, jumped out of the car, and was taking hard, quick steps toward him, her right hand tightening into a fist as she went.

"What the fuck!" Carlos said, when his brain finally allowed him to comprehend that it was really Livvy he saw heading toward him. "Bitch! Are you—"

But before he could get another word out of his mouth, Livvy hit him squarely across the chin. From the impact of the punch, he fell. He dropped, and Livvy felt the urge to burst out in laughter, she was taken so much by surprise at how quickly and easily he was put down. But he had only fallen to one knee, caught off-guard, and he quickly sprang back up, grabbing her by her shoulders and shaking her furiously.

"What the fuck's wrong with you! Are you crazy, hittin' my shit!"

"Fuck you!" Livvy said, then spat in his face. The saliva landed in his eyes. Carlos took a step back, wiping at them.

"You said you loved me! I put up with your ass for all these years, listened to all your promises that you never kept, and I got to catch you runnin' around wit' some trick-ass bitch!"

The girl was out of the car now, and she gasped at the remark.

"What you gonna do, bitch?" Livvy challenged, spreading her arms out, inviting a fight.

The woman looked away, and Livvy was about to go after her anyway, before she was snatched by the arm and dragged back by Carlos to the rear of his car.

"You see this? You gonna pay for this shit. You hear me?" Carlos shook her. Livvy didn't respond. He shook her harder. "You hear me!"

"No. I don't hear shit," Livvy threw back. "This don't even compare to all that I gave to your sorry ass. You want it fixed, pay for it your damn self. Or get the bitch to fix it." Livvy then turned to walk off. But Carlos grabbed her again.

"No, you're gonna pay for it," Livvy heard him saying, and she was being forcefully spun to face him. When he'd spun her all the way around, she didn't meet him with words, but with a heavy swipe of her hand, gouging his face with her nails. Carlos fell away again, backpedaling, his hands shooting up to his face. He pulled them away, saw the blood, and then he lost it.

He raced after Livvy, grabbing her by her shirt, and hitting her with the back of his fist. Livvy whirled around, tripping over her feet, falling hard to the ground. She rolled onto her knees and tried to crawl back toward her car, but was grabbed by the hair, pulled up, and again, Carlos hit her—this time with his fist, straight on, and Livvy felt his knuckles dig into her eye. She saw bright, starlike explosions. Her body gave. It wanted to fall, but it was being held up against its will by Carlos so he could continue pounding her.

"Bitch, you wanna fuck wit' me?" he yelled, and he slapped her with his palm this time. "Who the fuck you think you are?" And she was slapped again, this time with the back of his hand. "You ain't shit but a fuckin' piece of old pussy, bitch!" he yelled, and was rearing back his fist, still holding her by the hair, as if he was sizing her up for his most deadly blow, when the other woman threw herself on him, grabbing his arm.

"No, Carlos, don't. Don't. Let's just go," Livvy heard her say.

Livvy tried to look up at that girl, up at Carlos to see if he was listening, but her left eye had already ballooned completely shut, and tears blurred her right.

Livvy didn't hear a response from him, didn't know what was going to happen next, until she felt him release her hair. As if she didn't have a bone in her body to support herself, Livvy crumpled to the ground, there in the middle of the street, the one working headlamp of her car illuminating just how badly she had been beaten.

THE CAR was wrecked, but it was able to get Livvy the few blocks back to her apartment. She stumbled out of the car, onto the elevator, feeling as though her head was not her own. As she rode up, she gently explored with the tips of her fingers the damage done to her face. She could feel how grotesquely puffy and distorted her face had become.

She stepped off the elevator, unlocked the door to her apartment, and walked in.

Ally was on the sofa again, watching TV, and after hearing her mother walk in, she said, "I'm turning it off now." Pulling herself off the couch, she turned and caught sight of Livvy. Ally screamed, rushed over to her.

"Mama, what happened?" she cried, tears already spilling down her face.

"Nothing, baby," Livvy said, taking Ally's hand, and walking gingerly toward the sofa.

"Mama, I said what happened!" Ally asked again, nearly hysterical. "What happened to your face!"

"Baby, I said it'll be all right." Livvy sat down with Ally's help. "Now just get a frozen hamburger patty out of the freezer and bring it to me."

Ally rushed into the kitchen, brought back what her mother asked for. Livvy took the frozen, plastic-covered piece of meat and gently placed it over her swollen eye. She winced from its cold touch.

Ally stood there over her, still crying, looking helpless.

"Mama, I'ma call the police."

"No," Livvy said. "Just sit down, and don't do nothing."

Ally did as she was told. Livvy leaned back into the couch, trying to get accustomed to the cold burning on the side of her face.

"Mama, who did this? Who did this to you, Mama?"

The sound of her daughter weeping for her was killing Livvy. The fact that she had to see this was not right. All those years her children had seen her mistreated and had felt sorry for her. And now, Ally had to see her mother abused and feel the pain of seeing her suffer. It wasn't right, and it was all her fault. All her fault.

Livvy turned to her child. "Alizé, it doesn't matter who did it."

"It was Carlos, wasn't it?"

"I told you—"

"Wasn't it, Mama? Let's call the police. Or I know some people. It won't cost much, and they can—"

"Ally, dammit!" Livvy yelled, pulling the frozen meat from her eye and slamming it on the table. "It wasn't his fault," she said, lowering her voice some. "I let him do this to me. Do you understand?" She looked into her child's eyes with the one eye she was able to see through. "I allowed him to do this to me because I wasn't strong enough to stop seeing him. I wasn't strong enough to be on my own. I couldn't just love myself. I had to have someone else say they loved me before I could see any worth in me. And look what it's gotten me, Ally."

"Mama," Ally cried, reaching for her mother's face but not knowing where to touch her.

"I want you to look at me. I mean really look at me, and see what can happen when you don't value yourself—when you place a man over you and everything that's important to you. Do you see me, Alizé?"

Ally tried hard to look directly at her mother's beaten face, but it was too painful for her, and she kept looking away. Livvy reached out and grabbed her chin in her hand, physically forced her.

"Look."

And the girl did. Through the tears that flooded her eyes, she looked at her mother.

"Do you see, baby?"

Ally nodded.

"This is why I'm so hard on you, why you always thinkin' I'm being mean to you. It's because I want better for you, sweetheart," Livvy said, placing an arm around Ally's shoulder and bringing her close. "I have to protect you, baby, because you just like I was."

"I am?" Ally said, looking into her mother's eyes, almost sounding proud.

"Yes, you are. You're an affectionate, loving person who needs love and affection back."

"Is that why you're always harder on me than on Henny?"

"That's right," Livvy confirmed. "Henny's not as much like me as you are. She doesn't need that security as much as we do, so I didn't have to ride her as much. But it never meant that I loved you any less, baby." Livvy leaned forward to look into her daughter's face. "I do it because I love you oh so much."

Alizé threw her arms around Livvy, hugging her as tight as she dared. "I love you, too," she said, still weeping for her mother. "I love you, too."

FORTY-ONE

RAFE pulled the Jaguar into the parking lot of the Marriott Suites hotel. As he pulled the key out of the ignition, he wondered why he was here, thought of just turning around and going back home. But what would be there? Just that empty room and thoughts of Henny he couldn't do anything with but be sad about.

This was what he had been doing since the night he had last seen her. She had called him a zillion times, but he never picked up. She left him voice mails, but he could only bring himself to listen to the first few words of the first message, because he knew if he heard her out, he would go running back to her, and that he couldn't do. Bottom line, Livvy's mother was right: they were wrong for each other. End of story.

Things weren't any better on the work front. Smoke had called recently.

"Had enough time off, pimp. Time to come on back," he'd said.

It wasn't enough time, because Rafe still hadn't found a way to get out of this situation.

"I don't know what you're talkin' about," was what he said.

"Stop playin' games, Rafe. I gave you your thinking time, and that should've been enough for you to know that that little shit that happened at the club had nothing to do with you. It was happening before you got out of prison, and it's gonna keep on happenin' when it has to. You can't change it, and you don't cause it. So stop fuckin' freakin'. Put some clothes on and meet me at the Marriott off of I-80. Suite 216. Picked up some bitches from a club, and I'm sure it's something you'd be interested in."

"I don't think so, Smoke."

"C'mon, Rafe. Get yo' ass up. You ain't doin' nothing, and I know you ain't got no ass there, so c'mon."

And Smoke was right about that. He wasn't doing anything but thinking about Henny. He needed to stop that. He wasn't with her anymore, and eventually he would have to get used to being with other women, so why not start tonight? It was the last thing he wanted to do, but he agreed.

"Yeah, all right. See you there."

"My nigga," Smoke said.

RAFE climbed the stairs to suite 216 and really didn't have to see the numbers to be sure that it was Smoke's room, for the music was pounding hard against the inside of the door.

Rafe knocked. There was no answer. He knocked harder. Still no answer. He pounded with the side of his fist, and just before he hammered down on the door for the third time, it quickly swung open. Smoke stood there, his shirt off, a drink in his hand, a huge grin on his face.

"Damn playa. I know you frantic to get in, but I wasn't gonna start wit'out you. Enter," Smoke said, holding the door wide for Rafe to pass in.

Rafe walked through the large room, a sofa and chair on one side, two queen beds on the other. All the lights were off except for a blue bulb burning in one of the bed lamps. Erotic music with a hard hip-hop beat blared out of a portable stereo atop the dresser.

Smoke walked up behind Rafe and slapped a hand down on his shoulder, squeezing it.

"So whatcha think?" Smoke asked, and he was obviously referring to the four women wearing nothing but thongs and T-shirts, dancing and fondling each other on top of the beds.

"Wow," Rafe said, in a tone lacking emotion. "Not bad, I guess."

"That's what a tight pocketful of loot will do for a brotha. Now grab you a drink, take yo' shit off, and let's have some fun."

Rafe watched as Smoke jumped onto one of the beds, watched as the two girls there started to undo his pants, strip him down.

Rafe walked over to the dresser, grabbed himself a plastic cup, and reached for one of the three open bottles that was there. He didn't know what it was—it was too dark to see—but he poured his cup half full and replaced the cap, thinking how much he didn't belong here.

He turned around to face the bouncing, frolicking girls. He saw one

of them seductively motioning with a finger for him to come to her. As
he took a step forward, an image of Henny flashed before him. He saw
quick snippets of their first meeting, the first time they kissed, the first
time they made love. He stopped for a moment, thinking of backing
away, putting his cup down, but then he remembered the talk he had
with Henny's mother. Rafe looked up at the girls again, brought the
cup to his lips and kicked it back, drinking its contents down in just
one swallow. Then he walked toward the girls atop the bed, taking off
his shirt, and undoing his pants as he went.

FORTY-TWO

WADE would've gone after her that day, but he was too busy trying to wipe scalding coffee from his face and at the same time save the sale of the car, which he had been certain was a sure thing.

It wasn't. He saw this as soon as he had finally smeared enough of the liquid away to open his eyes and speak like someone who hadn't been set afire.

"So, I'll take an additional five hundred dollars off the price of the car for all the trouble you guys have just had to go through." But Wade could see by the looks on their faces that they were no longer interested in doing business with him.

They walked toward the door, not saying a word.

"How about a thousand?"

They walked through the door and were gone.

"Dammit!" Wade threw the now-soaked tie he had taken off to mop his face with to the floor. He had lost the sale. Worse, he had lost a very special woman.

TWO DAYS later, Wade picked up his phone for what seemed the one-thousandth time, dialed Livvy's number, and waited as it rang. He stood by his dresser, tapping his foot, telling himself that Livvy should've been home from work because it was after eight. He was pissed the hell off. Not pissed off like when he called her the first time, two days ago, still thinking about losing his sale, and not like when he called her half a dozen times yesterday, angry because she hadn't called him back yet. No, Wade was truly and extremely pissed because of the time they'd spent together, the moments they shared, and all the personal things he had told her, and now she wasn't even picking up the phone.

He waited the final two rings, knowing the voice mail would pick up, and when it did, he angrily slammed down the phone.

"Forget this!" Wade said, grabbing a jacket out of the closet, snatching his keys off the TV, and heading out the door.

He got to Livvy's building in record time, his anger making him speed. He pulled into the parking lot and decided he would go up to her apartment even though he didn't see her car. She was probably parking it down the street or something to make him think she wasn't home, just like she wasn't answering her damn phone, Wade thought.

Wade stepped off the elevator, angrier than when he had got on, thinking about her treatment of him, and when he got to her door, he didn't hold back his rage, pounding heavily at it.

There was no answer, so he pounded three more times. When still no one answered, Wade pressed his face into the crack where the door met the frame and yelled, "I know you're in there, Livvy. Open the door." After a full minute, he heard nothing and turned around, about to leave. But then he heard the faintest noise behind the door. He spun back around and banged at the door again.

"Livvy, I heard you in there. Open the damn door."

"I ain't opening nothin'," he heard Livvy call from somewhere in her apartment.

"C'mon. I called you a thousand times. Why haven't you called me back?"

"Because I obviously don't want to talk to you."

Wade turned in a circle, not knowing what to do next. "I lost that sale because of you. That was money in my pocket. You know that."

"Good," Livvy said sarcastically. "But I'm sure that didn't hurt you since you own the place."

"Look. I told you that for a reason."

"I don't care."

"Look, I had no problem lying to you at first, but now I regret that I did it," Wade said. "I was just telling you what you wanted to hear."

"What do you mean, what I wanted to hear?"

"Just let me in, and I'll tell you."

"No. You can say what you need to say from out there."

"Livvy, I'm not going to spill my guts out here so all your nosy neighbors can know what's going on between us."

"They won't know, 'cause it's probably all lies you telling anyway."

Wade shook his head, frustrated. He looked at the door angrily, as if he was seeing through it, directing his stare at Livvy.

"Fine, Livvy," he said. "You want me to tell you everything. No problem!" And now he spoke at the top of his lungs, loud enough for all the people in the neighboring apartments to hear, as well as a few above and below. "I told you that I owned that dealership. I lied about where I lived because when I met you, you were the most beautiful, honest woman I had met in a long time."

"Wade, what are you doing? You don't have to yell," Wade heard Livvy say under the sound of his booming voice, but he continued.

"I knew in order for someone like you to spend time with someone like me, there were rules. I thought I needed money to be with you. So I lied and said I had it, even if it was just to get you in bed. To have sex with you."

"Wade!" Livvy said, her voice just right behind the door now. "Stop puttin' my business out like that," she said in a high whisper.

"And man, I got to say that was the best sex I ever had!" he yelled.

"Wade! Stop it."

"Open the door."

"No."

"So anyway," Wade continued, now pacing up and down the hall so all Livvy's neighbors could hear. "When we had SEX, it was like the most incredible thing I had ever experienced. You showed me things I hadn't seen in all my years. That one position where you turned around and grabbed your—"

"Wade!"

"Yes," Wade said, in a sing-songy voice.

"I'll open the door. But you say what you have to say, then you're outta here."

"Fine." Wade heard the chain loosened and then a bolt turn, and the door was cracked open.

Wade pushed his way in, closing the door behind him, then turned around to see Livvy with her back toward him. He knew things hadn't been resolved yet, but just being inside her place made him confident that everything would be okay. He was so happy to see her that he quickly walked up behind her, threw his arms around her, and squeezed.

Livvy cried out, shrinking away from him in pain.

"Livvy, what's wrong?" Wade said, worried, thinking that he had harmed her in some way. When she turned around, big dark glasses hung on her face, but they did not come close to covering all the damage.

Wade gasped, shocked, not believing what he was seeing. "Livvy, what happened?" He reached out to grab her, but again she shied away.

"It was . . . it was nothing. I had a car accident," Livvy said, turning her head down, trying to hide her face.

"A car accident," Wade said, skeptically, seeing the bruises, cuts, and scrapes on her face. He knew what a beating looked like both from getting a couple of them over the years and dishing plenty of them out. "Was anyone else involved?"

"No. I mean yes," Livvy said. "A little old lady."

"Was she hurt?"

"No."

"She wasn't hurt," Wade said skeptically. "But you come out looking like this. Must've been some tough little old lady."

"Yeah. Tough," Livvy agreed.

Wade didn't say anything, just stood there in silence, looking at her. Livvy peered at him from over the top of the dark glasses. "What?"

"You been to the hospital for this?"

Livvy shook her head.

Wade reached for the glasses off Livvy's face, but she pulled away. "Let me see," Wade asked gently. "Please."

Livvy brought the shades down from her face to reveal a left eye that was swollen almost completely shut, with blackness that had spilled over to the right eye.

Wade shook his head, feeling both sympathy and a steadily growing anger in him. With a calm voice, he managed to say, "Livvy who did this to you?"

"I told you. I was in an accident."

"Livvy, don't lie to me."

Livvy tried to shift his attention. "What are you talking about? You the one who's been doing all the lying."

"This isn't about me. Who did that to your face?" Wade asked, stroking one of Livvy's hands. "And I want to know the truth."

Livvy shook her head again, tears spilling from her eyes, as she appeared to try to tell Wade everything that happened but couldn't.

"Was it a man?" Wade asked, hoping for god's sake that it wasn't.

But when Livvy nodded her head, he felt a pain in his heart he could not describe, envisioning Livvy on the end of punches strong enough to damage her face like that.

"Was it someone that you used to see . . . someone that you still see?" And Wade hesitated to ask the second part of that question, but it was something he had to know.

"I used to see him," Livvy said softly, ashamed that it had come to this.

"The police pick him up?"

"No."

"Did you call the police?" Wade asked, sensing he knew the answer already.

"No."

"He did this to you, and you didn't call the police?" And the anger was back again, even stronger than before. "So this man beats you up and you just let it go?"

"It's done, Wade. It's over now."

"No. It's not done. It's not over," Wade said, with an intensity in him that had him up, pacing in front of her like a caged animal. "But it'll be over when I see him. What's his name?"

Livvy didn't even look up at Wade, but shook her head.

"What's his name, Livvy!" Wade asked more forcefully.

"I'm not tellin' you. What's done is done, Wade."

"No!" Wade said, passionately. "I can't just stand by while some man lays his hands on the woman that I love and be expected to . . ." Wade paused, not knowing that he was going to say what he had just said. It had to be his emotions getting the best of him. He hoped Livvy hadn't heard that, but judging by the look on her face, she had.

There was a moment of silence—not awkward but contemplative. Then Wade said, "Tell me his name, Livvy, so I can make sure this fool never does this to you again."

Livvy looked up at Wade, hesitating for a moment, then said, "Carlos Tillman."

FORTY-THREE

AFTER LIVVY reluctantly gave Wade the address, they pulled up in front of Carlos's house. Wade was fuming, having to listen to Livvy questioning him all the way over there. "Wade, why are we doing this? What's going to happen? You aren't going to hurt him, are you?"

When they pulled to a quick stop at an intersection, Wade spun around to face her. "What do you think I'm going to do? And after what he did to you, you should *want* me to hurt him, should be *praying* that I hurt him. What? Is there something still going on between you two? You still have feelings for this man? Because if you want, I can drop everything right now and leave you two alone."

"No, Wade, it's not like that. I've just known him forever, and . . ." Livvy trailed off. "But no," she said, sincerely, "I don't care nothing about that man anymore."

"Good," Wade said, punching the gas pedal and speeding through the intersection. "I'm glad to hear that."

Wade jumped out of the car so fast after parking in front of Carlos's house that the push he gave the car door didn't even close it all the way. It hung slightly open as Wade took the stairs up to Carlos's door two at a time.

Livvy leaned over the driver's seat of the car, reached out and pulled the door shut, as she looked on, hoping nothing truly bad would happen.

Wade rang the doorbell, knowing the man was home.

"Yeah, that's his car," Livvy had said, when they pulled up. "The Cadillac."

Wade clenched two anxious fists at his sides, eagerly awaiting the moment he would see this bastard's face. Wade knew there would be little talking. He stabbed a finger into the doorbell again, ringing it twice this time.

Carlos had beat the shit out of Wade's girl, and there was no need to find out the reason. All there was need for now was to deliver the punishment, and Wade was ready as he would ever be for that.

Wade heard approaching movement from behind the door, heard locks being turned, and then the door swung open. A man in his mid-thirties, with black wavy hair and a sun-baked gold complexion, stood in front of him. It was no wonder Livvy was taken by this guy. He was good looking, Wade thought. But he wouldn't be for long.

"Can I help you with something?" Carlos asked.

Wade flashed a quick, fading smile at Carlos, then quickly threw his hand into his chest, grabbing him by his knit pullover, and yanked him out of the house. Wade threw him against the brick wall just beside the door, and he was surprised at how easily he was able to handle him.

He knew he had to have had fifty pounds on the man, but also felt his adrenaline pumping, knew that his rage was fueling his strength as well, and hoped that he could control just how much pain he'd put this man through.

"What the fuck are you—," Carlos tried to say, shock and anger on his face. But before he could finish, Wade drilled him with a hard shot to his stomach. Air and spittle rushed out of Carlos's mouth as he was forced over, cradling his middle.

After a second, his eyes looked up, only to see another one of Wade's fists flying at him. This punch hit Carlos on the side of the face, on his cheekbone, knocking him off balance. He stumbled sideways, then fell to the porch floor.

He rolled over once, quickly spun to his stomach and looked up at Wade again, a sickly, frightened look on his face.

"Who the fuck are you, and why you doin' this!" Carlos yelled, half crazed.

Wade walked toward him as if nothing registered, as if he hadn't heard a word Carlos said.

He came down on Carlos with an overhand right, hitting him squarely in the left eye.

Carlos fell flat to the porch again, flailing around blindly, reaching out, trying to get ahold of Wade. Wade sidestepped one of the weak attempts, then hauled himself back, and kicked Carlos in the gut, flipping him to his back.

"Who are you!" Carlos yelled again between coughing fits.

Wade kicked him again in the ribs, two more times, then stepped over him, grabbed him by his shirt with one hand, and punched him in his left eye as hard as he could, hoping his eye would swell up and shut too, so he could see how Livvy felt.

Three more hard blows, and Carlos didn't even cry out in pain after the last shot, couldn't even hold up his arms to try to defend against any more blows. His body was limp, and Wade let him go, allowed his body to flop down on the porch.

Wade continued to stand over him, looking down, the anger still coursing through him, but starting to ebb some now.

"Why did you do this?" Wade heard Carlos say, his voice weak.

Wade kneeled, so he could look into Carlos's eyes, allow Carlos to look into his.

"You want to know?"

Carlos nodded his head.

Wade looked out toward his car, saw Livvy looking worriedly up at him.

"Look up, out there," Wade said, pointing toward the car, but Carlos didn't seem as if he wanted to put forth the effort it would take to raise his head. Wade reached down, grabbed the man's face, and raised his head for him. Carlos moaned in agony, but through his quickly swelling eyes, he saw Livvy sitting there in the car, her face still a mess from the beating he had given her.

"You see her there?" Wade said.

Carlos didn't respond.

"I said, do you see her?" Wade asked again, more forcefully, squeezing Carlos's face.

"Yeah!" Carlos yelled from behind clenched teeth.

"That's why I did this to you, and if I ever hear word of you touching my woman again, if I hear that you've even been near her, you can bet your little sun-tanned ass that I'll be back, and what just happened will seem pleasurable compared to the beating I'll have for you then." Wade dropped Carlos's face from his hand, his head slamming against the porch surface.

Wade stood and was prepared to return to the car when he heard a final question seep out of Carlos's mouth. "Who are you?"

Wade turned. "I'm Livvy's new man," he said, then turned back around and walked away.

* * *

"HE DESERVED IT, Livvy," Wade said, pouring Livvy and himself a drink. He had taken them back to his room, telling Livvy that he wanted her with him and also wanted her to see him for what he really was, find out if this relationship could be salvaged.

"He laid his hands on you, and he deserved to have it done back to him," Wade said.

"I know, but I just wish that I didn't have to bring you into this."

"You didn't bring me into this," Wade said, setting down his glass, moving closer to Livvy. "I came because I care for you, and believe it or not, that's why I told you those lies."

"Let's just forget about that, Wade. Okay?"

"No. I want to explain first. I'm not a lying man, Livvy. Please believe that. I don't have a lot, nothing that I can really be proud of, but I'm not ashamed. I'm doing the best I can. I have very little debt, and I work very hard, putting money away. By this time next year, I'm going to have a house of my own. Like I said, I guess I was just lonely, tired of being by myself, and I was willing to say whatever I needed to keep you with me. I hope you'll forgive me for that."

Livvy reached out and caressed his face. "If you forgive me for saying that a man with a lot of money was the only kind I wanted, and for making you think that I couldn't love and appreciate you for all the good things that you truly are."

"I can forgive you for that," Wade said, placing his hand over the hand that touched his face.

"Then I forgive you, too."

FORTY-FOUR

ALLY closed the book, unable to read any longer. Earlier when she came in from apartment shopping, she sat down in front of the TV and scanned the immediate area for the remote. It wasn't on the sofa with her, and she didn't see it atop all the junk that lay on the coffee table. She sank her hands in between the cushions of the couch, blindly feeling around for it, but when she felt nothing, she shuffled the magazines, paper plates, and other crap that was before her and finally found it.

She pointed the thing at the TV and was just about to click it on when she thought about everything she'd just had to do to locate it. She thought about what her mother said—how she comes in the house, sees Ally sitting around a pile of junk just watching TV, and Ally knew she was right.

Ally put the remote down beside her, telling herself the least she could do was clean off the coffee table, and then she could watch TV. If nothing else, this would give her a clean space to kick her feet up.

She did that, then stepped back and saw that there were crumbs and lint on the rug, so she brought out the vacuum cleaner and vacuumed—not only the living room but the dining area as well.

After that, Ally clicked on the stereo and found herself dancing around to WGCI as she washed all the dirty dishes and cleaned the kitchen. When she was finished with that, she took out some more cleaning supplies, products like Pledge, Windex, and Fantastic. Ally used them all, cleaning the living room, dining room, kitchen, hallway, and bathroom from top to bottom. She took out all the garbage, pulled out all the old stuff that they didn't use anymore that was just cluttering up the place, and dumped it.

When she was done, she felt good. She settled back down on the couch, grabbed the remote, pointed it at the TV again, and found herself hesitating once more. She didn't know why, but after all that work she'd done, she didn't even feel like watching TV anymore.

She set the remote down on the coffee table, sat there a moment, looking up at the ceiling, thinking. All of a sudden, she got up from the sofa and walked down the hallway toward her room that she shared with Henny.

When she returned, she sat down with one of Henny's big African history books, opened it, and started reading. She couldn't wait 'til her mother got home to see what she had done, especially after what had happened the other night. She needed to be able to relax, not worry about anything, and Ally understood that. She also understood now why her mother had treated Ally the way she always did. But things would change, Livvy told her. She would treat her better now. And at that moment, Ally made the same promise to herself. From now on, she would treat her mother with more respect, do what she was expected to do, and it was all starting with her cleaning up the house.

After ten pages of the book, which Ally surprisingly enjoyed, she closed it, looked at the clock, and seeing that it was after eleven, wondered where her mother was. Just then, Ally heard a key slip into the lock, and instantly got excited. Her mother would walk in the door, see how clean the place was, and would be so proud of Ally.

She stood from the sofa, then looked down at the book, quickly picked it up, cracked it open, and held it in both her hands, as if she was just in the middle of studying a thought-provoking sentence.

When the door opened, Ally looked up and was disappointed to find that it wasn't her mother but Henny.

Well, Henny would be surprised at the clean house too. She hadn't seen her in a couple of days, thought her sister was avoiding her for some reason, but now she would have no choice but to say something nice to her for a change.

Henny closed the door and turned to look at Ally with an angry glare. She quickly covered the room with her eyes, seeming to dismiss how clean it was, then focused on her sister.

"What are you doing with my book?" was all Henny had to say.

"Ain't you gonna say something about the house? I cleaned it up."

"Fuck the house," Henny said, walking toward her sister, extending her hand. "Give me my book."

"Fine," Ally said, handing it over. "What's your damn problem?"

"Rafe dumped me. Have any ideas why, Alizé?"

Ally looked at Henny as if she had just been asked a trick question. "No."

"Because Mama went to his house and told him he needed to. You want to tell me just how she got his address?"

Ally hesitated to answer, quickly trying to work out a response that would suit her sister, but when nothing came, she simply said, "I tried not to tell her, but Mama knew I was lyin'."

"Dammit, Ally!" Henny slammed the book to the floor. "She knew you were lying. So what? You lied to her a million times before, and when she caught you, did that mean you turned around and told her the truth?"

Ally didn't say a word.

"Well did it?" Henny demanded.

"No."

"Then why did you do it this time? Because you wanted her to know," Henny answered before Ally could. "You told her because you wanted him to dump me, because this was the one time that someone wanted me instead of you."

"It wasn't like that, Henny," Ally said, reaching out to her sister.

Henny waved her off. "I don't believe you, Ally. Every time I got a boyfriend, you would come around swishin' your big ass in front of his face, trying to lure him away, and you always did. All those times I didn't mind, because I always had an excuse to dismiss that. They weren't worth it anyway. I didn't really like that boy. I'd rather be studying than be with him. But, Ally this was different!" Henny said, her entire face trembling, her lip quivering, a tear quickly streaming down her cheek. "I love him!"

Ally grabbed her sister. "Henny, look. We can fix this."

"How? He won't listen to me, so he sure as hell won't listen to you. And Mama won't allow it because she knows he's been in prison. How did she find that out, when you and I were the only ones who knew about it, Ally?"

"I don't know," Ally said, but Henny didn't believe her.

"I always knew that there was a certain amount of dislike you had for me, and I never really knew why. You promised that you wouldn't tell Mama about Rafe being in jail, but you did anyway," Henny said, dropping her face in her hand. "I know now that I just don't mean shit to you."

"Henny, what are you talking about? You're my sister. I love you," Ally cried.

"I'm tired of always trying to be the one to make things right between us. You don't care about me, don't care about us," Henny said, wiping tears from her face. "So from now on, I don't care about us either. I don't even consider you my sister anymore." And she headed for the door.

Ally ran over to her, grabbing her and throwing her arms around her.

"Henny, please don't go. I'm sorry about all the bad things I did to you, but I only did those things because I was jealous of you. Because you were perfect and I couldn't compare to that. Because you got all Mama's attention and she never cared about me. But everything's cool now, Henny," Ally said, still holding tight to her sister, looking up into her eyes, hoping that some of what Ally was saying reached her. "I had a talk with Mama, and I understand, and things are gonna be better for everybody. I promise, Henny. I promise."

Hennesey continued to let herself be held, looked down at her sister as if thinking about what she'd just told her, then said, "Just like you promised not to tell about Rafe." Henny wrestled to free herself from Ally's embrace, turned, then left the apartment, slamming the door behind her.

Ally stood there, crying. She'd never really understood just how much her sister meant to her until that very moment. Ally was thinking about what to do next when the phone rang. She walked over to it, picked it up. "Hello?"

"Get your stuff, and come out to the Hyatt by the airport," Lisa said.

"What are you talkin' about? That's forty minutes away, it's almost midnight, and it's starting to rain. Besides, something just happened and I don't feel like doin' anything."

"Ally, this is it, girl. The last two. Got these two niggas in the hotel right now, and they loaded. Drove me over here in a Bentley. Puffy drive a Bentley, and you know how much money he got! Get over here!"

"I told you, I don't feel like it. Besides I ain't spendin' all that money for a cab."

"They said they got you. They just want me to have one of my girls come out here."

Ally paused, thinking about it. She looked over at the door her sister just walked out of, wondering if she could catch her. But what would she tell Hennesey to make her forgive her?

"Ally, this one last hit, baby, and we're done," Lisa said, desperation in her voice. "I need this, and I know you do too. Let's put in this one last night, all right. We came this damn far. Let's finish it off so you don't have to be sleeping on nobody's couch."

A frown covered Ally's face at the thought of Lisa's reference. She gave it another moment of thought, then said, "This is the last time, Lisa, and then it's over. I got changes to make."

"Fine. Just leave out now, okay."

"That's what I'm doin'. See you in forty."

Ally hung up the phone, grabbed her cell phone, and scrolled down through the directory for a number. She pressed Send and waited for someone to pick up.

"Hello," a voice answered.

"Rafe, this is Ally, Hennesey's sister."

There was silence for a brief moment. Then he said, "Yeah, so?"

"I think Henny's on her way over there. When she comes, let her in, will you?"

"Me and Henny don't got nothing to talk about." He paused again. "I'm done with her."

"C'mon, Rafe. You might be able to play her, but don't try to play me. You ain't the only one know the game. I know you in love with my sister, saw it when you came over here, and can hear it in your voice right now. I know my moms come over there talkin' a lot of trash, but that's not her place. If you love my sister, like I know she loves you, then forget what my mother said. As much as she wants to, she can't decide who my sister is with, and you shouldn't let her. You hear me?"

Rafe was silent.

"Rafe, you got that?"

"Yeah, Ally. I got it. I appreciate this," he said. Then asked, "How you been? You ain't still hanging around them ballers are you? That's bad news. You need to stop that before something happens."

Ally heard the question and Rafe's warning, but hung up the phone. *I'm doing what I got to do,* Ally told herself, grabbing her keys off the table, her jacket from off the back of the chair. She walked out the door, her sister still heavy on her mind.

FORTY-FIVE

ALLY must've been right, Rafe thought, as he quickly headed down-stairs to answer his doorbell. He stood there at the door for a moment without opening it, trying to get himself emotionally straight. How would he look at her? What would he say?

From the moment he took his first step down the stairs and toward the door, he told himself he would be strong. What he had said had to stand. They were over. There was no way they could be together, no way that it would work, and the sooner they both accepted this, the sooner they could get on with their own lives, go down their own paths, see other people.

But Rafe knew it wasn't that easy as he wrapped a hand around the doorknob, preparing to open the door. Henny had too much of a hold on him. He had found that out the other night in the hotel room with those girls. They were all over him, writhing about, practically naked on that bed. They were wanting him, or maybe it was Smoke's money that made it appear as though they wanted him. Either way, he could've had them.

But he didn't go through with it. He wanted to, wanted to so badly, because he knew it would've helped him rid himself of the thought of Hennesey. But he just couldn't. He felt the kisses of one of the girls down his neck, the other pecking him around the torso, slowing mov-ing south. He looked across to the other bed, saw Smoke working on the other two girls like some professional porn star, and he knew he couldn't be a part of that. Whether they were together or not, Henny meant too much to Rafe for him to go out like that.

Rafe turned the deadbolt on the door and told himself a number of times, silently in his head, he would not take her back. He would not take her back. It was for her own good.

When he finally opened the door, Henny stood outside, her body drenched from the rain, her long hair flattened against her head and face. She was not looking up at him but down at the ground, as if ashamed at the fact that she was standing there.

"What do you want?" Rafe asked, trying to sound firm, even though all he wanted to do was grab the girl, take her in his arms, and never let her go.

Henny slowly raised her head, rain and tears sliding down her face. "It's what Mama thinks, but it's not how I feel," Henny said, trying to be heard over the rain that was crashing down around her.

"Why did you come? We already talked about this. How did you even get here?"

Henny looked out toward the street. A cab sat there waiting, smoke streaming from the exhaust, windshield wipers moving back and forth, sloshing the rain away.

"Henny, get back in the cab. Go home, please." Rafe tried as hard as he could to sound convincing and get her out of there as fast as he could, because he knew his willpower would last only so long. "Just go."

"But we can make it, Raphiel," Henny said, stepping forward, grabbing him with a rain-soaked hand.

"Go home!"

"Not 'til you take me back. I love you."

"Well, I don't love you."

"You don't mean that. I know you don't mean it."

"It's not gonna work," Rafe said, stepping out in the rain, placing himself in Henny's face.

"How do you know? We've barely even tried."

And now Rafe was starting to get frustrated. It was bad enough that he loved this girl like he'd loved no other and couldn't be with her. But now he had to list the reasons he wasn't "the right man" for her.

"How do you know?" Henny asked again.

"Because I just do!" Rafe said, raising his voice over the sudden clap of thunder. "Because I'm from the streets. Because I don't read. Because as a kid, all I did was rob and steal and stay in trouble, and that's the total opposite of all you ever did. It ain't gonna work because you got a bright future ahead of you, and all I'm gonna do is stay here and fix cars, and I ain't trying to hold you back, Henny. I ain't trying to do that to you. So just go," Rafe said, but this time instead of just telling her that, he grabbed her by the arm and started to lead her in the direction of the taxi.

"No! What are you doing?" Henny said, trying to fight against him. "I told you, I'm not leaving."

"It ain't up to you," Rafe answered, continuing to drag her over the wet pavement, through the puddles on the ground, closer to the cab.

"Stop it! Stop it, Raphiel," Henny cried, fighting harder, becoming increasingly harder to hold.

"Just get in the fucking cab and go," Rafe commanded.

"I won't!" Henny yelled, then kicked him in the shin, which made Rafe cry out and release her. "Why are you doing this?"

Rafe was still bent over, both hands wrapped around his lower leg, trying to rub the pain away.

"Is it because you're afraid to love me, so you're using what my mother said to try and get out of this? Because if that's it, just tell me the truth, not some lie, and I'll leave you alone, if that's what you really want so much."

Rafe looked around himself. It was after midnight, raining like crazy. He was drenched down to his skin, standing outside on the front lawn of his aunt's place trying to explain to the woman he loved why he didn't want to be with her. He wanted to forget about her, turn around, and just go back up to his room. It would've been easier than doing what she was asking him to do, because that meant facing some things that he didn't want to face. But she deserved that much.

"It won't work because I don't want it to work," Rafe admitted, and he saw the shock on Henny's face after he spoke those words. "Ain't nobody ever love me like this before," he said, rain running down his face. "All the girls who wanted to be with me before loved me because I *was* a thug, but you love me in spite of it. You looking at me, loving me for me, because you must think I got something going, that there's something more to me than there really is, and I don't know how much longer I can keep you thinking that. I love you, baby," Rafe said, grabbing Henny by the shoulders. "But your mother is right. You gonna be getting all that education and experiencing all sorts of different things, and that's gonna make you look at me differently. I ain't gonna be the man that I once was to you, the man that you gonna need me to be when you become a doctor. You gonna start looking around and seeing what you should've had, comparing that to me, and I just won't be able to stack up. Then I'm gonna lose you, and I just won't be able to take that. I love you too much. I'd rather just stop it here than to think that we gonna be together forever and then have someone take you away from me. I just couldn't live through it." Rafe felt weak all of a sudden, needing to wrap his arms around Henny. He did, hugging her tightly.

"Do you want more?" Henny asked.

"What?"

"Do you want to do more than what you're doing now?"

"Yeah, but—"

"But nothing. Then just do it. You'll still come down to school with me, and we'll get you in some classes—if not next semester, then the one after that, and then we'll grow together. I'll love you for who you are and the man that you'll become, and I can promise that I'll never leave you."

"But, Henny—"

"What!" Henny snapped, frustration in her voice. "You'd give up someone you love now because of your fear of what *might* happen in the future? This could be the best thing that has happened to either one of us, but you'll only know if you give it a chance," Henny said. "Give us a chance, please."

He looked inside himself, fighting his urge to tell her no. But he knew that urge wasn't sincere. It would only be an action he would've taken because of the words Henny's mother had said to him. But this wasn't her life. It was his, and Rafe knew that running from Henny would only guarantee their not working, and he truly didn't want to do that. This was worth giving it a chance.

"Okay, Henny," Rafe said, taking her in his arms, kissing her wet forehead. "I'll do this. I'll go."

FORTY-SIX

ALLY paid the cab driver. It was forty bucks with the tip, and she was thinking that this hit better be worth everything Lisa said it would be.

Ally climbed the outside stairs to room 302, still thinking about Hennesey. She hoped everything was okay with her and Rafe. By now, she knew, either they had patched things up or Henny was probably on her way back to the apartment, hating Ally even more than she had when she left.

Ally prayed that that wasn't the case, because she couldn't take it when her sister was mad at her. Of course, Henny had been angry with her a million times before, but it was always over little things, like Ally sneaking out in one of Henny's new shirts before Henny had a chance to wear it, or stealing one of the boys that Henny didn't really give a damn about anyway. But this was different. Henny had said that she didn't consider her her sister anymore. How could she have said such a thing? There was nobody closer to Ally than Henny. It wasn't *like* they were twins. They *were* twins. Born only minutes apart. Ally had never been without Henny and couldn't imagine being without her now. Ally remembered them as three year olds in the bathtub together as their mother washed them. She remembered them in first grade together as they shared their birthday party at school, and the time they both learned how to ride the broken-down bike they'd found. And then there was the time that Henny had gotten hit by that car. They rushed her to the hospital. Ally could remember standing by her bedside, watching her sister sleep. She wouldn't wake up, and their mother said she was in a coma. Ally thought she was going to die, and that terrified her because she didn't know if she would be able to live without her sister. The fact that Ally had thrown the ball that Henny had chased out in the street, the one that may have cost Henny her life, made things worse. Even then, as an eight-year-old child, she knew that if Henny didn't live, she didn't want to continue living either.

Henny's harsh words didn't really hit Ally 'til she was in the cab, on her way out here to the motel. That's when the tears came. That's when she wanted to lean forward over that seat and tell the cab driver to turn around and head for Rafe's place. But she didn't. Henny needed time to take care of her business. In the meantime, Ally would just have to take care of hers.

Ally knocked on the motel door. When Lisa opened it, her smile suddenly changed to a look of shock.

"What's your problem?" Ally asked, reading the expression. "You did say come out here, didn't you?"

"Yeah, girl," Lisa said, whispering, even though loud music was being played in the room behind her. "But where's your stuff?"

"What stuff?"

"You're wig, glasses. Your stuff!" Lisa said, pointing at Ally's face and head.

"Whatever. There was too much going on, and I forgot it. Like I said, this is my last hit anyway, so what difference does it make?" Ally said, carelessly, trying to step in through the door. Lisa blocked the entrance with her arm.

"You sure you want to go in there like that? What if you get recognized on the street, later?"

"This place is way out in the suburbs. Ain't nobody out here gonna be hangin' where I'm at," Ally said, trying to enter the room again, and again Lisa stopped her.

"You sure?"

"You want me to be a part of this or not?" Ally said, becoming impatient.

"All right. C'mon in."

Lisa and Ally walked into the motel room. It looked untouched for the most part. Both double beds were still made, not a wrinkle in either of the spreads. There seemed a general order about the place, from the three bottles of liquor sitting on the dresser that looked as though they had come with the room, to the neat, straight lines of cocaine that stretched over the surface of the coffee table. Ally told herself this would be a quick night. She didn't have time for any wild exhibitions and close calls, but just in case, she'd made sure to pack the gun she'd taken from JJ the other night in her purse.

"So what did I tell you," Lisa said, speaking to one of the brotha's that was sitting behind the coffee table on the sofa. "Is my girl fine, or what?"

"Oh, hell yeah," the thin brotha with red slacks said.

"Turn around," the other brotha said. He was leaning back in the sofa, his hair braided in crazy, wild designs on top of his head.

"What?" Ally asked.

"I said, turn around so I can see what you got back there," the man said, his words barely making sense because of the huge cigar that was stuck in his teeth.

Ally did what she was told, sticking her behind out a little, telling herself that this would definitely have to be a quick night.

"You like?" Ally said, faking enthusiasm, turning back around.

"Yeah," the man said, squinting one of his eyes to avoid the cigar smoke he blew out the corner of his mouth. "You gonna be mine. What's your name?"

"Uh," Ally said, rattling off the first thing that came to mind. "Silky," she said.

"Well, Silky," the man said, pulling the cigar from his lips, a look of deep anticipation in his eyes, "I think we gonna have lots of fun tonight. So as I told your girl, this is one of my associates, Mr. Charles," the man said, pointing to him with his cigar. "And you . . . you can just call me Smoke."

FORTY-SEVEN

THE NEXT morning, when Rafe woke up, Henny was in his arms, smiling at him.

"What are you doing?" Rafe asked, his voice a little groggy.

"Looking at you."

"Why?"

"Just because. Got a problem with that?" she said, smiling.

"No," Rafe said, leaning in, and giving Henny a kiss on the cheek. "But I know who's going to have a problem."

"Who?"

"Your mom, when she finds out that we're back together and I'm still going down to school with you."

"I'm not worried about her."

"You're not worried about your mother?" Rafe raised a suspicious eyebrow.

"No. I don't care what she has to say about us, and to tell you the truth, I'm not listening to anything else she has to say."

"And how are you going to do that?"

Henny thought for a moment; then a smile appeared on her face. "We don't have to wait to leave."

"What do you mean?" Rafe asked.

"I mean my apartment is already leased and waiting for me. I got the paperwork a couple of days ago. Early registration isn't for another week, but we can always go down early."

Rafe didn't say a word, just looked at Henny, uncertainty on his face.

Henny nudged him. "Rafe?"

"Yeah, I'm here. I just wanna know, are you sure about this, about me?"

"Of course, baby," Henny said, scooting closer, kissing him on the lips. "I'm more sure about this than anything I've been sure about in my entire life."

FORTY-EIGHT

WHEN ALLY sprung up out of sleep, she had to look around to remember where she was. She glanced down at what she was lying on, saw that it was a couch, and realized that she was at JJ's place.

Last night had gone surpassingly smoothly, just like she had hoped. Although there was something scary about the guy Smoke, something that made Ally think that if he hadn't passed out when he did, there would've been trouble. Thank god he was a heavy drinker, and the drugs worked on him almost immediately.

Ally had been buck naked on the floor before him, crisscrossing her legs, open and closed. He wanted a show, he said. No. He demanded a show, and he said it as though if his demands weren't met, she would've paid with something very close to her life. So she did as she was told.

Smoke took another swallow of the drink Lisa had made for him, twirled his finger, making a little circle in the air, instructing her to roll over as if she were a dog. Ally did that, slapping her ass cheek with one of her hands, continuing to watch him over her shoulder as Smoke's eyes slowly became heavier and heavier. Moments after that, he was totally knocked out.

Ally looked across the room at Lisa. She was in Mr. Charles's lap. His head was slung back over the top of the chair, and he was snoring loudly. Lisa raised one of his hands and let it go. It dropped heavily back onto the arm of the chair, letting Ally know that he was gone as well.

They grabbed everything the two men had, and they sure had a lot—more than seven thousand dollars between them. Smoke had most of it, a chunk of it in his pocket, a thick rubber band wrapped around it. He had more in his right sock, and some clipped to the waistband of his underwear. The man was a gold mine.

They took the jewelry the men were wearing as well and were just about out of there when Lisa said, "Hold on a minute."

Lisa went back into the motel room and grabbed Smoke's keys off the dresser.

"What did you forget?" Ally asked when Lisa came back out.

Lisa didn't reply, just jiggled the keys and smiled. "C'mon."

Ally stood outside the passenger side of the burgundy Bentley as Lisa hit the switch for the alarm. There was a quick chirp, then the four locks on the door simultaneously popped up.

"I ain't gettin' in there," Ally said.

"What? What you mean, you ain't gettin' in?" Lisa said, half in the car herself.

"I ain't gettin' in that car. You crazy if you take it."

"You act like we ain't already take all that man's money and everything else he had. What, you thinking he ain't gonna be mad if we leave his car? You thinking he gonna wake up, come out here and be like, 'Damn, those girls got me for all my loot, but they left my car, so how can I be mad at them'? It ain't gonna happen."

"The man looked evil. There was something not right about his ass. I don't know what it was, but it scared the shit out of me." Ally felt a chill run through her even now.

"Good. All the more reason to get your ass in this car and get out of here before he wakes up."

Ally told Lisa not to take her home. After everything they'd just gone through, she wasn't ready to bump into Henny.

"You can stay at my place," Lisa said.

"Naw, that's okay. I ain't seen JJ and Sasha in a while. Drop me off over there."

"JJ gonna whup your ass for knocking on her door at three in the morning."

"She's just gonna have to be mad," Ally said.

When Lisa dropped her off, Ally got out of the car and walked around to the driver's side.

"What you gonna do about this car, girl?" Ally asked.

"I don't know. Think I should keep it?"

"Girl! Don't lose your damn mind."

Lisa posed, leaning over to one side of the seat, extending a limp wrist over the steering wheel, the other grabbing her chin, looking like a pimp. "But it's so me, though. Ain't it? Say it ain't me, Ally."

"All right. It's you, Lisa." Ally was unable to help herself from laughing a little at how ridiculous her girl was acting.

"This car is tight. I could say, screw getting a new place. I can bring my kid out here, and we can live in this. This could be my house."

"It could also be your casket if dude find you in it," Ally warned. "So you gonna dump it, right?"

"Yeah, yeah."

"Tonight."

"Naw, not tonight. How the hell am I supposed to get back home? First thing tomorrow morning, though. I'll take it up north, then jump the train back. All right?"

"All right." Ally leaned into the car window, gave Lisa a hug and kiss. "Love you, girl."

"We did good tonight, Ally. We do it another year, we'll be living in mansions instead of apartments."

"We're through. Now get out of here."

Lisa winked at Ally, then drove off.

Ally had to knock on JJ's door five times before someone answered. When the door was finally opened, JJ looked as though she wanted nothing more than to reach out, grab Ally by the throat, and strangle her to death. Her hair was flattened on one side, her eyelids hanging low over her eyes.

"Looks like you were getting some good sleep," Ally said.

"I *was*. What the fuck are you doing here interrupting it?"

"If you can let a sista' in, maybe I'd tell you."

She filled JJ in on everything that happened. She told her that this was her last job, and that she never wanted to do anything like that again, because, for some reason, she was starting to see things differently.

JJ brought Ally out some linens to throw over the couch.

"Take your ass to bed. And if you wake up before us, leave quietly, please."

Now, when Ally sprang up out of sleep and realized she was in JJ's place on her sofa, she relaxed a little, her heartbeat slowing some. She had been having a nightmare, and that guy Smoke was in it. She couldn't really remember what it was about. All she knew was that it was bad. Really bad.

Ally was about to climb off the sofa and head toward the bathroom, when she heard a dull rumbling in her bag.

She reached out, hooked her purse, and pulled it over to her. The phone was ringing on vibrate, and when she looked at the caller-ID, she saw that it was Henny.

She reluctantly picked up. "Hello, Henny. Calling to curse me out some more? Tell me that you hate me even more than last night?"

"No, Ally. I've been trying to call you all night to tell you that I'm sorry. I know that it wasn't you who told Mama about Rafe. He told her himself."

Ally was quiet for a moment, still hearing the hateful words her sister had said to her echo in her mind. "I told you I didn't tell her."

"I know you told me that. But I was just so mad at you that I couldn't hear a thing you said. Ally, I need to talk to you, see you, so I can apologize in person. I didn't mean what I said. I couldn't mean it. You've always been my sister, always been my best friend. Always will be. I don't know what I would do without you."

Ally wanted to tell her sister that she felt the same way, but for some reason she couldn't. Not then.

"You know, you always say that I've been mean to you, but you've been mean to me a lot too," Ally said.

"I know that, Ally."

"You act like just because I'm not as smart as you, that I don't want to do better, that I don't want to have a nice life, that I don't want to accomplish things like you. But I do, Henny. I do want those things."

"Ally, I know. I know," Henny said, and to Ally, it sounded as if her sister was crying. "Just come home so we can talk all this through. I have a bunch a stuff I have to tell you."

"I don't want to come home right now. I just need a break from being over there, all right."

"Then let's meet. Have you eaten yet?"

"No," Ally said.

"Then let's meet at Lenny's. We'll get some barbecue. My treat."

"When?"

"I don't know, twenty minutes."

"Un-uh. Need more time than that. I gotta get all the way over there," Ally said.

"All right, half an hour."

"Forty-five minutes."

"Sounds good. I can't wait to see you," Henny said, and now it sounded as though she was smiling.

"Yeah. You too," Ally said, then hung up.

"Damn, whoever that was, tell them to call me next. I wanna be happy like that," JJ said, walking into the living room, seeing the huge grin on Ally's face.

"What's up, J? Sorry I woke you up last night."

"Don't worry about it. You my girl, and you ain't wake Sasha up. She can sleep through an earthquake. You want something to eat?" JJ asked, walking toward the kitchen.

"Naw, but thanks. I'm supposed to be meeting Henny for lunch," Ally called back into the kitchen.

A moment later, Ally's cell was vibrating in her hand again.

"Hello."

"Girl, where you at? I'm gonna come swoop you so we can do some shopping," Lisa said.

"How you gonna come swoop me on the bus?"

"Well, see, this morning when I got up, I knew there was shopping that I wanted to do. And I was thinking which would be better: Bentley or bus? Bentley or bus? You'll be surprised to find out I chose the Bentley."

"Lisa, I told you to get rid of that thing. What if somebody sees you, or they report it stolen?"

"Like you said. Those guys were way out west, and shady-ass niggas like them ain't tryin' to go to the police to report something stolen when they probably stole the car themselves. Now are you rollin' or not?"

"Not," Ally said. "I'm supposed to be meeting my sister for lunch."

"Let me guess. Lenny's?"

"Yeah."

"Well, let me pick you up. You can roll to the ghetto rib spot in style," Lisa said. "Everybody'll be looking at you, asking 'Ooh, who dat is? Who dat is?'"

"Not a chance. Dump the car, Lisa. Okay? Will you do that for me?"

"All right, all right. But, girl, if you could see all the heads turning to check me out. It's a shame. A damn shame."

FORTY-NINE

THIS WAS the life that Lisa always wanted to live. She made a slow
right turn on Jefferson and thought that if she had just finished school,
or if she hadn't gotten pregnant, then maybe she would be driving a car
like this on the regular, and not having to steal it from the guy it
belonged to.

What the hell, she thought. She was driving the Bentley right now,
and most people can never say that they've ever done that.

She turned into the parking lot of a Pier One store, thinking she
was going to need some stuff for her new place, and once again some
brothas were scoping her. They were in a nice car themselves. She
didn't know what kind it was, but it was red, sporty, and had a little
crown emblem on the hood.

Lisa parked the Bentley, and the red car pulled up behind her. The
brotha on the passenger side threw his elbow out the window.

"Whassup, baby? Dope-ass ride."

Lisa blushed, smiled, giggled, and took the compliment as though
the car was really hers.

"Thanks, sweetheart. So's yours."

"You doin' some shopping today?" the brotha asked.

"Yeah, probably pick up a few things. Why you wanna know?" Lisa
prepared herself to go into her purse, reach for her pen and paper,
because she knew he would ask for her number next.

"Just askin'," the brotha said. He gave Lisa and the car another look,
pulled his arm back into the window, and the car sped off.

Lisa watched them as they raced out of the parking lot.

"Stank Negroes," she muttered, still watching the car as it cruised
into the busy flow of traffic. "Just because they got a nice car, they

think they can act any way they want. Well, I got a nice car too." Lisa hit the switch to enable the alarm, then walked into Pier One.

THE RED Maserati stopped at a red light as the brotha on the passenger side spoke into his cell phone. "Yeah, it's yours," he confirmed, craning his neck to look back at it. The car was now parked across the street, facing the direction of the Pier One store.

"Yeah, I'm sure. Same plates. Yeah," the brotha said. "So what you want us to do?"

The brotha received the instructions. "All right. Well, if she move, then I'll ring you back and let you know what's up. Otherwise, I'll just wait 'til you get here. Peace."

FIFTY

LIVVY walked into her apartment from spending the night at Wade's. She had to get ready to go to the hospital and hand in her essay. But when she looked up, she was shocked. The place was clean! Not just straightened up, the cushions readjusted on the sofa, or the clutter stacked in neat piles on the coffee table. The place was spotless, like someone had come through with a huge vacuum cleaner and a bucket of disinfectant, sucking up and wiping away all the grime. All that remained was the faint scent of pine freshness.

Livvy stepped farther into the apartment, the smile on her face growing wider and wider with each step. She hesitated to lay her purse on the couch for fear of cluttering the place up again. She walked through the living room and headed for the kitchen to see just how far this trail of spotlessness went.

The kitchen was immaculate. The toaster, the fixtures on the sink, even the floor gleamed as though it was covered with glass. Livvy told herself not to do it, knowing that she would be asking too much, but she pulled the door to the fridge open anyway, and instead of the pile of food that was normally thrown any which way in there, everything was neatly organized. Eggs were placed in the egg bin, fruit in the fruit crisper. Everything was in its proper place.

Unbelievable! Livvy thought, closing the door, and resting her back against it. This was the nicest thing anyone had done for her in a long time, and it was just what she needed after all that nonsense that had gone on with Carlos. Thankfully Wade had been around, and thankfully they had gotten past their differences, and everything was cool with them now.

Seeing her place clean like this, knowing that one or both her daughters was responsible and remembering the night she had had with Wade, she realized that life now really wasn't so bad.

Livvy called out to her daughters, wanting to thank them. She would take them out to dinner that evening to show her appreciation.

"Hennesey, Alizé," Livvy called, walking down the hall toward their room. She clicked on the light, peeked into the bathroom on the way, and yes, that was clean too.

"Hennesey, Alizé," she called again. She knocked on the girls' door, and when she received no answer, she walked on in. The room wasn't as neat and tidy as the rest of the place, but they were entitled to a little mess, Livvy thought, smiling. This was their private space.

She wondered where both of them were, but she wouldn't worry about that right now. She had to jump in the shower, put on some clothes and . . . Livvy froze. She stood there in the middle of the girls' room, trying her hardest but almost afraid to remember all she had seen when she walked in the front door of her apartment. Or rather, all she had not seen.

"It's still there. It's still there," Livvy said softly to herself, but starting to panic because she knew that it wasn't. She commanded her feet to move out of the room, down the hall, and in the direction of the living room.

She continued to tell herself that it was still there, because she knew that if it wasn't, then all her hard effort, all the time she'd devoted, would've been lost. What would hurt her most would be losing the opportunity to dream. Livvy's head had been in the clouds ever since she had undertaken this challenge for the scholarship, thinking about all the possibilities for the future. Getting an education, a new job, more responsibility, self-respect, and respect from others. So many nights before going to bed, she couldn't help but smile, hoping, almost knowing, that she would win this scholarship to nursing school. She knew how strong her essay was, and for all the sacrifice she'd made, all the hell she'd been through, if there was anything fair about the world, then she knew she deserved to win.

Livvy stopped just before turning the corner that would give her full view of the living room. "Please, God, let that stack of old magazines still be there, and let me just have missed them when I walked in, because I was so taken with how clean the place was. Please, God, please," she prayed.

She closed her eyes, walked out into the living room, and then opened them. What she saw was an empty book shelf cleared of all the magazines that had been there just a couple of days before. Her heart sank, and all her hopes and dreams drowned with it. But wait! There were four or five magazines stacked neatly on top of the television. Maybe . . .

She practically ran across the room, hoping that one of the magazines would be the old '88 *Ebony* with Billy Dee on the cover. But when she stood over them, she saw that they were all recent issues.

Livvy picked up the one on top. It was a copy of *Essence*. Jada Pinkett and Will Smith were both smiling on the cover, looking as though they had not a care in the world.

Livvy focused on the attractive short-haired actress, her white teeth, her flawless skin, the man's arm around her, holding her close, as if protecting her from even the slightest little trouble that might come up.

"Life must be nice for you, hunh?" Livvy said to the magazine cover. "Ain't got a fucking worry in the world. Got you a good man, got you money, got you a big-ass house, and you never have to worry about your kids, 'cause I know you got motherfuckers paid to take care of 'em," Livvy said, clutching the magazine in both her fists, becoming angrier and angrier with each step she took across the living room floor.

"Everything's fine with you, because *you* got a job. *You* a big-time actress, but *you* don't even have to do that, because your husband can do it for you. *You* don't got to worry about your kids gettin' pregnant, or gettin' raped, or gettin' shot, 'cause *you* don't live in the 'hood. *You* don't have to worry about if you gonna make rent next month, or if you gonna still have a job tomorrow 'cause you two seconds from going off on some bitch for treating you like you they child when you know ten times more than they do," Livvy said, tears falling from her eyes. She pushed them away with the heel of one of her hands.

"*You* don't got to worry about that, because *you* didn't get pregnant with twins when you was sixteen and sacrifice your whole life for those girls. *You* didn't have to give them everything you had, even shit you don't got, make them your priority, put them first, because you love them so much. Then when you try to do something for yourself, try to make it out of the hole you been digging yourself in for all your life, you don't have to find out your children are the ones killin' your chances, burying you in that hole."

Livvy stopped her pacing, looked back one last time with tear-clouded eyes, just to make sure that the magazines really weren't still there. No. There was nothing, and Livvy felt her heart drop lower than she ever thought imaginable. She looked at the magazine in her hand, thought she saw Jada wink up at her, then she slung the thing with all her force across the living room, into the big mirror, hoping it would break it, but it didn't.

"Fuuuuck!" Livvy screamed out, hysterically.

FIFTY-ONE

RAFE dropped Henny off at the train station. "Why you want to ride the train? Just let me take you home."

"Because I'm not going home. I'm meeting Ally for lunch, and you know I like riding the train. It'll give me some time to think about everything we're about to do and find a way to tell my mother about this in a way that even she'll understand."

"You sure about this?"

"Of course, baby." Henny took his face in her hands and kissed him on the lips. "So you're gonna start packing, right? Because that's what I'm going to start doing as soon as we get back from lunch."

She was so excited that she could barely contain herself. All they did on the way to the station was talk about how wonderful things would be once they got down to school, how they wouldn't have to worry about what Henny's mother said or have to worry about this guy who was tormenting Rafe.

"And you better not change your mind" was the last thing Henny said when she jumped out his car. That's one thing she didn't have to worry about. He was just as excited as she was. The first thing he did was go to the store and buy some luggage and some other things he needed for the move. He wanted to get everything out of the way before he got rid of the car. He would park it somewhere, didn't know for sure where, and call the job, leave a message for Smoke, letting him know exactly where it was.

Rafe was riding through an area near his old neighborhood and decided to stop for gas, considering the fuel light had been on for some time.

He jumped out the car, swiped his debit card, and was about to grab one of the pumps when someone stepped up behind him.

"Pump that gas for you, sir?"

This happened every time Rafe used to stop for gas in the 'hood, and more times than not, he would always allow whatever kid or old man was down on his luck to pump the gas for a dollar or two.

"Go ahead, man," Rafe said, stepping away from the pump.

The weathered man stepped around Rafe, "Thank you very much. Thank you," he said, looking up into Rafe's face quickly, then grabbing the pump.

He didn't know if it was paranoia or not, but Rafe felt the man looking out the corner of his eye, studying him.

"Is there a problem, man?"

"Rafe, that you, man? Raphiel Collins?" The man turned to face him.

Rafe took a good look at the man. He appeared to be in his forties, painfully thin, his long hair a mess on his head. He wore clothes that looked as if they hadn't been washed in months, and the same could've been said for his body. He shuffled closer up to Rafe, grinning.

"Man, how you doin'? Remember me?"

Rafe looked at him, trying to place his face.

"C'mon, Rafe," the man said, showing a smile that lacked about half a dozen teeth.

"I was your biggest customer 'til you got sent away."

Rafe knew now. It was Jimmy Kingsly. Never had any money, but Rafe would toss him the occasional dime bag of weed to wash his car while he and Smoke took care of business.

"How you doing, Jimmy?"

"Fine, man. Glad to see you out. Look like you rollin' even better now. Got that fine Jag," Jimmy said, salivating over the convertible. "You need that washed? I see a little dirt trying to stick to the hood. I can get a bucket and some water from the gas station," he said pointing in that direction. "I can get started right now."

"Sorry, Jimmy. I really got to be running. I got some stuff to do." Rafe opened the car door.

"How about a complimentary bag, then? I'd really appreciate that."

"I'm out of the game, man. I don't do that no more. Sorry." Rafe gave Jimmy a couple of crumpled singles, then got into his car.

"It's because your brother got killed doing it, messing with them drugs, ain't it?" Jimmy said, replacing the pump and screwing Rafe's gas cap back into the car.

Rafe closed the door of the Jag, but not before he had heard what Jimmy said. It took a moment for it to register, but when it did, Rafe threw open the door. "What did you say?"

"Yeah. I know about that, and I'm really sorry."

Rafe jumped out the car and grabbed Jimmy by the arm, looking intently into his face.

"Know about what, Jimmy? What do you know?"

"That Eric was running drugs for Smoke. I stopped him one time after I ain't seen you in a while. He said you was locked up, but that he was running for Smoke, you know, carrying weight. He said soon Smoke would be lettin' him sell. So I told him that it wasn't no big deal that he ain't have no car yet. I'd wash his bike every now and then if he kicked me down with a dime bag. Know what I'm saying?" Jimmy chuckled through his missing teeth. "It was a damn shame. He got shot by those Puerto Ricans up on the West Side. A damn shame," Jimmy said, bowing and shaking his head.

Rafe snatched Jimmy by the shirt, shook him hard. "You sure about this! You know this for a fact!"

Jimmy looked frightened all of a sudden.

"Rafe, yeah. Everybody know. Didn't you?"

"No," Rafe said, under his breath, pushing Jimmy aside, hurrying back into the car, starting the thing, and forcing it into gear. He didn't know. But it all made sense now. That's what Eric was doing on the West Side, and that was why he got killed. That wasn't Smoke's territory, but knowing his ass, he was trying to expand: using Rafe's little brother to open a new market without drawing attention to himself. But he got Eric killed. He got Eric killed, and now Smoke had to pay.

FIFTY-TWO

LIVVY could cry only so long, and she knew that ultimately it would do her no good. Regardless how many tears she spilled, it wouldn't help her get that scholarship.

Livvy wiped the tears from her face and looked over at the clock. It was a little after ten. She was hoping that by now one of her daughters would've come in and told her that they hadn't thrown the magazines out—just put them in storage somewhere. Livvy had run outside, out to the trash to see if they were there, but the dumpsters had been emptied this morning, so if they had been there, they were gone now. She had the superintendent take her down to the basement to check if they were there as well. Nothing.

She had also thought to call Alizé on that cell phone of hers, but she didn't have the number. It was becoming apparent that there was nothing Livvy could do but lie there and cry. Her will wouldn't let her, though. At the very least, she could go to the hospital and appeal to the doctor in charge, tell him what happened, and ask for an extension.

"HE'LL BE right with you, Ms. Rodgers," Dr. Ranick's secretary told Livvy. Her eyes lingered about Livvy's face longer than they should've, and Livvy knew she was checking out the results of the beating Carlos had given her. Livvy sat down and during the ten minutes she was waiting, saw three other women who worked at the hospital come in and give the secretary brown envelopes. Livvy knew that their essays were in those envelopes, and she knew her chances of winning were becoming less and less likely.

The door to the doctor's office opened, and Dr. Ranick, a white man in his early forties, stuck his head out.

"Livvy. Sorry to keep you waiting. C'mon in." He held the door open for her, as Livvy walked in and had a seat in front of his desk.

Livvy felt awkward there. She felt small, like she did when she was a child and was sent to the principal's office for doing something wrong.

Dr. Ranick sat down behind his desk, wearing his white lab coat. He smiled at her, his beard, neatly trimmed, his hair, long but controlled. Livvy was glad that it was him who was in charge of this contest. She had known Dr. Ranick since she had started working at the hospital, and she liked him, thought he was fair, and felt he liked her too.

"What can I do for you today, Livvy? Coming in to turn in your essay?"

Livvy looked down at her hands, once again feeling like that child, this time singled out for not having done the assigned homework.

"I don't have it," she murmured. Then when she saw that he didn't fully understand her, Livvy cleared her voice and spoke the same words louder. "I don't have it. I think my daughters might have thrown it out by mistake."

Dr. Ranick seemed sympathetic to what he had just heard, but said, "So what would you like us to do about that?"

"I was wondering if I could get an extension. If I could turn it in later."

"Livvy," he said, already shaking his head.

"Even if it's just one day. Tomorrow. I think I can remember most of what I had down."

"Livvy, if I could, you know I would. I've known you a long time, and I think you're a fine nurse's assistant. And if anybody deserves this scholarship, it's you. But giving you an extension would be unfair to all the other applicants. The rules are clearly stated on the application, and I can't go back on those."

"Dr. Ranick, please. I know there's something that you can do. Something, anything. If you only knew how much I was relying on this to change my life."

The doctor looked at Livvy, sorrow in his eyes, but said, "I'm sorry. There is nothing at all that can be done. By chance, did you save a copy of the essay on disk?"

"I did it longhand. It was the only copy I had," Livvy said, sounding as though there was no hope for her now.

"Livvy, if you can possibly rewrite one and have it in by five this evening, I might—"

Livvy spun around, looked at the clock on the wall. "It's already eleven fifteen. There's no way."

"Then I'm sorry, Livvy," Dr. Ranick said, genuine sadness in his voice.

Livvy sat there, feeling beaten, helpless, and powerless. She needed to get up, get herself out of that office, but she just couldn't find the strength. After all she had recently been through, she couldn't find the energy to do anything but cry, and that's exactly what she did.

HALF AN HOUR later, Livvy was driving home. She had accomplished nothing that she had set out to do. Instead, she had done something else. She had quit. She sat there in front of Dr. Ranick and cried for only a moment, and then that sorrow turned into frustration and anger, and she told him that if she couldn't be a nurse, then she would have nothing to do with that hospital. She told him that she was tired of taking shit—and that's exactly what she said, "shit"—from all the nurses when she knew she could do their job as good as or better than they could. She told the good doctor this, but only after she had told him everything else about her life as well. She spoke of her two daughters, about the criminal her college-bound daughter was dating, and about the breakthrough she had just had with her other, less successful daughter. She even told him where the bruises and swelling on her face had come from. She told the doctor everything, and then before leaving, said, "All I wanted was a chance to provide for my children and to prove to myself that I could've accomplished something that was important. I would've been a good nurse, Dr. Ranick. I would've been a very good nurse." Then she got up and walked out.

FIFTY-THREE

LISA never saw it coming. She had finished her shopping and put some nice pieces of furniture on layaway for her new place. She was proud of herself for being able to afford those things, being able to afford the new place she would be getting soon. She was proud of herself because she needed money, and she had done what it took to earn it.

On her way home, she took the shortcut like she always did, and as she pulled into the mouth of the alley, she thought to herself that it would be really nice to keep the Bentley. It would fit her new lifestyle perfectly. Lisa was so lost in thought that she had no idea what was happening around her. When the big 7 series BMW quickly pulled in front of her from an intersecting alley, she slammed both feet down onto the brake pedal, but the car wouldn't stop in time.

It slammed into the side of the midnight blue car, her head pounding into the steering wheel of the Bentley. Everything was a blur after that. She heard doors opening, heard them closing. And then she felt her door open, felt someone reach in, undo her seat belt.

"I'm sorry," Lisa felt herself saying, her voice groggy, still disoriented, unable to see clearly.

She was hoisted out of the car by two men, but she sensed there were more around her, maybe three or four.

"Exactly what are you sorry for, sweetheart?" she heard a familiar-sounding voice ask her. Her head was spinning, trying to account for her injuries, but she found herself concentrating more on where she had heard that voice before.

The two men dragged her weakened body over to a short trash bin and sat her on top of it.

"You better be sorry for more than slamming into my car, baby," the voice said again.

"What . . . what are you talking about?" Lisa asked.

"Look at me."

Lisa's eyes were on the ground, but she raised her head, trying to clear the cobwebs out, trying to focus on the man who was speaking in front of her.

The man raised his voice. "I said, look at me!"

Lisa squinted her eyes, forcing them to focus, and when they did, she was terrified by who she saw.

FIFTY-FOUR

TWELVE MINUTES later, Rafe's car screeched to a slanted halt in front of his aunt's place. He yanked the keys out of the ignition, bolted out of the car, and flat out ran to the side door. The adrenaline in his blood made him fumble with the keys, trying to force them in the lock. The key finally went in, and with the aid of the banister, he was bolting up two and three stairs at a time.

Once on his floor, Rafe turned the corner and raced down the hallway. He passed Wade checking his mail but said nothing to him, concentrating on getting to his room.

"Hey, what's the hurry, Rafe?" he heard Wade say.

Rafe opened his door and ran to his closet, ready to open it, but looked over his shoulder to see Wade standing in the doorway.

"Rafe, everything okay?"

"Yeah, everything's cool. But I gotta talk to you later."

"Okay, that's cool," Wade said, backing away from the door.

Rafe kept his eyes there for a moment until he didn't see Wade anymore, then opened the closet door, reached up to the top shelf, and brought down a cardboard shoe box. He opened it to expose a folded leather holster, which he quickly threw on, and the .45 that Smoke had recently given him. Rafe had turned it down, but Smoke insisted he take it.

"Just in case something goes down, and you need to get my back."

Rafe never carried it, even though Smoke had always told him to. Instead he had dropped it in the cardboard box and shoved it up on the closet shelf. He slid it into his holster now, reached in the closet, yanked out the first button-down shirt that he laid his hand on, and threw it on over the weapon.

When Rafe spun around to leave, he jumped at the sight of Wade standing there in front of him. He had a serious expression on his face. "What's going on, Rafe?" Wade asked, the lighthearted tone no longer in his voice.

"I said, I gotta talk to you later. I got some serious business to take care of, okay?" Rafe tried to step past Wade, but Wade placed himself in front of Rafe, blocking him.

"Serious business of what nature, Rafe? The kind that demands you carry a gun?" Wade pulled open the halves of Rafe's shirt, exposing the weapon.

Rafe snatched the shirt closed.

"This ain't shit you need to concern yourself with."

"Let's talk about this. I don't want you to do something stupid, okay?"

Rafe didn't say anything, just brushed roughly past Wade.

"Now hold it, son," Wade said, reaching out, grabbing Rafe by the arm, and spinning him around. By the time Rafe faced him, the gun was drawn, the barrel shoved into Wade's ribs.

"I don't want to talk about it, and I ain't your son, okay!" The words seeped slowly and raspy out of Rafe's mouth. "You understand?" And with the question, he pressed the barrel of the gun further into Wade's ribs.

Wade took a small step back. "Yeah, I understand. But do one thing for me."

Rafe looked at him, narrowing his eyes. "What is it?"

"You got my numbers, home and cell, right?"

"Yeah."

"If anything happens, if you need my help. Call me, all right?"

"Yeah," Rafe agreed, slipping the gun back into the holster and turning to go.

"Be careful," Rafe heard Wade say to him, but to Rafe, safety was no longer a concern. If he died as a result of getting revenge for his brother, he wouldn't care. As long as Smoke died first.

FIFTY-FIVE

LISA wasn't sure, but her jaw had to have been broken. Her face was pressed to the hard ground of the alley, and every time she tried to move her mouth, blood flowed out of it, and it hurt like hell.

She didn't know how long she had been beaten, and didn't know if four men had done it or just Smoke himself. He was there, standing in front of her when her fuzzy vision became clear.

He said he wouldn't hurt her, that he just wanted to know where the other girl who robbed him was. But she knew he was lying. What? He would just let her go and hurt Ally enough to get back at the both of them? She knew that was bullshit, so she didn't tell him a damn thing.

Lisa could open only one eye. The other one had swollen shut, and it felt like a big rock had been shoved into her socket. She looked around for her purse, praying that they hadn't taken it and that it was somewhere close, because she knew she could move only a few inches, if at all.

Smoke had been pretty convincing, and Lisa wanted to believe him, thought she might even walk away from this alive if she just did as she was told. But tears came to her eyes when common sense told her that that would never happen.

"Baby, don't cry," Smoke said, gently smoothing a tear from her face with one of his fingers. "Just tell me what I need to know, and everything will be just fine."

"Bullshit, motherfucker!" she yelled, and then spat in his face. That's when the beating started and never seemed to end. It was pain that she never thought possible, but she wouldn't sacrifice her friend. She was the fool who didn't dump the car like Ally had told her to.

Lisa stretched out her arm now, felt the pain from her stomach injury telling her to give up, but she had to get her purse. It was there, just in front of her. Only inches away. It had fallen over, and the contents had spilled out. She saw her cell phone on the ground.

She thought, after a while, that she would've gone numb during the beatings, or unconscious, or into shock, but none of that happened. It just went on and on.

"The beating will stop if you just tell me. The pain will stop if you just tell me. Tell me, tell me, tell me, and it will all stop," Smoke said over and over again.

Lisa didn't want to give up Ally, but if she didn't, she knew she would die. She had a son. A fucking son. He was the reason she'd done all this to begin with, and she had to think about him, she realized.

"I don't know where she is now," Lisa said, regretfully, struggling to get the words out across her swollen lips. Through the blood covering her face, she saw Smoke rear back again, ready to hit her, but then she said, "But I know where she . . . where she gonna be."

Smoke dropped his fist, and Lisa told him. Told him that she was supposed to be at Lenny's, the barbeque place off State. That was it. All she knew. She was going to be at Lenny's anytime now.

"That's my baby," Smoke said. Lisa couldn't really see him, but heard the softened tone of his voice. She felt him rub his hand across her hair, caressing it.

"You did good. You kept your part of the bargain. And I'ma keep mine. I said if you tell me, you wouldn't feel no pain no more, and that's what I meant." Then she heard Smoke say, "Trunk, give me the gun."

Lisa screamed, tried to move, but couldn't.

"Goodbye, bitch," she heard him say. She heard the gun go off, and then she felt her belly being torn open by the bullets.

HER MIND was pulling away from her now, but she had managed to reach the cell phone. It was in her hand, and thank god Ally was the last person she called, because her mind was so messed up that she couldn't remember the girl's number. She pressed the Talk button, which automatically redialed the last number. Ally picked up.

"Hello."

"Ally, it's me, Lisa," she breathed painfully into the phone, her voice barely above a whisper.

"Lisa, is that you? I can't hear you too good."

"Ally, listen to me."

"I can't hear you. You have to speak up."

"Ally!" Lisa said, yelling as loud as she could, her voice still coming out as only a harsh whisper. "Listen to me. They caught me. The men from last night. Smoke, they caught me, and they beat me up. They shot me," Lisa said, starting to cry, coughing up blood. "I didn't want to tell them, but they beat me. They were going to kill me." She said the words, and they were vaguely comprehensible through her sobbing. "My son . . . I got a son, Ally . . . I need to be here for him, so I told them where you . . . where you goin' to be. I told them, Ally, and they comin' for you, so don't go to the place. They comin', so don't go!"

FIFTY-SIX

ALLY whirled around to look at the clock on the wall. It had been half an hour since she had spoken to her sister. They weren't going to get Ally, she thought, because she wouldn't be there. She was running late. But Henny was punctual, never late for shit, Ally thought, as she punched in her home telephone number, trying to catch her before she left. And she hoped that maybe, maybe this one time, Henny was held up.

The phone rang once, twice.

"Come on, Henny, be there," Ally urged, feeling herself on the verge of tears. "Be there, goddammit!"

And she knew that since her sister didn't have a cell phone, that if she had left the apartment already, there would be no way to tell her of the danger she faced.

The machine picked up, delivered its greeting.

"Henny, if you're there, pick up the phone," Ally said. There was no answer. She disconnected the call, hit the Redial button, and waited as the phone rang, hoping this time her sister would answer.

The phone rang three times again.

JJ walked in the room as the machine was picking up. "What's up, Ally?" she asked, noticing the distressed look on Ally's face.

"Hennesey, pick up the phone! Pick up!" Ally practically screamed into the phone.

"Ally, what's wrong?" JJ rushed over to her, sitting next to her on the sofa.

Henny wasn't picking up. She had left already and Ally knew it.

"Henny, if you ain't left yet, don't go. Do you hear me. Don't go to Lenny's! Something bad will happen if you do. So please, don't go. Call me as soon as you get this."

She disconnected the call, her face wet with tears when she looked up at JJ.

"Baby, what's going on?" JJ now looked as worried as Ally.

"The guys me and Lisa hit last night. Lisa kept their car, and they found her."

"Did they hurt her? Is she all right?"

"I don't know. I called 911, but I don't know where she is. And the men are lookin' for me now. Lisa told them where I was gonna be."

"Then just don't go. You'll be safe here," JJ said, grabbing hold of Ally's hand.

"But JJ, they know what I look like, and I was supposed to meet Henny there for lunch."

It took JJ only a second to understand what this meant. "Oh, my god. They gonna think she's you!"

"Dammit!" Ally screamed. She was at least twenty minutes away from there. JJ didn't have a car. It would take that long just for a cab to show up at JJ's place, and the bus was out of the question. "If something happens to her because of me," Ally cried. Then it came to her. She scrolled through her cell phone directory, pulled up a number, and pressed Send.

"Please, pick up the phone," Ally prayed. "If there's any chance for my sister, you'll pick up the fucking phone."

FIFTY-SEVEN

HENNY couldn't get the smile off her face. She was happier now than she could ever remember being. Everything was fine again with Rafe, and to think Ally had something to do with that! Henny couldn't believe her little sister had called and threatened Rafe to take her back. It didn't take all that, Henny thought, smiling even wider. But she was glad that Ally had done it. It let her know how much her sister did truly love and care about her.

When Henny was about four blocks away from Lenny's, she picked up her pace because she was excited to make up with her sister. She was going to tell Ally that she didn't have to worry about getting kicked out of the house after all, that she could come down to school with her as well. They could always get a two-bedroom 'til Ally got on her feet. Maybe she could even talk her into taking a few classes herself.

The second reason Henny thought of hurrying along was that she thought someone was following her. Twice when looking over her shoulder, she saw a big, blue banged-up car behind her. Whenever she spotted it, it would quickly turn a corner and disappear. She didn't know what was going on, but she just wanted to get to Lenny's, apologize to her, sister, grab her, and get home so they could all start packing and get out of there.

Henny continued down the street of rundown storefronts and vacant lots, then just stopped all of a sudden. She stood there a moment, not moving at all, then quickly whipped her head around. There it was. The banged-up blue BMW.

She quickly turned her head back around, hoping they had not seen her spotting them, but knowing they had. She almost felt unable, but she took one slow step forward, then another, and another, until she felt herself moving very quickly across the pavement. She had to get off the street, she told herself, and ducked between two buildings. That put her on an empty, narrow street that would take her through a few abandoned lots and straight to Lenny's.

She walked fifty feet, looking back over her shoulder the entire way. She had lost them. Henny let out a long, heavy sigh of relief. She didn't know what all that was about, but everything would be all right now, she thought. But she would've thought differently if she had turned her head back around, because there in front of her, the BMW with the banged-up driver's side had silently rolled up, stopping just in front of her. The driver's side window powered down, a gun extended out, Smoke behind it, taking steady aim at Henny.

She stopped again, still looking over her shoulder, unaware of the car in front of her. She was too busy making sure that it wouldn't all of a sudden turn the corner behind her, come barreling down that street. When she was certain it was no longer there, she turned around.

Henny froze, seeing the car stopped in front of her. She saw the gun aimed at her, saw the face of the stranger behind it, one eye closed, his sights set, and at that moment, she knew she was going to die.

The world went silent around her, her breathing stopped, and images of her life flooded her brain. Henny and her sister as toddlers. Henny graduating top of her grammar school class. Then Rafe. Him looking at her over that library book. Him standing in the rain telling her to walk out of his life, even though he loved her. The two of them making love, she knowing then she would forever love this man. Now she knew she would never see him again.

Again, Henny tried to tell her legs to work, but as in a dream, they didn't respond. She could not move, and even if she was able, she knew it would've been too late. She tried saying her good-byes before she died, then heard the shots. Two of them. Loud cracks, splitting the silence that was once around her. A second later the bullets had ripped through her. One through her chest, the other through her belly. All went brilliantly bright, the world inverted. The ground flew up to meet her. There on the pavement, her farewell to her mother, her sister, and her lover spilled with blood, silently out of her lips.

FIFTY-EIGHT

RAFE was racing toward the car dealership looking for Smoke, the gun still nestled in the holster at his side, when his cell phone rang. He picked it up, but couldn't understand what the woman on the other end was saying, didn't even know who it was, she was crying so hysterically.

"Hold it, hold it. Who is this?" he yelled into the phone.

"Rafe, it's Ally! Henny's in trouble. Something bad is gonna happen," Rafe heard her say frantically through her sobbing.

Rafe swung the Jag off to the side of the street. "Ally, just slow down, and tell me what the hell you're talking about."

As quickly as she could, she explained what had happened—how it was her fault.

"Goddammit, Ally. What did I tell you!" Rafe yelled into the phone, punching the gas, the tires squealing as he sped away from the curb.

"You got to get to her before she gets there. Please—"

Rafe shut the flip phone, threw it into the passenger seat, and bore down even harder on the gas. Rafe didn't know who they had robbed last night—Ally hadn't said—but if he was anything like the guy he had seen her with at that club, Rafe knew she was right. Something bad was going to happen if he didn't get there in time to stop it.

Rafe skidded to a stop in front of Lenny's. He looked quickly through the windows, but Henny wasn't there. He took off, circled the small building, then headed off in the direction of her house.

No sign of her after coming down the street. Could they have taken her? Rafe asked himself. The image of Henny being dragged screaming into a car raced through his mind, but he shut his eyes tight, blanked it out.

"No," he said under his breath, spinning the wheel hard to the right, forcing the car around in a cloud of gravel dust.

He would find her because he knew she was around there somewhere. She had probably taken a shortcut, stopped off to make a phone call or something. He raced up every other street leading to Lenny's except for one, and still no sign of her. Rafe turned down the last street, which wasn't a street at all but a narrow alleyway, opening up to some abandoned lots. He stomped on the gas, the engine roaring in front of him, shooting him down the street, until he saw something out in the middle of the pavement.

He slammed on the brakes, the car skidding to a stop ten feet in front of what now Rafe knew was a body.

No, he thought. It can't be her. The head was turned so he could not see the face. But the hair . . . the hair was the same, Rafe thought, jumping out the car. And her hand . . . her arm was thrown across her body as it lay on its side. The skin on her hand was Henny's complexion, he thought, feeling an overpowering sadness descend upon him. But it couldn't be her, he prayed, tripping, stumbling to the ground, falling just inches before the body. And then he knew, before he even reached out to turn her over, he knew that this woman, lying slain in the street, an ever widening blanket of blood stretching out from under her, was indeed the woman that he loved.

Rafe pulled himself up to his hands and knees, kneeled over her, then rolled the limp woman's body over. It was Hennesey. A line of blood crawled down from the corner of her mouth, her hands covered with the same red, as if she'd tried to cover the bullet wounds, tried to stop them from killing her. But there was no way, Rafe thought, looking down at those two wounds. One through her chest, the other through her stomach. The entire front half of her shirt was thick with her own blood, and as he scooped her up, wrapped his arms under her, he could feel his skin being coated with what came out the back of those wounds.

But she could still be alive, he told himself. He prayed that somehow she survived this, that someway there was just a little life in her still, just enough to keep her going until she was taken to the hospital.

He brought her up to him, lowered his face down to hers. He had done unlawful things, things that put him behind bars, things that got his little brother killed. He knew he was not deserving of a favor from God, but if it was granted, just this one time, he would change all that. He would change.

"God save her. Please, just save her!" Rafe cried, turning his head up, looking toward the skies, tears streaming down his cheeks. He looked down again into Henny's face.

"Henny. Henny, wake up, baby. I know you're still there. C'mon."

He lowered his ear down to her nose, listened, and felt for the most shallow of air coming from there. Nothing.

"Come on, baby. I know you're still with me," he said, laying her down, placing the side of his face to her bloody chest, but there was no heartbeat. He dug his fingers into her neck, but there was no pulse, and he knew then, as he fell backward covered with her blood, that it was useless. She was gone.

Someone had killed her, and Rafe would find out who that was, he told himself, feeling rage start to build within him.

He had to find Ally, get the name from her. She was the reason this happened, so she would know. But he didn't have to look far, because a second later he heard a piercing scream. When he turned, he saw Ally, both hands clawing into her scalp, a look of sheer horror on her face at the sight of her sister torn open on the street.

"Noooooooooo!" Ally screamed, standing fifteen feet away.

Rafe glared at her, hatred in his eyes. "I told you to stay away from those men. I told you!" he yelled. "Do you see this!"

"Nooooooooooo!" Ally cried hysterically again, not moving from the spot she was in. "It can't be. It can't!"

"It is! I told you to stay away from them!"

"Hennesey, I'm so sorry," Ally cried hysterically.

"Tell me who you robbed last night," Rafe yelled, looking back at Ally as he kneeled over Henny's body.

"I don't know. I can't remember."

"Try hard!"

"I can't!" she screamed.

"Goddammit, you have to remember!"

Ally got quiet all of a sudden. The crying stopped, and the expression on her face went blank as if she wasn't there anymore, but somewhere deep in her subconscious. She concentrated, and finally it came to her.

"His name was Smoke," she said, her tone even, calm almost. Then, "I'm sorry, Henny."

Rafe gasped. "What did you say?"

"Smoke. He said his name was Smoke," Ally said. "I'm so sorry, Henny."

"Smoke," Rafe said under his breath, feeling the rage from before growing to the point where he could no longer contain it.

"Ally, call 911 so they can come for Henny," Rafe said as calmly as he could, looking down at Henny's face. He lowered himself, kissing her gently on her forehead, saying his last good-bye.

Rafe pulled away from her, then commanded, "Did you hear me, Ally?"

When again he got no response, Rafe demanded, "Ally!" then turned to see what was wrong. When he turned, he saw Ally pulling something from her purse.

"I didn't mean for this to happen to her, Rafe. I know I should've listened to you, but you gotta believe me."

Rafe saw that it was a gun.

"Ally, Ally, listen to me." Rafe tried to calm her, easing his way toward her. "It wasn't your fault, it just—"

And before he could take another step, say another word, he heard Ally sadly say once again, "I'm sorry, Henny," before she shoved the barrel of the gun into her open mouth and pulled the trigger.

FIFTY-NINE

LIVVY'S DAUGHTERS still weren't home when she walked in the
door an hour later, and she felt both glad for that and disappointed.
She didn't want them to see her like this after she had failed herself the
way she had. But she could've used the comforting she knew she
would've gotten from them. It wouldn't have taken much. A hug
would've done it. She just needed to know that even though she
wouldn't get the scholarship, she was still loved by her family.

Livvy stood alone in the middle of the silent room, feeling as
though there was nothing left to do but feel pity for herself and cry 'til
she couldn't anymore. And then the phone rang.

"Hello," Livvy said.

"Hello Livvy, it's Dr. Ranick. Do you have a moment?"

"How can I help you, Dr. Ranick?" Livvy's tone was bland.

"I just wanted to tell you again how sorry I am about your not being
able to apply for the scholarship. Like I said before, giving you that
extra time wouldn't have been fair to the other applicants."

"I completely understand," Livvy said, not wanting to hear another
word. She was ready to lower the phone from her ear, hang up, when
she heard him say, "But what you told me . . . the things you said were
very compelling, very touching. I was thinking that if you could handle
all that, still come to work, and do the outstanding job you've always
done, then I think you'd make a fine nurse. I can't proclaim you winner
of this scholarship, because that wouldn't be fair. But I can recommend
you for a full scholarship to our nursing school. How does that sound?"

Livvy, shocked by what was just said, climbed on the sofa, and
started jumping joyously up and down, yelling at the top of her lungs.

"Livvy, are you still there? Is everything okay?" Dr. Ranick asked.

"Are you joking! Everything is wonderful!" Livvy said, catching her breath. "Are you sure this is true? I don't want to go telling my family, and this doesn't happen, Doctor. Don't go playin' with me about something like this."

She heard the doctor laughing over the phone. "No, you don't have to worry. This is true. And the recommendation is really just a formality. But I'm vouching for you, so don't make a liar out of me."

"Not a chance, baby. I mean, Doctor. Good-bye."

"Good-bye."

Livvy hung up the phone. "I got it!" she yelled, spreading her arms, jumping around some more. She couldn't wait to tell Wade and her girls. Finally things were starting to go as she had always dreamed they could've. Finally, everything was going to be all right.

SIXTY

RAFE tried to stop Ally, yelled, ran toward her, tried to reach out for her, but before he could get to her, Ally pulled the trigger.

It was the loudest silence he had ever heard. Not complete silence but a deafening click! *No bullet in the chamber,* Rafe thought. He was already in motion toward her and fell into her, tumbling with her onto the ground.

Rafe wrestled with her, trying to get the gun out of her hand before she could try to fire it again.

"Just let me do it!" Ally cried, fighting him. "This ain't got shit to do with you!"

He was careful not to get shot himself, but finally he tore the gun out of her grasp and flung it aside. He was straddling Ally at this point, and she was still tussling with him, trying to scratch and bite him, tears in her eyes.

"Ally, listen to me!" he said, still dodging her fists and sharp swipes at his face. He got hold of both her wrists and pinned them down on either side of her head.

"Look!" he said. "You ain't killin' yourself! Now that Henny's gone, you the only one your mother got left. You need to be here for to help her through this. You understand? Call 911!"

She nodded.

Rafe left her. There was nothing else he could've done about the situation from there. He had to find Smoke. The man had more than just Rafe's brother to answer for now.

He ended up at the dealership, entered through the service department, stormed down the hallway, his chest, his arms, his hands covered with Henny's blood, now dried. Outside Smoke's office door, Rafe pulled his gun and held it high, ready to fire. He took a deep breath, exhaled in an attempt to slow his pounding heart, then burst through the door.

Rafe had the gun aimed between the eyes of Smoke's secretary. If it had been Smoke there, he would've been dead by now. The woman's eyes inflated in her head. She threw her hands to her face, about to scream, but thought better of it when she heard Rafe say simply, "Don't."

He stepped in the office, slammed the door behind him, then moved around the desk, the gun on the woman's face as if he intended to kill her if she didn't give him the information he was looking for.

"Where's he at?"

"Who?" she said, frightened.

"Smoke."

"He's not here. He called, said he'd be at the warehouse, checking inventory." She spoke the words in a crying, quivering, voice.

"Are you sure?" Rafe said, stepping closer to her, giving her a better look at the gun.

"Yes! Yes!"

"Don't tell him I came by here looking for him," Rafe said, taking one last step, aiming the tip of the gun barrel between the woman's neatly trimmed eyebrows. He heard her gasp.

"Because if you do . . ." he trailed off, giving her a terrifying look, then ran out of the office.

He jumped back in his car and sped toward the warehouse, while thoughts of Henny lying on the ground entered his mind. Should he have left her there? There was nothing more he could do than take the gun from Ally and call 911. She said she would watch over Henny until the ambulance came. But Rafe called Wade just to make sure.

"Hello," Wade said, as if expecting the call. "Is everything okay?"

"No, it's not," Rafe said, his tone low and mournful. "I need you to go to Lenny's off State, then a block east."

"Why? What's going on?" Wade said, fear in his voice.

"Hennesey is dead."

SIXTY-ONE

"HENNESEY'S DEAD," Wade heard Rafe say.

"What! What did you just say?" Wade said, knowing he couldn't have heard him correctly, knowing this couldn't be happening.

"I said she's dead."

"How?"

"She was shot. She was shot, and now she's dead."

When Wade had gotten to the scene, a crowd of people had gathered.

"Excuse me. Pardon me. Let me through!" Wade said, pushing his way through the thick throng of people looking for Ally. Rafe said she would be there. When he got through, he looked down and saw nothing more than a wide puddle of blood.

This will kill her, Wade thought, thinking about Livvy, digging out his cell phone, knowing he couldn't hold this information from her. He dialed her number.

"Livvy, it's Wade," he said when she picked up.

"Baby, baby! I got the scholarship!" Livvy bubbled, and then shrieked.

"That's good, baby. But something happened."

All of a sudden, there was silence on the other end of the phone. Livvy must've known something was gravely wrong by the tone of Wade's voice.

"What do you mean, something's wrong?"

"Just be ready to go. I'm coming to get you, and I'll tell you then."

SIXTY-TWO

THE DOOR of the warehouse was open when Rafe arrived. He walked down the long corridor, his gun drawn, listening. He stopped when he heard voices.

He pressed himself up against a door, placed his ear to it. He heard Smoke's voice, then heard Trunk. Rafe adjusted his grip on his gun, placed a slightly shaky hand on the doorknob, counted to three, then barged through.

Inside, he quickly aimed the gun at Smoke, keeping an eye on Trunk just in case he decided to make any sudden moves.

"What the fuck, Rafe, bustin' through my shit like T. J. Hooker? Is there a damn problem?"

"Shut up, Smoke!" Rafe commanded. His eyes were still on Smoke, but he was aiming the gun at Trunk now. "Big man, show me your hands."

Trunk looked to Smoke for instructions.

"Don't look over there, motherfucker. I got the gun. Show me your hands."

The big man started to raise his hands, but then attempted to go into his jacket.

"Hold it!" Rafe yelled. "Open it up."

Trunk opened his jacket, revealing a gun.

"Slide it this way. Easy."

Trunk lifted the gun from his holster with two fingers, placed it on the floor, kicked it over. Rafe picked it up and now held a gun on both Trunk and Smoke.

"What the fuck is this about? Why you coming up in here like this?" Smoke demanded, standing from his chair.

"Sit down," Rafe commanded.

Smoke remained standing.

"Sit down!" Rafe yelled at the top of his lungs, raising the gun higher and pointing it at Smoke's head.

Smoke sat back in his seat. "Then tell me why you in my office, pointing guns at me and my man, with what looks like blood all over your ass."

"This *is* blood. It's from a girl you just killed. My girlfriend."

"Bullshit! The bitch I just deaded was a trick who robbed me for my car and all my shit last night."

"No, Smoke. That's who you *thought* you got," Rafe said, taking two steps closer to him, aiming both guns at him now, both his fingers on the triggers, preparing to pull. "Who you really killed was her twin sister. Someone who ain't have shit to do with that, don't even know you. You killed my girl, and now I gotta kill . . ." But before Rafe could pull the trigger, he saw Trunk go behind his back, dig in the waist of his pants. Rafe whirled the guns around as Trunk pulled his second gun, firing a shot.

The shot whizzed past Rafe's head, as he ducked and started firing at the same time. His bullets found their mark, the big man screaming out in agony, his lower limbs exploding in bursts of blood and splinters of bone. He fell slow and heavy, toppling over, the gun falling out of his grasp.

Rafe ran across the room, grabbed the gun, pointed it in Trunk's face, but the man was no longer a threat. He had passed out from shock and was lying there unconscious. Rafe shoved the gun down the small of his back.

"Goddamn man! What's your fucking problem?" Smoke said.

Rafe didn't answer but raised the guns to Smoke's face again. "Good-bye, Smoke."

"Wait. Wait!" Smoke threw his hands up. "Look, I ain't plan on killing your girlfriend. It was supposed to be the girl who robbed me. Ain't my fault she had a twin sister who was in the wrong place at the wrong time. If there's anybody to blame, it's the girl who stole from me. She's the reason her sister's dead."

Rafe held the guns on Smoke. "There's more."

"What, I kill somebody else now?" Smoke said, sarcastically.

"Yeah, my little brother. You had him running for you."

Smoke looked shocked by what Rafe had said. He looked as though he was thinking of trying to lie his way out of it, then just admitted,

"Rafe, he wanted to be down. You was sent up. He wanted, needed to make some money. It's all he ever wanted to do was be like you, so I—"

"You sent him to the West Side. You knew you ain't have no business there. Why the fuck did you do that!" Rafe yelled at Smoke, closing what little distance there was between the two of them, pressing both barrels into Smoke's cheeks.

Smoke raised his hands even higher, reared back in his chair, trying to distance himself from the tips of the guns.

"I never meant for it to happen, man. You got to believe me. I sent him on two, maybe three runs. Then I was gonna pull him. You got to believe me. I didn't think they'd suspect a kid like him to be carryin'."

"You suspected wrong, and they killed him." Rafe cocked both guns, preparing to make Smoke pay for all the death he'd caused.

"Rafe!" Smoke yelled in a last attempt to save his life. "Think about this, man. Do you think I wanted Eric to die? That was my little man. After you went down, I cared for him like he was my little brother. Why would I want him to die?" Smoke asked, the tips of the gun barrels still shoved into his cheeks. "Hunh, Rafe? Why would I want to cause you pain? We came up together in the 'hood, poor as hell. We brothers. I love you, man. You know that."

"None of that matters now," Rafe said, his fingers still trembling on the triggers of the guns.

"Ain't a day gone by that I wished I couldn't bring him back, wished that I was there instead of him. It's why I was giving your folks money, why I couldn't let you go. I needed to give you something back to at least try to make up for what happened."

"Money can't make up for my brother's life. Nothing can," Rafe said, his eyes narrowing, his fists tightening around the guns. He was going to kill Smoke now, and Smoke seemed to know it.

"Rafe. Ain't worth it, man. Kill me, you're back in prison. You don't want that."

"Don't have nothing more to live for," Rafe said, glancing down to see that Trunk was still out, before turning back to Smoke. "Close your eyes."

"Your parents!" Smoke said quickly, tossing out his final attempt at living. "The three years you were in prison tore them up. I was there to see it. How you think they gonna feel with you doing fifteen to twenty? Gotta ask yourself, Rafe. Will they even be alive when you get out?"

Would they be alive, Rafe thought. And even if they were, would it have been worth putting them through all those years of pain just so he could have his revenge? Rafe thought about Henny, what she would want him to do, and he knew the answer. Adding to the death toll would only do him harm and disgrace both her memory, and that of Eric.

Rafe stared down at Smoke. Saw the huge beads of nervous sweat crawling down his face. Smoke had killed, but if Rafe did the same he would only be stooping to Smoke's level. Rafe lowered his weapons, forced himself to back away, slipped one of the guns into his waist.

"You made the right decision, man. Jail ain't the place for you no more."

"I know it's not. But it is for you," Rafe said, walking toward the door. "I'll see to that."

Rafe grabbed the doorknob and was about to turn it when he heard a metallic click. He glanced over his shoulder, saw the gun Smoke was holding, and heard the shot as orange fire spewed from the barrel.

SIXTY-THREE

WADE had called around and found out that Hennesey was taken to Cook County hospital. He had parked the car, sat there in the driver's seat as Livvy continued to cry. She started before Wade even told her the news. From the look on his face when he walked through the door, she knew something terribly wrong had happened to her babies.

Without saying a word, Wade hurried to hug her. She fell into his arms, the sobs coming even harder. Livvy didn't want to hear the news, but she had to know what had happened. She had to know just how bad it all was.

"Tell me," she said between her sobs, her face pressed into Wade's shoulder.

"Livvy, maybe you should calm down a little before—"

"Tell me!" she screamed. "Just tell me what happened to my children!"

"Hennesey was shot, Livvy. She's dead."

"God noooooooo! Please no!" Livvy cried out. Everything drained from her body. Every reason for living, for ever having lived, was now gone.

An hour ago, life was what she always wanted it to be. Now it was nothing, and neither was she. She wasn't even a mother, for what real mother would let her child die like this? The image of her daughter's slain, bloody body flashed through her head. She saw her eyes open, her bloody hand reaching out for Livvy, heard Henny's voice cry out, "Mommy!"

Livvy went numb. Her legs collapsed, her body slipping through Wade's arms, as she fell to the floor, crying at the loss of her daughter.

* * *

ON THE way to the hospital, Livvy asked Wade who had done this to her daughter. How he had found out about this?

"Rafe told me. He called and told me."

And Livvy knew that it was going to have something to do with him. She cried even harder now, because she knew if she had just done more to keep that man away from her, Henny would still be alive.

AT THE hospital, Wade pulled the keys out of the ignition.

"Livvy, are you ready?"

"Yeah," Livvy said, wiping tears from her face. "I'm ready."

SIXTY-FOUR

WHEN SMOKE had shot at Rafe, the bullet missed, but it had come so dangerously close to him that he thought he heard it whistle past his ear. Rafe was left there standing dazed, both guns in his hands, bringing them up, squaring them on Smoke as Smoke fired off two more shots.

Rafe threw himself to the floor, repeatedly pulling the triggers of both his guns. The sound was deafening as the guns exploded, bullets ripping through the wall behind Smoke, into the desk, and a couple cutting through his body. Under the gunfire, Rafe heard him cry out when he was hit, saw the red mist spray from the wounds. But Smoke continued firing, Rafe seeing the bright flashes from his gun, hearing the bullets zip by his head as he fell, praying that he would not get hit but knowing he would.

When it was over, Rafe was on the floor in front of Smoke's desk. He couldn't see Smoke but heard movement behind the bullet-riddled desk, heard him moaning, gasping. Rafe crawled, peeked around the corner of the desk. Smoke was down, had fallen backward in his chair, looking with dead eyes blankly up toward the ceiling. His arms were splayed out to his sides, the gun no longer in his grasp, blood spilling from gunshot wounds in his chest, his arms, and his stomach.

Rafe scooped his arms under Smoke's head and elevated it. Smoke's eyes whirled about, finally finding Rafe's. He looked deeply into them.

"I'm sorry about your little brother, Rafe," Smoke said, his breath shallow, words barely audible.

"I'm gonna call 911. We gonna get you out of here."

"Ain't gonna happen. It's okay." Smoke tried to smile but was overcome by a short coughing fit, blood spilling from his lips. "I lived my life. It's all good."

Smoke's body tightened, his eyes clamped shut as he winced in pain. He grabbed Rafe's arms, squeezed, then slowly opened his eyes.

"Let me try and call someone, man. We can still get you out of here!"

"Un-uh," Smoke said. "Don't."

His body seemed to be getting lighter, Rafe thought. His eyes no longer focused on Rafe but looked past him, toward the ceiling.

"The gun," Smoke said, the words a whisper now.

"What gun?"

"You shot the cop with."

"Yeah."

"There," Smoke said, looking over at the gun he had fired at Rafe. It lay a few feet from them. Rafe grabbed it.

"I was never gonna turn you in. Just pullin' your chain, man," Smoke said, laughing a little, the laugh turning into a cough, then more blood from inside him. "You believe me?"

"I believe you, Smoke."

"Call my attorneys," Smoke said, grabbing Rafe's arms.

"What? Why?"

"Me dying is trouble for you." Smoke was wheezing deeply now between each word. "They know everything. Tell 'em the truth. They'll get you off. Don't want no more pain to come to you."

Smoke's grip tightened even more on Rafe's arms, as if something was trying to take him away, but he wasn't trying to go. He had no choice, and as Rafe felt his grip loosening, saw his eyelids lower, felt his waning breaths become shallower and shallower, Smoke said, "We was brothers. Weren't we? We was . . ."

"Yeah, Smoke. We was brothers," Rafe answered, then watched Smoke die.

SIXTY-FIVE

RAFE would call Smoke's lawyers, answer all the questions he could, deal with what he had to deal with, but first he called Wade.

"Come to the hospital, Rafe," Wade told him.

"Henny's dead. Ain't nothing there for me."

"Come, anyway. Her mother wants to speak to you."

"She probably thinks I had something to do with Henny getting shot. Tell her I didn't."

"Tell her yourself. Give the girl's mother that much respect. She deserves it."

Rafe thought about it for a moment. "Yeah, all right."

WHEN RAFE walked through the hospital doors, he saw Wade there waiting for him. He walked toward Rafe, his arms out, as if preparing to give him a hug. Rafe made no similar movements, but Wade hugged him anyway.

"I'm sorry about all that's happened," he said softly in Rafe's ear. "Let me take you to see Livvy."

Wade led Rafe to a room on the third floor, the door open, Livvy sitting inside.

Rafe looked at Wade as if afraid to go in, questioning what terrible things would happen once he did.

"Do it in your own time. But know that everything will be all right," Wade told him. He rested a hand on Rafe's shoulder, then walked off down the hallway.

Rafe took another look in the room, saw Henny's mother again, her head down, grieving.

He should just go, he thought, but stopped himself, knowing that

Henny's mother did deserve the right to speak to him. He stepped into the room.

"I'm glad you didn't leave," Livvy said, as if she was watching him the entire time he was outside the door, even though her head was down. "Have a seat."

Rafe took the chair across from her.

"No. Here," she said, placing a hand on the sofa cushion next to her.

Rafe slowly stood, stepped over, and lowered himself down beside her. Only then did she look up at him, pain and sadness in her eyes. He could tell she had been crying and knew that she blamed him for that.

She pulled her eyes away from his, looking at the blood that covered his shirt, that stained his forearms and hands.

"That's hers, isn't it?"

Rafe tried to cover his arms with his hands, as if to hide the reminder of the terrible thing that had happened to Henny. But he couldn't. "Yeah, it's her blood—and somebody else's," Rafe added.

"Whose?"

"The man who killed Henny."

"How is he?"

"Dead," Rafe said, looking away from Henny's mother.

"You killed him for her?"

"Yes," Rafe answered, annoyed. He stood up. "Look, Ms. Rodgers, I know you blame me for this, and I'm sorry about that. Sorry about everything that happened. I answered your questions. Ain't nothing left for me to do around here, so you take care." Rafe headed toward the door.

"You really loved her, didn't you?" Livvy asked.

Rafe stopped but did not turn around.

"You killed a man, could've gotten yourself killed because of how you felt about my daughter."

"Yeah, that's right." He still didn't turn to face her.

"You don't like me much, do you, Raphiel?"

Rafe turned around.

"It's because I told you you couldn't see her anymore? Because I said you weren't good enough for her, isn't that it?"

"Yeah, that's it." Rafe slowly sat on the coffee table just in front of her.

"You have to understand. I did that thinking I was protecting my daughter from something that would ruin her life, from something like this happening. I been through the things that I thought someone like you could put her through and ain't nothing good about it. She deserved better than that, better than you," Livvy said, pulling at a tissue she had crumpled in her hand.

"Alizé told me everything that happened. I know you're not to blame for this." Livvy looked up into Rafe's eyes. "I know now that I was wrong about that."

Rafe stood, glad that she had finally came to that conclusion, but Henny was dead. It was too fucking late now.

"I want to know if you can forgive me."

"Whatever," Rafe said, standing, anger thick in his voice.

"I don't understand that, Raphiel. I don't understand what *whatever* means," Livvy said, looking up at him above her.

"*Whatever* means it don't make no difference now if I forgive you or not. It doesn't matter anymore."

"You're wrong about that. It matters a lot."

"What are you talking about?" Rafe said.

"Wait here a minute." Livvy stood from the sofa and stepped out of the room. When she came back, she grabbed Rafe's hand, intertwined her fingers with his.

"I want you to come with me," she said.

Rafe felt he had no choice but to follow her. She led him down the hallway. There was a nurse standing outside another door.

"Go right in," the nurse said, and then she smiled at Rafe. Or did he imagine that?

"What is this, Ms. Rodgers? Where you taking me?" he asked.

They stopped just outside another door, inside the room they had just walked into.

"Raphiel," Livvy said, letting go of him, reaching up, taking his face in her hands. "I'm sorry for those things I said to you. I didn't know you. I had no right. And I should've known that if my daughter trusted herself enough to love you, then I should've trusted *her*." A tear came to Livvy's eye, streaming down her cheek. "Unlike her mother, she obviously knows a good man when she sees one," she said, and chuckled a little. "You are a good man, Raphiel. When Alizé told you Henny was in trouble, you went to try and save her. And when you saw that she had been shot, you called the paramedics, and they came. And if it had been only minutes later . . ." Rafe could feel Livvy's palms trembling on his face now, see more tears coming to her eyes, ". . . then they wouldn't have been able to save her."

Hold it, Rafe thought.

"But they were in time."

"No. What are you talking about?"

"I'm saying that my baby is alive." Livvy smiled through her tears.

"No," Rafe said, pushing her hands away from his face, stepping back from her. "I saw her there. She was dead. I listened to her heart, checked her pulse, and there wasn't one! She was dead, so why you tellin'—"

"Her heart was beating, but it was so faint because she was in shock. They rushed her to surgery and were able to save her. Because of you."

Rafe shook his head, tried to hide his face, because he felt the tears coming. "She's alive?" he asked, incredulous.

"Because of you. And that's why I need for you to forgive me. I want to know you. I want to be friends with the man that my daughter is in love with. Can that happen, Raphiel?"

"Yes," Rafe said, the tears pouring freely down his face now. "Can I see her? I want to see her."

"Of course, you can," Livvy said, grabbing his hand again, pulling the door open. "She's been waiting for you."

Rafe walked into the room and immediately wanted to turn around. She was alive her mother said, but she didn't look like it. All those machines beeping around her head, the tubes attached to her, pumping fluid in or draining it out.

He took steps closer to the bed. Alizé was on the other side, holding one of her sister's hands. She was crying, but a smile was on her face.

Alizé was torn up over this, was willing to die when she thought Henny was dead. She was on the wrong track, but something told Rafe that this event would change everything for her, that she would do better because now she knew how fragile life was.

Rafe looked to the other side of the room, saw Wade there, the old guy who was so understanding of everything Rafe was going through. He was happy for Wade. He liked him. He was a good man, and felt he and Henny's mother would have a good future together. Rafe just wished he could've said the same for himself and Henny.

After another reluctant step forward, Rafe stood directly over Henny. The blankets were pulled all the way up to her neck. He knew that if he pulled them down, he would see what he had seen the last time he was with Henny—the bullet wounds, the blood that had covered her. It was his fault. All of that. He knew he had that sordid past, that past that could come back to the present, threaten him or anyone near him, but he let Henny get involved with him anyway.

When he saw her body there on the pavement, when Rafe knew that she was dead, he tried to blame it on Ally, but it wasn't her fault. If Henny had died, it would've been his fault. It would've been his doing, and her mother was right. He didn't deserve her. He should walk away, and he knew it. There was just one thing stopping him: he loved her too much.

Rafe lowered himself over Henny. Her eyes were closed. She looked peaceful, almost dead, but he told himself he wouldn't think that.

"Hennesey," he whispered softly, and when she didn't respond, he looked up at Ally, then to her mother, worry on his face.

They both held fragile smiles on their lips, as if knowing all was still well.

He turned back to Henny, spoke her name again, a little louder this time. She stirred the slightest bit, her eyes slowly opening. Upon seeing his face, something near a smile flickered.

"Hennesey, I love you," Rafe said softly, a tear spilling from his face. "But I'll leave if you want me to. I love you, but I don't deserve you, and I'll leave if you want me to."

It took Henny a moment to respond, a look of disappointment and pain appearing on her face.

"What happened is over," Henny said, her voice raspy. "But I'm alive, and I love you. We can still make this happen if you want to."

Rafe felt Livvy, Ally, and Wade moving closer to the bed, circling around him as if so much depended on his answer, the answer that he didn't have to think twice about. He looked in their faces, felt their support for him, and knew everything would be all right.

"Of course, we can make it happen. Because I love you too, Hennesey." Rafe kissed her softly on her forehead. "I love you too."

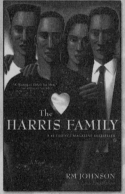